SOMETHING BETWEEN US?

Sammy's voice was low, his fingers warmly persuasive. He wore heavy silver rings, a thumb ring and two others.

"I'd like to get to know you better, Nicki." He squeezed my hand, not letting me pull away. "I'd like to make love to you."

My body throbbed, bringing a surge of guilt along with a surge of juices.

What was it about this guy that made him so sexy?

The old Nicki would've jumped his bones in a heartbeat and worried about guilt and explanations later.

Those blue eyes were incredible, and he smelled like forbidden fruit—juicy, and just within reach. I could stretch out my hand . . .

By Terri Garey

A MATCH MADE IN HELL
DEAD GIRLS ARE EASY

TERRI GAREY

A MATCH MADE IN HELL

AVON

An Imprint of HarperCollins*Publishers*

For my sisters,
who always make me laugh,
sometimes drive me crazy,
and forever keep me grounded.

AVON BOOKS
An Imprint of HarperCollins*Publishers*
10 East 53rd Street
New York, New York 10022-5299

ISBN 978-0-06-113616-0
www.avonromance.com

First Avon Books paperback printing: July 2008

Printed in the U.S.A.

10 9 8 7 6 5 4 3 2 1

ACKNOWLEDGMENTS

I'd like to thank the people in my life who've held my hand as I reached for the stars: my husband, my children, my fabulous agents Annelise and Christina, my immensely talented editor Erika, and some very special friends at The Writer's Playground.

I think it was the late John Lennon who said, "Life is what happens while you're busy making other plans." The part he left out is that death happens, too.

Just ask John.

I used to find the idea of an afterlife intriguing, but a near-death experience changed all that. I now find the world of spirits unavoidable, in more ways than one. Not only can they see me, but I can see them.

My name is Nicki Styx. A few weeks ago I went from worrying about business and boyfriends to worrying about spooks under the bed. Skeletons in the closet. Bones in the cellar, and . . . well, you get the idea. When the lights went out, the psychic lightbulb went on, and I became an unwilling "ghoulfriend" to the dead.

Ask me about vintage fashions and I know all the answers. Ask me how to save a lost soul, and all I can do is play it by ear.

I have a feeling I'll be lucky to save my own.

CHAPTER 1

"Too many freaks, not enough circuses."

The fat old man in sandals and socks didn't seem to care if I heard his rude comment. The old woman with him craned her neck to check out the pink streaks in my hair, widening her eyes at my heavy eyeliner and Midnight Blue lipstick.

Okay, so maybe the lipstick was a bit much, but I'd been feeling funkier than usual this morning. A little outrageousness never hurt anybody.

Besides, in Little Five Points, Georgia, I fit right in.

I gave the old man and the old woman a cheerful smile as I finished unlocking the door to my shop, Handbags and Gladrags. There was nothing freakish about my outfit—white vintage ruffled blouse with a vee neck, worn with jeans, cute sandals, and some clunky jewelry.

Let the old couple eat fashion cake.

I stood for a moment on Moreland Street, taking in the laid-back scents and sounds that defined Little Five Points. Tourist trap by day, party place by night, surrounded by picket fence neighborhoods full of quaint old homes. The smell of coffee drifted out the open door of Moonbeans—most of their sidewalk tables were already filled. Dreadlocked rastas chatted in the sun with tattooed punks, while freaks and stoners rubbed elbows with pudgy tourists in socks and sandals.

It was all good.

Unlocking the front door to the shop, I propped it open to the street, then flipped on the overhead lights with my usual thrill of pride.

Every item in the store had been handpicked, of course. My friend and business partner Evan and I love nothing more than finding timeless fashion gems among the dross of thrift stores and estate sales, cleaning them up and sharing them with those cool enough to appreciate them. The gorgeous gowns of the thirties and forties, the sparkling jewelry of the forties and fifties, the funky jeans and tie-dyed T-shirts of the sixties and seventies—Handbags and Gladrags stocked them all.

Five minutes later I had the register open and coffee brewing. I was busy giving the display cases a quick wipe-down, when I glanced up to see the second "looky-loo" of the day; a middle-aged woman was staring at me through the front window.

I gave her a friendly smile and went back to my counter polishing; we'd had a gaggle of teenage girls come in yesterday and they were all over the glass of the jewelry section. When I looked up again, the woman had entered the store.

"Good morning." It never hurt to be friendly with the customers. "Let me know if you need any help."

She didn't answer, and she was still staring.

Whatever. I turned away to stash the cleaning supplies and find my favorite coffee mug, certain the pot was ready by now. When I turned back, she was standing on the other side of the counter, two feet away. Late forties maybe, unnaturally black hair, carefully styled and hair-sprayed into place. Her pink sequined blouse was a bit gaudy, but to each her own.

"Can I help you?" The way she was looking at me was starting to creep me out.

She finally spoke. "You can see me?"

My heart sank.

"You can, can't you?" The woman smiled in relief, pressing a hand to her chest. Her nails were long, painted bright red. "You can see me. Thank goodness."

Oh, I could see her. I could hear her, too. She had a broad Southern accent—the word "can" was stretched into two syllables. I could even smell the scent she used . . . a mixture of fruit and flowers, like peaches.

"I've been at my wit's end," the woman said, with a flutter of fingers. "I didn't know what to do, but the good Lord hasn't abandoned me, after all. I need your help."

"Oh, crap," I muttered, flattening my hands on the counter.

It was déjà vu all over again; I'd been here before, and it always started the same way.

I need your help, Nicki.

The old man on the sidewalk had been right—I *was* a freak, because I knew something most people didn't; despite the red fingernails, the pink sequins, and the smell of peach body lotion, the woman on the other side of the counter was not a living, breathing human being.

Do unto others as you would have them do unto you, Nicki.

Double crap. My unexpected trip to the Light may have been canceled, but here I was, still paying the cost of the return ticket. And yet . . . being allowed to survive heart failure was no small favor, even if survival came with strings attached.

As if reading my mind, the woman blurted, "In spite of everything I've done, the Lord has put you here to help me. You're a good person. I just know it."

I had no idea what she'd done, and I could hardly argue with her about what kind of person I was, but I wished I had her certainty. Having had run-ins with at least four spirits in the past month, all with varying degrees of intensity, the only thing I knew for certain about seeing the dead was that it sucked.

The only question left was whether this lost soul was going to go gently into the Light, or be an undead pain in the ass.

"My daughter is hurt." The woman's statement took me by surprise. "But I don't know where she is."

I eyed her narrowly, hoping against hope she was just a crazy person. Of course I'd do my best to help a troubled spirit move on, but I'd much rather let the cops handle the loonies.

"We were in an accident," she said. "The car went off the road and down a hill . . . "

Yep. Dead. She was dead.

" . . . I could hear my daughter screaming and glass breaking . . . "

Goose bumps rose on my arms, and my guilt level rose along with them. Why did I always have to be such a smartass, even to myself?

" . . . and when I woke up I was wandering the streets." The woman gestured toward the front window. "I've tried to talk to people, to get help for my daughter, but everybody acts like I'm invisible."

Damn. My perfect morning had been perfectly ruined, but this lady had an even bigger problem than she thought she did.

She didn't know she was dead.

How was I supposed to tell her?

I sighed, feeling sorry for her and sorry for me at the same time.

One of the hardest parts about dealing with spirits was that there were no manuals for this type of stuff. I had to dance on the head of a pin, every time.

Hard enough for an angel, and I was no angel.

"Um . . . maybe we should call the police." I was stalling, of course. The local police would never buy the "I see dead people" routine. "What's your name?"

"Lila," she answered. "Lila Boudreaux."

I picked up the phone. "Where should I tell them to look for your daughter?"

Lila made an impatient noise. "I don't know! That's the problem! I've never been here before . . . I'm not even sure where I am!" She was clasping her hands now, long nails crossing and uncrossing. She wore a big opal on her right index finger, a pinky ring with a dangle on the left.

"You're in Little Five Points, near downtown Atlanta."

She frowned, obviously confused. "Atlanta? That's right! I came to Atlanta to . . . " Her face paled, looking very white beneath her rouge, emphasizing the inky blackness of her hair. A little less makeup and better quality hair dye would've done this lady some good—but it was too late to make fashion suggestions.

Lila had gone silent, and was staring at me again. A thought occurred to me, and since I was very busy going with the flow, it seemed as good a thought as any. "Why don't you talk to the police yourself?" I held out the phone.

Lila started to take the receiver, but hesitated. Her fingers hadn't quite reached the phone before she closed them, letting her hand drop. "I can't," she said, and her eyes filled with tears. "I've already tried to use the phone." Her voice trembled. "What's happening to me?"

I took a deep breath, hoping she was ready for what I had to say.

"It doesn't matter." She cut me off. "My daughter's still out there. You have to help her."

A brief *beep* sounded as the back door opened, then Evan's voice. "Good morning." The happy trill told me my partner had enjoyed a good night.

My head swiveled automatically in his direction, and when I turned back, the woman was gone.

"Lila?" I was speaking to thin air. "Ms. Boudreaux?"

I scanned the store, certain I'd never get used to the way the dead could come and go. Leaning way over the counter, I even checked the floor where she'd been standing. Nothing.

"Nice ass, Nicki, but you're not my type," Evan said from behind me. "I told you that in middle school." I turned, and he gave me his customary naughty grin. He was wearing his blond hair longer these days, and the look suited him.

Knowing how frightened Evan was of ghosts, I had no plans to tell him he'd just missed one. Pulling myself together, I gave him a crooked smile instead. "Morning, sunshine. How are things in Peachtree City?"

Evan grinned happily over the box he was carrying. "We stayed at the Hyatt last night. Butch was working security for some big corporate function and didn't get off until after midnight. Driving all the way out to Peachtree City and back was out of the question." He put the box down on the counter and leaned in for a quick peck on the cheek. "I think he likes me."

I snorted. "Likes you? You two have been glued at the hip for weeks now. I think he's in love."

Evan looked thoughtful. "Glued at the hip . . . what an interesting concept."

I rolled my eyes. Evan's wicked sense of humor kept me on my toes.

"What's in the box?" Eager to see his latest find, I reached for the lid, but he slapped my hand away.

"Patience, devil doll. I picked these up at an auction last weekend. I've barely had time to look through them." Evan opened the box to reveal a jumble of purses, leather mostly, with some velvet and canvas thrown in. "Ooh, look at this one," he crowed, holding up a raspberry velvet clutch. He snapped it open to check the lining. "Perfect condition. Probably never been used."

"I like this one." I dug beneath the leather, pulling out a gold lamé evening bag, studded with green glass cabochons. "Very Sonny and Cher—definitely seventies." There was a small makeup stain on the inner lining, but a little dry cleaning fluid would take care of it.

Digging for treasure took my mind off invisible women with long red fingernails, so I started piling purses on the counter. There was nothing I could do for Lila Boudreaux unless she showed up again, which hopefully wouldn't happen while Evan was here.

"What'd you do last night?" Evan asked absently. "Did Dr. Feelgood come over and make you feel good?" He picked up a bag made of tooled leather, inspecting the design before putting it aside and reaching for another.

"Yes, Joe was over for a while," I said, keeping my tone light. My boyfriend of one whole month, Dr. Joe Bascombe was the man who'd brought me back to life, in more ways than one.

I smiled just thinking about him. Tall, dark, and handsome just didn't cut it for Joe—dark-haired and handsome, yes, but the naughty twinkle in those green eyes was his most appealing quality.

Well, that and the way his butt looked in scrubs.

"We grilled steaks before he left for the hospital. He's on graveyard shift in the E.R. this week." I hesitated, then told Evan the rest. "He expects to hear from Kelly any day now."

Kelly was Joe's soon-to-be-ex-wife.

"You sound pretty blasé about it," Evan said, giving me a look. "Are you sure you're okay with this? I mean, having a boyfriend who's married to your long-lost twin sister could put a crimp in anybody's relationship."

"I don't know for sure she's my long-lost twin sister," I snapped, "and how can I lose something I never had?"

While I'd had a little time to get used to the idea, I wasn't sure which had been more difficult to accept—the fact I might have a twin sister I'd never known about, or the fact that my new boyfriend was married to her.

"Touchy, touchy." Evan shook his head. "Is it that time of the month again?"

I gave him the Evil Eye, and he wisely shut up.

"It could still just be a coincidence," I added. "Joe told me about her before we ever got involved, you know." Surely that wasn't a defensive tone in my voice? "She never said anything to him about having a twin sister, so she doesn't know about me either. They haven't even seen each other in four years. Just because we're both adopted . . . "

"Share the same birthday, the same birthplace, the same face . . . " Evan wasn't gonna let me out of this one.

"Who says we share the same face?"

Evan raised a perfectly groomed eyebrow in the manner that had earned him the nickname Queen Supreme.

"What?" I asked, getting testy. Being spooked first thing in the morning can do that to a girl.

"You've seen Kelly's picture," Evan said. "*I've* seen her picture. She looks just like you."

We'd been over this before, but Evan apparently needed to hear it again. "I haven't had long brown hair since I was in the sixth grade, and I sure wouldn't wear it in such a messy knot if I did. She wasn't wearing any makeup, and her idea of fashion is baggy jeans and oversized T-shirts." I shrugged. "She *so* does not look like me."

"You're talking about style, Nicki, not looks."

"Well, it's not my style to leave my husband and run off to join the Peace Corps, either, so I don't think we have much in common. Joe says it was a mutual split, and since she was on the other side of the world, they just never bothered to sign the divorce papers." I frowned, not liking that particular train of thought. "Anyway, I was perfectly happy being an only child. I'll deal with Kelly Bascombe when I have to."

He gave me raised eyebrows and a shrug, knowing when to let a subject drop.

I rummaged around in the box, looking for more flashy evening bags to put in the display case.

Back in work mode, Evan held up a bulky tapestry bag, turning it this way and that as he checked it for snags.

"Ugh. Hideous," I said.

He gave a long-suffering sigh. "Something else is bothering you, Nicki. Spill it." Trust Evan to pick up on the slightest snark.

"Nothing's bothering me," I lied.

"Liar."

"Nag."

"Spill it," Evan repeated.

"Okay, okay." Losing interest in purses for the time

being, I spilled it. "Don't freak out, but a woman came in this morning—a spirit. She said her daughter was hurt, that they'd been in a car accident."

"A ghost was here? In our shop?" Evan put down the bag he was holding, glancing around nervously. "I'm going straight over to Crystalline Blue and buy some sage sticks. Butch heard they can be used to purify a place from evil spirits."

I wanted to laugh at the idea that burning herbs would solve the problem, but I didn't.

"You do that," I said, "but don't blame me when they set off the smoke detector."

Evan gave me a look. "Have you got a better idea, Miss Spooky?"

I sighed, picking up my abandoned coffee mug. "No. No, I don't." Finally pouring myself a cup of caffeine, I looked for a place to sit. And there, in the chair behind the counter that Evan and I called the "catbird" seat, sat Lila Boudreaux.

"I remember now," she said to me. Fat tears were streaming down her cheeks. "I remember everything."

"Um . . . Evan?"

Evan glanced up from his box of purses, totally unaware that there was a ghost in his favorite chair.

"Maybe sage sticks wouldn't be such a bad idea."

He opened his mouth to say something, but the look on my face stopped him cold. Blue eyes widened.

"Here?" The word came out as a squeak.

I nodded.

"Now?"

I nodded again.

"Holy shit," he said. "Here we go again."

* * *

"I can't call the police yet, Joe. What am I supposed to tell them? That a dead woman just walked into my store and told me her daughter is missing?" I shot a guilty glance toward Lila, but she was staring blankly out the window of my car, watching the Georgia countryside whiz by.

"She's there with you now? In your car?"

I didn't blame him for being skeptical, though he, of all people, should know better—one dark night in the graveyard had recently proven that the dead don't always rest in peace.

"Yes, she is. Her name is Lila Boudreaux, and she says that she and her daughter were in a car accident."

"It was dark," Lila murmured. "We went off the road, down a hill."

She seemed so distant, as though talking to herself. The empty look in her eyes gave me the heebie-jeebies. My little red Honda was moving fast down I-85, but not fast enough for me.

"I wish you'd wait until my shift is over, Nicki. I could go with you—"

A muted sob came from the woman in the passenger seat. She pressed a chubby hand, red fingernails gleaming, to her mouth.

"Sorry, Joe. This can't wait."

"Nicki." Joe's frustration was evident. "Remember what happened the last time you tried to help a lost soul?"

Poor guy. What had he gotten himself into by getting hooked up with me? When I wasn't dodging voodoo queens and evil spirits, I was out doing favors for the dearly departed.

"Guess you could call me a high maintenance kind of girl, huh?" My attempt to be lighthearted came out kind of wimpy.

I could practically hear Joe roll his eyes. "High maintenance, high drama—woman, you are nothing but trouble. It's been a roller-coaster ride since that first day in the E.R." He chuckled a little to take the sting from his words. "I don't normally have to use electric shocks to get a girl's attention."

That made me smile, but I wasn't really in the mood for teasing. My life had changed in an instant a few weeks ago, and I was still missing the old one, the one where things made sense.

"Everything's different now, Joe. I see and hear the dead. I can't pretend I don't. I don't know how it works, but it is what it is." I swallowed hard, trying to concentrate on the road, but failing miserably. "I have to learn to live with it, and if you wanna be with me, you have to, too."

Silence for a few moments.

"Do you want to be with me?" Joe asked the question very quietly.

I hesitated, and answered as honestly as I could. "For now I do." Romantic commitment had never been one of my strong points, but for Joe, I was tempted to throw caution to the wind.

And that scared me.

Joe heard the hesitation. He was quiet for a minute. I hadn't turned the radio on, and the silence in the car was laden with tension.

"I'm not sure how much longer I can accept that as an answer, Nicki. Are we a couple, or is this just a casual thing for you?"

Lila turned her head and looked at me. Mascara streaked her cheeks, and the sadness in her face tugged at my heart. "Please hurry," she said.

I gripped the steering wheel harder with one hand, pressing the phone to my ear.

"Joe, I—" I cleared my throat nervously. "This is not the best time for this conversation. I'm not alone."

Another brief silence. Then, "Has it occurred to you that you're probably already too late to save this woman's daughter?"

I breathed a silent sigh of relief, recognizing a change of subject when I heard one. "Yes."

"*If* you find the car, and if you find *her*, the girl will have been trapped inside for who knows how long. Chances are she's already dead."

"She isn't," I said stubbornly. If Lila's daughter was dead, she'd probably be speaking for herself instead of having her mother do it for her.

"How do you know where to look? I-85 is a long stretch of highway."

"Lila said they'd just left the airport, and were looking for the I-20 exit. It has to be somewhere near there."

I was driving well over the speed limit, and checked my rearview for the umpteenth time, hoping I wouldn't get pulled over. Georgia state troopers were not known for their open-mindedness.

Sorry I was speeding, Officer, but there's a ghost in my car and she says I need to hurry.

Joe sighed in my ear. "Nicki, please be careful. If you find this girl, call my beeper number, then 911. Tell the operator to dispatch from Columbia Hospital, and I'll be on the ambulance before it leaves the E.R."

"You're the best," I said, smiling into the phone.

"I'm crazy," he answered. A hesitation. "Crazy about you."

My heart hammered against my ribs, but I wasn't sure if it was adrenaline or euphoria. This was the closest we'd come to using the L word. Either way, I needed to calm down or risk another cardiac event.

"I'm crazy about you, too," I murmured, wishing I didn't have an audience. "I'll call you as soon as I can."

Then I hung up, snapping my cell phone shut with one hand and dropping it into my lap.

"Was that your beau?" Lila had pulled herself out of her sadness enough to give me a small smile.

"My what?" For a moment I had no idea what she was talking about.

"You know . . . your boyfriend." Lila's Southern belle routine was no put on—for many Southern women, *Gone With The Wind* was never really gone. "He sounds nice."

"He's awesome." I pictured Joe as I'd first seen him, all serious and intent, trying to save my life; then another flash of him—naked and sexy, dark hair mussed—laughing down at me as we tickled each other silly after great sex. "Joe's an E.R. doctor at Columbia Hospital. He's promised to meet us with an ambulance if we—" I caught myself "—*when* we find your daughter."

Lila's lower lip trembled, then steadied. "I've made such a mess of things," she said. "Now here I am, caught between the devil and the deep blue sea. I never meant to hurt anybody."

"This isn't your fault." I hated to see anybody so sad. "Car accidents are called that for a reason."

"You're very sweet," Lila said, "and pretty as a picture." She cocked her head, eyeing me closely. "I love those pink streaks in your hair. Tell me . . . " She hesitated, just a moment. "Are you happy with your life?"

An odd question coming from a total stranger, but then again—maybe not so odd given the circumstances. This woman's life was over.

"I'm very happy," I said. "Happier than I've ever been." As I said it, I knew it was true. "I own my own business, run it with my best buddy, and have a great boyfriend. Life is good."

Lila smiled at me, a little wistfully. "You're a lucky girl, darlin'."

A sudden lump rose in my throat. I swallowed hard to get past it.

"Yes, I am." *Luckier than you know.* I'd been given a second chance at life. Lila Boudreaux hadn't.

"Your friend—back at the store—he's a little light in his loafers, isn't he?"

Despite the tenseness of the situation, I burst out laughing. "Yes, Evan's gay."

"That's all right," Lila said comfortably. "To each his own, I always say." She fluttered a red-nailed hand in my direction. "Don't mind me, honey, sometimes my mouth outruns my good sense."

"I know the feeling." And I did. My mouth had gotten me into trouble on more than one occasion.

The sign for I-20 appeared, and as we neared the exit, I slowed, pulling over to the side of the road.

"Does anything look familiar?"

Lila was staring at me. She blinked and drew in a deep breath, as though waking from a dream. Then she turned her head and scanned the roadside to our right.

It was pretty steep there. The grass dropped off quickly into a ravine choked with undergrowth, sparse trees draped with kudzu vines, scrawny crepe myrtles just touched with color.

Then I saw the skid marks on the blacktop, about twenty feet in front of us.

"I think this might be it, Lila."

She didn't answer. I glanced over to find the passenger seat empty.

With a sigh, I checked the sideview mirror to make sure I didn't become road kill, then got out, wishing I'd changed my shoes. Sandals would have a tough time on this hill. Then I remembered something useful—a pair of binoculars I'd bought for a Blondie concert the year before were still in my trunk.

I dug them out, shoving aside empty boxes and left-over garage sale junk from the weekend before, ignoring the whizzing of cars and the occasional honking of horns.

"Woo-hoo, baby!" A red truck with mud flaps and a Dixie flag in the back window came a little too close for comfort. I glanced up as it drove past to see a guy's head and arm hanging out the window.

Stupid Georgia rednecks.

Using the skid marks as a reference, I scanned the wooded area to my right. Tightening the focus on the binoculars, I followed a straight path down the hill. The undergrowth got thicker and the trees more numerous as my view of the hill changed. It was green, everything was green, except for the occasional gray rock or patch of red clay, a flash of pink crepe myrtle here and there.

And then I saw a glint of something shiny where there should be nothing shiny. Buried beneath fallen branches and hidden from easy sight by a wild tangle of bushes was a car's sideview mirror. Looking closer, I could see the car itself. It was green, too.

Things happened pretty quickly after that.

I speed-dialed Joe's beeper number as fast as I could. Once I heard the tone, I entered 666—our personal code—then hung up and called 911. I gave them the exit number and asked specifically for an ambulance from Columbia Hospital, but the dispatcher got a little snippy with me when I wouldn't stay on the line. "I've told you exactly where to find us. Now get your ass in gear and send somebody out here." Then I hung up, shoved the cell phone in my back pocket, and started down the hill.

It was pretty steep, and the ground kept shifting beneath my feet. Snatching at the bushes and using my butt as a counterweight, I scrabbled down the hill, wishing again for tennis shoes, or boots. Despite the dirt and clay between my toes, I managed to reach the crumpled car in just a few moments.

There was an oily smell, grease and gasoline. Broken branches covered the roof and hood, so I snatched away whatever greenery I could, revealing shattered glass and twisted metal. A few seconds later I could see the woman in the driver's seat. She was lying almost flat, the seat in a reclining position. Good thing, too, because the roof of the car was crushed. She had less than a foot of breathing space. There was blackened blood in her hair, and her eyes were closed.

It wasn't Lila, and I was glad. I didn't want to see Lila's dead body. The passenger side of the car was completely crushed against a tree, and there was no way I could get to it.

Lila's final task was done—finding help for her daughter—and her spirit was nowhere to be seen. I could only hope she'd crossed over.

"Miss?" I kept pulling branches off the car so I could get closer to the woman in the front seat. "Help is on the way," I said, knowing she couldn't hear. She was young—late twenties, maybe, brown hair, white T-shirt. Her face was turned toward me, cheeks pale except for a big bruise along the jawline, mouth slightly open.

"Where the hell is that ambulance?" I muttered. The window was shattered, jagged pieces of glass still stuck in the frame. Very carefully, I reached a hand in until I could touch her wrist, feeling gingerly for a pulse.

Like I knew what I was doing.

She moaned slightly, fingers twitching. Relieved, I said again, "Help is on the way. Just stay still." Her eyes didn't open, but her fingers twitched again, harder.

Without thinking, I took her hand in mine and squeezed. The faintest pressure answered me, and that was that. I stayed in that position, bent over awkwardly, holding her hand and hoping I wouldn't cut my arm on broken glass, until the ambulance arrived.

I never thought the wail of a siren could sound so good.

And then there was Joe, white lab coat flapping as

he scrambled down the hill with a first aid kit, two guys in blue shirts carrying bright orange boxes not far behind.

"They're here," I said to the woman. "Hang on." This time there was no answering pressure when I squeezed her hand.

As Joe reached us, I let her go to move out of the way, oddly reluctant to break contact.

"Oh my God," Joe breathed.

"Is she dead?" *Please don't let her be dead.*

"No." Joe's face was as white as a sheet. "It's Kelly. It's my wife."

CHAPTER 2

The nurse behind the emergency room admissions desk stared at me, stone-faced. Gray-haired and plump, she seemed glued to the chair, and completely unconcerned by my demands for information.

"Her name is Kelly Bascombe." I was insistent, unwilling to settle for "have a seat." I'd followed the ambulance in my car, but there was no way I could keep up. Now that I was here, I wanted to see her, dammit. "She's a car accident victim. They just brought her in."

The nurse's stern expression never changed. "You'll have to take a seat, ma'am. All I can tell you is she's being taken care of. The doctor will be out to speak with you as soon as he's able." The woman's cheerful scrubs didn't go with her drill sergeant personality; cartoon flowers and butterflies all mixed in with the words "Get Well Soon." Her ID badge said BETTY WALKER, RN, CNAA.

"Can't you at least tell Dr. Bascombe I'm here? My name is Nicki Styx. Joe—Dr. Bascombe—is a friend of mine."

She eyed me coolly, unimpressed. "I'm sure you understand that Dr. Bascombe is very busy at the moment. Please have a seat, and he'll be with you when he can."

Battle-Axe Betty was about to get an earful, but Evan stepped in. I'd called him on the way, and he and Butch got to the hospital at nearly the same time I did. Evan took me by the elbow and pulled me toward a row of chairs. "C'mon, Nick. We're gonna have to wait a little while. Joe knows we're out here."

A "little while" turned out to be three and a half hours. By that time, Nurse Betty was shooting me dirty looks every time I got up from my chair. There was a TV droning over in one corner, but I spent the wait pacing, nagging the nurse, and whining. Butch went for snacks, sodas, and magazines, so he and Evan managed to occupy themselves with fashion and fitness for a while. I wasn't hungry, and for once I didn't care about Lagerfeld's spring line *or* photos of buff, sweaty men.

"You'd think somebody could figure out how to make waiting room chairs more comfortable." My butt and hard plastic weren't a good fit. "I'm sick of this place. Seems like I've been here at least once a week for the last month."

"Three times." Supremely bored, the Queen Supreme flipped lazily through the current issue of *Muscle & Fitness*. "Once for you, once for me, and now for Kelly," Evan said.

Kelly. My twin sister. Supposedly. Maybe.

I'd know when I looked her in the eye.

Wouldn't I?

The chair next to me creaked as Butch sat down. His big, bald bouncer image was the perfect cover for a heart of gold and a teddy bear personality. He slid an arm around my shoulders, offering me a cold can of soda. His bulk was solid and reassuring, and he wore great cologne. Armani, maybe.

"Does she look like you, Nicki?" Butch asked.

"I don't know. Her face was bruised, her eyes were closed—she had blood in her hair. Long brown hair. She was unconscious."

I remembered watching Joe take her pulse, and how he said "She's alive" as if it were some kind of miracle. I'd watched him open the first aid kit and start pulling out tubes and needles. I'd backed up, away from the car, mostly to stay out of his way, partly so I wouldn't have to see the look on his face.

Would he have been that absorbed, that focused, if the woman were a stranger? Had I been watching a doctor trying to save a patient, or a husband trying to save his wife?

"I could only see the side of her face anyway." I took a teeny sip of soda. *She'd been wearing a white shirt and jeans.* "When the paramedics got there they had to wait for the police to bring a pair of metal clippers to cut through the roof of the car. They peeled it back and got her out, but she never woke up. She never moved."

"Wow," Butch said. He gave me a squeeze. "You *have* had a day, haven't you?"

I didn't need to be here. What could I do? Stand

around and watch while my boyfriend held his dying wife's hand?

"Hey now." Evan put down his magazine and slipped over to take a seat on my other side, while I covered my eyes and tried not to burst into tears.

I'd cried enough lately. Three funerals in a month, and my own near death experience. Twin sister shows up, she's near death, too. But if I were going to have a sister, I'd prefer a live one to a dead one. I had enough *ghoulfriends* as it was.

"Miss Styx." Nurse Betty finally called my name. She hung up the phone as I hustled over, ready to behave and be quiet if she'd just tell me *something*.

"Dr. Bascombe would like to speak with you privately." She came out from behind the desk where she'd been planted. "If you'll step in here," she opened the door to a side room just a few steps away, "he'll be with you in a moment." Was that the teeniest bit of softening I heard in her voice? The room was small, nothing but a few chairs, cushioned ones this time, and a couple of side tables. There was a big box of tissues on one and a Bible on the other. *Oh, shit.*

I looked at Evan, a wave of panic closing my throat.

That was the signal he'd been waiting for. Both he and Butch shot up and came toward me. The nurse subtly positioned herself between us and asked, "Are you both family members?"

Oh, shit. Privacy? Family members?

"This is my brother." I spoke up before anyone else could, and reached out to catch Evan's hand. There was no way I was gonna be able to pull off both of them as relatives. Butch would understand.

Evan's fingers squeezed mine, and I squeezed back.

"Well, then." The nurse didn't question us further, ushering the two of us into the little room. "Dr. Bascombe will be right with you," she said, and closed the door.

Claustrophobia immediately set in, making the panic worse.

"Oh my God, oh my God, oh my God . . . Kelly's dead," I blurted. "She's dead, I know she's dead."

Evan gave a horrified gasp. "You do?" He grabbed my hands in both of his, glancing suspiciously around the otherwise empty room. "Did the nurse tell you this or did she?"

Even in my panicky state I knew what he was worried about. One ghost today had been enough for poor Evan.

The door opened and Joe stepped in, looking haggard. He checked when he saw us both standing there, then came in and shut the door behind him.

"Let's all sit." He wasn't smiling. Panic gave way to a kind of numbness as Evan and I sank into the cushioned seats, not letting go of each other's hand. Joe sat on my other side.

"How's Kelly?" My voice sounded surprisingly normal.

Joe reached for my free hand, and I gave it to him without thinking. "She has a concussion, two sprained ankles, some broken ribs. She's dehydrated and very weak."

I blinked. Nowhere in there did I hear the word "dead."

Joe was still talking. "Ironically enough, the dehydration is probably what saved her. It kept the brain swelling under control and a blood clot from forming. The head injury could've been much more serious otherwise. But another day or so and dehydration would've killed her. Her kidneys would've shut down. All in all, she's in surprisingly good shape."

The numbness persisted, so I tried to focus on Joe's warm grip on my hand. "She's going to be okay?"

He nodded, but he still wasn't smiling. "She's going to be okay."

"Hallelujah." Evan blew out a noisy breath. "You had us scared to death! Why couldn't you just tell us that in the waiting room?"

Really. I closed my eyes and let my shoulders slump, surprised at the amount of tension they carried.

"Because there's something else."

Joe's answer brought my eyes open again. I looked at him, waiting for the other shoe to drop.

"She's been in and out of it, but we were able to talk a little." He hesitated. "She knows about you, Nicki."

"What? You told her already?" I stared into Joe's eyes, not knowing quite how to feel about that. Seems like he and Kelly had already done quite a bit of catching up. I couldn't help but wonder if they'd done some *making* up, too.

Joe was shaking his head. "I was too busy trying to save her life," he said. "I'll tell her about us as soon as she's stable."

His gaze never wavered, but the detached calm that made him such a good doctor made me nervous. Despite his promise, a little stab of jealousy hit. Was this a doctor being considerate of his patient, or a man putting off the inevitable with his wife?

"If you didn't tell her about me, then who did?"

He sighed. "The woman who was in the car with her." He paused, then added, "The woman who died. They were on their way to find you."

Now I was really confused.

"Lila? The woman in my store?"

"Nicki . . . " Joe glanced briefly at Evan, who was being uncharacteristically quiet. "I don't know any easy way to tell you this."

My fingers were numb from the death grip Evan had on my hand.

"Lila Boudreaux, the woman who died, was your mother."

Emily Styx was my mother.

Brown hair, plump cheeks, and sweet hugs. Adoring smiles and fresh-baked cookies for husband Dan and daughter Nicki. Advice and acceptance for me and my friends. Encouragement and pride. Love and warmth and laughter.

Those were my memories of my mother, and nobody could take them away.

I felt bad about Lila Boudreaux, but she was a stranger. A stranger who'd given me away without bothering to get to know me first. Even if she'd managed to survive the accident, she'd shown up far too late.

Although she could've at least said good-bye.

The corridor smelled strongly of whatever pine-scented soap the hospital used to mop the floors. I stood outside the door to Kelly's room at 9:00 A.M. the next morning, wondering what to say to her. My feelings for Joe, my thoughts of Lila, sympathy for what Kelly must've been through . . . everything was tangled up into a big knotted ball of curiosity and nervousness, curdling my stomach. I was about to meet my twin and my boyfriend's soon-to-be-ex-wife, all in one. This was *huge*.

I didn't have time to worry about the past. I had to deal with the present.

Before I could lose my nerve, I tapped at the door and went in.

Kelly was staring out the window, propped up against the pillows with her legs elevated. Her head was bandaged and so were both ankles. A smear of bluish-black bruises covered the side of her face, ugly twins to the ones on her arms.

She'd been crying. A box of tissues sat beside her on the bed, and she dabbed at her eyes, sniffling, as I came in. As soon as she got a good look at me, she froze, and so did I.

I had goose bumps. This was my *sister*.

"I'm Nicki." The words felt weird on my tongue, but I made myself say them. "I think I'm your sister."

Kelly sucked in her breath, eyes widening. I watched them fill with tears, while mine prickled uncomfortably. She pressed a bruised hand against her mouth while we stared at each other.

Then she held out her hands. They were shaking. Tears escaped her lashes and rolled down her cheeks.

"You look like her," she whispered. "She was so pretty." Her voice caught on a sob. "She's gone, you know."

I didn't need to ask who she was talking about, even though I didn't think Lila looked at all like me.

I moved toward the bed and took Kelly's outstretched

hands, careful to let her do the squeezing. Then I sank down beside her on the edge of the mattress. Her hands were cold, while mine were sweating.

We were only a couple of feet away now, staring into each other's face. Her expression was impossible to describe—a mixture of wonder and sorrow that made *me* want to cry. But I was determined not to. I'd been through enough mascara lately.

I couldn't deny it—even with the bruises and bandages, looking into Kelly's face was like looking into a mirror. *An ugly, bruised mirror, but whatever.*

"How can this be?" she murmured.

My normal personality asserted itself. "Well, the way I understand it, the fertilized egg splits in two."

She smiled, her first one. "So you're a smartass, too. What a relief. At least we'll have something in common."

I smiled back, finding it surprisingly easy. Kelly laughed a little through her tears, ending on a watery hiccup. Then she let go of one hand to swipe at her cheeks.

"I can't believe you're here." She squeezed my hand again as fresh tears threatened. "I wish she could've—" A choked sob kept her from finishing the sentence.

I wished fiercely for Evan, or even Butch, to tell me what to do. I'd never been very good at tea and sympathy. I supposed I should be crying, too, but then I'd be crying for a total stranger, and that just didn't work for me.

Then I remembered what comforted me the most in those dark days after my parents died.

"Tell me about Lila," I said.

Kelly closed her eyes. Her throat moved as she swallowed.

"Peaches. She wanted us to call her Peaches."

My heart fluttered, then throbbed as the beat picked up. I'd smelled peaches when Lila came into the store.

"That was her nickname, and she thought it would be easier than calling her Mom. She was funny and sweet and had a ridiculous Southern accent. I couldn't believe it when she tracked me down—I got a letter from her about two weeks ago." Another hard swallow. Kelly's eyes opened, seeking mine. "After that, we talked on the phone almost every day. I had to come back to the States anyway to take care of some unfinished business, and when I flew into Atlanta, Peaches was there to meet me at the airport." Her voice cracked.

Kinda weird how she referred to Joe as "unfinished business," but I could imagine the scene; a tearful reunion of mother and daughter, thrilled and happy to find each other. Where did I fit into the picture?

Oh yeah, there I was, the gloomy one in the corner with the pink streaks in her hair.

"She was so happy to see me." Kelly swiped away tears, hand trembling. "She said the only thing that could possibly make her happier was if we found you."

It was still hard to believe that all this time I'd had a sister and a mother I'd known nothing about—even harder to believe they'd been looking for me.

Kelly drew in a deep breath. Her voice was stronger after she let it out.

"She was so excited. So was I." A tinge of irony crept in. "We'd find you, and then we'd all be together—one big, happy family."

I didn't know what to say, so I kept quiet while Kelly picked at the hospital blanket. "The adoption agency told her they'd keep us together. She was pretty upset to find out things didn't turn out that way." Kelly blinked back more tears, swiping them away.

"Why did she give us away in the first place?" The burning question, the one I'd wondered about all my life, came out before I could stop it.

Kelly waved a bruised hand. "Same old story. Too young, not married, boyfriend dumped her."

I had a sudden image of poor lonely Tammy, the teenage spirit who'd been haunting the Star Bar since the eighties because of guilt over an abortion. If Peaches had chosen that route, I wouldn't be here.

"You're very pretty," Kelly said.

"So are you," I lied. The bruises on her face would have to fade and the swelling go down before that statement could be remotely near the truth.

"I look like hell," she answered. "The night nurse was kind enough to lend me a mirror. But that's sweet of you to say."

An awkward silence descended as we stared at each other. She was nervous, and so was I.

"I can't believe you're here. You don't look anything like I imagined," she said. "You look so . . . so stylish. Like a model."

I'd been going for a cheerful, upbeat look when I chose the outfit, a vintage paisley halter dress in watercolor shades of aqua and pink. I hoped my nervous sweat wouldn't leave pit stains on the vintage material.

"Thanks." Kelly was definitely more of the "nature girl" type. Her brown hair was straight, worn long and parted in the middle. Aside from the bruises, she looked pretty much like what I expected. "I guess I have an advantage," I answered. "I've seen your picture."

Kelly blinked, tiny frown lines appearing between her eyes. "You've seen my picture?"

I took a deep breath. "Yeah. Joe showed me."

"Joe?" Kelly looked at me blankly.

Holy freakin' Mother of . . . she didn't know.

I stood up so fast I knocked the box of tissues to the floor. "Um . . . hasn't Joe explained things to you?"

Kelly's confusion got deeper. "How do you know Joe? Explained what?"

At that moment I knew how a deer in the headlights must feel. Kelly was no dummy, and within seconds, comprehension dawned. Her mouth fell open.

"Are you kidding me?" Her voice rose slightly. "You and Joe? *My* Joe?"

"*Your* Joe?" The words were out of my mouth before I could stop them. "When's the last time you saw him, or even spoke to him?"

"Last night," Kelly shot back. "How about you?"

My heartbeat responded to the hostility in her voice, speeding up.

"This morning," I said calmly, "and pretty much every day for the last month. He told me he was free to date anyone he wanted. Are you telling me different?"

Kelly's face had reddened beneath the bruises, giving her a mottled look. I held my ground, meeting her eye.

She looked away first.

"Joe's his own man," she murmured. "But that doesn't mean I want him dating my sister."

"I see."

Charged silence for a moment, then her face turned back in my direction.

We stared at each other.

"You still have feelings for him." I made it a statement, not a question.

"He's a great guy." Her chin quivered, just once, then firmed. "He didn't deserve what I did to him."

"No, he didn't." I wasn't giving an inch. There was too much at stake. "But he's over it."

"Then why didn't he tell me this himself last night?"

Good question, though I didn't care for the way she asked it.

I shrugged, playing it cool. "Maybe he didn't want to upset you. You've been through a rough time."

Kelly blinked, and it was like a shutter came down, veiling her thoughts. Her gaze flicked over my bare shoulders and the neckline of my halter dress. In an abrupt change of subject, she said, "I can see why Joe likes you."

Was that some kind of backhanded slap, or a genuine compliment?

"I'm sure he likes you, too." I forced myself to answer her lightly. If she wanted to play nice, I could play nice. "He married you."

She shrugged, then looked away. "Our marriage has been over for years, and I was the one who threw in the towel. You can have him."

"Gee, thanks." This time I couldn't keep the sarcastic edge out of my voice if I'd tried.

There was a silence, then she said, "I'm sorry." She bit her lip, still not looking at me. "I have a tendency to be a bitch sometimes."

"I know the feeling." I knew that feeling, and a few others. Right now I had the feeling I should leave.

But I didn't.

Kelly seemed fascinated with the crappy hospital curtains.

There was a chair in the corner opposite the bed. I took a seat without asking.

"You and Joe have every right to be seeing each other, even if it is kinda weird," she said after a moment.

Tell me about it.

"I mean, what are the odds of that? Joe dating my twin?" Kelly eyed me curiously, and I returned the favor. If she were waiting for me to venture an opinion, she'd just have to keep waiting.

She sighed and let her head fall back against the pillows. "It was just a shock, that's all. It's been a pretty bad week."

I couldn't help but feel sorry for her. She was lying in a hospital bed, black and blue and white all over. Those bandages made me itch just looking at them.

"There are so many things I wanted to talk to you about, Nicki. Hearing from Peaches was like a dream come true, but the dream seems to have turned into a nightmare."

I tried not to let that comment hurt my feelings, but it kinda did. True, Peaches was gone, but what was I, chopped liver?

"I think my pain medication is kicking in." Kelly's face was pale, making the bruises all the more noticeable. "I'm really tired. Can we do this later?"

I got to my feet, surprised to find my knees a little wobbly. "I'll come back tomorrow."

"Thanks. By the way, I like your outfit. It looks . . . nice. Very colorful."

Then she ruined it by adding, "If that's the look you're going for."

"I hate her. And I hate Joe, too."

I'd called Evan on my cell phone as soon as I got to the car.

"What do you mean 'you hate her'?" Evan ignored my comment about Joe, knowing a lie when he heard it. "You can't hate her—she's your twin sister, for God's sake. Hang on a minute." I could hear the beep of the cash register in the background, so I waited until I heard him give a cheery, "Thanks so much. Come back and see us."

"Okay, so I don't hate her, but she's not making it easy." Evan would still have the phone cradled to his ear. I was barely paying attention as I drove my car out of the hospital parking garage.

"C'mon, Nicki, she can't be that bad." He was using his "let's humor the crazy chick" tone. "You barely met her."

"She dissed my outfit."

A horrified gasp, then a momentary silence. "What are you wearing?"

"The pink and blue paisley halter dress."

Evan sighed. "Well, no wonder. That thing's hideous."

"It is not," I shot back. We'd had this argument before. "I like it."

"It looks like the Easter Bunny threw up on you," he said. "Why in the world did you wear *that*?"

"You're not helping," I snapped.

"Okay, okay. But next time I'm picking the outfit."

"Next time? Who said anything about next time?"

"Nicholette Nadine Styx, there *will* be a next time, because she's the only family you have in the whole world. Which means *you're* the only family *she* has in the whole world. You're going to get over yourself, and you're going to get to know your twin sister, even if it kills you."

"Now there's an idea," I said glumly. "Can't I just kill her instead?"

Evan proved yet again how well he knew me by saying, "Quite frankly, I think you're just in a snit because God saw fit to create two of you instead of just one. You never could stand to share the spotlight. Then there's the guilt over the 'sleeping with her husband' thing."

"Who are you all of a sudden, Dr. Phil? Have you been going to some gay psychology class I know nothing about?"

"Don't get snippy," he warned. "I'm only trying to help."

"Stop taking her side and listen to me, Evan. First she was all sweetness and light, but as soon as she heard about Joe and me, everything changed."

"Excuse me, girlfriend, but your bitchy slip is showing." Evan was cutting me no slack. "She almost died. You were no Susie Sunshine the day after your heart failure, you know."

I remembered that day. I'd woken up in the hospital, not knowing how I got there, wondering if the dream I'd just had about a white light and a disembodied voice telling me it "wasn't my time" had been real. Stiff, sore, and cranky as hell, I awoke with the words "do unto others as you would have them do unto you" still resounding in my head. I was pretty unhappy to discover that the people I was supposed to "do it to" were people who'd died with unfinished business.

Evan was right, damn him. I shouldn't hold Kelly's crankiness against her.

"Has anybody ever told you that you're a pain in the ass?"

He laughed. "Well, actually . . . "

"Don't say it," I warned.

Evan laughed again, and I couldn't help but join him this time. Whatever issues lay ahead with Kelly and Joe, at least I had someone to adjust my bitchy slip.

"Kelly thinks you're cool. Colorful, she said."

I held the phone out at arm's length and stared at it. Then I put it back to my ear and asked Joe, very calmly, "What?"

"I was worried you and Kelly wouldn't like each other. You're so different."

Gee, ya think?

"Kelly's responding well, Nick. Her fluids are stabilized, the brain swelling is already subsiding. The ankles will heal. She'll be ready for discharge in a few days."

"And then what?"

Joe must've been tipped off by something in my voice, because his answer was wary. "What do you mean?"

My conversation with Kelly had left me edgy, and despite the tough stance I'd taken with her—claiming that

Joe was mine now—I couldn't help but wonder where I really stood. "I mean, what happens next? She's your wife. I'm your girlfriend. Where do we go from here? You didn't even tell her about me—I walked in there blind."

His hesitation made me even edgier. "Nicki, things have been happening pretty fast. I was going to tell her today. I didn't plan on you being at the hospital so early."

Not the right answer. At least, not the one I wanted to hear.

"She still has feelings for you," I said flatly.

"Did she say that?" No hesitation that time—in fact, Joe sounded a little too eager to find out the answer.

"She didn't have to." My heartbeat began to rise, anger or fear, I didn't know which. "The question is, do you still have feelings for her?"

He blew out a breath in frustration. "I believe I asked you about *your* feelings yesterday, and you never answered me."

I didn't plan on answering now, either. If I were going to declare myself to Joe, it wasn't going to be during a discussion about another girl.

"Is this some kind of stand-off? You won't tell me how you feel unless I tell you how I feel?" I didn't like pressure, yet I couldn't deny I was guilty of applying a little myself.

"Nicki, I've told you what happened between Kelly and me. I told you from the beginning, before we got involved, remember? You knew we were going to have to deal with this situation sooner or later."

"Not like this." I didn't know why I was being so pushy. Well, maybe I did, but I wasn't well-versed in jealous behavior; I'd always been the love 'em and leave 'em type, moving on before things got to this stage. "I didn't expect Kelly to be all hurt and vulnerable when she showed up. I mean, she needs a doctor, and here you are, a doctor. How convenient is that?"

Joe didn't answer at first, and I found myself gripping the phone so hard my hand hurt. "You're going to have to trust me, Nicki," he said quietly.

I drew in a shaky breath. The last time I trusted a guy, I'd caught him in the backseat of a car with a skanky blond cheerleader named Cindy.

"I've always trusted you," Joe said, "even when you've come up with some pretty unbelievable tales."

He had me there. Dead people, voodoo queens, grave digging—I was hardly your ordinary girlfriend.

Which was one of the reasons I was so worried.

"Let's talk about this later tonight," he said, sounding weary. "I'm going to catch a few winks in the sleep room before my next shift, but I'm off at eight. How does wine and pasta sound? I can stop by Mama Mia's on the way to your house."

"Sounds great." I meant it. Joe might not have said exactly what I needed to hear, but he hadn't said anything negative either, and I was tired of feeling insecure. "I do believe I'll be feeling the need for an emergency house call by then, Doctor."

He laughed, and it made me smile to hear it. His voice lowered. "Better that than another emergency need to visit the graveyard. I know what happens at the graveyard."

I laughed, too. "Yep, I remember. All kinds of horny devils come to life. Meet me there at midnight."

Joe's chuckle caught. "You're kidding, right?"

Poor man. I laughed again, enjoying his reaction. "Yes, I'm kidding!" I waited a few heartbeats and said, "But if I really did wanna go, you'd go with me, wouldn't you?"

I wanted to hear him say it, even if I had no intention of going near Trinity Cemetery in the middle of the night ever again. Joe and I had our naughty little walk on the wild side, but we'd also wound up in the middle of a voodoo ritual, and nearly wound up dead.

"You're a wicked, wicked woman, Nicki Styx." There was no way to miss the appreciation in Joe's voice. "And I guess if I'm gonna be with a wicked woman, I better be willing to be a bad boy once in a while. I'd go if you wanted to."

"Why, Joe . . . " I felt the prick of my own horny little devils. "Next time you feel like being a bad boy, you just let me know."

He cleared his throat and whispered hoarsely, "If you don't stop teasing me I'm going to be arrested for indecent exposure. How am I supposed to treat my patients when it looks like somebody pitched a tent in my scrubs?"

I giggled, feeling no guilt whatsoever. "Tell them you're doing a clinical study on those little blue pills, Dr. Bascombe. And if you come by later, I'll do my best to relieve the problem."

And oh, what a relief it was. By ten o'clock that night Joe and I had proven, to our own individual satisfaction, that he had no need for little blue pills.

And now he lay warm and solid in my bed, half-empty bottle of red wine on the nightstand, candles flickering. "I love this music," Joe murmured. "Who is it?" He sounded tired, but happy.

"Luscious Jackson," I answered drowsily, sliding my hand over his bare chest. "A girl band called Luscious Jackson." My shoulder was tucked beneath his shoulder, my right leg draped over his left, head nestled just beneath his chin. It was, as I liked to think of it, the sweet spot.

"Never heard of them," Joe said, "but I think Luscious is my new favorite word." He chuckled, chest rumbling beneath my cheek. "Music to make love to."

The word "love" brought me fully awake. "Is that what we just did?"

He gathered me even closer and pressed a kiss to the top of my head. "That's what I just did," he said softly. "How about you?"

I could barely breathe, but I wasn't sure if it was the way he was holding me or the way the conversation was going. "The word scares me," I whispered. "I'm not sure I know what love is."

He sighed. "I'm confused, Nicki. One minute you're pulling me closer, and the next you're pushing me away."

"That's me," I murmured. "An enigma, bound up in a riddle, wrapped inside a paradox." I'd heard that phrase once and never forgotten it; it seemed an accurate version of the weirdness that was me—now more than ever.

Joe tried to draw back so he could look me in the face, but I snuggled even closer and said, "You know my pathetic little story, Joe. Engaged at eighteen, lied to and cheated on, broken heart, broken dreams."

How lame it sounded. And it was, when you thought about it. I mean, who gets engaged at eighteen?

Ignoring my halfhearted resistance, he rolled me over and pressed me back against the pillows. "That was a long time ago, Nicki." His hand trailed down to the tattoo of a broken heart on the curve of my right breast. "You were way too young, and the guy was a creep who didn't deserve you."

The tenderness in his tone was enough to break my heart all over again.

The only light in my bedroom came from the candles on my dresser, but I could see Joe's face, serious and intent. I tried to lift the mood with a little teasing. "And you think *you* deserve me? You must've done something really bad to wind up with a girlfriend who sees dead people."

Joe didn't smile. He brushed the hair from my eyes and said, "I don't know what I did, but I'd do it again in a heartbeat if it meant I had a chance to be with you."

What could I do but kiss him? And then I kissed him again, because he tasted as sweet on the outside as he was on the inside—cherry chocolate cake, dripping with warm syrup and dusted with sugar.

And when the kiss was over, he rested his forehead against mine, breath warm on my lips. "Nicki, I—"

"Shh," I whispered. "I don't wanna jinx anything."

He sighed. "This from the girl who faced down a voodoo queen and dug up a zombie."

The smile in his voice made me smile, too, though the memory of that night wasn't funny.

"I think you just need a little more time and a little more proof that not all men are jerks," he murmured.

I ran my fingers through his dark hair, loving the feel of it. "I'm willing to do a little more research into the male psyche, Dr. Bascombe. Is there any probing involved?"

"Most definitely," Joe said, and then all conversation stopped for a while, as a band called Luscious Jackson engraved itself in my memory as part of one of the best nights ever.

CHAPTER 3

I was feeling a lot better about things by the time Evan and I went to the hospital the next day. After all, Joe'd spent the night in my bed, not by Kelly's bedside. He was still sprawled under my goose-down comforter, catching up on lost sleep and recuperating from our late night "research."

Evan, as usual, looked fabulous. Black linen trousers, creased in all the right places, with a blue and white striped dress shirt, untucked and tapered to fit. He even carried a matching bouquet of blue irises, the big fairy. He'd insisted on khaki cargoes and layered tees for me, an okay look but not my favorite.

"Now be nice," he hissed under his breath as we approached Kelly's room. "And get that smug look off your face. Not everybody needs to know you've been doing the nasty all night."

He gave me a warning glance, so I pasted a fake smile on my face and flashed it at him.

The door was open. I tapped the door frame and stuck my head in. Kelly was watching television, looking virtually the same as she had the day before. Her legs were still elevated on pillows, bare toes peeping from the bandages.

"Can we come in?" I deliberately made myself sound as cheerful as possible.

"Sure." Kelly clicked off the set. She looked curiously at Evan as he followed me into the room.

"This is my best friend and business partner, Evan Owenby. I hope you don't mind, but he's been dying to meet you."

"Oh my God," Evan gushed, "you two look exactly alike!" He shook his head in amazement as he stared at Kelly, completely missing my dirty look.

Kelly didn't look too happy at the comparison either, which I found pretty insulting. At least I didn't look like somebody'd beat me with an ugly stick, and right now she did. Her bruises were slightly more green than blue today, but that was hardly an improvement.

"Nice to meet you, Evan." She recovered quicker than I did.

"These are for you." Evan held out the irises, completely oblivious, or at least pretending to be.

"Thanks." Kelly took the irises and admired them, even holding them to her nose. "No one's given me flowers in a long time."

Evan melted, the big marshmallow. "Aww, poor thing. Have you been on a deserted island or something?"

Kelly gave him a genuine smile. "Kind of. I've been

in the Peace Corps. Romance tends to take a backseat when you're dealing with issues like poor sanitation and a lack of clean drinking water."

"Ick." Evan's shudder was just as genuine. "Speaking of water, let me put those in some for you." He bustled around like the Florence Nightingale of florists, taking the water pitcher from Kelly's bedside table and refilling it in the bathroom sink, talking the whole time. "No boyfriend? No significant other? Or doesn't the Peace Corps allow fraternization between the troops?"

Kelly's gaze flicked toward me, then away. She and Evan were chatting like old friends—I felt like a third wheel.

"I was seeing someone in Santo Domingo for a while, but it didn't work out. It's just as well—he turned out to be a jerk."

"I hear ya, honey. Sometimes it's better to be alone than in the wrong company. But you're here now, with us. Of course, this has got to be one of the strangest things *ever.* You guys should write to 'Ripley's Believe It or Not' or something. I mean, what are the odds that Nicki would lead the paramedics to her own twin sister?"

"Evan . . ." We'd agreed not to talk about this. There was enough stuff going on without announcing I was a freak who talked to the dead. Joe had been willing to keep it to himself, and so was I. I'd told the paramedics I just happened to see Kelly's crushed car from the highway.

"What?" Kelly lowered the flowers and glanced at me, then at Evan as he stepped from the bathroom. "What are you talking about?"

"You didn't know?" Evan was already in high gossip mode, taking the irises and unwrapping them as he spoke. I knew immediately he'd intended to tell Kelly this all along, the big meddler.

"Evan. This is stupid. Stop it."

He ignored me.

"Nicki knows things."

Kelly shot me an unreadable look.

"She knew there'd been a car accident." He gave me an innocent glance over his shoulder as he arranged the irises in the pitcher. "Nicki knew exactly where your car went off the road. She knew there was someone trapped in the ravine."

"Shut up, Evan." Rarely did I use that tone, and despite the fact that he deserved it, I could see immediately that he didn't appreciate it. It didn't stop him, though.

"She didn't know who you were, of course, but Nicki is the one who insisted on going to look for you. If she hadn't, you'd be dead by now." Evan gave the purplish blooms a final adjustment and turned a sweet smile on Kelly. "So you might want to remember that before you two get off to a bad start."

Unbelievable. Un-freaking believable. I was so pissed at Evan's move that I couldn't even speak.

He turned and brushed imaginary pollen from his fingers as he walked toward the door. "My work here is done," he quipped. "I'll see you both later." And then he was gone, the big coward.

At least he hadn't told Kelly about Lila coming to see me. For that I'd let him keep at least one testicle.

"What was *that* all about?" Kelly was frowning at me. "Was he telling the truth?"

I didn't know what to say. I sighed, and settled for, "It was just a coincidence."

She paled, bruises like mushrooms under the skin of her cheek. The look she gave me was suspicious. "Are you some kind of psychic or something?"

Nervous at how close she'd come to the mark, frustrated by Evan, my temper flared. "I said it was just a coincidence," I snapped. "Let's leave it at that."

Kelly apparently had a temper, too. "You don't have to bite my head off."

"Look—" Frustration made me say more than I probably should. "This whole thing has been a shock to me, too, you know. It's hard enough to grasp that I have a sister," I crossed my arms, trying to get a grip, "but as soon as you found out I was dating Joe, everything turned sour."

Kelly flushed, but didn't look away. "What did you expect?"

I steeled myself, preparing for the worst. "Are you telling me you want Joe back? After all this time?"

"No."

I waited, not very patiently, for her to say more.

All she offered was, "I was rude yesterday. I'm sorry."

Not quite willing to let it go, I said, "You dissed my outfit."

She flared again. "You came in here all glammed up the day after you find out your mother just died!" She looked away, staring resentfully at the crappy curtains. "It was inappropriate."

I didn't believe for one second that my clothes were at the heart of Kelly's hostility. "Well, excuse me, Mother Teresa."

"Ladies, is there a problem in here?" A black nurse, easily two hundred pounds of no-nonsense, came into the room. "This is a hospital, not the little girls' room at the high school prom." By the look on her face I knew I was in danger of being told to leave.

I wasn't ready to leave. Kelly and I had things to talk about.

"Sorry." I spoke first. "We'll keep it down."

I expected Kelly to say something different, but after a brief pause, she added, "Sorry, nurse."

A final glare of warning, and the nurse left. I waited a few seconds, then closed the door behind her and leaned against it.

I wanted to get back to the subject of Joe, but there was something else that needed to be addressed. "I don't mean to sound heartless," I said quietly, "but Lila Boudreaux was *not* my mother. She was a total stranger, and I don't usually go around dressed in mourning for total strangers." I had a brief flashback to my goth days, when that might've been the case, but that was a long time ago, before I learned that death was nothing to flirt with.

Tears filled Kelly's eyes and she swiped them angrily away. "Peaches had things to tell us, Nicki, things about our past that now we'll never know. I just can't believe that after all these years, when we finally meet, you don't seem to care that she's dead."

"I care." I just didn't feel the same way about death as I used to—not now, when I knew death wasn't the end of everything. "We can't change what's happened. I'm sure she's in a good place." *The Light was as good as it gets.* Peaches had seemed like a nice woman, and

I would bet she was doing just fine in the afterlife, but I didn't know how to communicate that to Kelly without sounding like a lunatic. I settled by being as honest as I could. "I can't miss someone I never knew."

Kelly broke down, covering her face with her hands. Her upper body shook with sobs, bandages pinning her legs to the pillows.

I felt like a big meanie. *Was I supposed to pat her shoulder or something?* I missed Evan—he'd know what to do.

In the end, I picked up a box of tissues from beside the bed and held them out. She snatched the box from my hand and helped herself to several, continuing to cry.

I sat down awkwardly on the foot of the bed, and after a minute or two the crying jag eased. Kelly wiped at her face with the wadded tissues and lay her head back against the pillows.

"I'm sorry," she said. "I survive a major car accident and find my long-lost sister, and instead of being grateful to be alive, I'm mad at the world. I've made a mess of everything, just like always."

I liked her much better this way, but I was still wary.

"You seem to have a lot of friends around here," she went on, "and I'm in the middle of feeling pretty sorry for myself. Maybe I'm a little jealous."

At this point, honesty surprised me, but it was so much easier to deal with. Jealousy was something I could understand.

"Maybe I'm a little jealous, too." I went with the flow. "After all, you were Joe's first love, and you're still married. Little things like that can make a girl nervous."

She sighed, giving me a watery look. "You've got nothing to be worried about. He's obviously crazy about you."

Silence for a moment. *He was, wasn't he?*

"Truce?" she offered.

Relieved that particular issue had been dealt with, at least temporarily, I took a deep breath. "Truce."

Kelly gave a final sniff, reaching for another Kleenex. "By the way, your friend Albert came by to see me early this morning."

For a moment the name didn't even compute.

"Albert?" I repeated it, in case I'd heard her wrong.

"Older black man? Very thin, dressed in a suit?" Kelly could read the confusion on my face.

I nodded, not certain where this was going. *What was Albert doing here?*

"He said he had a message for you"—the hair on the back of my neck began to prickle—"from somebody named Granny Julep. He said to tell you 'you did good' and 'thank you.'"

Why would Albert come here, and how could he have a message from Granny Julep?

Granny Julep was dead.

Uh-oh. The little chill I always associated with the phrase "someone just walked over my grave" went up my spine.

Maybe Albert hadn't come to the hospital just to visit Kelly.

"I gotta go," I blurted, rising from the foot of the bed.

Kelly frowned, dabbing at her nose. "He *is* a friend of yours, isn't he? Seemed like a nice old man."

"I really have to go," I said again.

Her eyebrows shot up but she didn't argue.

"Are you coming back?" Kelly's voice had a note of something that sounded suspiciously like hope. I wasn't ready to analyze whether it was hope that I *would* or hope that I *wouldn't*.

"I'll be back. But right now I gotta go." And I left it at that.

As soon as I was outside in the corridor, I started walking toward Joe's office. If there was an elderly black man named Albert Johnson somewhere in this hospital, Joe would be the one who could help me find him.

Even if my suspicions were correct, and Albert was in the morgue.

"Fascinating." Ivy looked elegant today in beige silk. A chunky amber necklace and earrings in shades of honey, gold, and green were the perfect accents. I'd already decided this would be my last therapy session, even though I'd grown to really like Ivy over the last few weeks.

"So you think your twin sister has the ability to speak with spirits, just like you do?" Ivy slipped her chic little reading glasses off the tip of her nose and held them in her hand. "That would imply the trait is genetic, yet you've always maintained it was the result of your near death experience. Does this change your thinking at all?"

"I don't know." Did it matter? "But Albert Johnson did indeed pass away yesterday morning at five-thirty A.M., in Columbia Hospital. I've seen his death certificate." I hadn't found it in my heart to be sad for Albert.

I knew he'd rather be with Granny Julep than anywhere else. "Maybe something happened to Kelly when she got hit on the head. Or maybe she had a near death experience, too, but just isn't talking about it." *If so, she was smarter than I was. I wouldn't be sitting in a shrink's office right now if I'd kept my mouth shut.*

"Why don't you ask her?"

Ivy had such a way of reducing the complicated down to the simple.

"We don't seem to communicate very well. Either she's crying or she's accusing me of being an over-dressed whore. Puts a kink in the whole sisterly bonding thing."

"And how are you to her?"

I shifted in my seat. "I've tried to be nice."

"Hmmm."

"What's that supposed to mean?"

"Nothing. I'm just listening." Ivy spread her hands, and I noticed the amber ring she was wearing on her index finger. Very cool.

"Okay, so maybe I'm not really ready to give her a chance either," I said. "But I didn't go looking for a fight."

"Didn't you?" Ivy was more direct this time.

"No, I didn't," I snapped. "I didn't go looking for anything. She started it."

"*Now* you sound like sisters." Ivy smiled, and put her glasses back on her nose. "I think there are deeper issues at work here, Nicki."

No shit.

Ivy flipped through her notes, going back to the first few pages. "You were very clear about something that happened during your near death experience. Ah, here it is." She read, "'I saw the fabled "grand design" stretched out before me like an infinite spider web.'" Ivy looked at me over the edge of her glasses. "That means you believe there *is* a grand design. Given everything that's happened to you since, isn't it possible that meeting your sister is part of it?"

She didn't wait for my answer, flipping another page and continuing to refer to her notes. "You said the voice told you to 'do unto others as you'd have them do to you.'" She smiled to herself, then pinned me with an innocent look. "Interesting that you'd meet your sister while she's injured and vulnerable, isn't it? How would *you* want to be treated in that situation?"

"Now wait just a minute." I didn't like where this was going. "*I'm* the vulnerable one here. She rides in on her broom and tries to play on everybody's sympathies, and before I know it she steals Joe right from under me. I've watched enough Lifetime movies to know how this works."

Ivy laughed out loud. "You're a funny girl, Nicki."

"Lotta good that'll do me when I'm throwing rice at Joe and Kelly's second wedding," I said glumly. "She'll probably ask me to be her maid of honor just to make me suffer." I could see it all now; me dressed in acres of lavender taffeta with a big bow on the butt, Kelly radiant in white with Joe at her side.

Ivy cocked her head, a sure sign I wasn't going to like what she had to say.

"Have you ever heard of a 'self-fulfilling prophecy'?"

"What am I now, an oracle?" Visions of crystal balls and black velvet reared their ugly heads.

Ivy shook her head, still smiling. "That's not what I meant. A self-fulfilling prophecy is an outcome that happens because you *believe* it's going to happen. The theory is that a person becomes so invested in the outcome itself that they behave in subconscious ways that actually make the outcome occur." She gave me a bland look. "You're a smart girl. You figure it out."

Damn, damn, and double damn.

Ivy was *good.*

"So you're saying that if I let Kelly piss me off to the point that I come off as a bitch, I could drive Joe right into her arms." Ivy's mild expression had probably come at the cost of thousands of hours of training, and thousands of dollars of somebody's money.

Worked for me. Maybe I'd keep coming to her for another week or two.

"Let's analyze the situation with an eye toward the future," she said. "Kelly's injuries will heal, though the ankles will be a problem for a while. I imagine she'll be discharged soon. She's been in the Peace Corps?"

"Yes." I knew this was leading to something.

"No permanent home? No significant others?"

I ignored a stab of guilt. It wasn't my fault Peaches died. "I haven't heard of any, except the guy she left Joe for. She said she's not with him anymore."

"Where will she go? What will she do?" Ivy's curiosity seemed genuine.

I shrugged. "I haven't asked her. Like I said, we have a communication problem."

"So I guess that means you haven't told her that your friend Albert Johnson was a ghost." Ivy's look was as direct as her comment. "What if she sees more spirits?

What if they start popping up in her life the way they pop up in yours? For people who have a communication problem, you two might have a lot in common."

I didn't answer.

"You have to decide if you *want* a relationship with your sister, Nicki. Whether you do or you don't is entirely up to you. I'm not here to sit in judgment, merely to help you think it through." Ivy recrossed her legs. Her crocodile heels were gorgeous. "Feelings are fluid . . . they change. And I'm not going to lie to you. If there comes a time that you *do* want to get to know your sister, you're going to have to work at it. There isn't going to be an easy solution, because this isn't an easy situation."

Nothing was easy anymore.

What I wouldn't give for the good old days, when I laughed and flirted and drank a bit too much, not a care in the world except getting my business off the ground. Evan and the store were all I cared about.

Well, that, plus fashion and Chinese food.

"Doing unto others" was hard work.

I headed straight home from my session with Ivy, having told Evan I'd be back at the store later in the afternoon. Business had been slow that morning, and he could handle things alone for a while.

Traffic was a little heavy on Paces Ferry Road, but I didn't mind. Sitting through stoplights gave me time to think. The quiet was nice, until a voice from the backseat nearly gave me a heart attack.

"She's a smart woman. You should listen to her."

"Shit!" Heart pounding, I took a quick glance over

my right shoulder, glad the car wasn't moving. "You scared the crap outta me!"

Lila Boudreaux's form was vague, not as solid as she'd been the other day. I could see right through her, straight to the upholstery, which was kinda creepy. She was in shades of gray, all color muted from her face and clothes.

"I don't have a lot of time, so you need to listen very carefully," she said hurriedly.

"What's going on?"

What was Lila doing here? I'd been certain she'd passed into the Light.

"He's coming," she said. "He's coming for you both, but you mustn't let him in."

"Who's coming?" The hair rose on my arms, tingling into goose bumps. The flow of traffic moved, then stopped. I tried to keep one eye on the rearview mirror and one eye on my driving.

"He's a liar. Don't listen to anything he says." Lila sounded rushed, worried. "He'll strike where you're weakest . . . he'll go after Kelly first. Promise me you won't listen to him."

The car in front of me flashed its taillights. I had to slam on my brakes to keep from rear-ending it. "What are you talking about? *Who* are you talking about? What's going on?"

At a full stop, I twisted around, but there was no one in the backseat.

Lila was gone.

"Great," I muttered, turning back to my driving. "Show up and get all cryptic on me, then disappear. Just what I need."

Who was Lila talking about? Was there an anonymous father out there, too? Stood to reason. Maybe Kelly and I were about to get a visit from our long-lost sperm donor daddy. *Oh, goody . . . more relatives.*

This situation just seemed to keep getting worse. I had a sister now, a true, flesh and blood sister—who I didn't know at all. And a birth mother who was haunting me. Now I was supposed to be worried about some guy showing up and telling lies. Hardly your typical family reunion.

I sighed, thoughts returning to Kelly. She was married to my boyfriend, and given her reaction to my pink and blue paisley outfit, obviously considered "fashion" a dirty word. The only things my sister and I had in common were that we both saw dead people, and we'd both slept with Joe.

She sees dead people, too.

I didn't think Kelly knew it yet. She'd seemed to accept Albert's visit at face value—a quick visit from one of my friends. Not that Albert was ever truly my friend. He'd done me a favor once, but only because it served his own purpose. I had no hard feelings, though, and I was glad to know that he didn't have any either.

I hoped he and Granny Julep were at peace now, together in the Light.

Kelly was in for some surprises. I couldn't help but remember how bewildering it was to wake up in the hospital to a whole new reality. It had been hard to accept that nobody saw the little Yiddish grandmother beside my bed except me.

But I'd accepted it, and dealt with it, even if dealing with it wasn't easy.

I popped in a Siouxsie and the Banshees CD, tired of silence and introspection. But while my fingers automatically tapped out the beat on the steering wheel, my mind was still working.

Before I reached the streets leading to my Ansley Park neighborhood, I'd decided to be bold. There was no way around this situation with Kelly except straight through it. No matter what she thought of me, and no matter what I thought of her, we needed to deal.

So I went home and used a little trick I'd taught myself long ago. *Look like a million bucks, feel like a million bucks.*

Whatever the situation was, there was an outfit for it, whether Kelly thought so or not.

Even though I'd already gotten dressed once that morning, I did it again. Only when my bedroom resembled the frenzied remains of a sale at Bloomingdale's was I satisfied; low-slung jeans embroidered down one leg with black thread, paired with a black off-the-shoulder blouse, sexy yet not overdone. The jeans looked great with stilettoed boots.

Then I spiked my hair a little, playing with the pink streaks until they were just the way I liked them. I redid my makeup, heavy on the eyeliner and mascara, and used my favorite shade of dark red lipstick.

I looked at my reflection in the mirror one final time. If Kelly and I were going to deal, then it was time to get real. This was me—"glam" and all. She could take me or leave me.

So for the third time in three days, I went to the hospital to see my sister.

"Hey." The television was off today, and Kelly was reading.

"Hey," she answered. Her eyes were wary.

I walked in and took a seat in the chair next to the bed, crossing my legs and resting my black velvet Rosenfeld bag in my lap. "I've been thinking about what you said yesterday, and you have every reason in the world to feel bitchy. You've been through a lot." Despite my sense of resolve, I wasn't ready to blurt out to Kelly that she and I could see the dead. I doubted she'd believe me, and if her experience was going to be anything like mine, she'd figure it out sooner or later anyway. I took a deep breath. "I'm really sorry about what happened to Lila. I know it has to hurt."

"Peaches," Kelly said, laying down her book. "She wanted us to call her Peaches."

"Okay, Peaches." *Don't get sidetracked, Styx.* "What I'm trying to say is I'm sorry she's gone. You barely had a chance to get to know her, and I didn't know her at all." Not entirely true, but there was no need to go into that yet. "Let's not miss the chance to get to know each other."

The swelling on the side of Kelly's face had gone down, but she still looked like someone had used her for a punching bag. Her hair was clean and straight, brushed neatly behind her ears.

She looked me in the eye, searching for the truth, and I met her gaze evenly.

"The police came to see me again this morning." Her statement threw me off. "They wanted to know if Peaches had any relatives or friends who needed to be notified. She didn't have any identification—they haven't been able to find any other next-of-kin."

"Does she have any?" Despite the way Kelly'd brushed off my apology, I was curious.

"Not that I know of. She must have some friends at the insurance company where she worked. I told them about that. But Peaches lived alone. Never married, no other kids. No family, except for us."

The way Kelly said "us" told me something. Suddenly certain what she was getting at, I answered, "Then I guess we'll have to make the funeral arrangements for her, won't we?" It was stupid of me not to have considered this sooner. I had no problem with laying the dead to rest with all the pomp and ceremony they deserved—especially if it helped them stay that way.

Kelly blinked a couple of times, then looked away.

"I don't have any money," she murmured. "I used the last of it on my plane ticket." She was staring at the crappy curtains again. "I was going to stay with Peaches in Savannah, and get a job there."

I looked at the bandages on Kelly's legs and the mottling of bruises on her arms and face. A job was a long way off.

"You can pay me back for your half of the funeral expenses when you're back on your feet." Fair was fair, and I had the distinct feeling she didn't want my charity.

"Why?" Kelly was looking at me again. "Why would you do that? Feeling sorry for the ugly duckling loser who's been dumped on your doorstep?"

That set me back. Kelly obviously had her own demons . . . and I was beginning to wonder just how well they were gonna get along with mine.

"No," I said, very calmly. "I'm doing it because it's the right thing to do." And I meant it, every word. Maybe I was getting the hang of this "do unto others" thing, after all.

"And you're not ugly. Or a loser." *Although the loser part remained to be seen.*

In a crash course on mental skydiving, I took the biggest plunge of all.

"Maybe you should come stay with me when you're discharged from the hospital. I have an extra room."

Kelly's lower lip quivered, just once. "And what about Joe?"

"What about him?" If I didn't offer her a place to stay, my sweet Dr. Do-Good would probably end up taking her in himself, and *then* where would I be? *Uh-uh. No, thank you.* "Joe told me you'd agreed to sign the divorce papers. We're all grown-ups, aren't we?" I shrugged, nonchalant on the outside but hoping I wouldn't throw up the granola bar I'd eaten on the drive over. "Joe and I are together now. I'm cool with it, and yesterday you said you were, too. Let's get past that."

Besides, I'd look awful in lavender taffeta.

"You surprise me," Kelly said. She didn't look surprised as much as suspicious. "If I were you, I'd be a little worried."

"About what?" If I was, I wasn't gonna admit it just for her benefit.

"About your boyfriend's soon-to-be-ex-wife showing up and stealing him away from you."

This chick's self-esteem bounced up and down like a rubber ball. I leaned in, tired of playing games. "If that's your plan, Kelly, you're going to be disappointed."

She said nothing, so I added, "If, on the other hand, you're being a bitch again just to piss me off, then congratulations. That particular plan worked." I stood, ready to walk out.

"Wait." Kelly reached out, then let her hand drop, curling her fingers tight around the book. "You're right, I'm doing it again. I'm sorry."

"Yeah, you are." I let that statement stand on its own.

Kelly flushed, face reddening. She waited a couple of heartbeats, and then I saw her chin go up. It was a gesture I recognized, because it was one of mine. "You were being nice," she said, "and the least I can do is return the favor. I'd like to come stay with you after I'm discharged, at least for a little while. It'll be a good way to get to know each other."

If we don't kill each other first.

"Good. It's settled. I'll come back tomorrow and we'll talk about the arrangements for Li—" I caught myself "—for Peaches."

"That would be nice."

I smiled at her, and she smiled back. I couldn't help but wonder which one of us was faking it more.

CHAPTER 4

Is that rigor mortis or are you just happy to see me?

Try as I might, I couldn't get the stupid funeral jokes I'd heard the night before out of my mind. The man with the clammy handshake who'd introduced himself as Mr. Bates was droning on about the benefits of mahogany caskets over oak, or perhaps we'd like to consider cremation?

He got where he is the old-fashioned way . . . he urned it.

"No, our mother would've preferred burial. Can you show us some casket choices? Only the high end ones, of course."

I didn't bother to ask how Kelly could've possibly known Lila's preferences in funeral arrangements. As it was, I'd been surprised when she asked to use this particular mortuary, but she'd seen an ad in the newspaper, and I had no desire to revisit the place where my parents' funeral had been held. Bad memories.

"Your mother would no doubt be pleased by your devotion to her memory." Mr. Bates could barely hide the gleam in his eye as he pulled out a thick leather book with the words *Going in Style* embossed on the cover. He reminded me of a cadaver himself with that pale skin and slicked-back hair. You'd think a guy who made the kind of money he probably did could afford a better suit.

I occupied myself with scanning the yellowed certificates on the wall and the dusty silk flower arrangements on the credenza behind the funeral director's desk. Forest Lawn Mortuary needed a new cleaning lady.

"The one with the pink satin lining is nice. What do you think, Nicki?" Kelly shoved the book under my nose and pointed to a particularly hideous white coffin with a Pepto-Bismol colored interior.

I wouldn't be caught dead in that thing.

"You choose, Kelly. You knew her better than I did."

Mr. Bates gave me an oily smile as Kelly flipped to the next page.

"What about these bronze or copper ones? They must last forever."

"Oh, they do." The funeral home director began to look positively cheerful. He reached across the desk and pointed to one with a white velvet interior. "We even offer vacuum sealing on this particular model."

I couldn't help myself. "Vacuum sealing? We're talking about a person here, not strawberry jam."

That comment earned me a dirty look from Kelly, and a raised eyebrow from Mr. Bates.

Kelly went back to looking at casket pictures while I contemplated a chip in my toenail polish. Time for a pedicure.

"It says the Queen Anne model is made of African mahogany," she said. "Is there a difference between that and regular mahogany?"

The funeral director opened his mouth, but I beat him to it.

"Yeah. About a thousand dollars."

Bates didn't bat an eye, but Kelly slammed the book shut, giving me a glare. "Mr. Bates, could you give us some privacy for a moment?"

"Of course." He rose from his seat, carefully avoiding looking at me. "Take all the time you need. I need to see about the lighting in the Serenity Chapel. We're hosting a rather large visitation this afternoon."

How many dead people does it take to change a lightbulb? None. They're always in the dark.

This was all Evan's fault. If he and Butch hadn't taken me out for sushi last night, I wouldn't be sitting here torn between a lingering sake headache and an urge to giggle.

The door shut behind cadaver-man, and Kelly burst out, "What's your problem? We agreed I'd pay you back for half the funeral expenses once I'm on my feet."

I stifled a grin. Considering that Kelly was sitting in a wheelchair, both ankles bandaged, that event was hardly likely anytime soon.

"This is funny to you?" Two red spots bloomed in her cheeks.

Kelly didn't know me well enough yet to realize that I'd rather laugh than cry any day.

"Our mother is dead. Show some respect," she snapped.

The sake headache took over, making me cranky.

"You mean like the respect she showed us when she put us up for adoption?" *Okay, so I had some lingering resentment about being given away like an unwanted puppy.* "And quit calling her 'our mother.' My mother's name was Emily Styx. She was the one who was there for me, and I loved her, and I buried both my parents according to their wishes."

Kelly's eyes filled with tears. "At least you had parents."

A stab of guilt, like a needle prick to my conscience. Just because I knew that Lila was doing just fine in the afterlife didn't mean I had to come off as such a bitch.

I closed my eyes and blew out a breath, exasperated with myself. "I'm sorry. I stayed out too late last night and I have a headache. Let's just pick something and get out of here, okay?"

"I don't understand you." Kelly obviously wasn't ready to cut me any slack. "This is really hard for me. It's like you want me to believe that you're a vain, selfish person without a heart."

Not entirely true. I had a heart, but it didn't work too well—heart failure and the residual side effects were what got me into this fix to begin with.

Do unto others, Styx.

"Look, I said I'm sorry. It's been a really weird summer."

Died, came back to life—check.

Nagging ghosts, voodoo queens, zombies, new love, old baggage—check.

A twin sister I never knew and a biological mother I never would—still working on it.

"Weird" was an understatement.

I glanced over and felt even guiltier. Kelly *had* just gotten out of the hospital.

"I'm not a heartless person," I said. Her face was expressionless, so I ventured a little joke. "Vain, maybe, but not heartless."

That didn't work, so I tried again. "Evan would tell me my 'bitchy slip' is showing."

"He'd be right." Kelly sounded more hurt than angry. "I was hoping that making the funeral arrangements for our mother would bring us closer, not drive us apart."

Guilt trip, anyone? And there was that "our mother" again.

"Okay, okay." I held out my hand for the casket book, secretly dreading even touching the damn thing. "I said I was sorry, didn't I? Show me the African mahogany . . . anything but the pink one."

"I thought you liked pink," Kelly said, eyeing the vivid streaks in my otherwise dark hair. "Peaches seemed to like it. She was wearing pink the first time I saw her."

"I do like pink," I answered. "I like lime green, too, but I wouldn't wanna be buried in it."

Kelly rolled her eyes, flipped open the book to a page near the back and handed it to me. I pretended to be fascinated at the differences between velvet and crepe bedding systems.

"What about the Angelica model? It has those beautiful guardian angel cornices."

I refrained from asking what a "cornice" was, and

dutifully flipped through the book until I found the Angelica model. It was white with gaudy gold trim, but at least the interior wasn't pink.

"Great. Let's take it."

"You're not even trying, are you?"

My patience was shot. Rather than say something else I'd have to apologize for, I handed back the casket book and stood up. "I think this one's just fine, but if you wanna keep looking, feel free. In the meantime, I need to find the little girls' room."

Kelly eyed me warily. "You're coming back, aren't you?"

"I'm not going to abandon you in a funeral home." I'd meant it when I said I wasn't heartless—there was no way I was gonna leave an invalid in this dusty, depressing place.

I might strangle one, but I wouldn't leave one.

I left the office and headed down a corridor to the right. The hallway was lined with glass cases full of bronzed sculptures and marbled urns, all apparently designed to hold ashes. *Like putting Grandpa's ashes above your fireplace was less creepy if you put them in something pretty.* Ugh.

Thankfully, I found the ladies' room and went inside.

There was a woman leaning over the sink, touching up her mascara. She glanced at me briefly in the mirror. The black cocktail dress she was wearing fit her size four figure like a glove, the perfect foil to carefully highlighted blond hair. Big freshwater pearl necklace and bracelet. She had a glamorous look, like she was used to money, and plenty of it.

That's all I noticed before I slipped into a stall, except for a glimpse of strappy black heels. *They couldn't possibly be Jimmy Choos.* Georgia wasn't exactly known for high fashion.

The woman was still there when I came out. She gave me a little smile as she dabbed at her lipstick.

"I love your hair," she said. "Very Kelly Osborne."

"Thanks," I said, though I'd never cared for that particular comparison. I smiled back as I washed my hands, emboldened enough to take a second look at the shoes.

"Great stilettos," I said.

"Thanks. When I bought them, I considered them to die for, and I was right . . . they're killing me." The woman gave a laugh, then pulled back from the mirror. She tucked her lipstick away into a tiny black bag and turned to face me. "You've got a great look, even if it is a little 'out there.'" She tilted her head, eyeing me critically. "Ever tried modeling?"

Out there? Modeling? I didn't know whether to be flattered or insulted. Cheerleaders and beauty queens were hardly the type of girl I usually hung out with. My style was darker—a holdover from my goth days, I suppose—even though I did have a girlie side. Today, my black leather jacket was paired with a perfectly lovely yellow sundress, circa 1950s.

"I own a vintage clothing store." I snatched a paper towel to dry my hands. "Handbags and Gladrags, down in Little Five Points." Anyone who lived in the area would know the neighborhood, and if she didn't, it didn't matter. She didn't look like the type of woman who'd wear vintage anyway.

The woman smiled. She was very pretty in a Barbie doll sort of way, and looked out of place in this shabby bathroom with its faded wallpaper and its smell of cheap potpourri. I wondered who she was there to say good-bye to. Nobody would get that dressed up just to make arrangements—she was obviously there to see and be seen.

"You run your own business?" the woman asked. At my nod, she said, "Good for you. Don't be stupid enough to depend on a man to support you, like I was." Bitterness crept into her voice. "If I'd had something to fall back on, I wouldn't be here."

Whoa. She hardly looked the part of a grieving widow, even if she was wearing black. Her makeup was flawless, unsmudged by tears. She was older than I'd first thought, tiny lines around her eyes and lips that makeup didn't quite hide. I wondered how much plastic surgery she'd had.

"I'm sorry." I wasn't exactly sure what I was sorry for, but it seemed the appropriate thing to say. "Did you . . . did you lose someone?"

Her laugh raised the hair on my arms.

"Oh, I haven't lost him yet."

I tossed my paper towel into the trash basket and started edging for the door. The conversation was starting to get weird—why would anybody be hiding in a mortuary? "Well, I hope you find him soon," I offered lamely.

"Ask your sister where he is."

I stopped, hand on the door. *I hadn't mentioned a sister.*

"She needs to tell that bastard something for me."

I turned, not liking the suspicion that crept into my head, or the acid that seeped into her tone.

"She needs to tell him that if I'm going to Hell, I'm not going alone. He was the one who lied to his wife all those years, not me." The woman's face wasn't quite as pretty now, and her voice was even uglier. Her eyes had narrowed into slits.

"Maybe you should tell him yourself." No way was I gonna get in the middle of somebody else's love triangle—not with one of my own going on. Kinda. Sorta.

"Oh, I intend to." She gave an ugly chuckle. "The car accident was his fault, too—he'd been drinking at the country club before he picked me up." Her cherry-red lips curled in a sneer. "Keith Morgan never could resist a drink or a chance to schmooze. He killed us both, the drunken idiot." She stabbed a finger in my direction. "Tell your sister to ask him about that, why don't you?"

My heart sank. Another lost soul with unfinished business, and this time it was a Barbie doll with a mean streak. Why did this keep happening to me?

"That slimy weasel may have gotten out of marrying me while we were alive, but I'll be damned if he's going to make me face the afterlife alone." The woman was working herself up. "Whatever punishment I deserve, he deserves the same and more for being a low-down dirty dog who cheated on his wife. And a big fat liar."

What was that saying about "hell hath no fury"?

She took a step closer, while I took a step back. "He's lying to your sister—enlisting her sympathy. He thinks he can save his soul in time to avoid paying for what he did."

He's a liar. Don't believe anything he says. Peaches's warning popped into my head. *He'll go after Kelly first. Promise me you won't listen to him.*

Oh, shit.

The blond woman's gaze turned inward, frustrated and bitter. "All those wasted years . . . getting older and older while I waited . . . " She spun back to the mirror, checking the skin around her eyes for wrinkles. Her voice hardened. "Now he wants to ditch me when I need him the most. I won't let him. I won't."

"Listen, I can't help you." I should've felt sorry for her, but I didn't. She wasn't very nice anymore, for one thing, and she'd been sleeping with another woman's husband. What kind of reward did she expect?

"Oh, yes, you can help." A sly expression came over the woman's face as she watched me in the mirror. "You can do a lot of things . . . more than you know."

"And just what do you expect me to do?" I stood my ground, unwilling to get involved with another pissed-off spirit. "It's not like I can order your dead boyfriend to 'go to Hell' and have him take me seriously."

She turned and looked me. "That's not what my master says."

Make that a Barbie doll with a mean streak and a taste for sadomasochism. "Um . . . yeah. Well, your master doesn't have any control over me."

"Are you sure?" I was *so* not liking that smirk. "What if he gave you everything you ever wanted, Nicki Styx?"

My blood ran cold. I'd never told her my name.

Hoping my voice sounded steadier than I felt, I said, "I have everything I need, thanks."

There was a silence, and then—before my very eyes—the woman became someone else.

Literally.

One moment she was a blond beauty queen, two seconds later she was a dark-haired young woman, dressed in glam couture—heavy makeup, sleeked 1920s hairstyle, fabulous clothes. I recognized the chocolate silk and velvet dress as one from Marc Bouwer's fall line—I'd drooled over it in the pages of a magazine the week before. Everything matched the model in the photo, except for the woman's face, and the vivid pink streaks in her hair.

The model was me. I was staring at *me*.

"Money, power, eternal youth." The other Nicki's voice lowered, took on a seductive note. "Fame and fortune. Fashion designers falling at your feet while the public screams your name . . . wealth beyond your wildest dreams . . . anything your heart desires, Nicki, anything at all."

"No." I shook my head, finding it hard to believe what I was seeing. "Leave me alone."

She took a step toward me and I jerked back. The tiled wall was against my shoulders before I knew it.

The woman returned to her original form while I stared, speechless. In a few seconds I was once again looking at a bitter-eyed blond in Jimmy Choos. She tilted her head and smiled like we were best buddies.

"You know my master already," she wheedled, making me remember nights spent sitting in the dark with my girlfriends, a single candle flickering on the wall and a chalk pentagram on the floor. "Where's the bad girl with a dark side who wanted to form a coven, hmm? The girl who put a hex on her ex-boyfriend to make him shrivel every time he looked at someone else?" She gave me the sly smile of someone who shared a secret. "You could have powers like that, Nicki Styx, and more. The Master rewards his servants well when they give him what he wants, and *you* have something he wants."

Still in denial, I insisted, "I was a teenager. That was all just make-believe."

She stared at me, then said flatly, "It's never too late to make it real."

"You actually expect me to make some kind of deal with the Devil?"

She smiled suddenly, in a dazzling display of white teeth. The perfect smile of a perfect woman, no doubt honed over perfect dinners with her married lover. The look she gave me was one of pity.

"Oh, honey . . . I sold my soul to the Devil long ago, and it didn't hurt a bit."

"Kelly, let's get out of here."

I'd made a beeline for Mr. Bates's office without once looking over my shoulder. Hopefully, Psycho Barbie would stay in the ladies' room while I got my sister and her wheelchair out to the car. The office was empty, except for Kelly, and I started rolling her out without waiting for her reply.

No dead guy filling her head with lies. Good.

"What are you doing?" Kelly grabbed the wheels with both hands, effectively stopping me in my tracks. "We haven't finished yet."

"Trust me—we're finished." I wanted to get as far away as possible from Psycho Barbie. Her boyfriend would likely end up in Hell with no help from me.

"I'm not leaving until we've picked out a casket. If you need to go, then go."

"I don't have time to drive all the way back out here a second time." Now was not the time to explain about pissed-off mistresses and deals with the Devil—now was the time to get the hell out of Dodge. "Evan's waiting for us at the shop. We were supposed to pick out a nice outfit for Peaches to be buried in, remember?"

Kelly shrugged. "I'm sure I can get Joe to pick me up and drive me back."

She said it lightly, but I didn't take it that way. "Joe's hardly yours to command anymore, now is he?"

"Well, he's not yours to command, either. The divorce papers haven't been signed yet."

Before I could respond, Mr. Bates walked back in, rubbing his hands briskly. He looked entirely too much like a man who enjoys his work. I couldn't help but wonder where those clammy hands had just been, and repressed a shudder.

"Well," he pulled out his chair, "made any decisions yet?"

"No," Kelly said, while I said, "Yes."

Cadaver-man checked in mid-sit, then let his weight carry him down. His chair creaked as he settled himself, but otherwise the silence was deafening. He gave us a fake sympathetic look and tried again.

"I know this is a difficult time. It's not unusual for families to disagree on the final arrangements. I'm sure we can settle on something that's agreeable to all parties." Cadaver-man patted the casket book like it was an old friend.

I leaned down and whispered in Kelly's ear. "I thought you liked the one with the guardian angel . . . um . . . *thingies*. Let's get it and go."

"I can't believe you," she whispered back. "And I like the one with the pink lining better."

Outmaneuvered and out of patience, I looked at Mr. Bates.

He gave me a bland smile, knowing perfectly well that whatever disagreement we'd just had, I'd just lost.

"Okay, okay. The pink one it is. Where do we sign?"

"What the hell was that all about?" Kelly was holding tightly to the armrests of her chair as I wheeled her toward the car.

I couldn't wait to leave Forest Lawn Mortuary behind. Just being outside was a relief, but I wasn't going to be satisfied until we were on the road.

Kelly kept talking. "You were very rude."

"I don't need a lecture," I snapped. I was jittery, mildly hung over, and had no idea how I was going to discuss with Kelly the dangers of talking to dead people.

"No, you need a chill pill or something." We hit a bump and she gasped, "Could you slow down?"

I bit my lip and walked even faster.

Kelly muttered something I pretended not to hear as I opened the passenger side door and positioned her wheelchair so she could lift herself into the seat. By the time I folded up the empty chair and stuck it in the back, she was buckled up and ready to go.

I got in and started the car for the benefit of air-conditioning, but I wasn't going anywhere just yet. Might as well jump in with both feet.

"We've got a real problem, Kelly. We need to talk."

She looked at me, then sighed. "Okay, I'm sorry about the 'divorce papers' comment. It wasn't very nice, but you deserved it for the way you were acting."

"That's not what I meant."

"Then what?"

"Have you been talking to a man named Keith Morgan?"

Her eyes slid toward the dashboard. "You know Keith Morgan?"

"No."

She shot me a glance. "So what's the problem?"

"So he's dead, that's what."

Kelly tried to laugh, but it came out wrong. "What are you talking about? He's not dead."

Was it possible she really didn't get it?

"You're the only one who can see him, Kelly. That's why he asked you for help."

She laughed again, a little nervously. "Dead people can't ask for help."

"Can't they?"

She looked at me, and this time I was the one who broke eye contact. I put the car in reverse and backed out of the parking space.

"What did he ask you to do for him?"

"He didn't ask me to do anything," she answered, sounding a little testy. "I met him very briefly, at the hospital. Apparently he'd been in a bad car accident, too, where somebody . . . "

Kelly's voice trailed off, so I finished for her. "Died."

She glared at me, but I kept talking.

"I'm telling the truth, Kelly, whether you wanna believe it or not. That guy was a ghost with some unfinished business, and he wants you to finish it for him."

Silence.

Reluctantly, I went on. "Listen, I know it's gonna sound crazy, but something happened to me about a month ago." If we were gonna share a house—share a life—particularly a life as strange as mine, then we needed to share some truths with each other, right? "I found out the hard way that I have a minor heart defect. That's how I met Joe, actually. He was the emergency room doctor on call that night."

"Oh." Kelly seemed relieved at the apparent change of subject. "What do you mean you 'found out the hard way'?"

"I died."

"You died." The skeptical note in her voice sounded familiar. We were twins, after all.

"White light, long tunnel, shadowy figures, music . . . the whole stereotypical near death experience, right down to the 'it isn't your time' speech." Kelly was staring at me, but I didn't dare look at her now, and kept my eyes on the road. "I was sent back. And when I woke up, I found out I'd been sent back with a little something extra. Something I'm apparently stuck with." Keeping my voice as light as I could, I said, "To quote the creepy kid in the movie, 'I see dead people.'"

"But you just said that *I* was the one who saw dead people."

I frowned. "It seems you do, too. I never said I understood it. It's complicated."

Kelly lowered her head and raised a hand to her face. Her dark hair spilled forward, so I couldn't see her expression even if I'd wanted to. I heard a muffled noise and glanced over. Her shoulders were shaking.

"Hey, you're not crying, are you?"

Kelly lifted her head. She was laughing.

"I get it." She threw back her hair, looking younger when she laughed, even with the bruises. "Joe put you up to this, didn't he? He knows I'm a sucker for the paranormal. What a way to get me back for running off to Santo Domingo with the Peace Corps." She shook her head, still grinning.

Unbelievable. This chick thought it was all about *her*. She actually thought Joe would bother to play a practical joke on her after what she'd done.

"He used to make so much fun of me when we were in college—the biggest scaredy-cat in the world, fascinated by ghosts and ghoulies and things that go bump in the night."

"You are?" Jealousy took a backseat to curiosity. Somehow I hadn't expected Kelly to have an interest in the occult. She seemed like such a goody-girl.

"Oh, yeah." She was nodding now. "Unexplained phenomena, ESP, séances, Ouija boards. You name it, I've read about it or tried it. I love that stuff."

"You do?" I couldn't seem to form a sentence more than two words long.

"Absolutely." Kelly was looking out the car window, watching the Georgia countryside go by. "Vampires, witches, poltergeists, hauntings . . . everything. Well, except Bigfoot. I've never really bought those stories about big, hairy 'skunk ape' sightings."

"Huh." Now I was down to one-word sentences.

"And UFOs. My internal jury is still out on aliens from outer space." She gave me a curious glance. "Don't know much about near death experiences, though. I'll have to read up on those." Kelly was grinning at me. "So you see dead people, huh?"

She didn't believe me.

Hell. I could hardly believe it myself.

"Tell Joe his little joke almost worked," she said. "That's too funny." There was a pause while she laughed to herself. "But I'm sorry about the heart thing. Are you okay? Is it serious?"

I decided I'd rather talk about my irregular heartbeat than be laughed at. Unless I missed my guess, she'd be convinced sooner or later, with or without my help.

"It's called mitral valve prolapse," I said. "And it's usually benign. An infection from some dental work affected a wimpy heart valve. Now that I know to take antibiotics and watch myself, I should be fine."

"Did you really have a near death experience?"

"Yeah, I did." She was serious now, curious, but I'd said enough. I was feeling off-balance, and I didn't like it.

She took the hint, and we drove to Handbags and Gladrags mostly in silence. Once we got into the rabbit warren of narrow streets and funky shops that was Little Five Points, it wasn't even awkward anymore.

The first street performer I saw was one of my favorites, a silver-painted ballerina who posed as a statue for the tourists. Her "artiste" name was Tina Ballerina, but her real name was Angela. She was perched atop an upturned bucket in Findley Square, a shaded courtyard of bricks and benches, the best place for tips.

"Wow," Kelly said. "She looks like a real statue. People pay her for that?"

"She's a college student, earning extra money for a boob job." Imagine, a delicate, graceful girl like Angela working her butt off for a big set of hooters. "She's a performance artist."

Kelly didn't answer, too busy taking in the extraordinary sights of my everyday world. I drove slowly down Moreland toward my normal parking spot, letting the first-timer look her fill.

Kelly pointed at the mural on the side of Blue Screw Tattoos, a vivid burst of psychedelic colors and images. "Look at that . . . and that!" She'd just spied the huge grinning skull whose front teeth formed the entrance to the Vortex, one of the neighborhood's hottest after dark spots. "Is this some kind of an artist colony or something? Everything's so . . . " She groped for a word. " . . . so unusual."

That might not have been the word I would've chosen, but she was right. The people who lived and worked in this funky old neighborhood were nothing if not unusual, which is exactly what gave it such a bohemian charm.

It was good to be home.

"Oh my God, that's hideous! What were you thinking?"

Despite the jingle of wind chimes over the front door, we could hear Evan's outrage loud and clear. Luckily, he wasn't talking to a customer, but to himself.

"Are those feathers in Courtney Love's hair or is it an actual bird's nest?" He held up the latest issue of *Faboo* magazine and waved it indignantly in our direction, not even bothering with a hello first.

"You mean the 'I just rolled out of bed in a crack house' look is already over?" I pushed Kelly's wheelchair through the doorway with no help from him, grateful for the cool rush of air-conditioning. It was September, but in Georgia the heat of summer tended to linger. "Maybe she passed out in a chicken coop."

"All that great bone structure just going to waste." Evan looked truly upset. "The woman needs to put down the lipstick and fire her stylist!"

"Oh, wow," Kelly said, unfazed by Evan's fashion fit. "What a great store!" She gazed around, taking in the clothing racks, the colorful hats and beaded purses, the glassed-in jewelry counter. "Is that Audrey Hepburn? Ooo, Marilyn Monroe! What a great idea!"

Nothing she could've said would've made Evan and me happier. The store mannequins at Handbags and Gladrags were our pride and joy. One of Evan's artist friends had turned bland figures into glamorous replicas of early film stars, and we kept them dressed accordingly. I tried to play it cool while Evan turned to mush.

"Kelly, hon." Evan put down his magazine and hurried over, giving me no attention whatsoever. "You're looking so much better." He leaned down and gave her a quick squeeze, which she returned. I wasn't surprised by the spontaneous affection so much as I was by Evan's unconcern about wrinkling his shirt. "First day out of the hospital, hm?" He beamed at her, patting her hand like she was an invalid or something.

Which she technically was, but whatever.

"Have you been to the house yet? Has Nicki shown you the guest room?" He took the handles of Kelly's wheelchair as if he'd done it a million times and wheeled her toward the counter. "Butch and I picked out the bedding ourselves, so don't let her tell you any different." Evan gave me a little wink as he passed, making it impossible to be mad at him. "Egyptian cotton will feel so much better on your skin than those cardboard sheets they use in the hospital. I hope you're not allergic to goosedown."

"Ahh . . . you're such a sweetheart," Kelly said. "A nice, soft bed sounds great. I've got bruises in places I didn't know I had." I was amazed at how easy these two were with each other.

My best friend and my sister—one I'd known forever and one I'd never known.

"We haven't been to the house yet. Nicki and I went straight from the hospital to make the funeral arrangements for Peaches."

Evan's eyes flew to mine, horrified. He'd obviously forgotten.

Kelly's voice sounded strained. "Then we came by here to find her an outfit to be buried in."

Evan's face changed. Now it looked as if *he* was the one about to cry. He reached out and snagged me with one arm, pulling me close, and put his other hand on Kelly's shoulder.

"It would be an honor," he said, "if you would allow me to help. What did you have in mind?" He gave me a reassuring squeeze, and I squeezed back, knowing I was comforting him as much as he was comforting me, the little drama queen. I was already mentally debating between a peach chiffon or a dark blue brocade. Both dresses were appropriate, and equally lovely.

"Pink," Kelly said. She glanced up at me over her

shoulder. Then she leaned back to look at Evan and said again, very decisively, "She liked pink."

"Pink it is, then," Evan said.

I sighed, not even bothering to argue. Evan wheeled Kelly toward the better dresses while I sank into the chair behind the counter.

"Don't get too comfy in the catbird seat, young lady," Evan called over his shoulder. "You can help, too."

The cushion beneath me was still warm from Evan's body heat. It had already been quite a morning, and there was a lot more of the day to get through. "You two go ahead. I'll be right here."

Evan shot me a look, but I gave him a bland stare in return. Let him take this one—he was the one who insisted I be sisterly, after all. Let *him* play nursemaid for a while.

"So," Evan's attention returned to Kelly and the clothing racks, "tell me about Peaches."

Kelly hesitated, then said, "She had dark hair."

Evan started sifting through the dresses. "Okay, dark hair, liked pink. What size do you think she wore? Eight, ten, twelve, maybe?" He held up a blush-colored suit dress with a short jacket, very Jackie O.

"Ten or twelve, I think." Kelly shook her head at his offering. "But that's way too conservative. Peaches was no wallflower. She was more like Nicki."

Evan's eyebrows shot up. He looked directly at me. "Oh, really?" he said to Kelly. "Do tell."

Kelly was looking at me, too. I was so surprised I kept my mouth shut.

"She liked bright clothes and she wore too much makeup"—Kelly smiled, though her eyes were shiny with tears—"and she was funny—I mean, *really* funny—without even meaning to be."

Evan's mouth dropped, and so did my heart. At least for a second . . . then it did that fluttery thing.

I wasn't sure I wanted to hear this—I'd been treating Peaches Boudreaux like a stranger. It seemed easier that way.

"We talked on the phone a lot the last couple of weeks, before she . . . well, you would've liked her." Kelly was still talking. "And she would've liked you."

To my horror, I teared up. I hate to cry—absolutely hate it—and I'd done enough of it the last few months. I wasn't about to join in a group hug, so I jumped up and went into the back office. I needed a minute.

"Hey, are you okay?" Evan followed me right in, baby blues full of concern. The man had a sweet side a mile deep.

"Yeah." I snatched a tissue off the desk and dabbed at my eyeliner, already finished with the waterworks. "I just didn't expect to hear that, you know?"

He tilted his head, and in typically blunt fashion pointed out, "But isn't it great? Now you actually know who you take after."

I shot him a look. "I take after myself, remember?" I'd always made it a point of pride to be different, unique. My adoptive parents and my upbringing might be pure middle-class Georgia, but not me.

Evan waved a hand in dismissal. "Style is one thing, girlfriend, genetics is another. If I'm not mistaken, that's your twin out there, and she just told you that you're a lot like your mother. That's pretty cool."

Trust Evan not to let me hide from myself, even when I wanted to. I changed the subject.

"I saw another ghost today."

Evan blanched. He hadn't gotten over what happened the last time. "What? I thought that was done and over with?" His eyes darted around the office.

"Not here, silly. At the funeral home." I lifted the coffeepot and checked the contents. *Still hot.* I poured myself a cup while I told him the rest.

"A woman in the ladies' room was looking for her married boyfriend . . . some local bigwig. They were both killed in a car accident." I stirred in some sweetener. "She said if she had to go to Hell, she wasn't going without him. They'd been having an affair for years, and she was pretty pissed about winding up dead instead of married."

I turned, and there was Kelly behind Evan, her wheelchair filling the open doorway.

Evan saw where my eyes went and attempted a graceful save. "Kelly, would you like some coffee? Nicki's feeling better now."

She turned down his offer with a shake of the head, eyeing me oddly. "You were telling the truth in the car, weren't you?"

I couldn't help it. I looked at Evan and he looked at me.

"We really do see dead people." Kelly was very calm, considering. "I have to go back to the mortuary."

Hot coffee sloshed over the rim of my cup, wetting my fingers. I held it away so it didn't drip on my shoes.

"Oh, no, you don't."

"Oh yes, I do," Kelly said. I recognized that stubborn look on her face as similar to one I'd seen in a mirror, many times. "I didn't tell you the whole truth." She rolled farther into the room. "He asked me to go to the visitation this afternoon. He wants me to talk to his wife."

I put down my coffee mug with a groan.

"You . . . you see them, too?" Evan breathed. He didn't have to say who "them" was.

Kelly glanced anxiously at Evan, her eyes begging him to be honest. "You'd tell me if this was all a big joke, right? 'Cause if this is all an act to get rid of me, you guys are going to way too much trouble." She looked at me again. "All you have to do is tell me the truth. I'm a big girl, I can take it."

"I did tell you the truth!" *Dammit.* "You're the one who lied!"

Evan made an exasperated noise. "Calm down, ladies." He stepped between us, helping himself to my rapidly cooling coffee. He took a sip, then grimaced, preferring it black. "Let me get this straight. You went to the funeral home and you both saw a ghost?"

Kelly didn't answer, so I nodded.

"Only not the same one?"

I nodded again, miserable.

"Oh my." Evan leaned against the desk, one Prada shoe crossed casually over the other. "You girls sure know how to put the 'fun' back in 'funeral.'"

CHAPTER 5

The parking lot of Forest Lawn Mortuary was packed with cars. All these people had come to pay their respects to Keith Gerard Morgan—local city councilman, admired businessman, and upstanding citizen. Evan had managed to dig the obituary out of the morning paper, and it seemed like Morgan was a pretty popular guy. If I had my way, there could easily be two less people at his bon voyage party.

Unfortunately, it didn't look like I was gonna get my way.

"You don't understand, Nicki." Kelly was trying to explain why she was honor-bound to help a rich sleazebag buy his way into Heaven. We pulled into a parking space at the far edge of the lot. "Keith is Catholic, and Catholics believe in Purgatory."

"Keith?" I raised an eyebrow at her. "You're on a

first-name basis with the dearly departed now?" I was still kinda pissed that she'd lied to me. I'd told her my biggest secret and ended up feeling like a fool—not a feeling I was particularly fond of.

Kelly sighed. "He came to see me again, while you and Evan were waiting on customers."

"I thought you were lying down on the couch in the back room."

"I tried to. Anyway, Keith can't move on from Purgatory until he's been cleansed of his sins, and because he died so suddenly, there was no time for confession or last rites. The only way he can be forgiven now is if regular Masses and prayers are offered on his behalf." She gave me a meaningful look. "Lots of them."

"If you've got some weird idea that I'm gonna start going to Mass and praying for this guy, you better think again." I popped the trunk and got out of the car. Retrieving Kelly's wheelchair and getting her into it took a minute, but we were already better at maneuvering than we'd been that morning. "I've never been to confession in my life, and I'm sure not gonna start now—I've got too many things to confess, some of which I haven't even done yet."

Kelly shook her head. "Don't worry. Your sins are your own problem."

I shot her a glance, but her expression was bland. *What did she know about my sins? Probably didn't have any of her own, the little goody two-shoes.*

"Listen, Kelly, there's something I haven't told you." I leaned a hip against the car while she settled herself into the wheelchair, then I reluctantly told her about my visits from Peaches.

"You've seen Peaches *twice*, and you didn't tell me?" Kelly's voice was a little shaky.

I sighed. "It's not exactly an easy thing to blurt out. I would've never told you at all except there's something you need to know. The first time she came because she wanted me to find you, but the second time she came to give me a warning."

Silence. Kelly's throat worked as she swallowed, hard.

Then, "She gave you a warning?"

"She said some guy was gonna show up and start lying, and that we shouldn't believe a word he says."

Kelly stared at me as if trying to decide whether I was telling the truth.

"And you think Keith Morgan is that guy?"

"I don't know," I snipped irritably. Her tone was a little too sarcastic for me. "But I do know that getting involved with restless spirits isn't always a good idea."

"I can't believe there's any danger involved in helping some poor guy get his dying wish, Nicki. All he wants is for his wife to have Masses held for his soul, Rosaries said for him, that kind of thing."

"Don't forget to throw in a few Hail Marys," I muttered, thinking Mr. Bigwig would need one or two of those to get past his ex-girlfriend and her "master." Morgan wasn't exactly the dedicated family man Kelly seemed to think he was.

She gave me a look. "I'm going inside and talking to Keith's widow. You can stay out here if you want to." She'd obviously made up her mind, and nothing I said was going to change it.

I sighed. "You really think you can help put this

man's spirit to rest?" I didn't want to get involved, but I couldn't abandon a bruised-up woman in a wheelchair, no matter how much I was tempted. If Kelly was going inside, I was going inside.

"Of course I can." Kelly was taking this "good Samaritan" thing very seriously. "Keith left his wife a very wealthy woman. She can afford to make sure his slate is wiped clean."

I'd already started wheeling Kelly toward the funeral home, but this comment stopped me dead in my tracks. "Are you serious? You really think his wife can *pay* to have his sins removed? How? Buy a 'get into Heaven free' card?"

"They're called 'indulgences,'" she said. "The Catholic Church can reduce Purgatory if they so choose, if they have a *reason* to."

"And you know all this how?" Not only did it sound complicated, it sounded ridiculous.

"Santo Domingo is predominantly Catholic, Nicki. I worked with the nuns to establish a school in the fishing village where I lived. When you're surrounded by a certain culture, you pick up a lot without even realizing it."

"Do you actually believe someone can *buy* their way into Heaven?"

A note of irritation crept into her voice. "It doesn't matter if I believe it. Catholics believe it. Keith Morgan believes it." She smoothed her hair as we approached the front door. "It's complicated."

"Sounds like a big fat bribe to me."

That was the last thing I said before the front door was opened by a somber man in a suit. He held it for us until Kelly and I were inside.

Forest Lawn looked a lot different when there were live bodies walking around. The foyer was full of people chatting in low tones while organ music played above our heads—at a respectable level, of course. The somber man in the suit pointed us toward a table near the door, which held a big black guest book and a stack of leaflets. The leaflet was titled A LIFE WELL-LIVED—KEITH GERARD MORGAN—1959-2008, and had a picture of praying hands on the cover.

Kelly signed the guest book while I looked around, hoping against hope I wouldn't see a glamorously dressed blonde in Jimmy Choos. There was something very scary about that woman, and it wasn't just that she was already dead.

"Doesn't it even matter to you that your good buddy Keith was cheating on his wife?" I whispered, still scanning the foyer. "His girlfriend died in that same car accident, you know. I don't see a memorial to her around here anywhere."

Kelly laid down the pen and looked up at me from her wheelchair. "That's funny. You never struck me as the judgmental type—particularly when infidelity is involved."

"What's that supposed to mean?" I kept my voice down, but people were starting to give us curious looks anyway. *Maybe it was the leather jacket.* Kelly avoided my question by rolling toward the open doors of the Serenity Chapel. I wanted an answer, so I had no choice but to follow.

And immediately wished I hadn't.

A wide aisle led down the center of the chapel, a red-patterned runway to a raised, circular dais surrounded by flowers: There—in all its African mahogany, gilt-corniced splendor—rested the coffin that held the corpse of Keith Morgan. The guest of honor himself was in a semi-reclining position, as though he relaxed on an overstuffed lounge chair, sleeping in a suit. While I watched, a woman rose from a kneeler beside the coffin, leaned in, and kissed the dead guy right on the lips before she turned, weeping, toward a seat.

Ewwwwwwwwww.

Kelly wheeled her chair over to the end of a pew, and I took a seat next to her.

"I hope you're not accusing Joe of infidelity." I counted on the organ music to cover my whisper. "You were the one who left *him*, remember?"

There was a flash of anger in her eyes, but she blinked, and it died. "I know." She looked away, toward the front of the chapel.

I couldn't help it, even though I knew this wasn't the time. "Maybe if you hadn't been gone for four years, he wouldn't be dating anyone."

I wasn't gonna take the blame for this muddled mess we were in, though I was willing to take some of it.

Kelly didn't answer me this time, and I shut up. Sometimes that's all you can do.

Keith Morgan had been a good-looking man. Late forties, nice head of brownish red hair with only a touch of gray; very dignified. Black suit, burgundy tie. The matching silk pocket handkerchief was a nice touch.

"Nicki." A whisper, like a spider crawling over my skin.

I looked at Kelly, but the whisper hadn't come from her.

"Don't let her do it, Nicki."

Kelly didn't react. She didn't seem to hear it.

"That bastard doesn't deserve to go to Heaven."

The people around me were total strangers, and none of them were even looking at me. No sophisticated blondes with a bitter streak.

But I had no doubt who the voice belonged to.

"Who does your sister think she is, anyway?" Barbie was there, even though I couldn't see her at the moment. *"Is she so perfect? She thinks that Keith should go to Heaven so he can end up with that mealy-mouthed wife of his. She thinks she can tie up the happily-ever-after with a big pink bow from Wal-Mart, and all that crap."*

"Leave me alone," I murmured.

The whisper went from pissed to taunting in the blink of an eye. *"Your sister wants her husband back."*

I jerked in my seat, fighting the urge to answer. All I needed was to have people see me talking to myself.

"She still loves him, Nicki." Barbie's voice turned sly. *"And she's jealous—she's jealous of you. She wants him back."*

Automatically, I looked at Kelly. She was watching a group of people in the front row of the chapel. A dark-haired woman sat closest to the coffin, one arm around a teenage boy who slumped next to her. I couldn't see their faces.

"I can help you keep Joe away from her." The ugly whispers went on and on, clear as a bell despite the drone of organ music and the muffled sounds of grief. *"If you help me first."*

I shot up from my seat, drawing Kelly's attention.

"Excuse me. I have to go to the ladies' room."

Her eyes widened. "Now? Are you sure?"

I stepped past her without answering and hurried out of the chapel. The foyer was empty now, and the front door beckoned.

I hesitated, knowing it would be better to have it out with Psycho Barbie in private, but not looking forward to it.

"Leaving so soon?" The voice was lilting, almost playful, and no longer a whisper. "You'll miss the eulogy."

I turned, and there she was, smiling politely, as though at a cocktail party. The blond hair was perfectly styled, the makeup flawless.

"So will you," I said. I wasn't going to let her intimidate me, even if my knees *were* a little rubbery. I'd learned that lesson well with my former friend, Caprice.

Alive, Caprice had secretly been a voodoo priestess; dead, her dark side made it impossible to remain friends.

"Why don't you go in and disrupt the show?" I was bluffing, of course. "Blow out a few altar candles, knock over a few flower arrangements. You'll feel better."

Psycho Barbie glanced toward the chapel. Her eyes went straight to the cross above the altar, not to her boyfriend's coffin. A flash of something ugly crossed her face. "That's okay. I know what happens next." She turned away from the cross. There was that smirk again, quickly hidden behind a fake smile. "Keith's good-old-boy buddies will get up and blubber about golf games and good works. They won't mention the strip joints or the stag parties or the one-night stands. They'll talk about hunting trips and ski vacations, but they won't bother to explain how most business trips are just an excuse for middle-aged men to behave badly." Barbie took a step toward me on those gorgeous stilettos. "They'll blather on about how much Keith loved his family, but they won't say how they'd all known for years that he was cheating on his wife." Her perfect smile remained perfectly in place. "You can say it, though."

No way in Hell. "I'm not saying anything to anybody. I'm sorry, but it's over. You're dead."

Her smile didn't falter. "Death is only the beginning, Nicki."

"Revenge isn't going to help." I had no idea if anything would, but it wasn't my job to figure it out. Just because I could see and hear this woman didn't mean I could save her.

I had a feeling it was too late for that.

"I'm not interested in making deals with the Devil." I'd been to the Light, and I already knew I preferred it to the Dark. "Leave me alone."

Her features tightened. Her smile became a sneer, the look in her eye turning sharper, more measuring. By the time she spoke, I was afraid of what she might say.

"You're making a mistake." Her voice was different now; deeper, raspier. I was left with the feeling that someone—or something—else was behind that flawless mask of makeup.

Whatever it was, it had a great sense of fashion. Even scared shitless I couldn't help but admire that perfect little black dress.

"Go ahead," the Barbie doll said, "keep 'doing unto others.' Let's see how long you last. But remember—we're watching."

And she was gone. Just like that.

Gone.

We're watching? Just who was this *we*?

And did I really want to know?

"So you think the Devil made her do it?"

Poor Joe. He must be getting so tired of phone calls like this.

"I don't know." I was hunched miserably in the front seat of my car, watching the entrance to the funeral home. Keith Morgan's service had been going on for at least ten minutes. "I've got a bad feeling. The way her face changed was weird." I'd already told Joe the whole story about the cheating councilman and his pissed-off mistress. "All I know is that I'm not gonna help her. No way, no how."

I knew Joe was working and he had patients to see and prescriptions to write, and I didn't care.

I was nervous, in more ways than one.

"What about Kelly?" Joe's question was very matter-of-fact, and went straight to the heart of my nervousness.

What about her? "She's still inside. I think her plan was to chat with the widow, talk up the cheating husband, and get some money donated to the Church in his name."

"You're telling me that Kelly can see ghosts, just like you?"

No, I'm telling you to forget about Kelly and focus

on me. Out loud, I said, "That's what I'm telling you." I paused, and couldn't resist a teeny bit of snarkiness. "Maybe she'll make another good case study for your paper on near death experiences."

"Maybe." Joe wasn't biting. "You left her in there by herself?"

"It's not like I abandoned her or anything. I just stepped outside for a few minutes." This conversation wasn't going the way I wanted it to. "She's a big girl." A big girl in a wheelchair. "She's bound and determined to help this Morgan guy. What I say doesn't matter."

"I know the feeling," Joe muttered.

"Point taken, smart guy." I could get mad, or I could turn the beat around. "But you like me anyway, don't you?"

"I'm crazy about you." I could hear the smile in Joe's voice. "Or else I'm just crazy. I'm not certain which."

Now we were talkin'. "Crazy enough to come over tonight?"

"Only if you promise to leave the whips and chains in the closet."

"Whips and chains? Don't you just wish."

Joe laughed. "My mother always told me to be careful what you wish for, because you might get it."

"Oh, you're gonna get it." I savored the words, made them a promise. "Whether you can handle it is another matter."

His voice lowered. "I think I'm doing a pretty good job so far. You're quite a handful, Nicki Styx."

"You know what they say." I smiled into the phone, enjoying the sexy teasing. "Anything more than a handful is wasted."

Joe corrected me automatically. "'Mouthful.' Anything more than a 'mouthful' is wasted."

"Hmm . . . an interesting concept." I toyed with the hem of my yellow sundress. "You'll have to prove it to me, Dr. Bascombe. Perhaps further research is in order."

When I got back inside I felt a lot better. Funny how flirting with your boyfriend can put a positive spin on things. The dead couldn't hurt me, and neither could Kelly. I slid into the pew beside her without a qualm.

"Behold, I show you a mystery." The organ music had stopped, and there was a priest beside the coffin, a chubby older man with thick glasses, reading from the Bible. "We shall all indeed rise again, but we shall not all be changed. In a moment, in the twinkling of an eye, the trumpet shall sound and the dead shall rise."

Not a very appealing image, if you asked me.

"Is everything okay?" Kelly leaned in, giving me a suspicious glance.

I nodded and smiled. I managed to keep smiling, even through the long prayers and dull stories about a man I'd never met. I just kept reminding myself it'd be over soon. The flower arrangements were nice, and the candles. As far as any grand expectations about learning how to "go in style," the only thing I learned is that I didn't wanna go like this. Give me a wild party and remember me fondly—don't make me wish I was dead already.

And when it was over, I was able to wait patiently while Kelly joined the line of people who waited to have a word with the family. I couldn't help but feel sorry for the widow and the teenager. The boy looked miserable, the woman shell-shocked.

"May I help you, child?"

I jumped, not having heard the chubby priest come up beside me.

"I'm fine." Off guard, I had no idea how to address him. *Was I supposed to cross myself or something*? "I'm fine, Father."

He gave me a kind smile, resting a hand on the back of the pew. "Are you sure? Something tells me you're in trouble."

I couldn't help but think of Psycho Barbie. *Something's been telling me the same thing.*

"Everything's fine, really. I'm just sad for the family." I glanced back toward Kelly and saw her in deep conversation with Mrs. Morgan. Both she and her son were paying rapt attention to whatever Kelly was saying, the grieving widow even smiling a little through her tears.

Father O'Reilly (I remembered his name now) was still standing at the end of the pew. I looked up to find him staring at me. "You have both darkness and light surrounding you, child. You must be strong enough not to let the darkness win."

"I beg your pardon?" I was surprised he could see anything through those Coke bottle glasses. I'd never met the man, and I was nobody's child . . . not anymore. "I said I was fine."

Father O'Reilly wasn't listening. He sketched a cross in the air and said, "Bless you, my child."

For some reason, it kinda ticked me off. "I didn't ask for your blessing, Father."

"Consider it a gift, freely given. After all, we must do unto others as we would have them do unto us."

Exactly what the voice inside the Light told me to remember.

Like I was ever gonna be allowed to forget.

"So did you get Mr. Morgan's eternal soul taken care of?"

I knew I sounded way too cheerful, but I was so happy to leave Forest Lawn behind us that I didn't care. The parking lot was nothing but a smudge in the rear-view mirror.

Kelly glanced at me from the passenger seat, but she wasn't smiling. "I think so. His wife was so relieved about the money that she believed every lie I told her."

"What?" Not what I expected to hear. "What lies? What money?"

"The money Keith Morgan stashed in a safety deposit box at a bank his wife knew nothing about. He hid the key under the water heater in their garage."

What a sleazebag, hiding money from his wife.

"I told her I worked for the bank, and that I'd been authorized to tell her where to find the key. I said her husband had left written instructions on file." Kelly didn't look too happy about her good deed of the day. "I wish I didn't have to lie to her, but I couldn't tell her about her husband's ghost. She would've thought I was a lunatic and then never known the money even existed."

I thought of Barbie, and all the lies Keith Morgan must've told to both women over the years. "Why in the world should she spend it on paying her husband's way into Heaven? I mean, the guy doesn't exactly sound like a prize." I'd never met him, true, and my perceptions were colored by an angry spirit's rantings, but anyone who could turn a soul as bitter as Barbie's was not cool with me. "Then he has the bad taste to get himself killed in a drunk driving accident, and takes his mistress out with him. Very public, very humiliating. If I were Mrs. Morgan, I'd spend the money on a vacation." A trip to Paris and a passionate fling with a Eurotrash boy toy would probably be just the thing, but I didn't say it.

Kelly sighed and shook her head. "I don't care what she does with the money." She stared out the window, the bruise on her temple still visible even after Evan's careful application of cover-up. "It's not up to me to play God. I did what an unquiet spirit asked and now he'll leave me alone." There was a silence as we sped along the highway. "Right?"

A simple question with no simple answer. I gave her the only one I had.

"I don't know." My fingers gripped the steering wheel just a little tighter. "I've only had this problem for a month. It's too soon to tell."

"Does it get any easier?" Kelly turned her head and looked at me.

Yeah, if you don't mind dead people bugging you until you take care of their unfinished business.

I stuck with the honest answer. "No."

"When did you see your first ghost?"

I thought of Irene Goldblatt and heard, in my head, her likely opinion of the situation: *Ech. Poor meshugeneh. What does she think—that you're an expert or something?* I grinned at the memory of the little Jewish grandmother who'd bullied me into accepting the inevitable, and the unbelievable.

"When I woke up in the hospital after my heart failure, there was a woman in my room who'd choked to death on her husband's matzo balls. She wanted me to tell him it wasn't his fault."

Kelly's eyes got big. "Did you do it?"

I nodded. "Yeah. But first I had to convince him the message came from his dead wife." Poor Morty would never be able to hear the theme song from *Laverne & Shirley* again without thinking of Irene, and neither would I.

"*Why* did you do it?"

Another simple question with a complicated answer. I thought about it a second, then realized it wasn't so complicated after all.

"Because it was the right thing to do."

"I knew it!" Kelly's outburst startled me. One minute she'd been depressed, and now she was crowing like she'd just won the lottery, rocking back and forth in her seat. "I knew it! You're not the vain, selfish person you want me to think you are!"

Gee, thanks. "I'm plenty vain, thank you."

Kelly laughed, settling back into the upholstery. "You're a nice person."

"No, I'm not."

"You like helping people."

"No, I don't."

She leaned forward again and said, "Then why are you helping me? You don't even know me. I could be an axe murderer for all you know."

Peace Corps volunteer, long-lost twin, axe murderer. Just my luck. I pretended to concentrate on my driving, but the car was finding its own way home.

"What about paying for a nice funeral for the mother you never met, huh?" Kelly was throwing out examples like confetti. "You even donated a three-hundred-dollar dress to bury her in. I saw the price tag. You've invited me into your home—into your life—even though you know how things used to be between Joe and me."

"'Used to' are the key words there." I couldn't really defend myself against her accusations of being a do-gooder, but I could insist on her getting the facts straight. "And I bought that dress on eBay for a lot less than three hundred dollars."

"See?" Kelly looked triumphant. "You've invited me to stay with you even though you're jealous about Joe. That proves you're a good person."

Puh-lease.

"I'm not jealous, because I have no reason to be jealous. And whether or not I'm a good person, well"—I shook my head—"you'll just have to come to your own conclusions."

Try and steal my boyfriend, and you'll find out what a good person I'm not.

"Why didn't you tell me she was such a Polly Purebread?"

I had my feet drawn up, snuggled against Joe on the couch. His hand was warm in both of mine, his arm trapped between my jean-clad thighs. He'd taken off his shoes and was resting his feet on the coffee table, not at all unhappy to find me waiting in his living room when his shift in the E.R. was over.

"You never asked me," came the typically male answer. "I did tell you she was in the Peace Corps." He gave me a tired grin before taking a swig of the beer I'd picked up on the way over. "What did you expect?"

I shrugged, enjoying the feel of his body against mine. "I don't know." I'd already told Joe about my day at the mortuary. I'd be going back for another funeral tomorrow, but thankfully, Kelly had agreed to hold a graveside service for Peaches, so I wouldn't have to go inside. It had been a relief to get Kelly settled into the guest room at my house, and an even bigger relief when she said she wanted to turn in early. "Somebody more like me, I suppose."

Joe laughed, risking a swallow of beer. "Like you?" He shook his head. His dark hair looked like he'd been combing it with his fingers. "There's nobody like you."

The simple way he said it made me feel better than anything had in a long time. I knew bullshit when I heard it—this wasn't it. Confidence gave me the courage to ask some of the questions I hadn't asked yet.

"If things don't work out, do you promise we can just be honest with each other?"

"Whoa." He put down his bottle. It hit the end table with a light *thunk*. "What do you mean, 'if things don't work out'? Are you planning to dump me?" He kept his tone teasing, but I could tell he wasn't thrilled at the direction the conversation was going. "You're not thinking about doing something *noble* or anything, are you?"

I made a rude noise, unable to believe how quick people were to accuse me of good motives today.

"That's the only way things won't work out, Nicki." Joe squeezed my hand, leaving it trapped between my thighs. "I've already told you, what Kelly and I had is long dead. She left me for another guy, and—" He shrugged and shook his head. "—I didn't even care. I was so wrapped up in my residency that it was almost a relief. I didn't have to feel guilty about neglecting her anymore." I could hear the sincerity in his voice. "Her showing up right now is great timing. I can get the divorce taken care of and move on with my life." He gave me a sideways smile, all the more sexy because of the look in his eyes. "Now that I have a reason to."

I leaned over and gave him a quick kiss, unable to resist a tired man in scrubs. This man, anyway.

"It might not be that simple." I gave him another kiss for good measure. "Life isn't always simple." I squeezed his fingers with one hand and ran the other up and down his arm, liking the rasp of hair against my palm. Joe had such strong, capable hands. I'm sure plenty of his patients noticed—I had, even while lying in a hospital bed, feeling like death warmed over.

Which, technically, at the time, I was.

"Let's be honest, Joe. Kelly obviously still has feelings for you, or she wouldn't be here."

He held up a finger. "Kelly came looking for *you*, not me."

"She knew you were in Atlanta. You were her 'unfinished business,' remember?" Joe looked away, impatient. "I want us both to see things clearly here. I want us to be honest with each other about what happens next. This can get *very* complicated." He sighed, but he was listening. "Your soon-to-be-ex-wife, who happens to be my twin sister, is living in my house. We're both either psychics or lunatics, your divorce isn't final, and my best source of advice is a gay man who plays with dolls." If mannequins weren't life-sized dolls, I don't know what was. "Somewhere in the middle of all this, you and I are supposed to have some fun, and my sister and I are supposed to become bosom buddies." *If we don't kill each other first.*

Joe laughed. He had the cutest crinkles around his eyes. "You have a real flair for summing things up, don't you?"

I grinned back, glad he didn't mind my bluntness. "Only one of my many talents," I teased. "I can also tie a cherry stem into a knot with my tongue."

That earned me a wicked grin. "Why does that not surprise me?" He leaned in, and a quick kiss turned into a mock-tickling match that left me pinned to the couch, laughing and helpless.

"I promise to be honest with you, if you promise not to forget about the fun," Joe said, grinning down at me. He looked awfully pleased with himself for somebody who'd just bested a mere girl. "You've spoiled me, Nicki Styx. Dr. Joe no longer wants to be a dull boy." He rubbed the tip of his nose against mine. "Everything will work out. You'll see."

I smiled up at him, wanting only to believe that it would. Then he kissed me, slow and deep, and I forgot all about twin sisters and cherry stems for a while.

CHAPTER 6

It was nearly two in the morning when I got home, nearly two-thirty before I fell asleep, and nearly dawn when I felt the mattress sag. Someone was sitting on the bed, near my feet.

Drifting, I kept my eyes closed. Morning light filtered through my lids, but it was faint enough to ignore as long as the curtains were drawn. It took a moment to dawn on *me* that since I was in my own bedroom, not Joe's, I should be alone.

I shifted, lifting my head to peer toward the foot of the bed.

There was a woman sitting there.

"Don't be afraid." She lifted a hand in my direction. An unmistakable Southern drawl, comforting and kind. "There's no need to be afraid." A sun-ripened scent, fresh fruit and flowers.

Peaches.

I was scrabbling, all elbows, arms, and knees. In two seconds I had my back against the headboard. The room was dim, and it was hard to make out her face. Then I saw what she was wearing, and my heart did a flip—the hot pink chiffon Kelly and I had taken to Mr. Bates, the cadaver-man.

A lump rose in my throat. This was my biological mother. *Bone of my bone and flesh of my flesh.* Funny, it had never mattered much to me that I was adopted. Now it was overwhelming.

"You must be so mad at me." Peaches put her hand down, folding it into her lap. "I've made a mess of things, as usual. I wouldn't blame you a bit if you were to tell me to go away. You girls were supposed to be together. I always thought you were together."

That lazy Southern accent was deceptive—she was doing some fast talking. "I made a terrible mistake giving you girls up. There wasn't a day that went by that I didn't wish I'd done things differently. And then I go and get myself killed just when I had the chance to make it right." She sighed. "All because I didn't want my seat belt to wrinkle my outfit. Vanity, thy name is Peaches."

Her friendly chatter left me numb. This was hardly an ordinary meeting. Lila Boudreaux—Peaches—might be the woman who gave me life, but she was still a stranger.

Besides, she was dead.

And I had no idea what to say to her.

"I came to say good-bye," Peaches said.

"Shouldn't you have said hello first?" The words popped out before I could stop them.

"I didn't know who you were when I came into the

store, Nicki. I was confused at the time, scared, worried about your sister. By the time I put it all together, what was I supposed to say? 'Hey, darlin'. . . it's me, your dead mama?' "

I bit my lip and said, "No offense, but showing up dressed for your own funeral probably isn't the best way to get to know me. Neither is popping up in my backseat with a cryptic comment about some guy lying to Kelly, and then disappearing on me." This was *way* too freaky—I didn't need a mother nobody could see but me. I'd had a wonderful childhood with wonderful parents. No childhood traumas, no abandonment issues here. "I don't mean to be rude, but this is never going to work. It's not like we can have a meaningful relationship at this late date, is it?"

"You're a feisty little thing, aren't you?" There was a smile in her voice. "And I like how you get straight to the point. I always had trouble with that. My mama would say 'Peaches, I asked you what time it was, not how a watch works.'" A flash of white teeth in the dimness. "And so pretty. Just look at you." I didn't know how she could see me when I could barely make out her face—all I could see was the pale oval of her cheeks, the bump of her nose. "You've got style. I always wondered what you girls would be like, whether you'd think the same, dress the same, act the same."

I ignored the phrase "you girls." There was no "you girls"—Kelly was still a stranger.

"I'm glad to know you two are so different. Kelly's the quiet one, and you're the spitfire. It makes for a nice balance. Good feng shui."

Feng shui? Please. I might technically be a twin,

but I still considered myself an original. I smoothed the sheets over my knees and kept my "unbalanced" thoughts to myself.

Peaches looked down, fingering the pink chiffon. "I love the dress," she offered.

"Good. I'm glad." I wished I had the nerve to turn on a light. "It's vintage," I added automatically, "1960s, chiffon with satin banding."

"It's beautiful. I thought you might like to see me in it, the way I would've looked if . . . " Peaches trailed off, while I swallowed the lump in my throat. Then she stood and held out her arms, modeling the dress. The room was lighter now, morning making its arrival known even through the curtains. "I'd like you to remember me like this—like a real person"—a graceful pirouette of hot pink chiffon—"not a wax dummy in a box." Her voice broke, then steadied. "Let this be both our hello and our good-bye, Nicki, and forgive me for being such a poor excuse for a mama."

I stared at her, trying not to cry. Dark hair, hot pink clothes, flair for drama. I had the oddest sensation of déjà vu. And then I realized—it was like looking through a glass darkly, and seeing an older, slightly different version of me on the other side.

"There's nothing to forgive." *I wasn't going to cry. I wasn't.* "I'm not mad at you, never have been. I had two great parents who thought I hung the moon, and I have a great life with great friends." I took a deep breath and added softly, "It's okay you gave me up for adoption. I'm okay. You can go into the Light with a clear conscience."

Peaches tilted her head. "Your parents must've loved you very much."

Another lump rose in my throat. I didn't answer.

"Their love fills this house even now, like the scent of fresh-baked cookies."

"Nicki's Amazing Chocolate Chunks," my mom had called them. Sunday afternoons, usually during football season, it'd been a ritual for her and me to make them for my dad.

"I know you'll be all right, Nicki. You were the lucky one." Peaches looked away, toward the curtained window. "Kelly's the one I'm worried about."

Of course. I resisted a roll of the eyes. I didn't know my sister all that well, but I already knew she was tougher than she looked.

"She doesn't have a great life with great friends and loving memories to fall back on." In profile, Peaches looked like Kelly—they shared the same stubborn jut of chin. "She doesn't have anybody now, except for you."

Uh-oh. I could see where this was going. *When did I become responsible for the whole world, hm?*

"Kelly will be okay. I took her in, didn't I? It's not like she's been thrown to the wolves or anything." Edgy, yet curious, I asked, "Have you been to see her since you . . . um . . . ?"

Peaches shook her head. "She can't see me. I've tried. Only you can see me. Haven't you figured it out yet?"

"Figured it out?"

"Kelly can only see men—male spirits. You can only see women."

That made sense. All the spirits who'd come to me so far had been women—Irene, Caprice, Tammy, Psycho Barbie.

"I didn't want this for you girls." Peaches moved toward the footboard, fingering the newel post. "It's one of the reasons I gave you up, you know, so that maybe you'd grow up lucky and not have to deal with it." She sounded almost as if she was talking to herself. "But Mama was right, blood will tell, every time."

A prickle of hair rose on the back of my neck.

"Only there's two of you. Two halves of a whole . . . two sides, two gifts. Two curses."

"Curses?" I wasn't liking the sound of that. I wasn't liking the sound of any of this.

Peaches laughed a little, but it wasn't a cheerful sound. "That's the way I usually saw it—a curse, though it wasn't all bad. I like to think I helped a few people along the way. Passing messages from the other side, giving comfort when I could. Besides," she shrugged, "it helped pay the bills."

A psychic. Great. That was just great. I could see the neon sign in my mind: MADAME PEACHES IS IN. FORTUNES AND FAIRY TALES TOLD HERE.

"Trouble is, sometimes the dead can be mighty determined to get the living's attention. And not always for good reasons. I wish you and Kelly didn't have the knack, but at least now you girls have each other." Peaches let go of the newel post and stepped back, away from the light filtering in through the curtains. "You're going to need to stick together, I think."

"The 'knack'? What does *that* mean?" This was a little too *All in-the Family* meets *Night of the Living Dead* for me. "You make it sound like it's something special to see spirits when I, for one, think it sucks. And since when did it become so important that Kelly and I stick together?"

Peaches took another step back, into the shadows. "You girls are bound to each other, two halves of a whole."

"I've known her less than a week. We don't even know if we're gonna like each other yet." I could barely see Peaches now, the hot pink chiffon losing its vibrancy to the dimness.

"Open your heart, Nicki. Good and evil exist, both inside and out. It doesn't hurt to have family on your side." Her voice was fading, along with the shadows. "Fate split you apart, but now it's brought you together again. The proof is in the puddin'."

Tired Southern homilies just weren't gonna cut it.

"Listen, I'll do my best, okay? You don't need to worry about us, we'll be fine. You can rest easy." I sincerely hoped she would. The last thing I needed was another ghost looking over my shoulder. Softening my tone, I added, "Don't be afraid to go into the Light, Peaches."

"I'm not afraid."

I couldn't see her anymore. Daylight suffused the room, driving back the darkness. With every passing moment her essence was fading. I could barely even hear her when she said, "I just wanted to say good-bye. You girls be good to each other, and we'll see each other again someday."

And then she was gone, leaving nothing but the lingering scent of peaches and regret.

I put my face down in my hands and cried like a baby for about five minutes.

Then I got up and took a shower. I had yet another funeral to go to.

* * *

Six people were gathered to lay Lila "Peaches" Boudreaux to rest, and one of them was a total stranger—the black-suited, balding minister Kelly had hired for the occasion. He was droning scripture from a well-worn Bible, and I couldn't help but wonder how many times he'd read the same passages about hope and glory and everlasting life over the graves of people he'd never met.

I took a deep breath and looked up, appreciating the view of blue sky and clouds more than the sight of the closed coffin, poised to be lowered. A beautiful Georgia morning in early fall—my favorite time of year. Joe squeezed my hand and I squeezed back, oddly at peace under the circumstances.

Not so Kelly. She cried steadily into a wad of tissues, a single white rose in her lap. The rose had come from the spray of flowers Evan and his boyfriend Butch brought, which now lay on top of the casket. Butch hovered over Kelly's shoulder like a muscle-bound mother hen, while Evan flashed me a worried, apologetic look.

But I was okay. All was as it should be . . . Kelly needed their support right now much more than I did.

"Amen, amen, I say to you, whoever hears my word and believes in the One who sent me has eternal life and will not come to condemnation, but has passed from death to life."

The minister had his eyes glued to what he was reading, or he might have seen what I saw—the black limousine that turned off the main road and glided to a stop right behind him, a few hundred yards away. Someone visiting one of Forest Lawn's dearly departed residents, no doubt.

"Do not be amazed, because the hour is coming in which all who are in the tombs will hear His voice and come out, those who have done good deeds to the resurrection of life, but those who have done wicked deeds to the resurrection of condemnation."

There it was again—"the dead shall rise again" thing. All I could envision was a bad zombie movie. *If corpses ever start clawing their way out of graves, I won't be one of the ones standing around shouting "Hallelujah."*

"Amen."

"Amen," echoed Kelly through her tears. Joe murmured the same and gave my hand another squeeze. Right on cue, a breeze swept through the cemetery, flattening the grass and sending fallen leaves dancing. I lifted my head and let the air cool my cheeks, breathing in the scent of early autumn and late peaches.

It felt like good-bye, and it felt right that Joe was there, that we were all there—my boyfriend, my sister, my best friend, and his partner.

An ending to what I'd known, and the beginning of something unknowable.

Life.

A pretty damned complicated one, too.

The minister came over to Kelly and shook her hand, then offered it to me. "I'm very sorry for your loss," he said.

"Thank you." Despite an ill-fitting suit and a bad comb-over, the man had a kind face. He turned to Joe and offered him condolences, too. Joe walked him aside while I turned to Kelly, who was swiping at her nose.

"You okay?"

She looked up at me, puffy-eyed. "I think so." Then, "Are you?"

I squatted so we were level and nodded, resting a hand on the arm of her wheelchair. "Did you smell it?"

She gave me a confused look. *Stupid question.* Her nose was red as a beet and still dripping.

"I smelled peaches," I said. "Just a second ago—right after the minister said 'amen.'"

"You did?" Her face crumpled. She scrabbled in her lap for a fresh tissue, eyes locked on mine. I was disappointed she hadn't smelled it. I was sure the farewell had been meant for both of us.

I snagged a Kleenex and handed it to her. She was crying harder than ever.

"Do you think it was her?" Kelly sounded so hopeful, I was glad to be able to give her an honest answer.

"Yes. It was her."

She blew her nose and her crying began to ease, but I was feeling guilty—it would be selfish to keep my predawn visit from Peaches to myself. Tempted as I was to keep the experience private, Kelly should hear about it.

"There's more."

Kelly immediately got the gist, eyes widening above the wad of tissue. I glanced toward the departing minister and murmured, "I'll tell you about it on the way home."

A mechanical hum began, and I turned my head to find the casket being lowered. Two men with a small backhoe—obviously funeral home employees—stood in the shade a discreet distance away, one of them holding a remote. Even funerals had become automated and electronic these days. How creepy.

The white coffin sank down, smooth as silk, until it disappeared. You couldn't see the actual hole in the ground, because green draping covered everything, including the framework that did the lowering. When the mechanical hum stopped, I knew it was done. It was finished.

I stood up, ready to go home.

"I knew it," a woman said sadly. "I knew my darling Peaches was gone. I felt it in my bones."

I turned, not having heard anybody approach.

The woman at the foot of the grave was elderly and plump. She wore black, including gloves and an old-fashioned hat, complete with veil. The veil was pinned to her hat with a glittering brooch, polished jet and sterling silver by the look of it.

Jet, for mourning.

"You knew our mother?" Kelly spoke for us both. I was relieved, because for a second I'd been afraid the woman wasn't real. If Kelly could see her, then I was safe—she was flesh and blood. The limousine I'd seen earlier was still parked by the road, rear passenger door ajar.

"Peaches was my daughter."

Kelly's breath caught in her throat, matching my shocked gasp.

The woman took a few steps closer, clutching a black beaded purse with both hands. "She told me she'd found her girls, and nothing would do but that she go after the two of you." The old woman's voice was pure Low Country Southern, all molasses and manners. "I warned her not to go looking for trouble, but she didn't listen." She stared at the grave, voice breaking. "She never listened to me once she'd set her mind on something. Always one to go her own way, was my Peaches."

The woman dabbed at her eyes with a handkerchief, and I couldn't help but notice that the handkerchief was black, too. The old lady had style—an old-fashioned style, but style nonetheless.

"Excuse me?" I wasn't sure I was hearing this correctly. "You're our *grandmother*?"

"Call me Bijou, dear," the woman said. As with many older ladies, her makeup was exaggerated—too much rouge and too much eye shadow. All the foundation in the world wasn't gonna cover those pouchy bags beneath the red-rimmed eyes. "Bijou Boudreaux. 'Grandma' sounds so déclassé, and I refuse to go by one of those silly, made-up names like 'Mimi' or 'Gigi.'"

I stared at her, speechless. The old lady had a lot of nerve if she thought I was going to start calling her anything.

"Peaches told me she lived alone." Kelly's voice was shaky, but I was glad she spoke up. "She said she had no family."

Bijou smiled. A sad smile, with a hint of irony. Lipstick was smeared over the edge of her lip, like her hand had been shaky when she put it on.

"She was angry at me. We didn't part on good terms." Bijou shook her head, the jet brooch on her hat glinting as it caught the light. "I'll never forgive myself for that." She swallowed hard, double chin wobbling. "A deputy from the sheriff's department called me from her cell phone two days ago. When I called the coroner's office, they told me—" Her voice faltered, then steadied. "—they told me that her remains had been released to Forest Lawn Mortuary. When I called here to make arrangements, I was told they'd already been made."

And you thought her funeral would be a good time to introduce yourself? I kept my snarky thoughts to myself, but I couldn't help it if they popped into my head. Whoever Bijou Boudreaux was, she was obviously grieving. Tears had left clean tracks through the makeup on her cheeks.

"I don't understand," Kelly said, shaking her head. "Why would Peaches lie about something like that?" Her fingers stroked the petals of the white rose in her lap.

Very gently, Bijou said, "I told you, dear. She was angry. But we loved each other, my Peaches and I, and I would've met you soon enough, I've no doubt."

Nobody moved. Kelly and I were silent as we stared at the old woman in black at the foot of the grave.

"I can't believe my poor, sweet Peaches is gone." Bijou's wrinkled face crumpled. She brought the black hankie up to cover her mouth, gazing tearfully at the green draping, the open hole in the middle. After a moment she recovered enough to say, "And now it's up to me to protect you girls. That's what Peaches would've wanted."

The ensuing silence was awkward.

I, for one, didn't need protecting, and Kelly was awfully quiet.

"There's nothing for it," Bijou said. She squared her round shoulders and nodded her head, black-veiled hat like a helmet atop her carefully styled gray hair. "You'll have to come back to Savannah with me." Her gloved hands worked the hankie, clutching and unclutching. "You'll have to come back to the Blue Dahlia."

This was too much. "I really don't mean to be rude, but we don't even know you." I glanced toward Kelly in her wheelchair, but could only see the top of her head. "I have a business to run. I can't just run off to Savannah." *What the heck was the Blue Dahlia?*

Besides, this woman was a stranger, and I'd learned to be wary of strangers who showed up and made demands. I didn't like being told what to do, and I didn't like being rushed. If Bijou Boudreaux truly was our grandmother, there would be time in the future to get to know each other.

Bijou's bleary-eyed gaze took me in from the tips of my black leather boots to the top of my pink-streaked head. She lingered on my face, looking for something that might remind her of Peaches, I suppose.

"You have your own business?" she asked, dabbing delicately at her rather large nose.

"I do." Evan shifted a little, and I took the hint, raising a hand in his direction. "My friend Evan and I are partners."

Bijou's gaze flicked over Evan, then Butch and Joe, all of whom stood by in silence.

"This is Evan's friend, Butch, and my boyfriend, Joe."

"Very nice to meet you all," Bijou said. "I'm sorry it wasn't under better circumstances." Then she turned her eyes back to me, effectively dismissing the men. "As a businesswoman, you can surely understand why I can't leave the Blue Dahlia unattended. You'll have to come to Savannah in order for me to teach you."

"Teach us what?" Kelly's voice held a note of skepticism, and I was glad she'd finally spoken up.

"Teach you how to handle the knack, dear."

My radar went up. I hadn't forgotten about the "knack."

Bijou cocked her head, jet brooch glinting. The gesture put me in mind of a plump black crow. "The gift of sight can be a dangerous gift, unless you know how to use it. My darling Peaches was extremely talented, but she lacked focus." Bijou looked sadly at the green draping. "And look what happened."

Kelly, however, had no clue what Bijou was talking about. "The knack? And what do you mean, 'look what happened'? It was a car accident."

Bijou looked at her sadly. "Oh, it was no accident, dear."

Joe murmured in my ear, "What is going on?"

I had an idea, but I didn't like it. Abruptly, I asked, "What type of business do you run?"

"My shop is called the Blue Dahlia." The old woman snapped open her purse, reached in and handed me a business card with one black-gloved hand. She handed a second card to Kelly.

Sure enough, the card read, in flowing script: *The Blue Dahlia, Savannah's Finest Blossoms.*

"A flower shop," I said stupidly. I'd expected something a lot more "cosmic," like "*Psychic Readings By Appointment*" or some such crap.

Bijou shifted the handbag into the crook of her elbow and said patiently, "So it is, dear. It's also my home. A lovely old place on the outskirts of Savannah's historic district. It was Peaches's home, too."

Joe chose that moment to slip his arm around my waist. I leaned into him gratefully. *Could things get any weirder?*

"You girls are in danger," Bijou said.

I felt Joe stiffen. *Apparently, things could.*

"That's why your mother tracked you down. She wanted to train you herself, but now she's gone, and the job falls to me."

"Nicki, could you take me home?" Kelly's voice was a little faint, but her request was a welcome relief. "I . . . I'm not feeling very well."

Bijou pinned me with a red-rimmed gaze, as if I were the one who'd said something. "Don't pretend you don't know what I'm talking about, child."

I *hate* it when people call me "child."

"I can sense things," Bijou continued. "And I can sense quite well that you know I'm telling the truth. Storm clouds are gathering. You're going to need my help to keep the darkness at bay."

Goose bumps rose on my arms. *You have both darkness and light surrounding you, child,* Father O'Reilly, the priest at Keith Morgan's funeral, had said. *You must be strong enough not to let the darkness win.*

Despite the goose bumps, and despite the offer of help, I was cautious. There was more to this old woman than met the eye, and I wasn't too eager to attach myself to someone who claimed to "sense things." As far as I was concerned, seeing was believing, and I'd already seen too much of the "otherworldly" stuff.

"My sister isn't feeling well," I said flatly. "I need to take her home."

"We'll call you." Kelly spoke up, though this time I wished she hadn't. "This is all just a bit overwhelming. Nicki and I need time to think things over."

I didn't need any time. I was staying in Atlanta, thank you, but I kept my mouth shut, hoping to speed our departure.

"I see." Bijou looked pained. "You girls have got your mama's stubbornness, as well as her looks. I hope those qualities serve you better than they did my Peaches." She drew herself up, clutching her black purse. Her voice trembled, and she pressed the black hankie to her lips, looking once again toward the grave. "Would you . . . would you mind if I stayed here a little while? It's a long drive back to Savannah, and I'd like to say my farewells first."

"Of course. Take all the time you need," Kelly said. "I'm glad you were able to come. I'm sure it would've meant a lot to Peaches to know you were here."

Bijou gave us a wan smile. "You're very kind. I'd like to think she's looking down on us right now, wouldn't you?"

Not really. I'd had my fill of spirits looking over my shoulder. Joe gave my waist a squeeze, and I touched his fingers, sensing he'd read my mind.

Bijou looked at Kelly, then me. "Your mama would've been proud of you girls," she said quietly. "I wish you'd had the chance to get to know her. She was very special."

Kelly broke down at that, giving way to tears.

In a few moments we'd said our good-byes to Peaches's only visitor and were heading toward our cars, Butch pushing Kelly's wheelchair between the headstones while Joe, Evan, and I followed. My two men flanked me, each of them taking one of my hands.

"Well, that was certainly interesting," Evan murmured. He tucked my fingers into the crook of his elbow and patted them absently as we walked.

Joe shot me a frowning glance. "No offense, but that lady seemed a little weird."

We'd almost reached the parking lot. Butch was already wheeling Kelly onto the blacktop.

"Why would *I* take offense? I don't even know her." And I wasn't sure I wanted to know her either. All this talk about "training" and the "knack" screamed bad news, with a capital B. I had enough problems without going to Savannah and looking for more.

I caught the glance Evan and Joe exchanged.

"She's your grandmother, Nicki," Evan said.

"Maybe. So she says. Whatever." I looked at Joe for reassurance, but he just shrugged.

Evan took a quick glance over his shoulder. "Trust you not to have a *normal* grandmother. A sweet little old lady who likes to bake would've been nice. But, no, you get the mysterious 'lady in black.'"

I stopped and looked back to where the old woman stood alone by the grave, a breeze ruffling the hem of her black dress. Despite my desire to avoid any more sticky family entanglements, I couldn't help but wonder about her. "What kind of a name is Bijou, anyway?"

"I don't know." Evan eyed the old woman a final time before moving toward the car. "But Joe's right—she's weird."

Kelly was very quiet on the drive home.

Evan and Butch had driven to the cemetery in Butch's SUV, so it was just the three of us in Joe's BMW—Kelly, Joe, and me. Joe was quiet, too, shooting me an occasional anxious glance when he thought I wasn't looking. I appreciated his concern, and rested a hand on his thigh as he drove. Other than a few stilted replies to a few stilted comments, Kelly sat silently in the backseat, staring out the window, as we made our way back to my Ansley Park neighborhood.

"You wanna come in?" I asked Joe when he pulled into the driveway.

"I think I'll go home and change out of this monkey suit," he said. "I'll be back in an hour, and take you both out to dinner."

The guy was so sweet—he was giving Kelly and me a chance to talk privately, to unwind a little after the funeral.

"Thanks, but I don't really feel like going out again today," Kelly said. "You two go ahead." She opened her car door and started to get out, moving her bandaged ankles carefully.

I gave Joe a shrug, opened my own door and waited while he got Kelly's wheelchair out of the trunk. "I'll see you later, handsome."

Joe grinned at me, and I couldn't help but smile back. He looked good enough to eat in his so-called "monkey suit," though I'd never refer to custom-tailored Dolce and Gabbana that way. I'd picked out the tie myself, a subtle gray and black geometric by Ralph Lauren.

"One hour," he said.

"Forty-five minutes." An hour was too long.

A quick kiss, and he was off, while I wheeled Kelly into the house.

"Well?" I pushed her into the living room and sank down on the couch. "What did you think of Bijou Boudreaux?"

Kelly looked troubled, her face pale. She was still holding the white rose from the gravesite. "Why didn't Peaches tell us we had a grandmother?"

I shrugged. "Bijou said they'd had a fight. Do you believe her?"

"I don't know," Kelly said. Her lip trembled. "Why would she think Peaches's death was no accident? Was she blaming me?"

The idea that there was any blame to be laid was a new one. Peaches hadn't blamed anyone but herself for what happened, and Kelly shouldn't, either.

"Of course it was an accident. Bijou wasn't there, how would she know what happened?" I gave a rude snort. "Oh yeah, I forgot, she 'senses' things."

"Maybe she does." The acceptance in Kelly's voice surprised me. "We 'see' things other people can't, don't we?"

She had me there.

"You don't seriously blame yourself for the accident, do you? Peaches didn't blame you—I swear she didn't." Nobody should have to carry around that kind of guilt.

Kelly wouldn't meet my eye. "Thanks for saying that. It means a lot."

We were both quiet for a minute. Then she said, "What if Bijou really does have some kind of psychic ability? What if seeing dead people is hereditary? What if Peaches could do it?" She was absorbed in thought, eyes distant. "Bijou said we were in danger, and you said Peaches came to give you a warning. What if this gift really *is* dangerous?"

"Gift?" I begged to differ. "This is no gift—it's a curse. And for the record, Peaches never said we were in danger. She said that a liar was coming, and not to believe him." I pinned her with a sour glance. "But you chose to believe that lying jerk Keith Morgan, and nothing bad happened." *Not yet anyway.* "You're making too big a deal out of some weird old woman's ramblings."

"Bijou called it the 'knack.'" Kelly was still lost in thought. "She said Peaches was talented, but lacked focus." Finally, she looked directly at me. "She said you knew what she was talking about."

Uncomfortably aware that I hadn't told Kelly everything Peaches had said to me, I found I couldn't meet her gaze very long. With a sigh, I said, "All I know is that Peaches said she used the knack to help pay the bills. She told me she didn't want that kind of life for us—that it was one of the reasons she gave us up."

Kelly made a strangled noise. "And you were going to tell me this *when*?"

"I didn't think it was important," I lied. The real reason I hadn't said anything was because it seemed like a private conversation between Peaches and me, and I didn't usually go around broadcasting the details of all my private conversations.

Or something like that.

"What else did she say?"

Kelly demanded details, so I went ahead and told her everything. "She said you can only see male spirits and I can see female spirits, and that we're bound to each other—two halves of a whole."

"Yin and yang," Kelly murmured, fascinated. "We're yin and yang."

"Would I be yin, or would I be yang?" I heard the sarcasm in my voice but couldn't help it. "I've always kinda liked being Nicki."

"And now Bijou wants to train us to use the knack." Kelly's mind was working. Her fingers moved restlessly on the stem of the rose. "But Peaches didn't want us to use it. This is weird."

"Thank you." I breathed a sigh of relief. "At least we agree on something."

"What should we do?" Her question surprised me. I supposed there would come a time when it became easy to think in terms of a *we* with my sister, but right now it was part of the weirdness.

"I'm not jumping into anything," I said. "If you want to get to know Bijou better, that's fine, but I'm not running off to Savannah to get 'trained.'" I leaned forward, resting my elbows on my knees. "I'm nobody's monkey."

Kelly looked at me thoughtfully. "I need to think about it," she said. "The first thing I need to do is get well." She touched her left rib very gingerly, then gestured toward her bandaged feet. "I'd like to have some time to recuperate before I go anywhere."

I couldn't help but feel sorry for her—she did kinda look like hell. She'd been crying and wore no makeup; there were dark circles beneath her eyes. It was obvious that Peaches's funeral had taken its toll.

"Let's just take it slow for now, okay? There will be time in the future to get to know Bijou, if that's what you want to do."

"Sounds like a plan," Kelly said tiredly. She maneuvered her wheelchair in the direction of her room, pushing herself along with both hands.

"Can I get you anything?"

"Answers would be nice."

I sighed. "Can't help you there."

CHAPTER 7

"Good Lord, woman. You said you'd be 'dressed to kill,' not maim."

I sauntered toward Joe on four-inch stiletto heels, slapping a leather riding crop against the palm of my left hand.

"What's the matter," I asked huskily. "Scared?"

He gave me the slanted grin that always set my heart tripping. "Absolutely," he said. "Scared stiff."

The avid way he was eyeing me was no joke, so I took my time modeling this year's Halloween costume, enjoying his undivided attention.

"What would a Wicked Witch be without her whip, hm?" I trailed the riding crop across my much-more-prominent-than-usual cleavage. I'd glued a single plastic spider on the curve of my right breast. "Or her black corset?" I could barely breathe in the thing, but it was worth it to see the look on his face. I flipped up the hem of my flirty orange and black skirt so he could see the garter belt I was wearing beneath it. Of course, I'd stayed true to my goth roots by making sure the fishnet stockings were ripped in all the right places, and added fake spiderweb tattoos on both shoulders for good measure. My hair was streaked with orange glitter gel beneath my pointed witch's hat.

"I can't believe how gorgeous you are," Joe said. He shook his head admiringly, obviously enjoying the view. "You are *hot*. Black lipstick might be my new favorite."

"Well, you know what they say." I gave him my sexiest pose, hand on hip, one leg forward. "If you've got it," a flirtatious wink, "haunt it." Then I blew him an air kiss.

He laughed appreciatively, and I felt good all over. We were going to have a great time tonight.

"It's a good thing I chose a 'tough guy' costume over 'Dr. Phil Good,'" Joe said. "I'm going to need to look tough to keep the other guys at the Vortex away from you."

"Are you kidding? When the girls get a look at you in those leather pants, I'll probably need to use this whip for real."

Joe had morphed into a sexy 'bad boy' in his biker clothes—all handpicked by Evan, of course. Tight leather pants, chunky black combat boots, and a sleeveless Harley-Davidson T-shirt. His beautiful body was usually hidden under surgical scrubs—I could get used to having a boyfriend with a regular gym habit. Nice shoulders, lean belly, and great biceps, now sporting fake tattoos even cooler than mine. He'd refused to let Evan style his hair, though, and slicked it back himself. The gel made it even darker than usual.

A flutter in my belly made me look forward to the end of the evening.

"Wow." Kelly thumped into the living room on her crutches, smiling. "You guys look great."

"You can still come with us," Joe said. "It's not too late for me to get a hospital gown and a wheelchair. You can go as an accident victim."

"Ha ha." Kelly gave him an exasperated look, but she was grinning. They seemed pretty easy with each other. The divorce papers had been signed with no fuss. She had even gone back to her maiden name, Charon.

Styx and Charon—the river of the dead and the boatman who ferried lost souls across it. Pretty weird when you thought about it.

"I don't want to go like this," Kelly said. "Maybe next year."

Next year. That's right. There would always be next year.

In the weeks since the funeral, Kelly and I had lived pretty quietly. She had the house to herself during the day, and at first she spent a lot of time watching TV in her room. She was an early riser, like me, so we'd fallen into the habit of having our coffee and newspaper together.

"You'd have fun." I tried to tempt her into getting out of the house. "Maybe even meet somebody."

Something flitted over Kelly's face before she looked away. "I guess I'd just prefer to meet Mr. Right when I'm looking my best," she said, still smiling. She looked back, and whatever it had been was gone. "You guys have fun for me. Tell me all about it tomorrow."

"You just wanna get back to that computer." I turned to Joe and said, "Kelly's been doing research into the paranormal, reading a lot of ghost stories on the Internet."

I normally didn't tease her about the amount of time she spent online, because I didn't blame her one bit. What else was there to do when you were recovering from two bum ankles and a couple of broken ribs?

"You should try reading up on the paranormal sometime, Miss Ignorance Is Bliss," Kelly answered, giving as good as she got. "Particularly now that we have to live with it."

I didn't wanna think about that tonight. After all, a ghoul's just gotta to have fun *sometime*, doesn't she?

"Presenting," Evan's voice boomed from the hallway, "the *incredible* Miss Liza Minelli," Evan and Butch stepped into the room in full costume, "and the love of her life, Mr. David Gest!"

We greeted them with the gasps of amazement they deserved, followed by bursts of laughter.

Evan was glorious as Liza, fake-eyelashed to the hilt, wearing a spiky black wig and a dramatically regal expression. "Liza" modeled a white fake fur over a tea-length black dress, heavy makeup, and stockings with high heels. No way was Evan gonna miss his annual chance to get campy—last year he'd gone as Cher, and looked damned good doing it.

But Butch stole the show.

Looking taller than usual in a heavy black overcoat, normally bald Butch wore a half wig, slicked straight back, and a giant pair of dark sunglasses. He was dressed in formal wear, white silk ascot around his neck, long white evening scarf dangling. He held his mouth as though he'd just tasted a lemon.

It was hilarious. Alone, Evan would just be another Liza Minelli impersonator and Butch a constipated goon in an overcoat, but together they were a celebrity freak show *event.*

"Wait, wait," Evan said between giggles, "you have to see him without his glasses."

Butch—trying hard to stay in character—took a moment to straighten his face, then pulled off his sunglasses without saying a word. Evan had taped his eyelids, stretching the skin on his forehead to a ridiculous degree. The result was a plastic surgery nightmare.

Joe was laughing harder than I was, and Kelly was dying. I saw her grab the back of the couch to keep from falling off her crutches. She looked younger when she laughed, and prettier, too. The bruises on her face were finally gone, her long brown hair freshly washed and tucked behind her ears.

"I've got to get pictures," Kelly said, when she could stop laughing. There was a camera on the counter, and she got some great ones of the four of us, then more of us as couples—Joe and I, Liza and Butch. Evan camped it up even more for the camera, and we all laughed again at how well Butch held his plastic escort pose.

Then we were off to the Vortex for some Halloween fun.

Atlanta's Little Five Points took October 31st seriously. An annual costume parade, a fall festival and pumpkin carving contest, lots of different bar parties. Halloween night was *the* night to get together and get weird—and in an area known for its weirdness, that was saying quite a bit.

We parked and walked down Moreland toward the Vortex, taking our time. "Liza" and her big goon strolled the sidewalk arm in arm, while Joe and I walked behind, admiring the other freaks we passed along the way.

The air was full of music and laughter, lifting my spirits like the smoke from the fog machines in Findley Plaza. Reggae music spilled from the open door of Hey Mon's, not quite drowning the thump of heavy metal coming from The Crypt. Two women dressed as vampires passed, eyeing Joe like he was a pint of plasma and they were a quart low. I gave them a cheerful "too late, girls" grin. SpongeBob SquarePants stumbled by, led by a woman in a harem outfit. Poor SpongeBob had either had too much to drink or was about to get lucky, I couldn't tell which.

A leering scarecrow with corn-husk hands and a burlap head jumped out at us from an alley between the buildings, and a guy in a Bill Clinton mask tried to pinch my butt. Once I realized what he wanted, I let him, then playfully smacked him with my riding crop, enjoying the anonymous flirting.

"See? What'd I tell you?" Joe shook his head, grinning from ear to ear. "Forget Dorothy and her ruby slippers, you're the sexiest Wicked Witch the Land of Oz has ever seen." He was watching the milling crowd of partygoers, looking everywhere at once. "This place is wild."

I laughed. "Good girls like Dorothy may end up with cute shoes, but bad girls have more fun." Joe was holding my hand, and it felt like it belonged in his. "Anybody can buy shoes."

We reached the Vortex, where an even bigger crowd was gathered. I was glad to see Fat Mitch was the bouncer tonight—he knew Evan and I both from the store. We were always good for an extra lunchtime burger from The Five Spot, or the occasional bottle of Grey Goose, and he let us in.

The place was jumping, all loud music and moving bodies. Constantly shifting purple and orange lights streamed from a giant disco ball; spotlights cast shadows of witches, black cats, and skulls over the crowd. Spiders and spiderwebs dripped from the ceiling, while skeletons and ghosts dangled from the rafters. The music was so loud it made the walls tremble. It was crazy and deafening, and I loved it. We made a beeline for the bar, easing our way through a seething mass of humanity.

I'd no sooner been handed my Black Magic when I felt a hand on my ass.

I whirled, pointed my whip at a man in a gorilla suit and threatened, "Watch it, buddy. Don't make me send my flying monkeys after you!"

Gorilla Man raised his hands and shook his head, backing off. I wasn't sure if he was claiming no responsibility or apologizing, but it didn't matter either way.

"What are you drinking?" Joe was right beside me, but he wasn't having much luck getting the bartender's attention.

"Vodka and Kahlua, with a twist of lemon." I took a greedy sip, savoring the rich flavor of Kahlua. I was restricting my mixed drinks for special occasions now—hard liquor isn't as good for the heart as red wine. "Want a sip?"

He shook his head. "I'll stick with beer, if I ever get one."

"There's another bar in that corner." I pointed. "The bartender's a woman. Go flash those dimples at her."

He laughed. "There you go, treating me like a sex object again."

I reached around and smacked him on the butt. "You love it."

Joe leaned over and spoke directly in my ear. "You're right—I do." He bit my earlobe, and my knees went weak. "Stay here, Little Miss Wicked. I'll be right back."

I watched him walk away, admiring the view, then took a sip of my drink.

"Hello, gorgeous."

The voice was unfamiliar.

I turned, and met the eyes of one of the hunkiest guys I'd ever seen in my life. Spiky blond hair, cheekbones a fashion model would kill for, and a wicked grin. He was wearing a sleeveless black leather vest, no shirt, and tight jeans with the cuffs laced into combat boots—the perfect "bad boy."

He winked at me like we were old friends, raising his glass. "Looks like we're kindred spirits," he said. "I can't get enough of that old Black Magic either."

Old habits die hard, I guess. *Besides, a little flirting never hurt anybody.* I tilted my head and touched the tip of my whip to my chin.

"Let me guess . . . Spike, from Buffy the Vampire Slayer."

He shook his head, still grinning. A silver earring glinted from one ear.

I guessed again. "Billy Idol?" *God, I loved a man in black eyeliner.*

"That old punk?" He laughed, pretending to be insulted. "Way overrated."

"Who are you, then?"

"I'm the man of your dreams, baby."

I'd heard that one before, so why did it sound so different when *he* said it? I watched as he took a sip of his drink, blue eyes never leaving me.

"How original. Is that the best you can do?" Despite the lousy come-on, I found myself intrigued, and more than just a little attracted. His eyes were an unusual shade of blue—very pale, and very striking. Warning bells should've been going off, but I felt wrapped in silk. Smooth, slippery silk.

He took a step closer. "Talk is cheap. Let me prove it to you." He smelled like cloves, a spicy scent that made my mouth water. I didn't pull away when he leaned in close to whisper in my ear. "I'll bet I know just how you like it: you on top, and me inside you. Hard, hot, and eager to please."

His breath was tickling my neck, and my belly fluttered at the mental image that popped into my brain. Up close, I could see that the silver earring was actually a small skull and crossbones.

Walk away, Styx. Walk away.

I wanted to, but my body seemed to have a mind of its own. One lean, muscular shoulder was right in front of me, and I wanted to lick it—just once—to see if he tasted as good as he smelled.

"Nicki? Yoo-hoo, Nicki!" Evan's voice broke the spell.

I jerked back, avoiding eye contact with Mr. Eye Candy.

Evan was at my elbow, looking garishly feminine in his wig and fake eyelashes. The look he was giving me was laced with warning.

"The costume contest is about to start." The look turned more pointed. "Where's Joe?"

"Joe?" I was flustered, off-balance. *What'd they put in this drink, anyway?*

"Joe." Evan was beginning to get that tone in his voice. "Your boyfriend—remember?" Someone jostled my elbow, and I glanced over to find Butch standing on my other side, giving my new friend an expressionless stare. I sighed, recognizing the drill. I was in the middle of an overly protective "Minelli" sandwich.

"He's right over there." I pointed toward the corner bar, and saw Joe watching me across the room. The crowd shifted, and I lost sight of him, but I'd seen enough to tell that he wasn't smiling anymore.

My Billy Idol look-alike glanced that way, then turned back to me. He ignored my gay security squad and raised his drink in an admiring salute. "'Abashed the Devil stood, and felt how awful goodness is, and saw Virtue in her own shape how lovely; saw and pined his loss.'"

My jaw dropped. It was weird enough to hear some guy spouting quotes in a bar, but his choice of quotes . . .

"Milton. *Paradise Lost,*" he added, with another wicked grin. His pale blue gaze flicked over Evan and Butch. "And apparently it is." He winked at me. "For now, anyway. See you around, Nicki Styx."

Then he walked away, his blond head quickly lost in the throng of people on the dance floor.

"Who the hell was that?" Evan didn't mince words.

"I don't know." And I wasn't sure I wanted to. "Just some guy, that's all."

I'd never told him my name.

The music seemed louder than ever, the bass from the speakers thumping in time with my heart.

"Earth to Nicki." Evan was getting impatient. "Put your

tongue back in your mouth, will you? The costume party is about to start." He hated being last in line for anything, and a group was starting to gather near the main stage.

I didn't bother to take offense. "Butch, put your sunglasses back on, and Evan, let me check your makeup." I used my thumb to wipe away a nonexistent smudge of lipstick and gave him a quick hug, sending him off to the spotlight. "As they say in show business, break a leg."

"Please," Evan said. "These legs are worth more than Liza's. Prettier, too."

Evan and Butch headed toward the stage, arm in arm. Heads were already turning in their direction, and I was glad. Evan adored being the center of attention, and camped it up as Liza. They drew howls from the crowd as they moved toward the stage, Liza pretending to trip and then smacking poor Butch on the head with her purse.

"Who was that guy you were talking to?" Joe was back, beer in hand. I found myself incredibly glad to see him. *What had I been thinking, flirting with that blond guy?*

"Just some guy," I answered, with a little stab of guilt. "He offered to buy me a drink."

"It looked like he was offering more than that."

Joe sounded tense, and I met his eye, surprised. He'd never shown any sign of jealousy before—but then I'd never given him any reason to.

Technically, I hadn't given him any reason tonight either. *Thinking* wasn't the same as *doing*.

"It doesn't matter what he was offering." Calmly, I took a sip of my Black Magic. "I wasn't buying."

It was hard to hear above the music, but I was fairly

certain that Joe gave a grunt of dissatisfaction before raising his bottle of beer and taking a swig.

"I thought you liked having a hot girlfriend," I reminded him teasingly. "You didn't mind when the guy in the Bill Clinton mask pinched me in the ass earlier."

"The blond guy was different," he said grudgingly, still not smiling. I raised my eyebrows at him, and he responded with, "I didn't like the way you were looking at him."

A round of clapping and laughter came from the stage area, reminding me that Joe and I were there to have fun. The urge to get defensive passed as quickly as it came, and I gave him a flirtatious grin. "Was it anything like the way I'm looking at you now?"

Wryly, he grinned back. "Unfortunately, yes."

"It couldn't have been," I said, and leaned against him. "Because I don't see anyone but you."

His free hand came around my waist. "I'm not very good at sharing, Nicki. I want you all to myself."

I raised on tiptoe to speak directly into his ear. "I want you, too . . . naked."

He chuckled, pulling me closer as I tilted my head to hear his reply. "Your wish is my command, but you'll have to wait until later." His teeth nipped my earlobe, making me shiver, and all was right with the world.

An hour later Evan and Butch were the proud owners of the "Cutest Couple" trophy, and I was pleasantly mellow from laughing and dancing with my hunky doctor/bad boy. Joe and I were taking a breather at a table near the wall.

He was eyeing me over the rim of his beer, smiling and

happy. A few dark strands of hair had escaped the styling gel to fall over his forehead, and his face was flushed from dancing. He looked hot, in more ways than one.

"Having a good time?" He had to raise his voice to be heard above the music. Purple and green strobe lights bathed the room in Halloween color, making a shifting kaleidoscope out of the costumed crowd.

I only had eyes for Joe, though. "I'm having a great time. I really needed to get out, have a little fun."

"Me, too." He smiled in the way that made his eyes crinkle, the way that made my heart twist. "I always have fun when I'm with you."

He leaned in, eyes roving over my face and hair. "I probably shouldn't say this, but I'm glad Kelly didn't come." Joe cocked his head, giving me a sexy grin. "Two's company, three's a crowd."

His tattooed biceps were distracting me. The faint sheen of sweat on his skin made me want to lick him right where the barbed wire crisscrossed his upper arm.

"I bought you a present," he said. "I wanted to give it to you in private."

"A private present?" I arched an eyebrow at him. "I think you've already given me that. Quite a few times."

He laughed, and the sound of it made me feel good. I wanted to make this man laugh every day. I took a sip of my Black Magic, smiling at him over the glass.

"It's a Halloween present." Joe leaned back in his seat and slipped a hand in his pocket. "For the prettiest ghoul I know."

Whatever the present was, it had to be small—there wasn't a lot of wiggle room in the pockets of those tight leather pants.

And I knew why. Lucky me.

Joe's hand came out with a small white envelope. He grinned as he gave it to me. "Not the fanciest packaging, but I hope you don't mind. I didn't want to carry a little box around."

The envelope was heavier than I'd thought. The paper bulged in a slight circle, like it held a coin. Or a ring.

My heart started to pound.

"Open it," he urged. "It won't bite."

The envelope was unsealed. I shook the contents into my palm.

It *was* a ring. Even in the dim light, I could tell it was vintage. The gleam of old sterling silver vied with the sparkle of marcasite, framing a single drop of black onyx.

I loved it.

"I saw it in the window of an antique shop over on Newberry Street," he said. "It looked like you."

I glanced up from the ring, touched. It was perfect—just perfect. No strings attached.

"It's gorgeous . . . absolutely gorgeous. I love it." I leaned across the table to kiss him, several times. I slipped the ring on my finger, but it was a little loose, so I moved it to my index finger. *Perfect.* "You are so gonna get lucky tonight," I said.

The grin that split his face was a sight to behold.

Then a look of disappointment ruined it. He glanced down at his cell phone, clipped to his belt. "Uh-oh."

Crap.

With an apologetic shrug, Joe unclipped his phone. He was a doctor, after all, so I didn't do anything but make a brief face as he answered. "Hello? . . . Kelly?"

The look he gave me was apprehensive. "Calm down. Have you called the police?"

"The police?" *How did Kelly get Joe's cell phone number?*

"Calm down . . . " Joe's eyes were on my face. "If there's someone in the house you should call the police." His shoulders eased and he shook his head to let me know there was no reason to worry.

"Okay, okay. Tell me what happened. Slowly." Joe listened intently, watching me all the while. "Yeah . . . uh-huh." One eyebrow shot skyward. "But—" he was obviously cut off mid-sentence. "I don't know. I think you need to talk to Nicki." He thrust the phone at me without waiting for a reply.

"Kelly?" *This had better be good.*

"I did something stupid, Nicki." Kelly's voice sounded shaky. "I did something really stupid."

Great.

"I decided to try and make contact with Peaches. I used a scrying mirror and a candle, and I think—"

"You used *what*?" The music at the Vortex was pretty loud. "What's a crying mirror?"

"A *scrying* mirror." She was nearly shouting. "Never mind, it doesn't matter what I used! I tried to call up Peaches's spirit, and someone *else's* spirit came through!"

I could've killed her. Things had been nice and quiet in the dearly departed department, but she'd had to go and stir things up . . .

"I'm scared, Nicki. Please come home."

I looked at Joe, how his sexy, carefree smile had been replaced by seriousness and concern. "We'll be right there," I said with a sigh.

CHAPTER 8

"What were you thinking?"

Kelly was sitting on the couch, looking chastened, but I had little sympathy for her at the moment. We'd arrived home to find the house brightly lit and nothing whatsoever going on. Joe was still checking the closets and making sure all the windows were locked—at Kelly's insistence—but Evan, Butch, Kelly, and I were in the living room, and I was pissed.

"Why did you have to go looking for trouble, Kelly? If the dead want to talk to you, they'll talk to you. I've told you that before." *Like she ever listened.*

"I wasn't looking for trouble," she insisted. "I just wanted to talk to Peaches one last time." A flash of resentment in her eyes, quickly veiled.

Joe walked in, shaking his head. "House is clear. What exactly did you *do*?"

Kelly sighed, gesturing toward a black candle on the coffee table. I'd put it there last week as part of my Halloween decorations, just like the pumpkin on the front porch. "I bought a scrying mirror on the Internet," she said.

There it was, a framed hand mirror, lying facedown right next to the candle. Curious, I picked it up and turned it over. Oddly enough, the surface of the mirror was black, not silver, but just as reflective. The frame itself was beautiful, a great example of turn-of-the-century Art Nouveau, depicting the profile of a young woman peering into the mirror from the bronzed flowers that ringed the mirror itself. The woman's gowned legs swept downward to form the handle, satiny with age. A gorgeous piece of vintage, yet it gave me the creeps.

"You bought this on the Internet?"

"eBay," Kelly said distractedly. "You're supposed to turn out all the lights and sit in the dark with a candle, thinking about the person you want to talk to. Then you stare into the mirror and wait for them to appear."

Evan was sitting in the wing chair, Butch standing next to him. He was already holding Butch's hand, but now he clutched it like a lifeline.

"That's the stupidest thing I've ever heard," I told her. Then the lightbulb went off. "Wait a minute. You've been *planning* this, haven't you?"

Kelly had the grace to look vaguely uncomfortable.

"You bought the mirror, you waited until Halloween, and then you lit the candle." I shook my head, thinking about the guilt trip she'd laid on me earlier. "That's why you didn't want to come with us tonight."

"So what if I did?" she flared. "Nobody likes to be a third wheel! I bought the mirror out of curiosity, but I hadn't used it. I was scared to, honestly. But, I—" She stopped, swallowed. "I had to try." She lowered her voice. "I wish I hadn't."

"What happened?" Joe pulled me down next to him on the couch, subtly getting me to ease off.

"I saw a man," she said. "He . . . he spoke to me."

"Oh my God!" Evan's outburst saved me the trouble. "What did he look like?"

Kelly shook her head. "I don't know. The mirror was cloudy, the room was dark." She crossed her arms tightly over her chest. "The man wouldn't let Peaches come through. He said Peaches owed him a favor, and he wouldn't let her go until we gave him what he wanted."

"What?"

"I'm just telling you what he said!" Kelly's voice rose. She stopped, took a shuddering breath, and rubbed her face briskly with her hands. "He said to go to the house in Savannah, the Blue Dahlia. He said there was something there he wanted, and that if we could get it for him, he'd let Peaches go."

"Let her go where?" Poor Butch sounded as confused as I felt.

"Into the light," Kelly said quietly.

"Get what?" I asked, still highly skeptical. The whole episode sounded awfully "smoke and mirrors" to me.

"I don't know," Kelly said. Her eyes slid away. "I was scared—I freaked out and put the mirror down as fast as I could." She shuddered. "I never want to look into it again."

We were all quiet for a few moments.

Then Kelly said, "We have to go to Savannah, Nicki."

Um, no. "I don't wanna go to Savannah."

"But we have to," Kelly insisted. She leaned forward on the couch, resting her elbows on her knees. "I think Peaches was here earlier—she was trying to get our attention, but the guy in the mirror wouldn't let her come through."

At my skeptical look, Kelly's chin went up. "I have proof. Look at these." The pictures she'd taken before we'd left for the party were scattered all over the coffee table. "I uploaded them to the color printer after you left." She thrust one at me.

There the four of us were in the picture, laughing and smiling, looking like rejects from the *Rocky Horror Picture Show.* Evan, Butch, Joe, and me. And someone else.

Someone was standing behind me, but I couldn't make out who, or even *how.* It looked like a shadowy face peering over my shoulder. Then I realized that the picture on my living room wall was still visible—*through* the person's head.

I pulled off my witch's hat and tossed it aside, wincing at the tug of glitter gel. *Peaches was supposed to be gone, crossed over or whatever.*

"We have to go to Savannah and talk to Bijou," Kelly argued. "Peaches's spirit needs our help. Bijou said she could train us to use the knack—maybe she could help us free Peaches so she can go into the light."

Joe, Evan, Butch, and I looked at the photos several times—there was definitely a foggy image in most of them. Evan was pale, and Butch's untaped eyebrows had gone back to their pretaped position.

I didn't want to go to Savannah. Kelly would drag me into something I didn't want to be dragged into, and I'd have to leave Joe and the store and Evan . . .

Besides, I wasn't entirely convinced that Kelly hadn't just spooked herself out and imagined some guy in the mirror. Peaches had said good-bye and been laid to rest. I was pretty certain she was gone.

"I'll think about it, Kelly, but I can't just pick up and leave the store, and I'm not going anywhere tonight, that's for sure. Let's talk about it in the morning, shall we?" I'd wanted to have a good time tonight, dammit. The party had been ruined, and I'd promised Joe—and myself—that he was gonna get lucky.

"Um . . . " Evan uncrossed his legs and rose from his seat as gracefully as the real Liza would, reaching out a hand for Butch. "I think we'll head on home. It's a long drive." He wasn't fooling anybody, but I didn't blame him. Let him go spend some quiet time alone with his man.

Wish I could do the same. I couldn't help but glance toward Kelly, who'd gone back to studying her spirit photos.

Inwardly, I sighed. Having a housemate who'd once been married to your boyfriend was a little inhibiting when it came to having wild sex in your own bed. I'd imagined Joe naked more than once that evening, and the image wasn't going away.

I gave Evan and Butch their good-bye hugs and watched as they shut the door behind them, wishing I could shut my problems out as easily. I felt edgy and unfulfilled by an evening's fun denied, and quite frankly, at this point I didn't care how those images had managed to show up on Kelly's camera.

It was Halloween, after all. If it *was* Peaches, maybe our mother just had a sense of humor.

"Maybe Joe should leave, too," Kelly suggested, surprising me. "Peaches might come back if it's quiet. There might be too many people here."

Yeah. At least one too many.

"You think I should go?" Thankfully, Joe looked to me for confirmation, not Kelly. Despite his words, he didn't seem in any hurry to leave.

"Not yet," I said, and was relieved when the subject was dropped.

"This doesn't make a whole lot of sense." Joe picked up one of the pictures, though we'd all been through them several times. "Yes, I see what looks like a shadowy figure in some of these pictures, but I can't swear that it's a *ghost*. It could just be a problem with the camera."

"How can you say that?" Kelly demanded. "It's obviously Peaches. There's two eyes, a nose, a mouth. See the outline of her head?"

"It could be a trick of the light," Joe interrupted calmly. "Maybe it was the flash from the camera."

"You're wrong," Kelly insisted, equally as calm. "She could be here—in the room with us—right now."

I hated to admit it, but she was right. Maybe it was harder for normal people like Joe to see and believe the unbelievable. I wouldn't have believed it myself a few months ago.

Joe sighed. "Every time Nicki's had"—he hesitated,

then settled for—"a problem like this, the spirits appear in person—she actually sees them." He looked at me, baffled. "Do you see her now?"

"It's not like I make them appear on demand, you know." I was already tired of talking about this. My fun evening had been ruined by the undead. Might as well start calling them the "fun dead."

Recalling the fun I'd *been* having reminded me of the guy I'd met at the Vortex. For a brief second I wondered if my spiky blond bad boy had something to do with this. I couldn't shake the feeling that he was more than just some tortured poet in a bar. He'd known my name, after all, and there'd been something about him . . .

I was being silly. I shoved the thought away, but other thoughts of him lingered. The memory of our encounter gave me a tingle. I'd been hot and bothered all evening, and it wasn't going away. The guy at the Vortex may have fanned the flames, but I wanted my sweet, sexy Joe, and I wanted him now. I hoped it had nothing to do with *Paradise Lost*.

Right now I would prefer some "paradise found."

I tapped my finger on the photo I was holding. It was the one where I was sitting in Joe's lap; I was laughing and showing a little leg while he held me tight, looking very pleased with himself.

I made myself a mental note to break out the Photoshop. The shadowy figure standing behind us ruined what was an otherwise fabulous photo. Maybe I could airbrush it out.

It might be the only satisfaction I was gonna get this evening.

I tried to keep my mind off sex, but Joe looked so good. The sleeveless shirt really showed off his biceps—he should keep that barbwire tattoo. And the way those leather pants strained over his hips was practically obscene. Deliciously obscene.

"I'm tired," I lied. The evening was still young, and there were better ways to spend it. "I'm gonna go get out of this costume—my corset is killing me." I shot Joe a flirtatious look. "Wanna help?"

His eyes flicked to Kelly, then back, but luckily for him, I chose to ignore that split second of hesitation. "You bet." He stood up and reached for my hand. "I've checked the house, Kelly. It's locked up tight. Nicki and I will be right down the hall."

"Oh." If Kelly sounded momentarily deflated, she covered pretty quick. "I'll just go watch some TV in my room. You guys have fun."

Neither of us looked back as I led him down the hallway, but when the bedroom door closed behind us, I couldn't help a little sigh of relief.

"This feels kind of weird, Nicki." Despite his words, Joe slid an arm around my waist, pulling me close.

"That's funny," I answered, "it's always felt pretty damn good before." I kissed him, loving the taste of his tongue. The cherry-chocolate scent of his aftershave drove me crazy. I was so hot for him I could've done it standing up, but the bed was close. I turned his back to it and gave him a playful shove.

"Oh, yeah." The mattress bounced under his weight. Elbows braced, legs splayed across the bedspread, Joe looked sexy as hell. "Impatient little thing, aren't you?"

"Tonight I am." I stepped closer, right between his knees. "It's your own fault for wearing those pants." I smiled wickedly, admiring the view from my particular angle. "Now take 'em off."

"Bossy, too."

Joe's lips were smudged black from my lipstick. I found the result very erotic, and wondered how he'd look with some eyeliner.

"That's me. Impatient and bossy." I started undoing the clasps on my corset.

"Are you sure we shouldn't go to my place? What if Kelly hears us?"

I felt a flash of irritation, but pushed it away. Joe was such a Boy Scout sometimes—but it wasn't worth losing the moment. I could care less if Kelly heard, particularly if she were nosy enough to listen.

"Impatient, bossy, and trying desperately to get your attention." My corset fell away, and Joe's eyes widened. I rested hands on hips, posing for him. "Selfish, too, because I can't wait the time it would take to get to your place."

If the growing bulge in his groin was any indication, he couldn't either. I had his attention now, but that didn't stop me from tormenting him further. I turned around and flipped up my skirt, giving him an eyeful of lacy panties and garter belt. "Maybe you should spank me for being such a bad girl."

Joe sat up and took me by the hips. He kissed each rounded curve, just once. His lips felt like fire. Then he slid his arms around me and pulled me into his lap, nuzzling the bare skin of my shoulders while his hands roamed wherever they wanted. "I have a better idea," he murmured. I caught my breath as his teeth nipped my earlobe. "How about I reward you by making you feel good."

His hands felt so strong as they kneaded my skin, sliding over my breasts and thighs, squeezing every curve. He drew a deep breath through his nose and let it out appreciatively, warm against my neck. "You smell like incense and flowers." I squirmed against him, pressing my softness against his hardness. "In naked beauty more adorned, more lovely than Pandora."

I tensed, not sure I'd heard him correctly.

"Mmmm . . . " Joe trailed kisses along my shoulder blades, leaving a moist path of heat that pulled me back into the moment. "Taste good, too."

My body felt heavy, pleasantly so. I didn't want the kissing to stop. "What was that you just said?"

I could feel Joe's chuckle against my naked back. He barely lifted his lips enough to answer, "I don't know . . . it just popped into my head. I was inspired." His fingers brushed my nipples, already pebbled into hard nubs.

Two men quoting classics in one night—what were the odds?

"I find you very . . . inspiring." He proved it by cupping a hand between my legs, making me gasp, while his hardness gave an answering throb against my bottom.

I was slipping, giving into sensation. Joe felt so good. His thighs were rock hard beneath my fingers, supporting all my weight as I arched against him.

He rubbed me there, through my panties. I bit my lip against a moan, closing my eyes. An image flashed into my mind—the blond-haired, blue-eyed guy with a killer smile, raising his glass of Black Magic in a salute. The memory was a good one, and so was the tingle that came with it.

I pushed the mental image away—Joe deserved my undivided attention. Opening my eyes, I twisted in his arms, determined to live in the now.

We spent the next forty-five minutes doing just that, and every time my Billy Idol bad boy popped into my brain, I shoved him back out.

I just wish he hadn't popped in so often.

"Nicki. Nicki, wake up." Someone was shaking my shoulder.

"What?" I cracked an eye to find Kelly leaning over me. It was morning, and Joe had left for his own apartment somewhere in the wee hours.

Kelly was still in her pajamas, long hair hiding part of her face, but she tossed it over her shoulder in an impatient gesture. "Look at this, Nicki." She thrust something at me.

I frowned blearily at whatever she held in her hand. It was the scrying mirror.

"Get that away from me," I mumbled. What was she doing, barging into my bedroom unannounced this early in the morning? Judging by the light seeping through the blinds, it wasn't much past seven.

"Look at it," she insisted.

I couldn't help but glance at it, though I didn't appreciate being ordered around any more than I appreciated the rude awakening.

"Did you do it?" Her voice was rising.

"Do what?" I pushed myself up in the bed, in full crank mode now. "What the hell are you talking about?"

Kelly thrust the mirror at me again.

I snatched it, ready to throw it at her. The bronze handle was warm beneath my hand. Reluctantly, I looked down, bracing myself. "It's cracked," I said, stating the obvious. There was a hairline crack running from the lower left to the upper right, marring the otherwise smooth black surface.

"It wasn't cracked when I went to bed," Kelly answered. "Did you do it?"

I thrust the mirror back at her, not wanting to hold it any longer than necessary. Mirrors were supposed to be silver, not black. "No, I didn't do it," I snapped irritably.

Kelly tried to stare me down, but I gave as good as I got.

"Haven't you ever heard of knocking, by the way? What if Joe had still been in here?"

She shrugged, taking the mirror from my hand. "Nothing I haven't seen before."

I glared at her, and it was then I noticed how pale she was. Dark circles beneath her eyes stood out like smudges.

"What's the matter with you? What's going on?" I ran a hand through my hair, snagging my fingers on glitter gel. Kelly looked away, pointedly, and I realized I was naked. I'd just given my sister a great boob shot, nipple ring and all.

I shrugged mentally, though I did pull up the sheet. She was the one who barged in—she deserved to be flashed.

"I woke up and found the mirror broken, that's what's

going on," she said. "I laid it on the table right beside the bed before I went to sleep, and this morning it has a crack in it." She kept her eyes averted, even though I was decently covered.

"I thought you said you never wanted to look at it again." I might've just woken up, but I hadn't forgotten that. "What were you doing with it right before bed?"

She sighed, hesitating. "I changed my mind," she said. "You were right—I'd had two glasses of wine last night and I probably got freaked out over nothing. Besides, it's pretty. I paid a lot of money for it."

I narrowed my eyes at her, though she wasn't watching. What was all the fuss about? Last night she'd been afraid of the mirror, and this morning she was pissed because it was broken?

"I know a guy who can replace the glass," I said. "Let's put a real mirror in it, slap a price tag on it, and sell it at the store." Good quality Art Nouveau pieces were pretty popular. I knew I could unload it pretty quick or else I'd never have offered.

"No," she said quickly. "I'm going to hang on to it."

"Well, hang on to it somewhere else, would ya?" I grabbed the sheet, ready to whip it off and head for the bathroom. "And you can make the coffee this morning," I added. "I wasn't planning on getting up for at least another hour."

She left, and I went to freshen up. I'd barely closed the bathroom door behind me when I heard her calling.

"Nicki!" Her voice was high-pitched, frantic. "Nicki, come here!"

I grabbed my robe from the back of the door and hightailed it toward the kitchen.

"What is it?"

She was standing in the middle of the living room, staring in horrified fascination at the breakfast counter that overlooked the kitchen. Every piece of china I owned was sitting on it, stacked precariously in a mishmash of plates and saucers, teacups and coffee mugs. Smaller pieces on the bottom, larger pieces on top, an inverted pyramid of breakable objects that appeared ready to topple at the slightest touch.

"What the—" What the hell had Kelly been doing? Were my dishes not clean enough for her? It looked like she'd been up all night emptying the cabinets. And maybe a bottle of Jim Beam while she was at it.

"Look," she whispered, pointing.

There was something written on the refrigerator. All my fridge magnets had been swept aside and replaced with bright pink letters about two inches high.

YOU WERE DRIVING, it said.

Kelly started to cry. The cabinet doors gaped open on their hinges, showing a jumble of spilled spices and tumbled cans. The silverware drawer was open, but empty—the contents had been dumped in the sink. I walked closer and saw that the floor was littered with broken glass.

So much for my favorite wineglasses. How could I not have heard the noise this must've caused? Joe and I had been having a good time, true, but I think I would've heard it if the earth literally moved. The kitchen certainly looked like an earthquake hit it.

Except for those precariously balanced dishes, and the pink lettering on the fridge. I hoped it was lipstick, not permanent marker.

Kelly's sobs grew louder, and if I'd only been able to think clearly, I would have tried to comfort her. As it was, I could only stare, dumbfounded, at what I'd woken up to, while a thousand irrelevant thoughts ran through my head.

"I knew it," Kelly said. She'd slumped to the arm of the couch, eyes full of tears. "She blames me. I killed her."

That snapped me out of it. "No, you didn't!" Peaches didn't blame anyone for her death except herself. *Vanity, thy name is Peaches*, she'd said, about not wearing her seat belt.

"That's why she came here last night," Kelly cried. "That's why she did this!" She swept an arm toward the kitchen. The wording on the refrigerator stood out, an accusation we couldn't ignore.

I wasn't buying it. If Peaches really blamed Kelly for her death, she'd had plenty of time and several opportunities to tell me so.

So who'd done this?

I backed out of the trashed kitchen and went to Kelly, but she'd buried her face in her hands and refused to look at me.

"Peaches doesn't blame you," I said firmly. "Why would she do this when she could've just told me whatever it was she wanted to say?" I put my hand on her shoulder, taking a deep breath. My therapy sessions with Ivy hadn't been completely wasted, but I was hesitant. "Blaming yourself doesn't help. I know a great therapist—"

Kelly gasped, then shrugged off my hand and rose to her feet. "You think *I* did this?"

"I just—"

She didn't let me finish. "Yeah, Nicki. I woke up in the middle of the night and decided to wreck your kitchen and write all over your refrigerator." Her voice was bitter. "Better yet, I was sleepwalking and I just don't remember doing it, right?"

"Well . . . " The theory wasn't *that* far-out. She'd been under a lot of stress these past few weeks, and if she was eaten up by guilt, too—who knows?

"I know, I know!" She was getting all worked up. "I was pissed off because you and Joe were getting it on in your room all night, so I took my jealousy out on your dishes!" Her voice was taking on a hysterical note.

Getting it on? Did people even use that phrase anymore?

"Calm down, Kelly." I filed what she'd said away to think about another time. Another interesting theory, though.

"I broke my own mirror, too, right?" She snatched the damn thing up off the couch and waved it at me.

The mirror.

An ugly suspicion formed. "Were you trying to call Peaches up in that mirror again last night after I went to bed?"

"No."

She'd said it too quickly. I didn't believe her.

"What did you do?" A feeling of dread settled over me, heavy as a cloak.

"I didn't do anything." Her face was red, cheeks wet with tears. But she was calmer now, and for that I was glad.

I eyed her suspiciously, but decided not to push it. It

was too early in the morning for all this emotional shit. With a sigh, I said, "Let's just get this mess cleaned up, shall we?"

"I'll do it," she said stiffly. "You go get ready for work."

I would've argued with her, but the idea of a shower was so tempting—my scalp itched from glitter gel and my bladder was about to burst. "It wasn't your fault that Peaches died, Kelly," I repeated gently. "It was an accident."

She brushed past me, swiping at her nose and cheeks with the sleeve of her pajamas. "Whatever."

I'd almost reached the bathroom door when she announced, "I'm calling Bijou in Savannah today. You may be able to see spirits without even trying, but I want to learn more about the knack."

Grimacing in frustration, I answered her the way she'd answered me.

"Whatever."

Either my house was now haunted or my sister was a nut job who needed therapy even more than I did. Neither prospect was appealing. Let her go to Savannah for a while, and take her issues with her.

"I've got a problem, Evan."

"What problem is that, sweetie?" he answered me absently, engrossed in his latest creation.

It was time to change the window display at Handbags and Gladrags, and we'd opted to celebrate fall in shades of brown and gold. Texture was the name of the game, and we'd designed a great look for our Jean Harlow mannequin. Jean was wearing an ecru cashmere sweater with a mink collar, a cute metallic-gold crocheted hat, and a brown corduroy skirt with velvet trim. The boots were faux snakeskin. With her platinum hair and kewpie-doll lips, Jean was the original "blonde bombshell." She still looked the part, only warmer.

"Besides your sister inviting spooks into your house and wanting to charge off to Savannah, of course," Evan added.

"Well, there's that." I'd already told him about the disaster in my kitchen. Neither one of us was sure whether it was evidence of paranormal activity or guilt-induced paranoia. "But there's more."

"More?" Evan arched a brow. "Greedy little guts, aren't you?"

"I cheated on Joe."

"What? Tell me you did no such thing!" Evan crushed the silk scarf he was holding against his chest, clearly worried I had. "Joe adores you!"

I opened my mouth to explain, but Evan wasn't done.

"It was that blond himbo at the Vortex, wasn't it? I saw the looks shooting between you two."

I shook my head, partly to clear a tickle of pleasure at the memory. "Only in my *mind*, Evan, not in person. I haven't slept with anyone else."

Evan made an impatient noise.

I rushed to finish my little confession. "But I was thinking about the guy at the Vortex while Joe and I were . . . you know."

"Oh, so what? You were thinking about another man while you were making hot monkey love with your smokin' hot doctor." Evan let his opinion be known with an exasperated wave of the scarf. "What's the big deal?" He adjusted Jean's mink collar, muttering, "You just about gave me a heart attack. For heaven's sake, why didn't you just say you'd been fantasizing about some guy instead of making it seem like you'd done something nasty?"

I reached out to snatch the scarf, belting it around Jean's waist. "Because it's been bothering me. I didn't expect it." I thought about what I was trying to say, and the words were out before I knew it. "I love Joe."

Evan's irritation vanished. "I knew it."

"You think you know everything."

"I do know everything."

"Yeah? Well, you love Butch." I had a pretty strong hunch I was right, though Evan hadn't officially said so. His boyfriends didn't usually stick around this long.

He smiled at me sideways, still fiddling with Jean's outfit. "Yeah, I love the big brute, but I knew that before you did." He gave the corduroy skirt a final twitch, looking smug. "'Cause I know everything."

My intended comeback was interrupted by the jingle of the front bell. We both glanced toward the door, and there was the guy from the Vortex, coming in to scan the racks.

"Well, speak of the Devil," Evan murmured.

A tingle went down my spine—lust, guilt, or surprise, I wasn't sure. Despite my feelings for Joe, I couldn't deny the blond guy was hot.

Even hotter than I remembered.

And he was here, in my store.

He hadn't noticed us in the window yet, or else he was doing a good job pretending he hadn't. I watched as he went straight to the winter coats and started flipping through the racks. A pin-striped trench coat caught his eye and he pulled it out, then put it back, moving on to a navy blue peacoat with jet buttons.

I had to admire his taste. Either coat would've looked good on him, but the peacoat had more personality.

"I'll take care of him," Evan said under his breath. "You finish up here."

"Oh, no, you don't." I'd had enough of the overprotective stuff. I was a big girl, and just because I found a guy attractive didn't mean I had to act on it. "I can handle him."

Evan shrugged and went back to window dressing. "Exactly what I'm afraid of."

I ignored Mr. Know-It-All and stepped out of the window alcove, heading for Mr. Eye Candy. He was wearing a bright yellow shirt today, under an old leather bomber with sheepskin lining. His jeans were low on the hips, faded at the pockets and crotch.

"Can I help you find something?"

He turned, and his eyes widened. I couldn't help but be glad I'd worn my cutest new find—a candy pink sweater, real angora. Fuzzy pink looked great with gray-black camouflage pants and my favorite Lucchese cowgirl boots, if I did say so myself.

"I need a new jacket . . . " he began. *There was that killer smile again, and those cheekbones.* "Hey, do I know you?"

He was older around the eyes than I'd first thought, but it didn't hurt his looks one bit. Those tiny crinkles gave him a jaded, worldly-wise expression . . . very intriguing.

"You're the girl from the other night, aren't you?" His smile got bigger. "The Black Magic woman."

He seemed so pleased to see me that I couldn't help but smile back.

"The Milton man," I said.

"Wow." He looked me up and down, totally unashamed to be checking me out so openly. "You're even more gorgeous in daylight."

I'd never seen eyes that color blue on a man before. A Siamese kitten, once, but not a guy. His blond hair was still spiky, but not as stiffly sculpted as he'd worn it at the Vortex. He wore a silver chain around his neck.

"Thank you." I kept my voice neutral, well aware of Evan's eyes burning into my back. "Looking for some vintage?"

"You work here?"

"No. I own the store." I couldn't help the note of pride in my voice. Like my outfit, the store was nothing to be ashamed of. "With my partner, Evan." A nod of my head to Mr. Nosy Pants, who flashed us both a fake smile and pretended like he wasn't listening to every word that was said.

"Oh yes, your partner and protector." Blondie raised his voice so Evan could hear him clearly. "Loved the dress."

How he recognized Evan out of drag was beyond me. Probably the overprotective vibe in the air.

I stifled a laugh at Evan's unimpressed sniff.

That killer grin was aimed at me again as the guy added, "I can't believe I was lucky enough to run into you again. I mean, what are the odds?"

He wasn't fooling anybody. "Let me guess," I said.

"You just happened to be walking down Moreland and saw this store. You decided you were in dire need of a vintage peacoat, and ducked inside." I crossed my arms over my chest, enjoying the feel of angora. "Imagine your surprise when you find the girl you were hitting on at the Vortex Halloween night."

"Was I hitting on you?" He looked so innocent it was comical. "I had no idea."

"You know I have a boyfriend. I can sell you a coat, but that's all I've got to offer . . . the rest is taken."

He heaved a sigh. "Okay, I get it." The grin reappeared. "Can't blame a guy for tryin'."

I laughed. "What's your name, Blondie?"

"Sam," he said. "Sammy, to my friends." *He should charge admission for that grin.* "Of which I hope you'll be one." He raised his hands in mock defense and added, "Platonically, of course."

"Sammy." I don't know why, but I'd expected something more provocative, like Spike, or Sting. "My name's Nicki." I hadn't forgotten how he'd known my name at the Vortex, and made a mental note to find out who'd told him.

"Evan here," Mr. Stick Your Nose Where It Doesn't Belong spoke up from the window alcove. "Evan Owenby."

"Charmed." Sammy acknowledged Evan with a brief glance, then caught my hand and lifted it to his lips. It was a courtly gesture—very old-fashioned and very unexpected.

"I'm sure," muttered Evan.

"Nice to meet you, Nicki," Sammy said, pressing a quick kiss to my knuckles.

I shot Evan a dirty look, letting my hand linger. Sammy's fingers were firm and his lips were warm. He touched me with the tip of his tongue; it felt like the brush of hot coals. My eyes were drawn to the heavy silver ankh around his neck. An ankh—the ancient Egyptian symbol of life.

"What time did you say Joe was stopping by, Nicki?" Evan's nagging was getting old.

"I didn't." I pulled my hand free, keeping my voice light. I turned toward Evan, letting him see the warning in my eyes. He knew me well enough not to ignore it, I hoped. "Don't you have something to do in the back?"

Faced with a direct hint, he had no choice but to take it or come off as an ass. His chin went up, and so did his high horse, which meant he might not be speaking to me for a while. "Well," was all he said before he disappeared into the back room.

It was okay. I'd make it up to him by buying lunch.

"Sorry about that. Evan can be overprotective."

Sammy had been watching the byplay. Now he said, "You seem like a girl who knows how to handle herself. No reason to be afraid of a guy like me."

"That's right. No reason." I flashed Sammy a smile and turned to the winter coats. "I had some heart trouble earlier this year. Evan's been acting like my mother ever since." Actually, my mom would've been *much* worse, overprotectively speaking. She'd probably still have me tucked up in bed, watching soap operas and eating homemade stew, even though the heart defect was benign.

I missed her so much. All this talk about Peaches left me missing Emily Styx even more.

"Ah. So he does this with everybody." Sammy rubbed the back of his neck. "Here I thought he was worried you wouldn't be able to resist me." He quirked an eyebrow, looking both sexy as hell and extremely hopeful.

"You're pretty cocky for a guy who's already been turned down twice." I pulled out an aviator jacket, brown leather with quilted lining, and held it up against his chest. Without asking his opinion, I put it back and reached for one with epaulets. "How's that 'Charming Billy' thing working for ya? I take it most girls fall into your arms when you turn it on, hm?"

Sammy laughed. "True." The twinkle in his eye urged me to join in the joke. "I don't usually have to work this hard. Billy Idol *is*, after all, a rock-'n'-roll god."

I flicked him an arch glance. "The other night you called him an 'old punk.'"

"Yep, I did . . . because that's what he is." Sammy's shoulder brushed mine as he flipped through the rack. Whatever scent he wore should've been illegal—spicy and masculine, but not overwhelming. "And so am I. An old punk."

"How old *are* you?" I was curious—I couldn't help it. I dragged out another trench coat and checked the size.

"Older than I ever expected to be." Sammy smiled when he said it, but didn't meet my eyes. "Die young, leave a good-looking corpse. That's always sounded pretty good to me."

Not to me. Particularly now that I knew that death wasn't the end. People should enjoy life while they had it—it could be over so quickly.

The next forty-five minutes proved my point, because the time was gone before I knew it. Sammy decided he needed an entire new outfit to go with the coat, and I was happy to help, knowing my accountant would be happy, too. I'd be lying to myself if I didn't admit it was a lot more fun dressing a good-looking guy instead of a blank-faced mannequin, particularly a guy who was unafraid of fashion. In the end, I'd sold Sammy not only the peacoat, but a pair of studded bellbottoms from the sixties, a red and black cowboy shirt stiff with embroidery, and a black leather belt with a huge buckle. He threw in some cool T-shirts and a pair of crocodile boots I'd been coveting for myself (too big) and a second pair of Levi's. Evan never made a reappearance, though I knew full well he could see us in the security monitors.

Not that there was anything to see—Sammy was a perfect gentleman. The only titillating thing to happen was when he came out of the dressing room in an unbuttoned shirt, giving me a glimpse of some fabulous abs.

Evan's bird's-eye view from the camera meant he'd probably gotten a better look than me, damn him.

Then I was ringing Sammy up at the register, wondering what his reaction would be to the total. Quality vintage isn't cheap. He didn't bat an eyelash, just whipped out a gold AmEx and leaned on the counter while I swiped it and waited for approval.

"He doesn't have to know." Sammy rested his chin on a hand. "Your boyfriend, I mean."

I laughed. "Are you kidding? Joe will be thrilled to hear I sold those cowboy boots."

"That's not what I meant."

I knew exactly what he meant, but I wasn't gonna play.

No matter how much I was tempted.

"The answer's still no, Sammy."

The swipe machine was ready, so I turned it for his signature. His hand covered mine before I could blink.

"Am I just imagining something between us?" His voice was low, his fingers warmly persuasive. He wore heavy silver rings, a thumb ring and two others. "I'd like to get to know you better, Nicki." He squeezed my hand, not letting me pull away. "I'd like to make love to you."

My body throbbed, bringing a surge of guilt along with a surge of juices. *What was it about this guy that made him so sexy?* The old Nicki would've jumped his bones in a heartbeat, and worried about guilt and explanations later.

Those blue eyes were incredible, and he smelled like forbidden fruit—juicy, and just within reach. I could stretch out my hand . . .

"Joe would never know," Sammy murmured.

Joe would never know.

I snatched away my hand and took a step back.

Sammy straightened, giving me the rueful grin of a thwarted rock-'n'-roll god. "Okay, okay. I get the message. You're a good girl and I'm a bad boy." He sighed. "Problem is, you don't look like a good girl. I'm sorry. I'll keep my hands to myself."

He signed on the dotted line while I bagged the last of his clothes, which I handed over with a rueful grin of my own.

"I'm not normally this good," I said, "and I can't deny I find you . . . attractive." Sammy's eyebrow arched hopefully. I hardened my heart and locked my knees. "But I love my boyfriend. I'm flattered, really. But I wanna give this monogamy thing a try."

"Damn," he said softly. There was a wicked glint in his eye, of lust and regret and appreciation. "So Satan, whom repulse met ever, and to shameful silence brought, yet gives not o'er though desperate of success."

I frowned. It was strange how this guy started quoting the classics whenever he got shot down in flames. "Milton, again? English, please."

Sammy laughed, and I was struck anew by how dangerously gorgeous he was—how sexy . . . how clever . . . how *cool.* Why wasn't this man on the cover of *Rolling Stone* magazine?

"It means you can resist the Devil, but he never gives up. It's better to make a bargain with him while you still have a chance."

My stomach turned to ice. The last person to urge me to make a deal with the Devil had been Psycho Barbie, and I wasn't fond of the memory.

He shook his blond head before turning to go. "Ah, women. Why are the good ones always taken?"

"Are you comparing yourself to the Devil?"

Sammy paused, one shoulder holding open the shop door. That killer grin had never been more blinding. He winked, and said. "I'm not comparing myself to anyone, sweetheart. If there were any comparisons to be made, I'd be comparing you to your sister. Twins, aren't you?"

I froze, never having mentioned I even *had* a sister.

"Guilt seems to run in your family, doesn't it? Too bad Kelly can't seem to get past that nasty little car accident. Maybe she might be a bit more receptive to a guy who just wants to show her a good time."

I opened my mouth to ask how he knew Kelly, but he cut me off with a jaunty wave of the hand. "See you around." And he was gone.

I'm not ashamed to say I now had a serious case of the creeps. I wanted answers, but I didn't want to call him back; it was best if he left, and I didn't want to encourage him. Still, I couldn't help myself—I went to the window to watch him walk away. He got into an old Mustang convertible and drove off down Moreland, his rock-star looks drawing plenty of second glances.

Who was he?

Psycho Barbie claimed that "they'd be watching." Was Sammy sent by the Devil to tempt my newfound morals, or was he just a case of incredibly bad timing? And that comment about Kelly—it had almost sounded like a threat. Was I a total paranoid, or just your average nutcase? Who knew?

I sure as hell didn't.

"So, do you need to change your panties now?" Evan popped his head into the room. "Or should I break out the bubble bath so you can enjoy the afterglow?"

I blew out a breath, shaking my head. Anything I might have said was interrupted by the jingle of the bell as the front door opened again.

"Oh my God, did you meet him?" It was Angela, the performance artist from Findley Square. "What's his name? Is he married?"

I heard Evan mutter, "Oh, Lord."

Angela hadn't applied her silver body paint yet. It was almost strange to see her without it. She was tiny and athletic, brown hair in a tight bun.

"Can you believe a guy like that will be right across the street?"

"What?" Evan and I spoke at the same time.

Angela nodded her head. "He bought Indigo, didn't you hear?" Clearly pleased by our stunned expressions, Angela kept talking. "Somebody said he's turning it into a music store, vinyls and CDs."

Indigo was the Jamaican grocery store that used to belong to my friend Caprice. It was the site of some bad mojo, in more ways than one. Caprice had died there, for starters. The touristy little market had been just a cover for Caprice's real line of work—she'd been a powerful "mambo," a voodoo priestess—a fact I unfortunately didn't learn until after she was dead. There was a scary, hidden "voodoo room" in the back of the store.

"Divinyls, I think he's calling it." Angela was full of information today. Maybe she was the one who'd told Sammy I had a twin sister. "Isn't that a cool name for a music store?"

The phone rang, and I answered it automatically, though my attention was on the bombshell Angela had just dropped. "Handbags and Gladrags, this is Nicki."

"Nicki, it's Kelly. I just called Bijou's number in Savannah and spoke to a man named Leonard. He said Bijou's been sick. He invited us to come. In fact, he *urged* us to come. Bijou was sleeping, but I told Leonard to let her know we were coming."

"Kelly, I—"

"She's an old woman, Nicki, and we're all the family she has left. I'll go without you if I need to, but I sure wish you'd go with me." She hesitated, then added, "I'm sorry I was so bitchy to you this morning. I was a little freaked out."

That made two of us.

"It's okay," I said. "Don't worry about it." I looked out the window again, staring at the familiar front porch of Indigo, and the steps where Caprice had been murdered.

Once the scene of a tragedy, those steps were now to be a source of daily unease. Dead people, guilt, weird family obligations—I never meant to look for trouble, yet trouble kept finding me. *Why was nothing easy anymore?*

"And whether you believe it or not, I didn't trash the kitchen. I wasn't sleepwalking, either. I think Peaches is trying to communicate with me, and I need to know why."

"Okay, Kelly." Destiny called, I supposed, and I decided it might be a good idea to take Kelly out of harm's way, at least temporarily. "You win. We'll go to Savannah."

CHAPTER 9

Wrought iron, like black lace, framing glimpses of gardens and courtyards. Brick streets, oak-shaded and wide, houses gleaming with trim and sentried with shutters. Savannah dripped with Southern charm and Spanish moss, particularly in the historic district.

"Beautiful town," Joe said. He'd insisted on coming with us, claiming he needed some time off anyway. I knew he'd done it because he was worried about what kind of trouble I'd get myself into without him, but that was okay with me. A night or two with my boyfriend at a cozy bed and breakfast sounded pretty good, even if Kelly was part of the deal. She'd have her own room. "I've always heard Savannah was worth a visit."

"Me, too," I said. "Aren't these old houses great? Look at those brownstones—they must date to the 1800s."

Savannah was a city of squares. Literally. The center of

each square was marked by either a fountain or a statue, green space all around. People sunned themselves on benches or hung out on the grass, the atmosphere lazy and unhurried. Even the tourists took their time, strolling in and out of quaint little shops and historic mansions.

It was cool—in a vintage kind of way.

"There's a big fountain in that park over there," Kelly said, pointing. "Let's stop and get a couple of pictures."

"Sounds good to me," Joe said. "I wouldn't mind a chance to stretch my legs." After a four-hour drive through a boring stretch of grassy Georgia low country, I didn't blame him. We found a parking meter with some time left on it near a sign that said FORSYTH PARK and left the car.

"Wow, look at the size of that." Kelly was admiring the two-tiered fountain. It was white stone, high and graceful, capped with the stone figure of a woman. Marble sea nymphs splashed at her feet.

A little touristy, but gorgeous.

"I'm glad you guys decided to come." Kelly smiled at me, taking a seat on a bench near the fountain. "And I'm so glad to be out of that wheelchair."

She was hobbling around pretty well without her crutches. Joe had pronounced one ankle almost healed and the other ready for a walking cast.

"I'm glad you didn't mind driving instead of flying," I said. "Those little commuter planes make me nervous."

Joe gave a snort. "Wimp."

I pretended I was gonna smack him, but he just grinned and grabbed my hand instead. I let him keep it.

"I've always wanted to come here," Kelly said as we

took a seat on the bench beside her. She looked relaxed and happy, soaking in the day.

Somewhere in the background I could hear band music—the old-fashioned, energetic kind—lots of horns and tubas. Judging by the flags and streamers in one corner of the park, and the cluster of tourists in that area, there was a festival of some kind going on.

"We have to have some fun while we're here, check out the nightclub scene," I said to Kelly. "I hear it gets pretty wild down on River Street. Can't have your memories of Savannah be anything less than spectacular."

She laughed. "I don't know if I'm up to 'spectacular.' I'll be happy with 'great' or 'interesting' or something like that."

I sighed. "You need to wave your freak flag higher, Kelly."

"My what?"

"Your freak flag—you know, whatever it is about you that makes you unique, makes you *you*." I glanced over, only half teasing. "You should let loose once in a while."

She looked away, staring toward the fountain. "I guess I should. It's just been a long time since I have."

I watched a woman in period costume stroll past a man with a big dog on a leash. The man was ignoring the woman's severe hairstyle and wide hoop skirt, chatting it up with two babes in jeans and tight T-shirts, each with a dog of their own. The dogs wagged their tails and checked out each other's butts while their owners did the same, only more discreetly.

"Let's throw a coin in the fountain," Kelly said.

"You go ahead." I was fine just where I was. The afternoon sun was warm, though the air was cool. I loved fall in Georgia. "Don't forget to make a wish."

Kelly got up and went toward the fountain, digging in her purse for change.

"I'd like to make a wish, too," Joe said, rising from the bench. He was smiling.

I gave him my archest look. "Really? What are you going to wish for?"

"If I tell you, it won't come true." He winked at me as he moved toward the fountain, diving one hand into his pocket. "And I can't have that."

I watched him walk away, enjoying the view. The man knew how to wear a pair of jeans.

"Have you seen any of the men from Fort McAllister?" The woman in Civil War costume was walking quickly toward me, skirts rustling.

"Excuse me?" Some people really get into these reenactments.

"The garrison," the woman said. "Major Anderson's men—Sherman's taken the fort. Have any of the men returned?"

I had to hand it to her—this woman was *in* character. I'd seen people like her before. They loved festivals, and usually belonged to some anachronistic society with a weird name, like the Society for Creative Underpants.

"I'm sure you can find them wherever the beer booth is," I said, smiling only enough to avoid out-and-out rudeness.

"You're dressed strangely." The woman looked at me suspiciously. "I thought you were a boy."

"*I'm* dressed strangely?" Mentally, I compared the woman's drab gray dress with my favorite flat-front khakis, worn with a beaded belt and cute blue corduroy jacket. "Move along, Miss Harriet Beecher Stowe—or whoever you are."

The woman was plain and wore no makeup. With her dark hair in a severe part, clubbed in a low bun, she bordered on homely.

"Elizabeth," she said. "My name is Elizabeth."

And that's when I knew. She wasn't pretending. She wasn't a member of any society.

She was dead.

"They say that Sherman will burn Savannah to the ground," Elizabeth said, looking around with a worried expression, "that we should pack up and run while we have the chance, but I can't go without William. Have you seen him? William Coleman?"

Poor woman. The only thing I could do to ease her mind was tell her the truth.

"Savannah won't burn, Elizabeth." I remembered that much from my history lessons. "And William is at peace now."

She looked stricken, raising a hand to touch the white cotton collar of her dress.

"He's not here anymore, Elizabeth." *At least I hoped not.* "But you can see him again—anytime you want to. You just have to be willing to leave this place behind."

"But . . . but Savannah is my home." Elizabeth spoke the words simply, like a child. "Where would I go? What would I do?"

I shook my head at her. "Don't worry. Don't be afraid. Just open your eyes and look—really look—around you."

Elizabeth's face was pale. I'm not sure how Southern women used to breathe in such tight-waisted gowns—hers was banded and cinched with layers of ribbon.

She met my eyes a moment more, then did as I'd suggested, looking around at the tourists in their shorts and tennis shoes, wielding their cameras. At the dogs on their leashes, and the people who walked them. At the cars parked along the streets that bordered the square.

I watched her face, seeing her expression go from guarded to puzzled, from puzzled to accepting.

"I don't belong here," she said.

"No, you don't." I kept my voice soothing. "But keep looking."

Her eyes scanned the trees that filled Forsyth Park, taking in the Spanish moss, swaying in the breeze, the shadows cast by the leafy green oaks. "I see something," Elizabeth whispered. "Something beautiful."

Those were the last words she said as she gathered up her skirt and walked away.

Within three steps she was gone, dissolved like a mist from times past.

"You look like you've seen a ghost," Kelly said. She'd come back from the fountain without me even noticing and was standing by the bench.

The look I gave her must've spoken for itself.

Her eyes widened. "You *did* see a ghost!"

"Nicki?" Joe was beside her, frowning.

"Shhh," I said, shooting up from the bench. The chicks with the dogs were sending us curious glances. "Let's get out of here. I'll tell you about it in the car."

* * *

"That is so cool," Kelly said. "You helped a woman from the late 1800s. It's like there's no time limit on this thing."

"This thing?" I wasn't sure what she was driving at.

"You know . . . " She waved a hand. " . . . how long a spirit can hang around after the body's gone."

Kind of a creepy train of thought, if you asked me. "I never thought about it," I said, and I really didn't want to now, either.

"Are you okay, Nick?" Joe's fingers gripped my thigh as I drove, his touch warm and reassuring. "Is this one over?"

I nodded a yes, keeping my eyes on the road. This encounter, this episode, was over. The look of peace on the woman's face as she walked into the Light assured me of that.

"It's over," I said. "I'm okay, except that I'm starving. It's almost one o'clock; let's get something to eat before we go to Bijou's."

"Fine by me." Joe glanced in the backseat at Kelly. "Are we expected at any certain time?"

"I just told Leonard we'd be there sometime this afternoon," she said. "I wasn't sure how long it would take us to get here."

We looked for a place to eat near the Old City Market. The smell of fried chicken lured us into a diner called Homebody's, where we pigged out on crispy chicken, mashed potatoes, and pot-likker greens. There was even fresh-baked corn bread.

Halfway through the meal Joe's phone rang. He checked the caller ID and sighed. "Sorry," he said. "I have to take this." Then he answered, "Dr. Bascombe."

I could tell by his expression that he was going to be a while. He confirmed it by putting his napkin beside his plate and rising from the table. "What does the MRI show?" he asked the person on the other end. He jerked his chin toward the window to indicate he was taking the call outside, then went out on the sidewalk.

Joe was being considerate. We both hated it when people yakked on their cell phones during a meal.

"It's weird how ham hocks can add such flavor to vegetables." Kelly sprinkled more salt on the last of her greens. "I'd love to learn how to cook like this someday."

"My mom used to make the best black-eyed peas you ever tasted," I mumbled through a mouthful of chicken. "And biscuits. She made the best biscuits."

Kelly said, "None of my foster moms were very good cooks."

The fried chicken suddenly tasted dry. I knew it wasn't my fault that she hadn't had the happy childhood I had, but still . . .

"What was it like, living in foster homes?" Might as well not dance around it. I took another bite. "How many were there?"

"Three, mainly. I don't remember the first one very well—I was a baby. They were nice, I guess. I was moved to a different foster home when I was four or five." Kelly put down her fork and reached for a glass of sweet tea. "The Bakers were nice people, too. I lived with them and a bunch of other foster kids until I was twelve or so." She took a sip of tea. "I knew they were never going to adopt me, though, so I was pretty happy when the Charons came into the picture. They picked me out of a photo album and came to meet me at an adoption picnic. A few weeks later they took me home."

Wow. I would have been scarred for life after being handed around like an unwanted kitten, but I didn't say it.

Kelly shrugged. "I'm not sure what happened. We never bonded, I guess. I tried to be a good daughter, but it just didn't seem to work out. We didn't get along. I even ran away a few times, but the cops always found me hanging around the bus station and brought me back. It's not like I had anywhere to go, anyway."

"Then what made you run away?" I was curious. She didn't seem angry at her adoptive parents, so they must not have been *too* bad.

"It wasn't their fault. I found out they'd lost a baby—a little girl—and I wasn't eager to be anybody's replacement kid. I always had the feeling they were disappointed in me, like they'd picked the wrong kid from the photo album and regretted it."

My throat tightened.

"I got good grades. Earned a scholarship, even, and worked my way through school." She glanced up, her look slightly sheepish. "I even married up, just to please them. But nothing ever did."

"Joe?"

Kelly put down her glass and leaned back. "I can't believe I'm sitting here spilling my guts like this." She gazed around the old-fashioned diner, empty but for a couple of guys in the corner. "We're supposed to be having fun."

"Oh no, you don't." No turning back now—fun could wait. "You married Joe to please your parents?"

"Partly." Kelly glanced at Joe through the window, then stared at the table. "I cared about him, but mainly I just wanted to get away. The Charons had never been further away than Macon, Georgia, and never would. Joe took me to Boston and I never went back."

How could she not have been wildly, madly in love with Joe Bascombe?

"I always felt like Joe deserved better," she murmured, as if reading my mind. "I was the doctor's wife who didn't know how to cook, dress, or make the right small talk at cocktail parties. He never complained, but then again, he wasn't home very much."

"So you ran away again."

She didn't bother to deny it. "Yep. I ran away and joined the Peace Corps." Her laughter surprised me. "My childhood dream."

"Really? That was your childhood dream?" Personally, the thought of visiting third-world countries was only appealing to me if there were white sand beaches, fruity tropical drinks, and palm frond huts that came with maid service.

Kelly nodded. "It's a great way to see the world and do some good at the same time. I've never regretted it."

Joe was still out on the sidewalk, so I felt safe asking the question. "Did you regret leaving Joe?"

She met my eyes evenly enough, though she took her time answering. "He's a great guy. I want him to be happy. But we made better friends than lovers," she said, and left it at that.

"Excuse me, ladies." The two guys from the corner had stopped at our table on their way out. One of them was offering a brochure. "We were wondering if we could interest you in a free ghost tour?"

Kelly and I looked at the brochure, then at each other, and burst out laughing.

"C'mon now," the guy said, obviously used to that reaction, "Savannah Spooks is a cool tour." He was short and chubby, mid-twenties, wearing jeans and a black T-shirt covered with skulls. "Spider and I know the creepiest places in Savannah. We usually charge ten bucks apiece, but for you lovely ladies, we'll do it for free."

His friend "Spider" was tall and thin, with a jet-black goatee and close-cropped hair, a silver crucifix dangling from one ear. He was by far the better-looking of the two. I noticed him staring at Kelly as he put in his two cents.

"Skully makes it sound like a bad pickup line, but it's for real. We give guided tours of some of Savannah's most haunted places, including Bonaventure Cemetery."

I couldn't help it—I laughed. *Spider and Skully, of course. What else would their names be?*

Spider frowned at me, obviously not amused.

"Sorry," I choked out, "private joke."

Kelly recovered quicker than I did. "That's really nice of you guys, but no thanks."

Spider looked disappointed, but Skully was obviously the persistent type. "Take one of the brochures." He urged it on me with a smile, chubby cheeks gleaming, and I took it. "Maybe you'll change your mind. We leave from the Velvet Elvis over on Congress Street every Friday and Saturday night at seven o'clock. We even provide the mosquito repellent."

Lovely. But I wasn't going looking for any ghosts. They found me easily enough as it was.

"You girls from around here?" Poor Skully wasn't giving up. "Need directions?"

I felt a little bad about the way I'd been laughing. They seemed like nice enough guys. "No, thanks," I said. "We have a map we got off the Internet."

"Those things are crap," Spider said. "Where ya goin'?"

Kelly surprised me by telling him. "The Blue Dahlia. It's a flower shop over on Victory Drive."

Spider looked at Skully, and Skully looked at Spider. Then *they* were the ones who burst out laughing.

"What? What's so funny?"

Skully was the one who answered. "Oh, it's a flower shop, all right. It's also one of the most haunted old houses in Savannah."

This time when Kelly and I looked at each other, neither one of us felt like laughing.

"What's going on?" Joe came in from the sidewalk. He snapped his cell phone shut, looking none too happy to find us talking to two strange guys.

Kelly spoke up. "Spider and Skully give ghost tours. They were just about to tell us about the Blue Dahlia."

Joe gave them the eye, then shot me a brief glance as he slid into his seat. "What about it?"

Skully was eager to share, unfazed by Joe's lack of enthusiasm. "It's haunted, man. Big-time. It used to be a bed and breakfast, but the old lady shut it down. We'd love to get some equipment in there—set up some recorders, a night vision camera. Probably get some orbs, maybe even some EVPs."

The way Skully said "orbs" and "EVPs" made them sound like religious experiences.

Joe wasn't impressed with the techno geek-speak, and

neither was I. He took a bite of his now cold chicken, while I held back a sigh.

Kelly, however, was fascinated. "EVPs? That's electronic voice phenomena, right?"

Spider gave Kelly an approving look. "That's right. Ever heard any?"

She nodded, surprising me. "On the Internet. Some of them are really spooky."

Spider's thin face lit up. Kelly was smiling at him, and I realized she was actually *flirting* with this guy. Compared to a wholesome guy like Joe, a guy like Spider hardly seemed her type.

"Tall, dark, and brooding" was usually *my* type.

"Cool," Spider said to Kelly. "Ever been to a site called Spooked? I helped set that one up . . . it's got some great EVPs in the audio section."

What the hell. Getting laid would probably do Kelly a world of good.

"Have a seat, guys." I grinned at Joe to let him know there was nothing to worry about, guywise. "Tell us about the Blue Dahlia."

A half hour later we knew most of what there was to know about the old house our mother had grown up in, and more about Spider and Skully than I really expected to.

"The house was built in the late 1800s—a classic Queen Anne—by a ship's captain named Horace Montgomery." One of the things I'd learned about Spider was that he took Savannah history, and its architecture, very seriously. "He built it for his wife and children, but they didn't get to enjoy it long. He came home from a voyage to find his entire family had been wiped out by yellow fever."

"He was a smuggler, actually," Skully chimed in. "Rumor has it old Horace was a rum-runner. Rumor also has it that he went nuts. He didn't believe his family was dead, and dug up the bodies, one by one. Then he reburied them, but no one knows where."

One of the things I'd learned about Skully was that he didn't seem to take *anything* seriously. He wiggled his eyebrows at me and said, "Maybe there's bones buried in the basement."

"The house has had a series of owners, but nobody ever stayed in it very long until the old lady bought it," Spider went on. "'Course, she wasn't an old lady then." He shrugged. "When she closed down the rooms to boarders, the bottom floor was converted into a flower shop." He shook his head. "There've been a lot of strange stories about that house."

"And you know all this because . . . ?" I didn't know diddly about the history of any old houses back in Atlanta, much less whether they were "Queen Annes" or had any strange stories connected to them.

Spider gave me an impatient look. "It's our job to know. We're tour guides, remember? Savannah's full of ghost stories and haunted houses, and we know them all. The Pink House, the Hampton Lillibridge house, the Pirate House—"

"It started out as a hobby," Skully broke in cheerfully. "Then it became an obsession." He glanced at Spider with a grin. "For some of us, anyway. I'm just along for the babes."

I rolled my eyes, glad to see Joe grinning good-naturedly at Skully's optimism.

"Don't get your hopes up here, Skull Boy," he said. "Nicki's got a boyfriend, and a pair of sharp-toed boots. She knows how to use 'em, too."

Skully's grin was still in place. He was no threat to a guy like Joe, and he knew it. "I like a woman who knows how to stick up for herself."

Confident the dweeb could take a joke, I said, "Be careful I don't stick 'em—"

"Nicki!"

I kept forgetting that Kelly was such a good girl. Besides, I was just teasing. It was hard to be offended by a chubby guy who thought you were hot, particularly when said chubby guy already knew he didn't stand a chance.

Spider gave a noncommittal grunt, then said to Kelly, "What about you? Boyfriend waiting at home?"

Her cheeks turned pink. She gave Spider a shy smile and shook her head, toying with her ice tea glass.

"Anyway," Skully drew us back to the topic at hand, "this town is full of weird places. The American Institute of Parapsychology has named Savannah 'America's Most Haunted City.'"

"The American Institute of what?"

"The American Institute of Parapsychology," Kelly said, earning herself another admiring glance from Spider. "I read about it on the Internet. It's an organization dedicated to scientific psychic research."

"Scientific psychic research? Isn't that like an oxymoron or something?"

"Ha, ha." Kelly had that look on her face that warned me I was close to getting another lecture about taking life, and death, more seriously. "It's a very well-respected organization."

"Respected by who, Gypsy fortune-tellers?"

Skully laughed, deepening the crease in his double chin. "You're spunky. I like you."

"Great," I murmured, watching Spider and Kelly exchange another glance. I wasn't used to being invisible to cute guys, even if I wasn't interested myself. Still, Kelly did look pretty good today. She rarely wore makeup at home, and her hair was out of its usual careless knot. "Just great."

Later on, while Joe paid the check at the register, I asked Kelly, "So why didn't you tell them about Peaches? After all, she apparently lived in a haunted house. You might've scored a few more points with Spider over that one."

She gave me a look. "Jealous?"

"Please. He was way too skinny for me, and I've got Joe, remember?"

"As if you ever let me forget."

"What's *that* supposed to mean?"

"Never mind." She went back to staring out the window, watching Spider and Skully amble away down the sidewalk.

The surest way to make me "mind" something is to tell me to "never mind."

"Seriously. What's that supposed to mean?"

Kelly sighed, glancing at me. "You keep Joe on a pretty tight leash."

"Excuse me?" I'd always considered myself the "free Willy" type—I'd never believed in leashes.

"Either you go over to his place or you both disappear into your bedroom. It's like you're afraid for Joe and me to be in the same room together or something."

She might have been right, but no way was I gonna admit it. Particularly when it was something I didn't like about myself. My chin went up. "Did it ever occur to you that I might just be trying to be sensitive to your feelings?"

Kelly turned her head and gave me a long, level look.

Then, without saying a word, she went back to staring out the window.

CHAPTER 10

"May I help you?"

The man behind the counter at the Blue Dahlia was shaped like an egg, bottom heavy and bald. The only hair on his head were his eyebrows. He smiled, peering at us through thick, horn-rimmed glasses.

"We're looking for Leonard Ledbetter," Kelly said.

The old man leaned forward, resting both hands on the counter. "I'm Leonard Ledbetter. Do you have something on order?"

I glanced around at the showy bouquets of roses, lilies, and hydrangeas, admiring the display. "I wish I did. These arrangements are gorgeous." The Blue Dahlia was an elegant little store, and smelled as great as it looked. Striped damask wallpaper in blue and gold, flowers and greenery everywhere, a big bowl of magnolia potpourri right by the front door. The shabby chic armoires were painted white and then "blued"—a nice touch.

I glanced at Joe and teased, "I like flowers, by the way."

"Point taken," he murmured, eyes twinkling with a smile.

The house had a warm, cozy feel—it sure didn't look haunted, inside or out. It was a white clapboard Victorian with gingerbread trim, cheerful with flowers, only a discreet blue and white sign on one end of the porch to indicate it was anything other than a private home.

"I'm Kelly Charon, Mr. Ledbetter," Kelly said. "This is my sister, Nicki Styx, and our friend, Joe Bascombe."

"Oh my." Leonard looked stricken. "Oh my goodness me."

"We spoke on the phone, remember?" Kelly did the talking while I admired an exotic orchid, bright orange with a pale yellow center. "We've come to see Bijou."

No reply. I looked up to see that Leonard had gone white as a sheet, and for a moment I wondered if he was about to stroke out on us.

Talk about making an entrance. *I'm sorry, Grandma Bijou, but we've killed your store manager.*

"Are . . . are you all right, Mr. Ledbetter?" Apparently, Joe was concerned about the old man, too.

"Leonard," he gasped. "Call me Leonard." The man looked like a "Leonard"—his pants were pulled up so high his belt buckle nearly met his bow tie. All he needed was an inch of white socks and a pocket protector.

"It's you," he said. He was staring at Kelly, though his eyes kept flitting to me. "Her daughters. Here, at the Blue Dahlia." Leonard gave a little cry—of grief, of surprise, I wasn't sure—and stumbled back a few steps. His generous bottom hit the cushions of an overstuffed chair with a *whoof.*

"Hey, take it easy," Joe said, moving around the counter. Kelly and I started forward, but Leonard gave us a weak smile, waving away our concern.

"I'm fine, really. Just a little low blood sugar, I expect." He stared, eyes going back and forth between Kelly and me. "You two girls may be twins, but you look so different. Took me by surprise."

The old man won points for that comment. I never wanted to be part of a matched set.

"Oh, you're both so pretty. So much like your mama." Leonard's smile faded. Even his bow tie seemed to wilt a little. "Sweet, sweet Peaches. God rest her soul."

If she were resting, we wouldn't be here.

"Fine woman. Such a tragedy." Leonard's voice wavered, then steadied. He pulled out a handkerchief and dabbed behind his glasses. The handkerchief was black silk, and very wrinkled.

"Mr. Ledbetter—"

"Leonard," he wheezed, "call me Leonard. Bijou said you would come, but I didn't believe her." He was babbling now, twisting the black hankie into a wad. "'Just wait,' she said, 'they'll come. They won't be able to help themselves.'"

I shot Kelly a look, which she studiously avoided. She moved to squat by the old guy's chair. "Are you okay?" She put a hand on his shoulder. "Can we get you anything?"

Her touch seemed to have a calming effect. Leonard took a few deep breaths and mopped at his face, even going so far as to remove his glasses. He blinked like a turtle before slipping them back on.

"You must forgive an old man," he said with a wavery smile. "But you're about to be very angry with me."

Leonard Ledbetter wasn't making much sense. "Um . . . is Bijou around? Maybe we should talk to her."

To my absolute horror, the old man burst into tears. He shook his head, pressing the black hankie to his lips. "She's gone," he murmured brokenly. "Passed away in her sleep, three days after Peaches's funeral. Her heart was broken, you know."

Kelly's eyes met mine over the old man's head. *Why was nothing ever simple anymore?*

"But I just talked to you on the phone—you said Bijou was sick, not—" Kelly's protest stopped before she said the word "dead." "Why would you lie to me like that?"

"Yes, Mr. Ledbetter." Joe's voice was grim. "Why *would* you lie about something like that?"

Leonard wept even harder. "I had to," he cried, "Bijou made me promise. When she came home from the funeral, she told me she felt the hand of death on her shoulder." He mopped at his face with the handkerchief. "She was a sensitive, you know. She knew these things. She said if the worst happened . . . " He paused, throat working. " . . . then I was not to notify you girls of her death unless . . . "

Leonard paused to blow his nose, noisily.

"Unless what?" I couldn't stand it. The poor old guy was obviously losing it.

The words came out in a rush. "Unless you came to Savannah on your own. To the Blue Dahlia. She didn't want you coming out of obligation, she said."

Bullshit. This was bullshit.

The dark look on Joe's face proved he was no happier by this turn of events than I was.

"Her heart was weak, you know." Leonard flapped a hand, not realizing how his words sent a chill through me. "A fluttering condition, life-long. I think it finally just gave out." He heaved a deep sigh, getting himself under control. "She left you something."

I was tempted to tell Leonard Ledbetter what to do with whatever it was, but one look at Kelly's face stopped me. She was deeply disappointed, tears in her eyes.

"My darling Bijou. Before she . . . before she passed, she left you both a letter."

"A letter?"

"One for each of you." Leonard pushed himself to his feet. "I put them in the bottom of the cash register drawer so I'd know right where they were when the time came." He punched some keys on the old-fashioned register, and the bottom drawer popped open. He pushed his glasses up on his nose and began to rummage beneath the change tray. "I was quite certain I put them in here," he said. His expression went from surprised to disappointed to vaguely embarrassed. After a moment or two more of rummaging, he gave a shrug, managing a weak smile. "It's possible I left them in the study. I do that sometimes."

Kelly and I looked at each other. I wasn't certain what she was feeling, and I didn't know what to say. First Peaches, now Bijou—it seemed like every time we met one of our long-lost relatives, they died before we could get to know them.

And just like that, a frisson of something . . . *bad* moved down my spine. Call it a foreboding, call it chicken guts, call it intuition—something was wrong. I just didn't know what.

"You must come inside the main house and make yourself comfortable," Leonard said. "Bijou would've wanted to show it to you—she was so proud of it. The place was a wreck when she bought it, but it's been completely restored. All the original trim and fixtures. My darling Bijou was quite the decorator—it was once a bed and breakfast, but in the end she couldn't bear to have strangers traipsing through it."

"We'd love to see it," Kelly said quietly.

I looked at Joe and sighed, wishing Kelly wouldn't take it upon herself to speak for everyone like that.

He quirked an eyebrow, clearly asking me what I wanted.

I gave a reluctant nod. Whether or not the Blue Dahlia was haunted remained to be seen, but Kelly didn't seem too worried, and she was obviously determined to look around. Might as well get it over with.

"You must forgive an old man," Leonard said, wheezing as he led us through the narrow corridor that led to the main house. "I don't move as fast as I used to."

Then he unlocked a door, and the house opened like a flower.

Beyond the corridor were gleaming hardwood floors, buttermilk-colored walls, and what seemed like acres of crisp, white trim. The furniture was an eclectic mix of junk-store gems and fine furnishings; a stained-glass Art Nouveau lamp sat on a battered antique dresser by the front door. The area rugs were worn, but still pretty, their colors muted by the sunlight flooding the house.

"I must let Odessa know you're here," Leonard went on, leading us all the way into the main part of the house. "She doesn't like to be surprised."

"Odessa?" Kelly asked.

Leonard blinked owlishly behind his glasses. "Oh yes. She's been here for years—longer than I have." He was nodding his head, deep in his own thoughts. "Housekeeper, don't you know . . . though she and my darling Bijou were very close. Bosom companions, in fact."

Bosom companions? Sometimes old-timers had a way of speaking that could just leave you scratching your head.

"It's a beautiful house." Kelly stood in the center of the living room, admiring everything—from the gilt-trimmed mirrors on the walls to the blue-striped chintz on the sofa—just as I was. "Does anyone else live here?"

Leonard smiled sadly, letting us look our fill. "Not anymore. Odessa stays in the cottage out back, and I'm only here during the day." He tugged a handkerchief from his pocket and used it to dab his eyes. "After nearly thirty years of opening the florist shop every morning, I just can't seem to kick the habit."

Poor guy. He really did seem torn up about Bijou. *Good for you, Grandma, to have a boyfriend who adored you till the end.*

"I know Odessa will want you to stay for dinner—we usually eat together before I go home." He inhaled a deep breath and let it out blissfully. "She's already started baking."

"We'd love to join you for dinner," Kelly said smoothly, ignoring my dirty look. "Maybe we could explore the house a little bit this afternoon? Take some pictures, go through old photo albums?"

Leonard perked up, mopping his face with his handkerchief and then tucking it away. "Absolutely. Would you like to see the rest of the main floor?" He started toward a door at the far side of the room, leading us that way. Kelly went eagerly, while Joe and I trailed behind, fingers laced together.

"You okay, babe?" Joe asked, beneath his breath. "Because if you want to go, we can go. I don't like this 'haunted house' stuff. Those guys at the diner were probably full of it, but if there *are* any spirits here . . . " He shook his head, not finishing the sentence. "Anything you can't handle, you let me know, and we're out of here."

I squeezed his hand, grateful it was there to squeeze.

Problem was, I now found myself curious—it really was a beautiful old house. I wouldn't have minded taking the grand tour if it weren't for the bad feeling I'd gotten in the florist shop. This place was too good to be true, and things that are too good to be true frequently aren't. But *feeling* wasn't the same as *knowing*, and I didn't want Joe to worry.

"I'm okay," I murmured. "No spooks so far."

"This is the dining room," Leonard said, proudly bringing us into a huge, silk-paneled room that overlooked the back garden. The table and chairs looked like original Chippendale, heavy and claw-footed, gleaming dark with age and polish. The fabric on the walls was, in contrast, a delicate Oriental pattern of water lilies and koi, picked out in pale green, coral, and cream. "Bijou did so love her dinner parties."

Pausing only long enough to let us admire the view of the garden, Leonard pushed open the swinging door that led to a sort of pantry, long and narrow, filled with closed cabinets and counters on either side. Then we were in the kitchen, a big room filled with the scent of bread and apples, wide slate floors and veined marble countertops. Something was steaming in a pot on the stove, and a heavyset black woman was stirring it. She didn't turn as we came in, giving whatever was cooking her full attention.

"Damn you, Leonard," she said. "Didn't I tell you to leave well enough alone? Those two girls are trouble, I can feel it."

Leonard seemed to wilt before our eyes, and an awkward silence ensued.

"I seen 'em getting out of their car. No question they belong to Miz Peaches." The woman turned around, wooden spoon in hand. She registered no surprise to see Kelly, Joe, and me standing there.

"What you lookin' at?" she asked. "Ain't you never seen nobody cook before?"

"Odessa," Leonard said, enunciating each syllable carefully, "we have guests."

"Huh," Odessa said, and turned back to the pot on the stove.

Kelly and I exchanged a wide-eyed glance while Leonard, obviously embarrassed, tried to smooth the moment over.

"You must forgive Odessa," he said calmly. "She can be a bit outspoken."

"Huh," Odessa repeated.

"I assume you'd like to start here, in Peaches's room," Leonard said. His lower lip trembled as he reached for the doorknob. The room was on the second floor, at the end of a long hallway. He took a deep breath, obviously bracing himself, and opened the door.

The room was just what one might expect. It was peach, from the color of paint on the walls—highlighted with the ever-present white trim—to the peach floral bedspread and matching peach floral curtains.

It even smelled like peaches, most of the sweet scent coming from a bowl of potpourri on the dresser. Right beside the bowl was a silver vanity set and bottle of body lotion, Peach Blossom, of course.

"Everything's just the way Miz Peaches left it," Odessa muttered grudgingly. She'd followed us up the main stairs and now stood like a dark, disapproving shadow in the doorway, hands clasped over her ample middle. "Miz Bijou done tol' me not to disturb nothin'."

Kelly moved slowly, looking around, while I stayed by the dresser. Joe had decided to stay downstairs in the library, reading, to give us some privacy while we searched for whatever bits of our past we could find. Leonard went to one of the windows on either side of the bed and raised the sash. Fresh air flooded the room, setting the floral curtains dancing.

He nodded toward the double doors of the closet. "Peaches had quite a few clothes. If you don't want them, we can donate them to any number of local charities."

"Huh." Odessa's opinion of that idea was quite clear.

"The bathroom is through here." Leonard was still nervously acting as tour guide, and seemed unable to stop moving or stop talking. "Though I'm not sure what you'll find in there."

Peach-scented soap and peach-scented shampoo would be my guess.

Kelly's hand touched the closet doorknob, but I noticed she didn't seem eager to open it. She glanced at me, then away, but not before I saw the sheen of tears in her eyes.

"Would it be possible for us to have a few minutes alone, Leonard?" I'd never liked to cry in front of strangers, and I doubted Kelly was any different. "This is kind of overwhelming."

"Of course, of course." He looked relieved, while Odessa looked like she regretted leaving her meat cleaver in the kitchen. "We'll just go back downstairs and leave you to it."

The old man scuttled past Odessa and out the door, but the plump black woman didn't budge.

I looked Odessa in the eye, refusing to let her gimlet stare intimidate me. "We're not here to steal anything, you know." She didn't answer. "Bijou asked us to come . . . " I hesitated briefly. " . . . before she died."

"Huh."

Just when I was beginning to consider the wisdom of shutting the door in her face, Odessa turned and walked away. The heavy clump of footsteps as she made her way toward the staircase left us in no doubt as to her disapproval.

"I don't know what her problem is," I muttered to Kelly, "but I'll bet it's hard to pronounce."

Kelly's tears overflowed.

"That was supposed to be funny," I said, uncomfortable.

Crying openly now, Kelly leaned forward, resting her head against the closet door.

"C'mon, now." I moved closer, glancing around for some peach-colored tissues, knowing they had to be there somewhere.

Aha. I snagged the box by the bed and offered it to her.

"Buck up, little cowboy." *Wow. I'd opened my mouth and my dad came out.*

"How can you joke at a time like this?" Kelly asked, snatching a tissue. "Doesn't it bother you to be here, in our mother's room, knowing that she's gone and we'll never see her again? And now Bijou's gone, too. We'll never know anything about them."

"We don't know that for sure, now do we?" I deliberately made my voice sound cheerful. "We see dead people, remember?"

Kelly gave me a dirty look, but it was worth it, because she'd stopped crying.

"That's all well and good for you, Nicki," she said, dabbing at her eyes with the tissue, "but it doesn't help me at all. I can only see male spirits, remember?"

"Oh. Yeah." What else was there to say?

"I'm starting to figure you out, you know," she said, sniffling. "You use humor to deal with things you don't want to deal with."

"Gee, guess I can fire my therapist now. I'm cured."

"Huh," Kelly said, sounding eerily like Odessa.

I bit my lip, making an effort to take the high road. After all, she was having a harder time coping than I was.

She touched the peach floral bedspread, smoothing her hand over one of the pillows. "Is she here somewhere, do you think?" The look she gave me made my heart twist. "Do you see her?"

Just to satisfy her, I looked around the room, even stepping inside the bathroom and giving it the once-over. There was a clutter of makeup on the counter, a big can of old-fashioned aerosol hair spray, and a fuzzy peach rug with a matching toilet seat cover.

But no Peaches.

"She's not here, Kelly." I hated to disappoint her, but remembering how Peaches had come to my room the morning of her funeral to say good-bye, I added, "I really think she's already gone into the Light."

"Then why did she show up in those pictures I took Halloween night? What about the man in the mirror?"

A vision of the pop star Michael Jackson popped into my head, but I knew Kelly wouldn't appreciate the song reference or the humor. "I thought you said you'd imagined him. Two glasses of wine, you said."

She looked away and shrugged. "I don't know. But Peaches was trying to communicate with us," she said stubbornly. "I know she was."

Tired of fighting a battle I knew I wasn't gonna win, I said, "Let's just look around and see what we can find. The sooner we get this over with, the sooner we can go home."

Kelly gave me an odd look—one I couldn't read, then said, "Yeah, I guess we better get started." She took a deep breath, and opened the closet doors.

"Wow," I said. "Looks like Peaches loved to shop."

Clothes in every color of the rainbow were crammed together so closely it was impossible to tell where one outfit began and another ended. Shoes were strewn all over the closet floor and crammed haphazardly on the top shelves. Belts and scarves dangled from hooks on the back of one door, and a broad-brimmed straw hat with pink flowers hung on the other.

"This might take a while," Kelly said.

As much as I was used to pawing through other people's discarded clothing, I found myself curiously reluctant to do it here. I mean, it looked like Peaches had just stepped out and might be back to change her shoes at any second.

"Can't we just look for the good stuff and go? I mean, these clothes are hardly going to tell us anything about Peaches." Eyeing the sleeve of a denim shirt covered in sequined palm trees, I added a silent, *Except for her questionable taste in fashion.*

"The good stuff?" Kelly was frowning at me.

I rolled my eyes. "Papers, Kelly. Diaries, letters, pictures, anything that will make you feel better and give you some closure."

An hour later we hadn't found a thing. No pictures, no papers, not even an overdue bill. Plenty of makeup, clothes, and costume jewelry, but nothing that told us anything about Peaches's past.

"Maybe Bijou cleared it all out after Peaches died," Kelly mused. "Do you think Leonard would let us take a look in her room?"

"Leonard isn't the problem, Kelly. Getting past the Dragon Queen in the kitchen, now *that's* a problem."

"There are still some boxes we haven't gone through in that chest over by the window," Kelly said.

I looked toward the chest, saw how deep it was and gave a sigh. "Knock yourself out," I said. "I'm gonna go check on Joe. Leonard's probably talking his ear off down there."

Kelly nodded, already moving toward the chest. It was a pretty piece, heavy yet feminine, delicately carved with doves and hearts. A trousseau, perhaps, for a turn-of-the-century bride.

A sudden twinge of sympathy hit. Poor Peaches.

According to Leonard, Peaches never married.

She'd lived here, in this house—alone but for her mother and a cranky, old black woman—her entire life.

And now she was dead.

Unexpected tears pricked my lids as I walked down the hall toward the stairs, but if I were being honest, they weren't for Peaches. They were for the loss of what "might have been," the thought of "what if?" I wouldn't trade my life for anything, but it made me sad to think about how different things might have been if she hadn't given us away.

I blinked the tears back, knowing in my heart that if anything had happened differently, I wouldn't be who I was. I wouldn't be Nicki Styx.

And I kinda liked being Nicki, myself.

I found my way to the library easily enough. The house was quiet, late afternoon sun streaming through the windows to make the wood floors gleam like gold. A faint clatter of dishes told me Odessa was still in the kitchen. Joe was in a leather chair by the window, sound asleep, feet propped on an overstuffed ottoman. A thick book lay open in his lap.

Poor guy. Doctors never get enough sleep.

I didn't wake him, but instead looked my fill, enjoying the sight of him sprawled in the chair, sunlight bathing his face. I'd seen him sleep before, of course, but only in the dark, close by on a pillow beside me. This was a different view entirely: a gorgeous man in the prime of his life, oozing unconscious sex appeal, laid before me like a banquet. One knee slightly raised, pointed toward the window. The bulge in the crotch of his jeans tempted my hand, and if we'd had the house to ourselves, I might've awakened Joe by cupping him there, bringing him to consciousness with the touch of my fingers.

To distract myself from such lewd thoughts, I focused on his face, loving the way his hair curled behind an ear—his hair was one of his most appealing qualities, dark and thick, soft. His cheekbones were all male, lashes surprisingly feminine. He'd shaved this morning, leaving his jaw smooth. I studied the faint lines at the corner of his eyes, wondering which creases came from laughter, which came from worry. Being a doctor must be so hard—everyone constantly depended on you to take care of them, to make them feel better.

Which made me feel guilty for depending on him, too.

"Do I pass the centerfold test?" Joe's sleepy murmur made me smile. He was watching me, eyes barely open. He lifted one hand in my direction, coaxing me closer. "I tried so hard to position myself properly before *Moby Dick* put me to sleep."

"I might've known," I said, settling myself into his lap, drawing a satisfied grunt as I wiggled against him. "You have no shame."

Joe pulled me down onto his chest, closer to his lips.

"You were looking at me like you wanted to eat me," he murmured. His breath tickled my cheek as he brushed my lips with his—once, twice, three times.

"You must be psychic," I breathed.

And then we stopped talking while he kissed me again, long and deep. A stirring against my hip revived earlier naughty thoughts, but a sudden clatter of pots from the kitchen confirmed that now was not the time.

Reluctantly, I pulled back a little, but kept my place

in his lap. He was hard where I was soft, and my body melded to his like butter—I didn't wanna get up yet.

"How's it going upstairs?" Joe asked, tucking a strand of my hair behind an ear. "Any progress?"

I shook my head. "Not yet. Kelly's still going through Peaches's things, but I needed a break."

He tilted his head, questioning, "You okay?"

I smiled, resting a hand on his heart. "I'm okay."

"Maybe I should take the car and go check us in at the bed and breakfast," he said. "It's getting late."

"Sounds like a plan." I would've liked to go with him, but felt I should stay with Kelly for the time being.

"You'll have to get up, then," Joe said. But neither of us moved. I laid my head against his chest and he drew me close, both arms around me as I listened to the thud of his heartbeat against my ear. Other than that, the house was still.

"Two rooms at the bed and breakfast, remember?" I trailed a hand up his arm, loving the rasp of hair against my palm. "Make sure one has a double bed."

Joe's chuckle made my body shake along with his. "Like I could forget something like that."

And then he kissed me again before reluctantly displacing me from his lap, and I walked him to the front door, where I waved good-bye.

Then I looked for a private place to use my phone, not ready to go back upstairs and dig through more of Peaches's belongings.

Evan was probably wondering how things were going in Savannah, and I couldn't wait to tell him.

Through the double doors at the back of the house, a bricked-in courtyard beckoned. A wrought-iron table took up one corner, so I went outside, pulled out a chair and sat. The bricks beneath my feet were bumpy with age and smattered with fallen leaves. The sun was getting low on the horizon, and the air held a chill, but the shadowed courtyard was just what I needed.

I took a few deep breaths and soaked in the quiet, the scent of wood smoke from somebody's chimney, the musty smell of damp leaves. Soothing, if the whole situation weren't so bizarre. Then I called Evan.

"Hey there, devil doll." Caller ID had long since eliminated the need for a simple "Hello."

"Hey."

"What's wrong?" Evan was alert to nuances. "Is the bed and breakfast okay? Sometimes it's hard to tell when you book a place over the Internet."

"We never made it to the bed and breakfast," I said. "We're still at the Blue Dahlia."

"What's it like?"

"It's a big old house full of empty rooms," I said. "And Leonard lied to us."

"Leonard." Evan kept his answers short, waiting impatiently for me to fill in the blanks.

"Leonard Ledbetter. He's the manager here. The caretaker, or something. Bijou wasn't sick. She—She's dead."

Silence from Evan. Then, a strangled, "Dead?"

"Died in her sleep a few days after the funeral. *Her* funeral was a couple of weeks ago."

"And nobody told you?"

"Nobody told us."

"Why not?"

"Your guess is as good as mine."

"The old guy Kelly talked to on the phone—"

"Leonard."

"*Sick* is a hell of a long way from *dead*."

"Tell me about it."

"Um . . . " I could practically hear Evan's mind working. "You need to get out of there, Nicki. The old guy could be a psycho or something. I'm having visions of Anthony Perkins and the Bates Motel."

"Ugh." I shuddered, partly from the thought of the famous shower scene, and partly from the cold wrought iron beneath my butt. "Enough with the visions. Believe me, being able to see things that aren't there ain't what it's cracked up to be."

Silence.

"That was a joke, Evan."

"It wasn't funny, Nicki. When are you coming home?"

"Kelly's determined to search through the house for keepsakes, and Leonard's invited us to dinner. I think we'll be here awhile." I hesitated, knowing Evan wouldn't like this next part any more than I did. "And just so you know, the house may be haunted."

I could hear his sudden intake of breath. "What did you see? *Who* did you see? You didn't talk to them, did you? You should come home, Nicki."

I was touched by his concern, but as usual, calming Evan down calmed *me* down. "It's okay. I didn't see anything. Not yet, anyway. Kelly and I met a couple of guys who give ghost tours and they told her the house was haunted, but who knows? At any rate, as soon as Leonard invited us in, she jumped on it."

"This Leonard guy sounds like a nutcase."

"I'm pretty sure he's harmless." Leonard might be a liar, but he didn't strike me as dangerous. "He's just a lonely old man. If you met him, you'd see what I mean. And Joe's here. It'll be okay."

"You be careful, Nicki. You know how quickly things can turn ugly."

Do I ever.

"And I'm not just talking about your hair," Evan added, making me grin.

"You're just jealous because pink streaks don't work for you, pretty boy."

"Neither does Vin Diesel, but I'll survive." I could hear the smile in Evan's voice. "Now Vin's personal trainer . . . *there's* somebody to be jealous of."

"Slut."

"Skank."

When I hung up the phone a few minutes later, I felt much better. Touching base with Evan always grounded me.

A rustle came from the bushes to my right, and I glanced over to find I was being watched. A pair of bright green eyes surveyed me calmly, those of a cat curled up in the fallen leaves. The orange and brown shading of her coat had rendered her almost invisible. The cat rose and slid from the bushes, giving me a cautious *mew* as she came to rub against my ankles.

"Hey you." I stroked her, enjoying the way she leaned into me. I'd always liked cats, but never had one. "Aren't you pretty?"

She answered with another *mew*, earning herself a scratch under the chin. Green eyes slitted in bliss, then shot wide at a sudden rattling sound. A leaf rolled by, and the cat pounced, swiping it with a paw and sending it careening across the bricks. She was after it instantly, her fickle attentions now focused on play instead of petting.

"I hate cats."

The woman's voice made me jump.

"Horrible creatures, leave hair everywhere."

Psycho Barbie took a seat in the wrought-iron chair facing me, crossing her legs in a choreographed slide worthy of a fashion model.

Conversely, I straightened, spine stiff as a ramrod. The hair rose on the back of my neck.

The bitter-eyed blonde from the funeral home. Here, in Savannah.

Red lips smiled a flawless smile, and my blood ran cold.

"Don't look so surprised, Nicki. Just because you've been left alone doesn't mean you've been forgotten." A tilt of a blond head, the perfect pose, très chic. "I told you we'd be watching." Barbie glanced idly around the courtyard, then back at me. "Nice house. I feel right at home here."

I was so screwed.

"Wha—" I licked lips gone very dry. "What are you doing here? What do you want?"

"It's time we had a little chat." Psycho Barbie's smile turned sly. "You met my Master the other night. Halloween is his favorite holiday, after all. One never knows in which guise he'll appear, but blond rock stars and leather-clad bikers seem to be among his favorites."

"Sammy," I murmured, not even realizing I'd said his name aloud.

"Strangely enough, he's quite taken with you." Her gaze flicked over my khakis and denim jacket. "He likes your sister, too, but you seem to be the one he prefers." She shrugged as if there were no accounting for taste. "And what my Master wants, he gets."

I stared at her, heart pounding, the way a mouse would watch a snake.

"You should've helped me with that lying bastard, Keith," she said. "His wife wasn't supposed to know about the money—that was *our* money, Keith's and mine, our little 'love fund.'" Psycho Barbie smiled as she said it, as though it were a joke, but it was an ugly smile. "Instead, you and your sister made him look like a hero to his family . . . a real saint. All those grateful, mealy-mouthed prayers have slipped him beyond my reach." Her flawless mask slipped for a moment while naked rage glowed in her eyes. "I'm going to love making you and your meddling twin pay for that."

"Wait just a minute!" The hostility in the air was palpable, like a shimmer of heat from the cold bricks beneath our feet. "This is between you and your boyfriend. You lived your life, you made your choices, and they had nothing to do with us." If they hadn't been out drinking at the country club, they'd probably both still be alive. "Don't drag us into it. It's not Kelly's fault for trying to do the right thing when somebody asked her to, and it's not mine either."

"Doing the right thing is *so* overrated," she sighed, touching a perfectly manicured nail to her chin.

"Listen . . . " I took a shot at blunt honesty. "I don't mean to be cruel, but you're dead. And so is he. It's over. It's done. You need to move on and leave me and my sister alone."

Psycho Barbie cocked her head, still smiling. "You don't understand," she said. "My Master has made me an offer I can't refuse. My eternal soul in exchange for one of yours." She shrugged a black-clad shoulder, toying with the freshwater pearls gleaming at her neck. "What's a ghoul to do?"

And just like that, anger replaced fear. I wanted to snatch those pearls and shove them down her throat, but I knew my fingers would find only empty air. The dead can manifest physically, sometimes even manipulate objects, but that ability didn't seem to go both ways. The living can't lay a finger on a spirit, no matter how much they want to.

The only thing I could do was call her bluff. I leaned in, bringing my face closer to hers. Her eyes held the cold flatness of a cobra's, but I refused to panic. "Back off, bitch." I pushed myself up from the chair and took a few steps away from the table, just in case the cobra decided to strike. "If you want my soul, you're going to have to kill me to get it, and I don't really think you're up to that." I made myself sneer, though my stomach felt like ice. "It might mess up your hair." That chic blond updo must've cost a pretty penny.

Barbie—for that was her name in my mind—lost her smile but not her focus. "I'm not going to kill you, little goth girl." She rose from her chair, languid, every movement a study in graceful control. "But by the time I'm finished with you, you'll probably wish I had."

CHAPTER 11

I rushed up the stairs to Peaches's room to find the door closed. "Kelly?" I didn't bother to knock, just opened it.

And there I found her, sitting in the dark. The curtains were drawn, sashes pulled down to block the light. A single candle guttered in the draft I'd created by opening the door.

"What the hell are you doing?"

Kelly gave me a look that was both guilty and defiant. She didn't say anything at first, not until I turned on the overhead light and saw what she held in her hand. "I had to try," was all she said then.

The scrying mirror. She cradled it in her lap, reflective side down, but I was sure she'd been staring into it just a moment ago.

"Are you nuts? What are you doing with that thing?"

"What do you think I'm doing with it, Nicki?" she said waspishly, obviously not happy at being caught. "I'm trying to contact Peaches, of course."

I stared at her, scared and frustrated beyond bearing. She was up here conjuring spirits while I was trying to keep one away from us. "*Why?*" I really didn't understand. "Peaches is gone, let her go!"

"Because I'm worried her spirit isn't at rest, and because I need to tell her I'm sorry, dammit!" Kelly's voice rose. "I was driving the car when she died, and I need to tell her I'm sorry. Don't you get it?"

I drew a deep breath. Here was the heart of the problem, the true reason we were in Savannah. *My therapist would be so proud.* "It was an accident, Kelly. It wasn't your fault."

Her face twisted. "Easy for you to say. You weren't there."

"No, but I've seen Peaches, talked to her. She doesn't blame you."

Kelly looked away, swiping angrily at her eyes. She still clutched the mirror. "You've seen her—good for you. I haven't seen her. Not yet, anyway." She drew a deep breath, then looked at the mirror in her lap, tracing the bronze curves on the handle with a finger. "Besides, what does it hurt?"

I sighed. Opening yourself to the spirit world was not a good idea.

I'd never told Kelly everything that happened with Caprice and Granny Julep. I didn't like to think about it, mostly, and liked talking about it even less. The fear was fading, but the hard lessons I learned were not, and I preferred it that way.

"A powerful voodoo woman once warned me against inviting the spirits in, and she was right." Granny Julep might have tricked me and tried to turn me into a zombie, but she'd never lied to me. "She said that just because spirits are drawn to your energy doesn't mean you have to give it to them. Not all spirits are good spirits."

Kelly made an exasperated sound, rolling her eyes.

This was my own fault. I didn't have the courage to say Caprice's name aloud, particularly in this house, so my telling of that story would have to wait for another day.

Instead of taking the blame for Kelly's ignorance, however, I said sourly, "You've spent *way* too much time watching *Ghosthunters* on the Sci-Fi channel. Dealing with spirits is not the glamorous job it seems." I was being sarcastic, of course—hanging around with nerds in dark houses at two o'clock in the morning was hardly my idea of glamorous. "Take, for instance, the nasty spirit I just met in the courtyard."

Kelly's eyes got big. She finally put the mirror aside, laying it facedown on the bed.

"Keith Morgan's girlfriend is here, in this house, and she's pissed."

"What did she do? What did she say?" Kelly seemed more fascinated than scared, the big dummy.

"She's really mad at you for telling her boyfriend's wife about the money." I wasn't above blaming everything on Kelly if it got her to move her butt. "She wanted him in Hell, with her, and you messed up her plans." I sighed, shaking my head. "I guess she followed us here."

"I was just trying to help," Kelly said. Finally, she looked a little nervous. "What was I supposed to do, ignore a dead man's last wish?"

"She's mad at me, too," I admitted reluctantly. Barbie's face flashed into my mind's eye, twisted with anger over Keith Morgan and the role Kelly and I played in his escape from her clutches. She was mad all right, mad enough to follow us to Savannah.

I'd known from the beginning that this house was trouble. The fact that Barbie felt "at home" here was a very bad sign as far as I was concerned. "I really think we need to leave."

"Poor woman." Kelly shook her head sadly, ignoring my last comment.

"Poor woman? She's a cobra." *A well-dressed, well-kept cobra.* Beautiful from a distance, vicious up close. "Whatever pity you're feeling, save it for someone who deserves it."

"Don't you see, Nicki?" Kelly's butt was stuck to the bed, and I was ready to leave it there. "We can't ignore this poor soul. We have to *do* something."

"Do what, exactly?" My temper was rising. "She's dead, she's pissed, and she's out to get us."

"Nicki, could you just calm down and *think* for a second? What could she possibly do to us? She's dead. A lost soul in need of our help. We have to free her from the earthly plane."

The earthly plane?

"Are you crazy?" I asked. "Because you're starting to sound it."

"You need to talk to her."

"I *did* talk to her!"

"You need to talk to her again," Kelly insisted. "She's confused. Her anger is clouding her judgment. You need to explain that she's dead now, that she needs to cross over."

I rolled my eyes, exasperated. "I told her that."

"Maybe you didn't do it right."

My mouth fell open. "*Didn't do it right*? Is there some secret, special way to tell somebody they're dead?" I was being completely sarcastic. "Gee, I'm sorry. Somebody obviously forgot to give me the course material. Maybe I should take a class on the Internet—'How to Talk to the Dead in Five Easy Lessons.' Smoke and mirrors extra."

Kelly ignored me and kept talking. "Her spirit needs to be put to rest, and I can't do it. I only see male spirits, remember?"

"And the point is?" *Besides you being an idiot?*

"*You* need to cross this spirit over. It's the only way to get her to leave us alone." She said that a bit too hopefully. "The very least you can do is try."

What the hell? "Do I look like an idiot to you? She threatened me, she threatened you. She followed us all the way to Savannah with revenge on her mind." Then it hit me. "I get it now—you're on some cockeyed quest to be the Peace Corps volunteer of the psychic world, aren't you?"

Kelly's lip twitched in the beginnings of a smile, but I wasn't trying to be funny.

"And if not this spirit, some other spirit. You're *hoping* to see a ghost. You're *dying* to see a ghost. You think all this psychic stuff is cool, and that we"—I moved my hand back and forth between us to emphasis my point—"*we* are special." I gave a snort. "We're freaks, that's all."

Kelly glared at me, defiant. "You told me to wave my freak flag higher, Nicki, and you just said it—we're freaks. 'Cut loose, be yourself,' you said."

She had me there. That's the problem with giving advice—you're too often expected to take it. I turned to the window, snatching aside the curtains and raising the sash, letting fresh air flood the room. An oak tree stood outside the window, still green despite the cool weather, draped with Spanish moss.

Kelly stood up. "You've got a chance to do something good here, Nicki, and all you're thinking about is yourself. What do you think Peaches would've wanted us to do?"

I could honestly say, "I have no idea."

But a teeny part of my mind said, *If she were anything like Emily Styx, she probably would've wanted me to do the right thing.* Dammit.

Do unto others as you would have them do unto you.

Kelly gave an exasperated sigh, shaking her head. "Please, Nicki. Help this poor woman find peace. What could possibly go wrong?"

In my opinion, that particular phrase was one of the top ten things people said before all hell broke loose. Kinda like "Trust me" and "I'm sure there's no boogeyman in the basement."

I threw up my hands and grabbed the curtains, staring morosely out at the oak tree.

"Okay, we'll stay a few more hours. If she shows up again, fine—but if there's a boogeyman in the basement, you're on your own."

* * *

Dinner at the Blue Dahlia was obviously an event. Late afternoon daylight was still streaming through the dining room windows, but candles were lit, both on the table and on the buffet that stood against one wall. Soft music played in the background, classical stuff that sounded like elevator music.

Joe had made it back from the bed and breakfast just in time for us to join Leonard in the dining room—I hadn't had the time or the privacy to tell him about Psycho Barbie, or about Kelly's stunt with the scrying mirror.

"Well, ladies, any progress?" Leonard had dressed for dinner, and was now wearing a dark green suit jacket, shiny with age. He'd even changed his tie, switching from the bow tie he'd had on earlier to a green and yellow striped one. Poor guy obviously needed a little help in the GQ department.

"Not really," Kelly answered. "We've been looking for pictures, legal papers, that kind of thing, but no luck so far."

"That reminds me," Leonard said, reaching inside his coat. He pulled two envelopes from his breast pocket and held them out. "These are yours. One for each of you. They were in the study, just as I thought."

I made no move to take them, but Kelly immediately reached out a hand.

Two white letter-sized envelopes, both blank on the outside.

"Which one's for who?" she asked.

Leonard shrugged. "I have no idea, my dear. Bijou said you'd know."

Kelly and I glanced at each other, then back at the envelopes.

"Ah, I think we'll open them later," she said. "If you don't mind."

"Of course not." Leonard looked a little disappointed, but he seemed relieved to have that obligation dealt with. "In the meantime, may I offer you a glass of wine?"

"Red for me," I said automatically. I had a feeling my wimpy ticker would need all the help it could get tonight. It was times like this that I missed hard liquor . . . a shot of Glenlivet would really hit the spot.

"For me as well," Joe said. There was a moment of awkward silence as Leonard poured. "I enjoyed some time in the library today," Joe offered, obviously making small talk. "Bijou must've been quite a reader. How big is this house, anyway?"

"Seven bedrooms, three and a half baths." Leonard handed Joe and I our glasses, then offered one to Kelly. "Speaking of bedrooms, I thought one of you might enjoy the Delft Room."

I shot Kelly a warning look. I had no intention of staying at the Blue Dahlia overnight.

"The Delft Room?" Kelly gave me a bland look that I took to mean *be patient*, but otherwise ignored my glare.

"Most of the rooms have names, you see, based on the color scheme. Delft is a particular type of blue and white pottery that originated in Holland." Leonard ushered us toward the table.

"It sounds lovely." Kelly smiled at the old man, encouraging him to talk.

Leonard pulled out her chair, a true Southern gentleman. He beamed like a university professor about to embark on a lecture about his favorite subject. "I'll show it to you right after dinner. It's a charming room, though a bit small . . . oh, what am I saying? We have four other bedrooms on the second floor—you must take your pick." He held my chair also. "I'm quite sure my darling Bijou would've wanted you to be comfortable."

Joe spoke up. "That's very kind of you, Leonard, but we've already arranged rooms at the Cabot House."

"The Cabot House?" Leonard's bushy brows shot toward the ceiling. "Whyever would you want to stay there? I have it on good authority that the owner rarely changes the linens. Besides, we have empty rooms just going to waste right here." The poor old guy looked so earnest, so hopeful. "Oh, do say you'll stay."

"I don't see why we can't stay here." Kelly's objection made me want to strangle her. "It would save us some money, and there's obviously plenty of room. No one seems to mind."

"Huh," came Odessa's voice. She waddled in with a soup tureen, placed it on the table with a thump, and waddled out the way she came.

"You mustn't mind Odessa," Leonard said, going red. "She knows my darling Bijou would have extended you every hospitality." He raised his voice here, so Odessa could hear it if she cared to, then lowered it again. "The poor dear is just protective of the old place, a bit set in her ways. A creature of habit, don't you know."

Creature, yes. *Poor dear,* my ass.

"I so wish you'd stay." Leonard looked a bit flushed, which was not a good match with his green and yellow tie. He shot a guilty glance toward the kitchen and leaned in, all but whispering, "My darling Bijou would be so disappointed if you allowed Odessa's rudeness to drive you away. It's a lovely old house, with plenty of room. Odessa is all bark and no bite." He straightened, speaking in a normal tone again. "Save the money for the bed and breakfast and buy yourself something nice with it instead."

Kelly smiled and nodded as if it were settled. Joe met my eyes, questioning, but those damn Southern manners of mine had already kicked in, and it would have been impolite to argue over dinner. Kelly had me at a disadvantage, and she knew it.

Odessa came and went, bearing platters of food and tons of bad attitude. I had to hand it to her on the food, though . . . the roast beef looked tender and juicy, the mashed potatoes fluffy, the vegetables steaming.

"This looks delicious," I said, suddenly dying for a biscuit.

Maybe I could kill the creature with kindness.

"Huh," she answered, and moved the biscuits closer to Joe before slapping down a gravy boat.

Leonard took a seat across the table from Kelly. The chair at the head of the table stayed empty.

"Looks wonderful as always, Odessa." Leonard rubbed his hands together and eyed the roast beef. "I can't wait to see what you've made for dessert."

"You know what I made for dessert," she grumbled. "I had to smack yo' fingers outta that pie all afternoon."

Leonard shoved his glasses back up the bridge of his nose, unfazed by her grouchiness. "It's your own fault. You know how I love apple pie."

"You love any kind of pie," she shot back. "You 'bout to split the seams on them trousers as it is."

"Aren't you going to sit down and eat with us, Odessa?" Kelly asked.

"I eat in the kitchen," Odessa said. "The dining room is for guests." She removed the lid from a steaming tureen of soup and waddled from the room.

"I thought you said Bijou and Odessa were friends, Leonard." Kelly was frowning. "Didn't they take meals together?"

Leonard looked uncomfortable. "Sometimes. But only in the kitchen."

Mystified, I raised an eyebrow.

"This is Savannah, my dears." He shrugged, bald head gleaming. "What can I say?"

"But this is the twenty-first century," Kelly said, obviously shocked, "not the pre–Civil War era."

A big bite of mashed potatoes kept Leonard from answering too quickly. Then he said, "I think you'll find that in Savannah, the past is very much alive." He took a sip of wine to wash down the potatoes. "In more ways than one."

Great.

Exactly what I was afraid of.

When it came to the past, I was tired of poking around trying to figure it out. I'd rather have some direct answers to some direct questions, and move on. Manners dictated I be polite, but nothing prohibited my being direct.

"So Leonard," I said, "tell us about Bijou and Peaches. Why didn't Peaches tell us about this house, about Bijou? And why was it so important to Bijou that we come to Savannah?"

Leonard blinked like an owl behind his glasses.

Trying to remain patient, I elaborated. "Peaches never mentioned that we had a grandmother. In fact, she told Kelly that she lived alone, with no family, and worked for an insurance company."

"They had a disagreement." He shrugged. "You know how complicated mother-daughter relationships can be."

"What did they fight about?"

"I have no idea," Leonard said. He took another sip of wine. "More mashed potatoes?"

He dabbed at his lips with a napkin while Kelly and I exchanged a glance.

"What's going on here, Leonard?" Something was up. The beads of sweat forming on that bald head weren't caused by hot soup.

"You done started it, Leonard, and now you gots to finish it." Odessa's voice from the doorway behind us made me jump. "Tell 'em. Go on, tell 'em."

Leonard looked at us helplessly, then laid down his napkin. "But that's the problem, you see." He wet his lips, glancing back and forth between Kelly and me. "You must forgive an old man, but I'm not supposed to tell you *anything*."

Huh?

"Dammit, Leonard." Odessa may've taken her meals in the kitchen, but she had no problem speaking her mind.

I swiveled in my chair to look at her, and Kelly did the same.

"What that old fool is trying to say," she waved a plump hand at Leonard, "is that you either got the knack or you don't."

The knack.

"Both your mama and Miz Bijou—they got the knack. If you got it, well and good. If you don't, they ain't nothin' here you need to know." She glared at us both, taking her time. "The house be the one to decide whether to tell you its secrets."

Odessa met my eyes one final time before turning away.

"Y'all enjoy your dinner."

CHAPTER 12

"A tarot card?"

I stared at the image in Kelly's hand; a burning tower, all black and gray and grim as Hell. Tarot cards were supposed to be colorful, weren't they? "Are you kidding me?"

My card was more like it, even if it made no more sense than hers—a hunky blond guy riding in a chariot, blue and silver on a bright yellow background.

Since neither envelope was addressed, we'd chosen at random, and I'd taken the one from Kelly's left hand.

"'The Tower,'" she read aloud from the bottom of her card, then glanced at mine. 'The Chariot.' What do you think they mean?"

I checked the now empty envelope again to see if I'd missed anything. "Senility comes to mind."

"We should have come here sooner. I really wanted to

talk to Bijou again, and now it's too late." Kelly looked sad, guilty even. "Didn't you want to get to know her better?"

I didn't know how to answer that, so I just shrugged.

"I was hoping she could tell us about Peaches, talk to us about the knack."

"You probably didn't miss much," I said. "If this is her idea of a letter to her granddaughters, she obviously had a screw loose."

I paced the floor of the Delft Room, a blue and white attic bedroom Leonard had shown us to after dinner.

"Why are you always so cynical?" Kelly sat on the bed—the only bed—which had a blue and white quilt as coverlet. The walls were papered in elaborate blue and white toile, taking advantage of the odd-shaped angles of the room. The garret-style windows were draped with lace.

"I'm not cynical," I said, "I'm pissed. I feel like I've just stepped into a frilly version of the Twilight Zone." Tarot cards? *This made no sense.* "What's going on here?"

"Hell if I know," Kelly said, surprising me with the casual profanity. She tapped her card with one hard. "But it'll be fun to find out."

"What the hell are you talking about?" I had no problem with profanity, especially if the situation called for it. "This is not *fun*. I've had a lot of *fun*," I made marks in the air with my fingers, "and this isn't it."

She shrugged, giving me a grin. "So you say."

"Thanks for setting me up at dinner, by the way." I crossed my arms and thrust out a hip, unamused. "You didn't even bother to ask if Joe and I wanted to stay here tonight before you agreed to it."

"I didn't think you'd mind. What's the harm?"

"What's the harm?" That innocent look of hers wasn't fooling anybody. "This house is haunted, and we see dead people. Do I need to spell it out for you?"

I did *not* need more drama in my life.

The Blue Dahlia had drama written all over it.

There was a tap at the door, which was open. "What's the verdict?" Joe asked, stepping into the room. "Do we stay or do we go? Leonard's asked me twice if he can help me with our luggage, and I'm not sure how much longer I can hold him off."

"I thought you took it to the Cabot House," I said.

He shrugged. "I checked us in, but the rooms weren't ready. Luggage is still in the trunk."

Damn.

"Look, Nicki, if you don't want to stay, then you and Joe just go on over to the bed and breakfast and I'll stay here," Kelly said.

"Are you nuts? Leave you here alone?" I don't know why, but I just couldn't do it. "Who knows what kind of trouble you'll stir up with your magic mirror while I'm gone?"

"You brought the mirror?" I was glad to hear Joe was just as appalled at Kelly's stupidity as I was. "Why?"

Kelly shot me a resentful glance. "Because Peaches's spirit may still be in this house, and if she is, I want to talk to her."

Joe shook his head. "Give it up, Kelly. Let it go."

She raised an eyebrow. "Don't tell me what to do, Joe. You know that never worked." Her gaze flicked over me. "I don't think it'll work for Nicki either."

True, but I didn't need Kelly to tell me how to deal with my own boyfriend.

"I don't like it," Joe said stubbornly.

"No offense, but I don't care. This house is all that's left of our family, and I'm not ready to leave. Besides," she shot me a quick glance, "Nicki's already seen one spirit, and everything's fine."

The look Joe turned on me made me squirm. "I haven't had time to tell you about it," I said, "and we haven't had any privacy." The look I passed on to Kelly was pointed.

Joe sighed. There was a pause, then, "I can't win with either one of you, can I?"

I wasn't sure what to say. Was he talking about the issue at hand, or something deeper?

"I'm going down to unload the car," he muttered. "But I'm going on record as saying I think it's a bad idea."

"I'll come with you," I said. To Kelly, I added, "And I'm not staying in this room. It looks like a giant blue and white doily."

"I knew it," Joe swore, shaking his head. "I *knew* it. So much for a peaceful weekend in Savannah." He strode down the hallway so fast I had a hard time keeping up with him. "I leave you two alone for five minutes and all hell breaks loose." He looked angry. "When were you going to tell me you'd seen another ghost?"

"Don't be mad at me," I said. "This is all Kelly's fault. I wanted to leave but she played the guilt card." I wasn't taking the blame for any of this. "She's the one who wants to see a ghost, not me."

He waited until we were outside on the front porch before asking any more questions. "Who was it? Who did you see?"

I winced at his abruptness, knowing it was rooted in worry.

"Remember the spirit who appeared to me at the funeral home? The blond woman?"

"The dead guy's mistress?" Joe unlocked the car with a *beep*, popping the trunk.

"Yep. She showed up late this afternoon, talking trash."

He gave me a look. "Talking trash?"

"Oh, you know," I said, giving him a nervous smile. I didn't really want to tell him that Barbie had promised to turn me over to her "Master." It sounded melodramatic and scary and stupid. "Girls talk trash all the time. Make snide comments, insult each other's taste in clothes. It's the girlie equivalent of arm wrestling."

"This ghost came all the way to Savannah to insult your outfit?" Joe obviously wasn't buying it. The trunk lid slammed as he finished unloading the bags. "What did she say? What does she want?"

Poor Joe. He probably missed the days when he was involved with someone bland and ordinary. Like Kelly.

Not liking that train of thought, I derailed it by going back to the problem at hand. "She's mad about losing her boyfriend, and she wants to cause trouble." I was talking about Psycho Barbie, of course. *Wasn't I?* "She's an angry spirit, very bitchy, but I don't think she can actually *do* anything to me—she's a ghost, after all. Ghosts have very limited access to the physical world." I'd almost said "plane," and wanted to bite my tongue off at the near slip.

Joe wasn't buying *that* explanation either. "Surely you haven't forgotten about Caprice."

"Caprice was being manipulated by a living person," I said quickly. "Her spirit was under the control of someone else."

Joe was quiet for a moment. "Why did this woman's ghost follow you here?"

I shrugged, not wanting him to know how worried I was. "I don't know, but she said she likes the Blue Dahlia. Maybe she'll stay here when we go back to Atlanta."

"You're afraid of her, aren't you?"

I sighed, not bothering to deny it any longer. "Yes."

He stared at me, and I wondered what he was thinking. Then he started walking toward me, and my heart did a flip. His big, warm hand covered my shoulder. "I'm here, baby."

I met his eyes, deep green and rimmed with fatigue. His dark hair needed a comb.

And just like that, I knew I was in love with this man. This man, who worked a fourteen-hour shift, then drove to Savannah to keep his crazy girlfriend and her crazy sister company in a haunted house. This man, who I first laid eyes on when I opened them in a hospital, fresh from a near death experience. This man, whom I'd spent the last couple of months getting to know and seeing in action.

This man. Joe Bascombe.

I opened my mouth to say those three little words.

Joe gave me a lopsided grin, squeezing my shoulder reassuringly. "Everything's going to be okay, Nicki.

We'll stay one night, and then if we have to drag Kelly kicking and screaming back to Atlanta, we'll do it."

Great. The image ruined the mood.

"But first, how about you and I go upstairs and pick out a room, hm? Kelly may like dollhouses and blue and white doilies, but I'm a king-sized bed kind of guy."

The mood returned, but with a slightly different vibe.

"That's because you've got some king-sized parts," I teased.

He wiggled his eyebrows suggestively.

"Your ego, for starters." I laughed as he made a mock effort to smack me on the ass. "Now show me your king-sized muscles, and carry those bags upstairs."

When we came downstairs an hour later, all the lights on the bottom floor were off. Which did not make me happy, because we'd left most of them on after Leonard had said his good-nights. Odessa had retired to her cottage out back, but it was a little early in the evening to be turning out all the lights.

"Kelly went to bed already?" Joe seemed surprised. "It's barely eight o'clock."

"Huh." The hair on the back of my neck prickled. "Something's wrong."

Joe didn't hesitate, and took the remaining stairs double time. "Kelly?" he called. "Are you down here?"

"In the living room," she answered.

"What are you doing in the dark?" I asked, annoyed. "Turn some lights back on." I pushed past Joe to do it myself, hating that she'd scared me like that.

The lights came on, and there was Kelly, sitting on the couch with Spider, one of the guys from the diner.

"Hey," he said. He nodded at Joe and me without smiling, looking like a brooding version of his name. Thin face, dark eyes, and neatly trimmed goatee. Barbwire tattoos on each wrist, silver crucifix dangling from one ear. A little too gaunt for my taste, but I did like his style. He was holding a beer, and Kelly had one in front of her on the coffee table.

She looked flushed. "Spider came by to see how we were doing," she said.

I'll bet he did. But it was none of my business if Kelly wanted a little action, so I just smiled and took Joe by the hand. "Cool," I said, ready to lead him away. "We'll be in the kitchen." Joe had expressed an interest in Odessa's apple pie, and I was more than willing to let Kelly enjoy her own dessert without having to share mine.

"What's with the candle?" Joe asked, resisting my tug on his hand.

I wasn't sure why he'd asked the question. We'd obviously interrupted a romantic little "getting-to-know-you" time. So what if they'd lit a candle? Was he jealous?

Kelly gave him a frosty look. "What about it? It's a candle."

Joe took a step forward, examining the objects on the coffee table. "You're doing it again, aren't you?"

"Doing what?"

"Dabbling."

"Leave me alone, Joe. You don't know anything about it."

"I *do* know about it," he said. "More than I ever wanted to."

Part of me was fascinated by the byplay between Joe and Kelly, and part of me was queasy. This must've been how they were to each other when they were married.

And that's the part that made me queasy.

"We were just about to do some dowsing, man." Spider moved his angular frame to the edge of the couch, setting his beer bottle down with a *thunk*. "It's no big deal."

I laced my fingers with Joe's, wondering if Kelly had mentioned to Spider that my boyfriend was her ex-husband.

"You're looking for water in the middle of a darkened living room?" Joe's skeptical tone made it clear what he thought of that idea.

"Looking for water is only one form of dowsing," Spider said tersely. "A very primitive form, actually."

"I think it sounds fascinating," Kelly said. "Spider's been telling me all about it." There was a teeny bit of challenge in her voice. "Sit down, Joe. Join us. Stretch that scientific mind of yours."

She was baiting him. Why was she baiting him?

Joe grunted, wiggling his fingers. Evidently I'd been squeezing his hand pretty hard.

"What the hell, Joe? Kelly wants to be entertained." I pulled him down beside me on the couch. If he was jealous over finding his ex-wife alone in the dark with another man, I'd rather know about it sooner than later. And if Kelly still cared enough about him to make him jealous, I wanted to know that, too.

Bait away, sis. Let's see what happens.

Spider and Kelly moved over to make room, but it was still a tight fit.

"It works better in the dark," Spider said, and Kelly jumped up and flicked off the light switch again before plopping herself back down on the couch.

Now *this* I did not care for.

The candle flickered, giving light to a very small area of the living room. Beyond its faint circle of influence, the house lay in darkness.

Spider picked something up from the coffee table. It was a chain, with a weight of some kind dangling from the bottom. The chain glittered as it caught the candlelight. "It's a pendulum. I made it myself with a malachite crystal."

Of course you did, spook boy.

I glanced at Joe, and he gave me an eye roll. I relaxed a little, relieved to know we were obviously thinking the same thing.

Kelly reached out to touch the crystal, peering at it in the dimness. "How does it work?"

"Simple," Spider said. "You hold the pendulum over a flat surface, like this." He let the chain dangle over the coffee table. "You ask questions, and the way the crystal moves gives you the answers. It's different for everybody, but mine goes in circles for yes, and straight back and forth for no."

I resisted another roll of the eyes.

Spider ran his hand down the chain, holding the crystal perfectly still. "If you really want to get specific, you can write the alphabet on a piece of paper—in a circle, of course—and let whatever spirit you're communicating with spell out words."

"Wait a minute." I wasn't sure I liked the sound of this. "Isn't that like using a Ouija board or something? I heard it's a really bad idea to use a Ouija board."

"Like you never have?" Kelly challenged me over Spider's lean back. "Tell the truth."

"When I was twelve, maybe," I said, remembering those slumber parties where my friends and I had scared each other silly. "I know better now."

"Very smart," Spider said, surprising me. "Ouija boards are bad news."

I felt like sticking my tongue out at Kelly in triumph, but since I'd just admitted I was no longer twelve, I couldn't.

Joe heaved a sigh.

"You got a problem with this, man?" That was the first time Spider had addressed him directly. "Because if you do, your negative vibes could throw everything off."

Joe waved a hand nonchalantly. "Knock yourself out. I think I can manage to keep my negative vibes to myself."

They had a mini-staring match for about three seconds before Spider, quite literally, gave Joe the cold shoulder. He turned to Kelly and asked, "You ready?"

She smiled. "I'm ready."

Spider moved forward to sit on the edge of the cushion, which gave us a little more room. "The idea is that by using a pendulum, the spirits can tap into the invisible electromagnetic fields that surround us, and use them to communicate." He seemed to be speaking for Kelly alone. "We ask them questions, and they guide the pendulum to give us the answers."

"Uh-huh."

I bit back a grin at Joe's lack of enthusiasm.

Spider ignored him and dangled his malachite crystal, or whatever it was, over the coffee table, resting an elbow to steady his hand. He pinched the chain between a finger and thumb and ran them downward until the crystal hung perfectly still. Then he let go, holding only the tip of the chain. "Are there any spirits here who would like to communicate with us?"

Slowly, the crystal began to move. Within a few moments it was going in a small circle.

"That's a yes," said Spider.

"You're doing that," I accused.

"No, I'm not." Spider kept his voice level and quiet. Kelly shot me a dirty look, but I was so used to them by now that I could care less.

Spider went on, "Spirit, are you trapped in this house?"

The house was dead quiet, the candle was flickering, and I was very, very glad to have Joe sitting next to me on the couch.

The circling of the pendulum became erratic, and within a few moments it was swinging back and forth, back and forth.

"No," Kelly said, sounding surprised.

Spider started to ask another question, but Kelly interrupted him. "Peaches, is that you?"

The pendulum swung no.

She frowned, concentrating. "Bijou? Is it Bijou?"

A continued slow, steady swing indicated no.

Kelly leaned back and shot me a look that was hard to read. Then she asked, "Is your name Sammy?" and the world went still.

Icy fingers trailed their way down my spine. "Sammy? You know Sammy?"

Kelly didn't answer.

I'd never said a word to Kelly about Sammy.

"It's changing," Spider whispered, enthralled. The pendulum slowed, then started swinging in a different direction. Within seconds it was circling again, indicating a yes.

"What are you doing, Kelly?" I grabbed her shoulder over Spider's lean back, forcing her to look at me.

"He needs our help," she whispered, keeping an eye on the pendulum. "I knew you wouldn't understand."

"He doesn't need our help," I said. "What've you gotten yourself into?"

"Do you need our help, Sammy?" Kelly was talking directly to the pendulum now, defiantly asking it to confirm what she'd said.

It clearly circled yes.

"Is what you want in this room?"

The circling seemed to speed up.

"Stop it!" I stood up, ready to snatch the pendulum from Spider's hand.

Joe rose, too, placing a calming hand on my back. "Nicki? What's going on?"

I couldn't hold still. Before I could lose my nerve, I plunged into the darkness outside the feeble circle of candlelight and fumbled for the light switch. Relief flooded me when it came on, and I leaned against the wall, aware I was trembling.

"How do you know Sammy?" I directed my question to Kelly, knowing Joe and Spider were wondering what was going on, but letting them wait for an explanation right along with me.

Kelly sighed. She looked at Spider, then at Joe, then sighed again. Reluctantly, she said, "He came to me in the mirror. He asked me not to tell you I was helping him because you'd try and make me stop."

I let my head fall back to hit the wall, mind working furiously. Brilliant. Simply brilliant.

"Are you talking about the guy you thought you saw in the mirror Halloween night?" Joe asked. "You think he's here? Now?"

"Cool," Spider said, sounding very impressed.

"Not cool," I snapped. "He's not who he pretends to be, Kelly."

She shot me a resentful glance. "He said you'd say that."

I wanted to strangle her.

But not in front of witnesses.

"Hey, what's this?" Spider moved his bottle of beer and picked something up from the coffee table. "I didn't see it here before."

A tarot card.

"Wow," he said, looking closer. "Look at that."

I couldn't help it—I had to see, so I came over to the couch and looked at the colorful card in his hand.

A horned demon sat on a throne, two chained figures at its feet.

"What is it?" Joe didn't seem any more pleased at the image than I was.

I read aloud from the bottom of the card, unable to stop myself.

"'The Devil.'"

CHAPTER 13

"That's it, Spider man," Joe said. "You're outta here." He stood up, looming over Spider, who was still sitting on the couch. "Grab your stuff and get out."

"Hey, man," Spider shot to his feet. "I had nothing to do with this."

"Right." Joe wasn't buying it. "You just happened to stop by, you just happened to carry a 'pendulum' in your pocket, and you just happened to find that tarot card. Scare the girls and make them cry. Probably works great with the tourists. Great way to meet chicks, huh?"

"Who's crying?" I snapped, nerves jangling. "Nobody's crying." I turned a fierce glare on Spider. "Did you put that card there?"

Spider kept his cool. "I didn't. I swear I didn't. It was just there." He glared at Joe.

"That's right." Kelly pulled her feet up onto the couch, hugging her knees. "This isn't his fault."

Joe's frustration showed in the way he ran a hand through his hair. "Whose fault is it, then?"

As if in answer to his question, a series of thumps and bumps came from the ceiling above our heads. I flinched at one particularly loud crash, then there was nothing but silence.

"Oh, man," Spider groaned, "I think that was the camera."

"The camera?"

"The one we set up in the Delft Room," Kelly said. She met my eye, unapologetic. "Spider was hoping to catch something on infrared."

I opened my mouth to tell her what she and Spider could do with their infrared, but there was a loud *pop,* and the lights went out.

"Shit," I muttered. Darkness enveloped the house like a cloak, thick with tension and heavy with silence. Now I was actually glad for the candle, though I didn't like the way it cast shadows high on the wall.

"Sounded like a blown fuse," Joe said calmly. "We need to find the fuse box." He held out his hand, and I took it, letting him guide me back to the couch. I sat down again, while he remained standing, but I felt a lot safer knowing he was close.

Kelly was still sitting at the other end of the couch, but I was so pissed I couldn't even bring myself to look at her. How long had she been talking to Sammy? What lies had he told her?

He's a liar. Don't listen to anything he says. I heard

Peaches's voice in my head. *He'll strike where you're weakest . . . he'll go after Kelly first.*

Oh, shit. She'd been warning me about Sammy.

Spider hesitated briefly, then moved toward the front door. "We'll need a flashlight to find the fuse box. I have one in the trunk of my car."

Joe gave a grunt, then plopped down on the couch, right between Kelly and me. "You do that," he said. He put an arm around each of us and pulled us closer. "We'll wait right here."

I couldn't help but notice that Kelly didn't seem to mind being handled like Joe's personal possession. I, for one, didn't care to be treated as part of a threesome, but I was too spooked to pull away. I snuggled closer to Joe, laying a hand on his thigh for good measure.

Spider glanced at Kelly, scowling as he turned away. He went out, leaving the front door wide open.

"You two okay?" Joe glanced back and forth between Kelly and me.

"Yes," Kelly said, while I said, "No."

Figures.

"Everything's fine." Joe gave us both a squeeze, but I wasn't sure I liked him squeezing Kelly. "The camera just fell over or something. That guy doesn't look like the brightest bulb in the pack."

And just like that, the lights came back on.

"Wow," I said, blinking at the sudden assault on my pupils. "Talk about the power of suggestion."

"He's actually very smart, Joe." Kelly seemed more concerned about Joe's assessment of her new friend than she did about the lights. "I don't think you're giving him a chance."

I sat up straight, easing from beneath his arm, and waited for Kelly to do the same.

Was it my imagination, or was she taking her time over it?

"Oh, really?" *Was it my imagination, or was there a hint of jealousy in Joe's voice?* "The guy walks around carrying a pendulum. And what kind of guy expects people to call him Spider man?"

Kelly gave Joe a sideways glance as she started to rise from the couch. "Spider. His name is Spider."

Another heavy thump came from upstairs, and all three of us glanced up at the ceiling.

"I guess we should go see what's making that noise," Kelly murmured.

"I guess we should," Joe said, but nobody moved.

Spider came in the front door, holding a flashlight. "Did you guys find a breaker?"

"No," Kelly said. "I thought maybe you did."

He shrugged. "No, but whatever. Let's go check out the camera."

"Uh . . . you go," I said. "The three of us will wait."

Kelly got up. "I'll go with you. I want to see what's going on up there."

To my surprise, Joe also got up. "Yeah, me, too."

I looked back and forth between Joe and Kelly, not liking the ugly thoughts I was having. Joe had never been particularly eager to confront any spirits—was he worried about Kelly's safety, or her obvious attraction to another guy?

"I'm staying here." I had no desire to go looking for trouble.

Joe frowned down at me. "Come with us, Nicki. I don't like leaving you alone."

"Don't go, then," I said lightly. "Stay with me."

Spider was already moving toward the stairs, Kelly following in his wake.

"Don't you want to see what was making those noises?" Joe glanced toward the stairs.

"Not particularly." *Stay with me, Joe.*

"Okay." He bent, patting my knee as he turned away. "I'll be right back."

In hurt silence, I watched as the three of them disappeared up the stairs.

Get a grip, Styx. Jealousy doesn't become you.

"Knock, knock."

I didn't move, didn't blink. I'd heard that slightly mocking, extremely sexy voice all too often in my dreams lately not to know who it was.

"You're supposed to say, 'Who's there,'" Sammy murmured, his breath warm in my ear. I shot up, twisting to find him standing behind me, leaning one arm casually on the back of the couch.

I opened my mouth to shriek, but nothing came out.

"Uh, uh, uh." Sammy waggled a finger at me like I was a naughty child. "This is between you and me, Nicki."

Swallowing hard, I found my voice, but just barely. "Wha . . . what are you doing here? Who *are* you?"

Sammy straightened, trailing a hand along the couch as he rounded the corner. "That should be fairly obvious by now, shouldn't it?" He gave me a wicked grin.

"Wasn't the tarot card enough, or do I need to draw you yet another picture?"

"This can't be happening," I whispered, feeling like a rabbit caught in a trap, watching the wolf get closer and closer.

Tight white T-shirt under a black leather jacket, even tighter jeans, showing off an impressive bulge. Big silver rings on both hands, a thick silver chain with a heavy cross.

"You're wearing a cross," I said stupidly. "You can't be wearing a cross if you're the Devil."

Sammy laughed, a throaty chuckle that should've made me run for the hills, but my feet were frozen to the floor. "An old wives' tale, Nicki. Probably one of my old wives, in fact." He waved a hand carelessly, rings glinting. "But it hardly matters. Out with the old, in with the new, I say."

"New wives' tales?" I was stalling for time, barely aware of what I was even saying.

"New wives."

Holy shit. Fear gave my feet the jolt they needed, and I was finally able to take a few steps back.

Sammy followed, grinning all the while. His blond hair was shorter than the last time I'd seen him, and stiffly spiked, the way mine felt at the moment.

"We'd be so good together," he murmured. "Just think of all the naughty things we could do." One bright blue eye closed in a wink. "But then, you've already been thinking about it, haven't you?"

I said nothing, taking another step back, but I couldn't stop the images that flooded my brain.

Sammy and I naked, my hands moving over his

broad chest and flat belly, the salty taste of him in my mouth, on my lips . . .

"Stop it," I said sharply, wishing I was safe in my bed, alone, so I could wake up and know that this was just a dream.

Sammy and I entwined on satin sheets, his hardness thrusting in and out of my softness while I threw back my head and screamed my pleasure to the world . . .

"That's not what I want." I shook my head, feeling a traitorous tingle between my thighs.

"Liar," Sammy whispered. He was only a foot away now, close enough for me to smell his scent, dark and rich, radiating heat.

"Get out of my head. Leave me alone."

"Don't worry, Nicki," Sammy murmured, leaning in. "A gentleman never kisses and tells."

Two steps back. "Now you want me to believe you're a gentleman?" Another step back, and the realization that I could go no farther—an overstuffed chair blocked my retreat. "How many mind-blowing revelations am I expected to handle in one night?"

Sammy tipped his head to the side. "Revelations. I've always loved that word." Thankfully, he came no closer, but the look he gave me sent a chill down my spine. "You should've taken me up on my previous offers, Nicki."

Another image popped into my brain, that of Psycho Barbie talking about her "Master."

Money, power, eternal youth. Fame and fortune. Fashion designers falling at your feet while the public screams your name . . . wealth beyond your wildest dreams . . .

Sammy finished my thoughts out loud, with a knowing smile. "Anything your heart desired, Nicki, anything at all."

I couldn't help but notice he'd used past tense.

"With your talents, I could've gained quite a few souls for my army. That pesky Light keeps drawing them away." Sammy shrugged, leather jacket creaking. "But if you won't help me, I'll have to focus my attentions elsewhere."

Swallowing hard, I rasped out, "What do you mean?"

His smile wasn't quite so charming this time. "You're not the only one who can see the spirits of the dead, Nicki."

Kelly. My blood ran cold.

"And she's so eager to be used, too," he said, knowing I understood the threat. "Give the girl a simple little mirror and she becomes completely mesmerized. I wonder what she'd do with some real power."

Without thinking, I blurted, "Stay away from my sister or I'll . . . "

"You'll what?" Sammy laughed, but it was an ugly sound. "What can you do?"

"What the H-E-double-L is goin' on in here?"

I spun, giving a small scream. Odessa stood in the open doorway, hands on her hips. A pink and blue flowered robe was belted around her ample middle, the cheerful print not matching the scowl on her face. She eyed the beer bottles on the coffee table. "You girls only been here one night and you throwin' a party like you own the place." She came inside the house, muttering and shaking her head. "Miz Bijou must be spinnin' in her grave." Catching sight of the still flickering candle, she snapped, "You trying to burn the house down?"

She leaned forward and blew it out with one quick breath. A thin trail of smoke curled toward the ceiling, leaving the not-so-pleasant odor of burnt string.

Or sulfur. Sammy was gone, and it was obvious Odessa had seen nothing but what she wanted to see.

"Well, where's the rest of 'em, girl? I know you ain't here by yourself."

Hurried footsteps on the stairs saved me the need to answer. I sank down in the chair, grateful I didn't need to go any farther to find a seat, as Kelly, Joe, and Spider came into the room.

"Nicki? Are you okay?" Joe looked worried, glancing at Odessa. "We heard a scream."

I nodded tiredly. "I was just startled, that's all." I'd tell Joe and Kelly about Sammy later, in private.

"And who might you be?" Odessa planted herself in front of the coffee table, eyeing Spider with disdain.

"Spider," I said sourly, "meet Odessa."

He offered his hand. "Pleased to meet you."

Odessa clasped her hands over her belly, leaving him with his arm outstretched.

"We met Spider earlier today," Kelly offered. "He told us there were rumors that the Blue Dahlia was haunted, and he came by to see if we were okay."

"Huh. Ain't that special."

Silence for a moment, then Odessa said to Joe, "You look like you could use a slice of pie."

How she pulled *that* out of the air was beyond me.

"And I *know* you could use one," she said to Spider. "You need some meat on your bones. A man ain't supposed to be so skinny. Them jeans about to slide off your behind."

Joe grinned at her. "I'd love some pie, Odessa."

"So would I," Spider added, not to be outdone.

"Come on into the kitchen, then, while I fix you up a slice."

She'd never offered to cut *me* a slice of pie.

"You girls get busy cleaning up that mess on the coffee table." Odessa turned away, waddling toward the kitchen. "Act like ain't nobody never taught you nothin' 'bout manners," she muttered as she went. "Beer bottles in Miz Bijou's parlor. I ain't never seen the like."

Joe was still smiling. "I like her," he said.

"So do I," said Kelly.

"Oh, geez."

I had the feeling that I was well and truly screwed.

And not in a good way.

"So you tellin' me you need this here fool to help you figure out this house is haunted?"

Odessa lifted her double chin toward Spider. Her hands were busy slicing up pie. "Huh. Anybody coulda told you that."

Spider didn't seem to mind her opinion one bit, taking a huge bite of crumbled apple, a blissful expression on his thin face.

We were sitting in the breakfast nook in one corner of the kitchen, staying out of Odessa's way while she fed and watered Joe and Spider. Nobody else was hungry.

"Why didn't you, then?" I dared ask. Having just sparred with Satan himself, I had no patience for Odessa. "You and Leonard could've saved us a few gray hairs. Instead, we got a lot of cryptic doubletalk and a couple of tarot cards."

The closest thing I'd seen to a smile yet flitted across Odessa's face. "Miz Bijou had her reasons for what she wanted done after she passed, and we honored 'em."

"Miz Bijou seemed to have a twisted sense of humor." I got a perverse pleasure in seeing Odessa's scowl come back. "She could've at least left us a letter or something."

"She did leave you something," Odessa said placidly.

"What? Where is it?"

"You girls want everything laid out all nice and easy, don't you?" Odessa sent me a scornful glance. "Sometimes you got to find things out the hard way."

I wished Odessa would quit referring to Kelly and me as "you girls." We might be twins, but we were hardly a matched set. And I wished she'd stop talking in riddles.

Kelly was sitting next to Spider, across the table from Joe and me. "You've lived here a long time, Odessa. What is it that Bijou wanted to teach us when she asked us to come to Savannah? What can you tell us about her? About our mother?"

Odessa shrugged, laying down her knife and reaching for the aluminum foil to cover what was left of the pie. "I could tell you lots of things, but Miz Bijou wanted you to figure it out for yourself first. I done told you all I can."

My patience was wearing thin. "What's with all the secrecy? We already know that Peaches and Bijou did more than just sell flowers. Why didn't they just hang a sign out front that said, 'The Blue Dahlia—Savannah's Finest Psychics,' and be done with it?"

I'd never seen the Evil Eye, but I'm sure the look Odessa gave me would qualify. "You don't know as much as you think you do, missy."

"Missy? Ow!" Somebody had just kicked me under the table, and I had no doubt who.

Kelly kept her expression bland and her voice even. "What about the tarot cards, Odessa?" She reached in the back pocket of her jeans and pulled out the card marked "The Tower." "Do you know what this means?"

Odessa glanced at the card, then away. "All I know is them cards don't always mean what you think they mean."

More double talk, and I'd had enough of it for one evening. "This is crazy." I stood up. "I need some sleep."

Odessa slammed the refrigerator door shut on the pie, making me jump. "Don't call me crazy, girl. I ain't the one going 'round here talking to dead people."

My mouth fell open.

"Huh. Ain't a whole lot of sleeping gonna be going on in this house tonight, neither."

With that as her closing volley, Odessa waddled out of the kitchen. A few seconds later we heard the front door slam behind her.

I wanted to tell Joe and Kelly about my visit from Sammy, but I was hesitant to talk in front of Spider. Instead, I asked, "What was all the noise upstairs?"

Spider answered gloomily. "We didn't find anything. Everything was just the way we left it, except the battery on the camera was dead."

"Yeah, you might as well call it a night." Joe spoke

up, wiping his mouth and tossing the napkin on his empty plate. "And don't worry about your stuff—your camera will still be there in the morning."

For once, Kelly seemed to agree with Joe. She stood up. "Thanks for coming over, Spider. Give me a call tomorrow, and we'll work out a time when you can come back and get your equipment." She smiled at him as he reluctantly unfolded his skinny frame from the chair. "Who knows? Maybe you'll get lucky and have something on the voice recorder."

"Yeah," Joe said with a perfectly straight face. "Maybe you'll get lucky."

Spider gave him a sour look but didn't bother to answer. He followed Kelly as she led him out of the kitchen toward the front door.

"I have to tell you something," I said to Joe.

He picked up his empty plate and carried it to the sink. "Why do I not like the sound of that?"

"Because it's bad. It's really bad."

He quirked an eyebrow at me, obviously in a better mood with pie in his belly and Spider on his way out the door. "Bad like in *good*? Or bad like in bad?"

"I'm serious, Joe." Biting my lip, I blurted, "The Devil wants to make me do it."

Joe looked at me quizzically. "Come again?"

"That, too," I said morosely.

"You're making no sense, Nicki." He leaned back against the kitchen counter, both hands gripping the edge. "What are you talking about?"

"The Devil. Satan. The Big Evil Kahuna. He's here, in this house. He wants me to sleep with him, marry him . . . oh, hell, I don't know!" The skeptical expression on

Joe's face was throwing me off, plus I was feeling guilty for some reason, as though thinking about sex with a horny devil was the same as having it. "I don't think he wants me to send any more souls into the Light."

"And you're just now telling me this?" Joe's good mood was gone.

"I just found out, while you were upstairs." Not entirely true, but this wasn't the time to go into details. I'd known Sammy wanted to sleep with me, but I hadn't known for sure who he was, or that he wanted me to help him recruit souls for his "army." "He calls himself Sammy, and he's posing as the owner of Divinyls." The lightbulb went off, and I almost laughed. "Pretty clever name, now that I think of it."

"You've got yourself all worked up over nothing, Nicki." Kelly walked back into the kitchen, obviously having overheard the last bit of conversation. "The Sammy I know isn't the owner of any store. He's just a poor, lost soul who needs a favor."

Poor, lost soul my ass. "No, he isn't," I said calmly. "He's the Devil."

She made a disgusted noise. "He isn't the Devil."

"Just because he doesn't wear a red suit and carry a pitchfork doesn't change the facts."

"What a thing to say. I can't believe you."

"You never wanna believe anything I say, Kelly," I shot back, out of sheer frustration. "You only wanna believe what you wanna believe. I've never seen anybody so stubborn in all my life."

"Look in a mirror," she snipped.

"You and your mirror are what got us into this mess!" I shouted.

Kelly flinched, but I wasn't finished. It all made sense to me now.

"Sammy said he wouldn't let Peaches go into the Light until he got something from this house?"

"He didn't mean it," she said quickly. Too quickly. "He was desperate for help, he said. Since we came to Savannah he's been very nice."

The hair rose on the back of my neck. "You've been talking to him since we got here?"

Kelly looked vaguely uncomfortable. "Only a couple of times."

Great. Who knows what he'd been telling her. "Do you know what he wants?"

She shook her head, frowning. "He hasn't been able to come through clearly enough to tell me."

"I know what he wants." My voice was rising again. "He wants *me*, and if he can't have me, he'll take you!"

Color rushed back into Kelly's cheeks. "You just can't stand it when you're not the center of attention, can you?" She put her hands on her hips, giving me look for look.

"Peaches tried to warn us—she said he was coming." I stared at her, remembering the morning Peaches had shown up in the backseat of my car, fearful and hurried. "She said not to believe a word he said." My thoughts turned inward, but I spoke them aloud. "He isn't holding her here," I murmured. "She's already gone into the Light. He just wanted to bring us here for some reason."

Both Kelly and Joe were frowning. Their glances met, and it pissed me off.

"Look, I'm telling the truth. Sammy is the Devil, and

he was here, in the living room, while you were upstairs ghost hunting." I curled my lip, giving Kelly a glare. "And I don't believe for one minute that Spider just stopped by. You probably called and invited him over on purpose so he could help you 'commune with the spirits.'" I waved my hands in a "woo-woo" manner.

"You're just pissed because Spider obviously likes me more than he does you."

"Stop it." Joe hadn't raised his voice the way Kelly and I had, and his words were all the more effective because of it. "You're acting like children."

At the exact same time, Kelly and I both said, "I'm not—she is!"

"You both are," Joe said calmly. "Now sit down and let's figure this out."

I'd had no idea that having a twin sister could be such a major pain in the ass. But I hadn't forgotten Sammy's parting words. Kelly was in danger, whether she believed me or not.

I sat.

Kelly hesitated, tucking long hair behind her ears in an impatient gesture. Then she sighed and sat down across the table from me, while Joe pulled out a chair.

I took a deep breath, pushing annoyance aside. "This has nothing to do with Spider." Kelly was frowning, drumming her fingers on the table, but I went on. "This guy Sammy—I first met him at the Vortex on Halloween night." Risking a quick glance at Joe, I saw that he was frowning, too. "He came into the store a few days later, bought some things, tried to hit on me, but I turned him down. Then I found out he was buying the store across the street—"

"Caprice's old store?" Joe asked sharply.

I nodded. Joe knew all about the hidden voodoo room at Indigo, just like he knew everything else about my old friend Caprice and her dark side. "I had my suspicions about who Sammy was at the time, but now I know for sure. He's the Devil. He admitted it."

Kelly gave a small roll of the eyes, but I caught it.

"He's using you, Kelly." That got her attention. "He told me so."

"Really?" Her skepticism was still there. "So tell me again. What does the Devil look like?"

I hesitated. Joe was sitting right there. "Picture a young Billy Idol, only way hotter."

Kelly shrugged, made a face. "Not my type."

My, aren't we picky for a girl who hasn't had a man in four years?

Frustrated as I was with her attitude, I kept the thought to myself. "Well, Spider sure seems to be your type. Maybe Sammy's using him as bait or something. He got you to try the dowsing, didn't he?"

Silence.

"I've never lied to you, Kelly." I looked her straight in the eye. "I'm scared. This isn't just a matter of helping a few lost souls find their way into the Light . . . it's a war." I swallowed hard. "We need to stick together on this."

Kelly's lip trembled. She glanced at Joe, then back at me. "I had no idea having a twin sister would be such a pain in the ass."

I said nothing—I could hardly blame her for saying what I was already thinking, now could I?

"Okay," she said, "I believe you. But I don't know

what we're supposed to do. What if Peaches *is* still here? What if we could help her somehow? And what about Bijou? What was it she wanted us to find out, but wouldn't let Leonard or Odessa tell us?"

I sighed, letting my shoulders sag. "I don't know, Kelly. We don't even know where to begin to look."

A clinking noise whipped all three of our heads toward the sink. Joe got up, walked over and looked down at the empty plate he'd just put there. "What the . . . ?"

Kelly and I both jumped up and went over, and there, on the plate, lay a small metal key.

"I guess we know what to do now," I murmured, glancing over at Kelly.

"Yeah," she murmured. "Look for something to unlock."

CHAPTER 14

Forty-five minutes later we'd been all over the house and found only one room that was locked—the bedroom that Leonard had already told us belonged to Bijou—and the key didn't fit.

I'd noticed that Joe hadn't said much during our search, and when he did, his words were terse and directed mostly toward Kelly. Something was bothering him, and I didn't think it was just the fruitlessness of our hunt. When the three of us found ourselves about to enter the kitchen, back where we started, I slowed him down by putting a hand on his arm.

"Everything okay?" I murmured.

Instead of looking at me, he looked at Kelly, waiting until she'd gone ahead of us.

She paused for a moment in the kitchen doorway,

holding the swinging door open, but let it swing closed when she saw us unmoving, my hand on Joe's arm.

He turned to face me, and it was clear my suspicion that something was bothering him had been right. His mouth was set in a grim line and he didn't look very happy.

"What is it, Joe?" I had an uneasy feeling that had nothing to do with the events of the evening. "What's wrong?"

"So Sammy was the blond guy at the Vortex on Halloween night. The one who was hitting on you."

My heart sank, though I wasn't sure why. I hadn't done anything wrong. Lusting in my heart wasn't the same as being unfaithful, was it?

Joe didn't wait for my answer, my expression apparently telling him all he needed to know. "You didn't bother to mention that he'd come into Handbags and Gladrags looking for you. Anything else you haven't bothered to mention?"

I put my hands on my hips, defensive without wanting to be. "Joe Bascombe, are you jealous?"

He didn't bother to deny it. "Hell, yes, I'm jealous. I'm also tired, frustrated, and mad as hell! You're keeping secrets from me, Nicki, and I don't like it."

"What secrets?" I tried to keep my voice lowered, but he wasn't the only one who was tired and frustrated. "I told you all about Sammy earlier, right there in the kitchen!"

His lip curled. "Oh, yeah. I particularly liked the way you described him—'Like a young Billy Idol, only way hotter.'"

I felt my face flush, and bit my lip to keep from losing

my temper. "I was just trying to describe him accurately, so Kelly would know we were talking about the same person."

He didn't answer, and I sighed, guilt winning out over any desire to fight. "You're right. I should have told you about him coming to the store."

"You didn't tell me about seeing the woman's ghost from the funeral home earlier today either," Joe pointed out, all too quickly. "I had to hear it from Kelly."

"I meant to tell you, really I did." Silence. "Every time I thought about it I got distracted . . . "

"By what? Or should I say who?"

I shook my head, not used to seeing Joe like this. He was always so calm, so in control—had I really given him reason to be so jealous?

"And what about Spider man?"

I blinked, not sure where *that* question came from.

"What about him?"

"Was Kelly right? Are you jealous because he seems to be paying more attention to her than to you? You've been needling her about him pretty hard."

My mouth dropped open, and I was—for once—speechless.

Joe turned away, running a hand through his hair. "Okay, okay. Maybe that was uncalled for," he muttered, "but he sure seems like your type." He shot me a look, adding defensively, "Goth. Edgy. Tattoos and all."

I opened my mouth to argue, but surprised myself with the realization that I didn't want to.

Joe had worked all night the night before, driven a long way, and despite the fact that he was mad, he was here with me. If he was jealous, well, so be it. I could handle a little jealousy.

So instead of biting his head off, I said, "*You're* my type." Moving in closer, I put a hand on his arm and added softly, "No tattoos and all." I squeezed his bicep, feeling the tension slowly drain from it as he looked me in the eye.

"I'm not used to this," he said. "It's been a long time since I've cared enough to get . . . " His voice trailed off, and I reached up a hand to touch his lips, letting him know there was no need to say anything more, but he shook me off, obviously wanting to. "I keep seeing things in my head, Nicki, imagining things I don't want to imagine, and it's making me crazy."

I frowned, knowing how jealousy could eat at a person. It had been a long time for me, too, but I knew what it was like to imagine the person with whom you were involved with someone else. I'd had to force thoughts of Kelly and Joe together out of my head all too often, and remind myself that whatever happened between them happened long before I met either one.

"You can trust me, Joe." I never broke eye contact with him. "I'm not going to do anything stupid."

He sighed, pulling me close until my head rested against his chest. "I sure hope not."

Not exactly a resounding statement of confidence, but it felt so good to be in his arms that I didn't complain. Actions spoke louder than words, and sometimes it was better to let them do the talking.

We just stood there, holding each other, while the future waited quietly, biding its time.

* * *

"What now?" Joe sank down on the living room couch, looking exhausted. It was late, and he'd been up longer than any of us.

"I have no idea." I was tired, too. "I just don't get it. Why doesn't Peaches or Bijou just show up and tell us what's going on?"

"Maybe we should split up," Kelly murmured.

"No way." I hadn't forgotten Sammy's little visit, and I wasn't eager for another one. "We're sticking together—like the three Musketeers. All for one, and one for all."

My comment was punctuated by the sound of a soft snore. I glanced over to see that Joe's eyes were closed and his head had fallen back. He was out of it.

"Okay, so we're the two Musketeers." I smiled, thinking how cute he looked when he was sleeping. I would've liked nothing better than to curl up next to him with my head in his lap.

"There's still one place we haven't looked," Kelly whispered. "The flower shop."

True. There was no entrance to the shop inside the main house. We'd have to go outside, to the far end of the porch to try the front door, or down the narrow back stairs to the courtyard to try the rear.

The front porch definitely had my vote—at least it was well-lit.

"Should we wake him up?" I wanted to, but Joe looked so peaceful. His dark head lay against the blue and white cushions, long legs sprawled, hands loose in his lap.

Kelly shrugged. "Let him sleep. We won't be far away."

She was right. Prince Charming had been on enough wild goose chases for one day.

I heaved a sigh. "Let's get it over with."

We let ourselves quietly out the front door. The night was still—no traffic on Victory Drive, no lights in the surrounding houses. Only a few crickets chirping somewhere in the darkness. Now that the electricity was on, a couple of porch lights made it easy to find our way past the old rockers and hanging plants . . . I tried to ignore the shadows beneath the oaks in the front yard.

A security spotlight lit up the entrance to the Blue Dahlia. Kelly slid the key into the lock. "It fits." There was an audible click as she turned it. "Why didn't we think of this before?"

I held my breath while Kelly opened the door, and gave a sigh of relief when no burglar alarm sounded. It was quiet, no green lights to indicate motion sensors. I felt for a light switch on the wall and flipped it.

The room looked just as it had when we'd arrived earlier in the day, minus Leonard, of course. The air was rich with scent, magnolia potpourri mingled with roses and other flowers. The blue and gold striped wallpaper looked darker without daylight to brighten the colors, but it was still a cheerful little store.

"I'm sure this is considered breaking and entering." I locked the door behind us, nervous about being in someone else's place of business after hours. "Nobody said we could come in here."

"Nobody said we couldn't." Kelly's logic might have been technically correct, but I doubted it would fly in a court of law. "But maybe we should keep the lights off, so we don't draw any unnecessary attention from the neighbors."

"Let's just look around and get this over with, okay?" Breaking and entering was one thing, wandering around in the dark was another. Who knew what kind of spooks hung around flower shops?

"Bijou? Peaches? Are you here?" Kelly was going for the direct approach this time. "What can we do to help you?"

A noise broke the silence, making us both jump. The hair on my arms rose as a door at the far end of the room creaked slowly open. Beyond lay darkness.

"Umm . . . " I slid my eyes toward Kelly. "Let's go back and wake Joe."

"Don't be silly," she said, though she looked as scared as I was. "We're finally getting somewhere."

Something touched my hand, and I nearly jumped out of my skin. But it was only Kelly, threading her fingers through mine. "The two Musketeers, right?"

Crap. That's what I got for watching old movies.

As I tightened my fingers, returning her squeeze, another old movie flashed into my head. Chain-saw massacres had never been my idea of great chick flicks.

Together, Kelly and I moved slowly toward the door. As we got closer, a brick wall with a handrail came into view, then steps, leading downward.

"Ever heard 'I Don't Wanna Go Down to the Basement' by the Ramones?" My lame attempt at a joke wasn't actually a joke—I *really* didn't wanna go down there. "Geniuses. The Ramones were musical geniuses."

"Here's another light switch." Kelly flicked it on,

then let go of my hand. "I'll go first." She started down the stairs, carefully holding the handrail. My palm was sweaty, so I rubbed it on my jeans before following her down.

Half a dozen, maybe eight steps, and we were in a small room—more of a ground level space beneath the front porch than a basement. Bookshelves lined two walls, and a round table with six chairs took up most of one corner. Worn Oriental carpets covered the floor. Instead of posters or pictures, swaths of purple and blue velvet were draped artistically over bronze sconces mounted on the walls. The air was strong with the lingering scent of incense. I would've admired the dramatic flair of the room except for one thing: the Ouija board sitting in the center of the black silk tablecloth.

"Wow," Kelly breathed. "Look at all these books." She moved to the nearest bookshelf and ran her hands over the titles. *"Embrace the Night: a Guide to Rituals, Spells and Hexes . . . Drums and Shadows: the Elements of Life, the Fundamentals of Death."*

The hair on the back of my neck prickled. I whipped around, but there was no one there.

"Lucid Dreaming . . . Omens and their Meanings, Past and Present . . . Candle Magic." Kelly was fascinated, but I wished she'd shut up. "Look at this one: *Daughters of the Moon—the Complete Guide to Tarot.*"

This was the lair of a fortune-teller. A palm-reading, tarot-card-spreading, talk-to-your-dead-loved-ones-for-twenty-five-dollars Madame Zelda. The only thing missing was the crystal ball.

What a nightmare.

Our mother had been the equivalent of somebody's loony old maiden aunt, reading tea leaves and telling fortunes in the basement.

Kelly pulled out the tarot book and laid it on the table, ignoring the Ouija board for the time being.

I tried to do the same thing, because the board creeped me out. The planchette, a triangular piece of wood, was like a dark eye pointed straight to my heart.

"'Rider-Waite deck,'" Kelly read aloud as she skimmed. "Seventy-eight cards, major arcana . . . here it is . . . " She tapped a finger on the page. "The Tower."

I tore my gaze from the Ouija board to look at the illustration of the card Kelly carried in her back pocket. A gray tower on a black background, lighting-seared, the night sky raining people and fire.

"'False concepts, denial . . . one of the clearest cards when it comes to meaning,'" Kelly read. Her face darkened. "'Earthly destruction or death of conviction, a war between the structures of lies and the lightning flash of truth. This card is a warning to the person being read for. Their world is about to be shaken up, their eyes opened, but there are none so blind as they who will not see.'"

There was a lot more to read, but Kelly flipped, frowning, back to the index. "'The Chariot. Page eighty-nine.'" She found the page, and there was my card, bright yellow and blue, a golden prince being pulled by two sphinxes—one black and one white.

"'One of the most complex cards to define . . . implies war, a struggle, obstacles overcome by control and confidence.'" Kelly raised her head. "'A balance of fate, a union of opposites, a harnessing of inner power. A sign that conviction will lead to victory, but a reminder that victory is not the end, it is only the beginning.'"

I drew in a deep breath, feeling anything but controlled and confident. As for victory. . . *huh*. This whole scene was way too freaky for me. Here we were, in the middle of the night, in a secret room in a spooky old house—spell books on the walls and a Ouija board on the table, reading about tarot cards.

"Well, aren't you the lucky one." Kelly eyed me thoughtfully. "Again." There was no mistaking the edge of bitterness in her voice. "I get death and destruction, you get victory and control."

"Neither of us knew what was in those envelopes, Kelly. You could've chosen that card as easily as me."

She didn't answer, merely returned her gaze to the book.

"Let's see about the third card. The Devil." She flipped to another page, and there he was—a horned, winged demon crouching on a pedestal, torch burning in one hand, chained slaves at his feet. "'A potent card, representing passion and abandon, obsession and greed.'" Her voice lowered, turned thoughtful. "'The Goat-god is a creature of great power, reveling in temptation and joyful excess. This card is a warning of enslavement, yet a reminder that chains are freely worn.'"

"Lovely." I looked around at all the books, rubbing my arms briskly. "Now I understand everything." I was being completely sarcastic, of course. "Don't know why I didn't get it before."

Knowing what the cards represented in the "ether of the universe" didn't help with the specifics of the here and now. I already knew there was a war, and I already knew the Devil could be very tempting . . . particularly when he wore faded jeans and a vintage bomber jacket.

What I didn't know was what to do about it, and I didn't know how to keep him away from my sister—who was acting pissy again just because my card was better than hers.

"You wanna know what I think? I think these tarot cards are just a way for Sammy to mess with our heads." I was more than ready to head home to Atlanta. If we drove straight through, we'd be there long before dawn. "And this house? This wild goose chase search for we-don't-even-know-what? What's the point of all this?" I gestured toward the fabric-draped brick walls, the books on Wicca and witchcraft, the Ouija board. "Family ties? Personal effects? Peaches and Bijou left us nothing but trouble." I saw the way Kelly's chin lifted, and my heart sank, literally, with a brief swooping sensation. It steadied, resuming an even beat, and I ignored it, as I had so many times before.

"Is this what you were hoping for, Kelly? Relatives who told fortunes for a living and a creaky old house full of ghosts?"

"No." She was very calm. "This is better than I'd hoped for."

"Are you kidding me?" In that instant everything clicked: this fascination Kelly had for the paranormal could be her downfall. Her curiosity, her eagerness to do good in the world, could lead her in the wrong direction, as it had with Caprice and her voodoo.

Good intentions aren't always enough, and haloes can get tarnished pretty easily.

"We've been given a gift," Kelly said. "We should find out everything we can about it. Develop it, use it. Maybe we can help the living as well as the dead."

There are none so blind as they who will not see.

"Listen, Kelly, I've helped a few spirits pass over, and I'll do it again whenever I'm asked." *Because they won't leave me alone otherwise.* "The point is, there's no need to go looking for trouble . . . trouble will find you."

"That's the problem, Nicki"—her voice was rising—"you see the spirits of the dead as trouble, and I see them as opportunities."

"That about says it all, doesn't it?" I was getting more frustrated by the second. "I say yes, you say no. I like something, you hate it."

"That's not always true." She closed the tarot book with a *thump.* "We both like Joe."

I couldn't help but notice the present tense, and just like that my temper snapped.

"Dammit! I knew it! You want him back!" The bland look on her face made me wanna slap her. "You said you were okay with the divorce, but you're not, are you? Tell the truth, dammit!"

"You are so paranoid," Kelly said mildly. "Are you always this jealous, or is it just me?" She dismissed me with a wave of her hand, turning back to the row of books. "I'm taking some of these books upstairs to read tonight," she murmured. "This stuff is fascinating."

"No, it isn't!" I snapped. "It's evil, and it's stupid, and it's bad news. Put that book down and let's get out of here."

Kelly looked at me like I'd sprouted horns, which at the moment wouldn't have surprised me. "Don't tell me what to do," she said. "You're always trying to tell me what to do."

"And you never do it!" I was completely out of patience, and quite frankly, nervous as a cat in that basement. Fear made me cranky. "I'd have better luck talking to these brick walls."

"Why don't you, then?"

She turned to the bookshelves and pulled out another book, entitled *Necromancy.*

"Unlike me, they might actually care what you have to say."

CHAPTER 15

I stormed up the stairs and through the empty shop, not caring if Kelly stayed down in the basement by herself. If she was so fascinated with all that mystical mumbo-jumbo, she could have it. I wanted no part of this house or that lifestyle—Madame Zelda I was not.

When I reached the front door, I wrenched it open and stepped out on the porch, in a hurry to get back to the main house and pack my things. A dark figure moved from the shadows, and my heart skipped a beat.

"Joe! What are you doing out here?" I could've killed him for scaring me like that, but I was so relieved to see him it didn't matter.

He moved toward the front steps as if I hadn't spoken. The overhead porch light caught him, and I saw his face, dark as a thundercloud. He was carrying his overnight bag.

"Joe! Where are you going?"

He paused, turning. The look he gave me was coldly furious, sending a shaft of icy fear into my stomach.

"What is it now, Nicki? More lies? More bullshit?"

His voice was so harsh, so raw—the tone stunned me so much I could hardly focus on what he was saying. "What? What are you talking about? What's wrong?" I took a few steps toward him, not even realizing I'd moved until he swung away from me and went the rest of the way down the steps.

"I should've known better than to get involved with a girl like you," he said bitterly, shocking me to stillness. "You warned me, and boy, were you ever right." He stopped in the driveway, giving me a tight, sarcastic smile. "Ghouls just wanna have fun, right? Guess that's the biggest difference between you and Kelly."

A punch to the stomach couldn't possibly have hurt more. The wood of the porch rail beneath my hand was all that kept me upright. That, and my immediate flare of rage.

"What the hell kind of thing is that to say?" I leaned all my weight on the porch railing. "What are you talking about?"

"I saw you kissing him!" Joe roared. "Don't act like it didn't happen!"

Dumbfounded, I yelled right back. "Kissing who?"

"Your ghost-busting goth boy!" Joe was furious. "In the kitchen, just now!"

"I'm not a goth," Spider said, stepping out the front door, "and I ain't a boy either. Or do we need to go another round to prove it?" He reached up and swiped a knuckle across his mouth, leaving a dark streak at one corner. Blood.

I had to be in the middle of a bad dream. Spider was glaring at Joe, and Joe was glaring at him, and then they were both glaring at me.

Spider shook his head. "I tried to tell him it wasn't my idea, Nicki. I just came back to get my pendulum, but when a pretty girl throws herself at me the way you did . . ." He shrugged. "I'm only human."

A cold chill went down my spine. He *was* human, wasn't he?

"I never kissed you," I gasped. "Why would you lie about something like that?"

"I saw you, not two minutes ago!" Joe roared again. A dog started barking in the distance—the entire neighborhood was probably awake by now. "I walked in the kitchen and caught you red-handed." The porch light showed me an ugly sneer. It looked out of place on Joe's face. "You looked me right in the eye before you ran out the door."

"You kissed Spider?" Kelly's voice came from behind me as she stepped from the door of the floral shop.

"No!" I snapped. "I didn't kiss anybody. It wasn't me."

It wasn't me. And with a mental click another piece of the puzzle snapped into place.

Psycho Barbie. She'd turned herself into me back in the ladies' room of Forest Lawn Mortuary, wearing that Mark Bouwer dress and tempting me with fame, fortune, and fashion designers. If she wanted to make my life a living hell, this was a great way to do it.

"It wasn't me!" I repeated, loudly. "It was her—the

ghost I was telling you about. Keith Morgan's girlfriend."

The look Joe sent me was withering, and my heart sank. "It's a little late to play the ghost card, Nicki." He flicked a contemptuous gaze over Spider. "I'm not coming to your rescue anymore. You've got yourself a new boy toy now."

And then he turned and walked out of the glow of the porch light and into the darkness.

"Joe!" Kelly brushed past me. "Where are you going?"

No answer, just the crunch of gravel beneath his feet, getting fainter as I listened.

"What's going on?" Kelly shot Spider and me both a bewildered look. She saw the blood on Spider's lip. "You're hurt!"

"It's nothing," Spider said. He gave me a sour glance, as if I were somehow to blame for everything "A major misunderstanding, that's all."

I couldn't take it. Tears threatened, and I fled before they could spill. I wanted to run after Joe, but pride wouldn't let me—he'd said some really ugly things.

And he hadn't believed me.

Into the house, up the stairs, down the hall, past the shadowed corners that would've frightened me ten minutes ago, to the room I'd chosen earlier in the day. I flipped on the light and slammed the door behind me, sagging against it.

"I warned you," Psycho Barbie said. She was lying in the middle of my bed, back against the pillows.

Or rather *I* was laying in the middle of my bed, back against the pillows.

The person laying there was my exact twin, and she sure as hell wasn't Kelly.

"Leave me alone!" I shrieked, completely out of patience. "Get out of my room! Get out of my life!" If I'd had anything in my hands I would've thrown it at her.

"Your eyeliner is running," she said spitefully. "You look like a raccoon."

I couldn't help it—I threw myself at her, landing belly down on the bed, a face full of pillows. She wasn't there, of course. Her mocking laughter came from behind me now.

"Stupid girl. Like taking candy from a baby."

I flopped over on the bed, propping myself on my elbows.

Psycho Barbie morphed back into looking like herself, her "cold blond bitch" exterior a better fit than mine would ever be.

I took a moment to get my anger under control. My heart was tripping double time, and that wasn't good. I wasn't going to let her win by giving me a heart attack.

"My mascara may be running, but your crow's-feet are showing," I returned spitefully. "No time for a touch-up with the plastic surgeon before you died?" If I couldn't hurt her physically, I'd use the only method at my disposal.

Her vanity.

By the narrowing of her eyes, it was apparent Barbie didn't like that method.

Score one for Styx.

"And those shoes are so last year," I lied. "Emilio Pucci is the new Jimmy Choo. Stilettos are for whores and paid escorts." I gave her a tight smile, feeling better already. "Oh, wait—that's what you are, aren't you? A paid escort?" I sat up, facing her. "Or *were*. You're dead now, remember?"

Normally I'd never be so mean, but she'd just cost me the best boyfriend I ever had.

I hated her.

"You're just pissed because your boyfriend dumped you," I said viciously. "In the end, he chose his wife over you, and you just can't stand it, can you?" I was past caring if my words hurt. Dead or alive, Psycho Barbie was a first-rate bitch, and I had no power over her except my words.

"Keith Morgan was never going to marry you—you're an icicle, an expensive piece of arm candy, that's all. Why don't you go away and leave me alone?"

Her face twisted with rage. She opened her mouth to spit forth some venom of her own, then paused, staring at a point behind me.

I turned, and saw us both reflected in a mirror above the dresser.

There I was, dark hair and blue jacket, vivid pink in my hair and streaks of black beneath my eyes; and there was Barbie, blond hair coiled in an updo, makeup flawlessly applied.

"That's not true," she whispered, distracted by her own reflection. "He loved me. And now I'll always be young, I'll always be beautiful."

And with a splintered crack, the mirror shattered.

I flinched, expecting glass to fly, but the frame held. The once beautiful antique mirror now looked like a glass crazy quilt. Open-mouthed, I looked from it to Barbie, and what I saw in her face *really* scared me.

Before I had time to say a word, my Louis Vuitton overnight bag flew across the room, hitting the wall with a loud *thud.* "Dammit!" The suddenness of it shocked me, but I was still more angry than frightened. It fell open on the floor, spilling its contents all over the rose-patterned rug. I'd chosen the "Scarlett O'Hara" room for its deep crimson walls and cool antique four-poster bed, but I would've seen red anyway. My cosmetics bag was open, mascara and lipstick scattered atop the jumbled clothes I'd packed so carefully back home, shampoo already seeping onto my favorite pair of jeans.

I didn't dare move, though, unsure of what might happen next. "Hey!" A peasant blouse hit me in the face, while my jeans flew into a far corner as if they'd been wadded up and thrown. The bottle of shampoo just missed my head.

"Stop!" I covered my head with my hands, cowering as a heeled sandal flew past my ear. I slid off the other side of the bed and crouched there, waiting for things to stop flying.

Then the room itself began to vibrate.

"Stop!" I shouted again.

A picture fell off the wall. It hit the floor in a tinkle of glass, followed by the picture on the opposite wall, which was bigger. All bravado flew out the window when the heavy antique dresser began to vibrate, rattling the beautiful porcelain pitcher and bowl that graced the top.

Surely someone would hear the commotion and come running—but then I remembered. I'd left everyone outside when I ran up the stairs.

I stood up, ready to bolt, but on impulse, I snatched up the pitcher.

"My Master says I have to give you a choice," Barbie hissed, taking a step toward me.

I froze, pitcher in hand.

She was practically snarling with rage, and for the first time, true fear crept in. "Choose to serve him and I'll leave you alone. Choose the life of a do-gooding doctor's wife, and he'll take your sister instead." Her eyes burned into mine, neck corded with the effort of rational speech. "It's up to you."

With a sound like the sharp crackle of electricity, Psycho Barbie vanished. But the smell of ozone lingered, stinking up the air.

It was a good ten minutes before I could pull myself together enough to pick my things up off the floor. I spent it slumped on the bed, at first trying not to cry and then giving in to tears completely. The rose-patterned pillowcase now had streaks of mascara and smears of lipstick on it, but Odessa would just have to get over it.

This was bad. This was really bad.

Joe thought I'd kissed Spider, and even if I ran after him and begged him to believe me, I couldn't explain the truth to him now even if I wanted to.

Which I wasn't sure I even wanted to, because he thought I was a slut.

But of course I wanted to, because I loved him. And I'd only just realized it and I hadn't had a chance to tell him yet. So he didn't know I loved him because I'd never told him, which probably made it a lot easier for him to believe I was a slut.

I rolled onto my back and stared at the ceiling.

But if I told Joe the truth now, then Sammy would go after Kelly, who was all too eager to be seduced by the dark side. She didn't stand a chance against a guy like Sammy—sexy, charming, with an edge of wildness that made you wanna see how deep it ran.

I already knew it ran straight to the depths of Hell. And because of that, hot as he was, I was pretty sure I didn't want the Prince of Darkness to be my sister's boyfriend.

But I didn't want him to be *my* boyfriend either.

"Shit," I sighed, scrubbing my face with my hands. I sat up, surveying the destruction in the room. A pair of my undies was lying on the floor right by the bed, and I snatched them up, still crying. A tube of lipstick rolled off and under the bed.

"Shit, shit, shit."

I bent to pick up the lipstick, but didn't see it, so I got down on my knees and lifted the dust ruffle.

And nearly had a heart attack.

"Holy—" I jerked back, scrambling to my feet. "What are you doing under there?"

Perfect. Just perfect. There was a little blond girl lying under my bed, head on her arm, like she'd hidden there a thousand times.

"You said a bad word," the little girl said, her voice coming from behind me now. "Lots of times."

I turned around, and there was she was, standing by the dresser. She looked about seven, blond hair in braids, bare toes peeping beneath the hem of a flannel nightgown.

I could see right through her.

Not past her. Through her—the dresser drawer pulls shone a dull gold behind her back, the top of the bureau level with her head.

"Why are you crying?" she asked. Her braids were mussed and tied with strips of blue ribbon.

My mouth went dry, my throat tight. Such a pretty little girl, so sweet, so young . . . too young to die.

I shook my head, lifted my chin. "It doesn't matter," I said, trying to smooth out my features. After the little pity party I'd just had, I probably scared her more than she scared me.

She looked at me solemnly, as though expecting a scolding. "Are you a lightskirt?"

"A what?"

"Chloe says lightskirts paint their faces and dress all fancy. You have all kinds of paint on your face, and pink stuff in your hair."

I was pretty sure I'd just been insulted, but I was too drained to care. What had happened to me today wasn't this poor little spirit's fault, and I wasn't going to take it out on her. My earlier anger had been washed away with tears.

"Who's Chloe?" I asked, swiping my damp cheeks with the undies I still clutched in one hand.

"Chloe sleeps in my room."

A maid, no doubt, maybe a nanny. Long dead, either way.

Careful to make no sudden moves, I squatted so the little girl and I were at eye level. "My name is Nicki. What's yours?"

"Sarah," she said, eyes cautious. "Sarah Montgomery." She paused, clasping both hands in front of her. "Have you seen my brother?"

Montgomery. I was pretty sure I'd heard that name earlier in the day, when Spider mentioned the man who'd built the house. The sea captain who'd come home to find his family dead of yellow fever.

"I haven't seen him," I answered truthfully. *And I hope I don't.*

"He was supposed to meet me here," Sarah said. "I've been waiting and waiting, but he never comes. Do you think he's forgotten?" An anxious look crossed her face. "Do you think he's lost? He got lost once at the market. Mama was very cross."

"I'm sure he's fine," I soothed, though I wasn't sure of anything. "You know how boys are. They get distracted easily. He probably found a—" I cast around in my mind for something a nineteenth-century boy would do, but the only image that came to mind was Huck Finn. "—a new place to go fishing or something."

Sarah gave me a shy smile, as though relieved by the explanation. "Old Cletus used to take him fishing. Johnny says Old Cletus knows all the good fishing spots."

"Well there ya go, then." I was happy to have that settled. I didn't wanna be the one to tell a little girl ghost that everyone she ever knew was long dead.

But if I didn't, who would? Sarah Montgomery had been waiting a long time for something that was never gonna happen.

Damn, damn, and double damn.

"That's a very pretty nightgown, Sarah." This might take some easing into. "Have you been sick?"

She looked down at herself and shrugged. "I was sick yesterday, but I feel better now. Mama never came to brush my hair or help me get dressed. Do you think she's fishing, too?" A giggle escaped the little girl, quickly stilled behind a hand. "No, that's silly. Mama doesn't like to fish."

This was gonna be hard. "Was your brother sick?"

Her smile vanished. "Yes, but Mama said he'd get better. She said he'd come play with me as soon as I could get out of bed." Sarah frowned, thoughtful. "So the next morning I got out of bed, but everyone was gone."

No, they'd probably still been here, grieving the beautiful little girl who'd died in her sleep. Or perhaps they'd all been stricken with yellow fever by then, unable to care for her, never knowing that Sarah was already gone. In a way, I hoped that was the case—she was a heartbreaker, this one.

"Sarah, would you like to see your brother and your mama again?"

Her face brightened. "You *do* know where they are! I was hoping you did—you look like the other one, the lady who knew things—but I can't find her anymore."

"The lady who knew things?"

"She was nice, even talked to me sometimes, but she couldn't see or hear me when I tried to answer," Sarah said. "You can." She took a few steps toward me, her tiny form a faded veil I could see right through. "Where's my mama?"

Without thinking, I reached out a hand, but stopped before I touched her, losing my nerve.

"Your mama is in a good place," I murmured. "She's waiting for you, and she can't wait to see you."

Sarah made a noise of frustration. "But where *is* she? Why doesn't she come get me?"

I smiled, giving a shrug. "Because you have to go to her. You have to be a brave, big girl, and go to her."

Solemn blue eyes, clear as water and almost as transparent, regarded me intently.

"Will you go with me?"

My heart skipped a beat, but I kept a smile on my face.

"I can't. I've already been there once, but I had to come back."

Sarah's face fell. I could see she was about to cry. She was seven years old, eight at best. "Where do I go?"

"You have to go into the Light." It was the only answer I could give her. "Have you ever seen the Light, Sarah? It's very beautiful, a bright white light, sparkling like the sun, only bigger. Your whole family is there, in the Light, waiting for you."

I watched myriad expressions flit across her face—dismay, disbelief, fear. "I won't go without Johnny." She turned her face away, lashes sweeping down to cover her eyes.

Then she was fading, until all I could see was the pale blond of her braids, and then nothing. Except her voice.

"He promised he'd meet me here—he *promised.* I won't leave without Johnny."

CHAPTER 16

I had no choice.

As much as I wanted to cry over Joe, to wallow in my misery, to pack my things, to leave the Blue Dahlia behind and go cry some more, I left my room and went down the hall toward the room Kelly had chosen. I couldn't leave poor little Sarah Montgomery alone to wander around this house for another hundred years, could I? I had to find out if her brother's spirit was still here, and I needed Kelly to do it.

Besides, it took my mind off dark-haired doctors and fair-haired demons. I was neither a slut nor a recruiter for Satan's evil army, and I was gonna "do unto others" if it killed me.

I sure hoped it didn't.

The upstairs hallway was wide and well-lit, hardwood floors gleaming on either side of a carpeted runner. The hall sconces were shaped like flowers, frosted glass tulip bulbs casting a warm glow on the cream-colored walls. The Blue Dahlia really was a beautiful old house.

Shame everything and everybody here was so whacked out.

A shadow moved at the far end of the hallway, where the corridor branched right.

"Kelly?"

No answer, so I walked closer. "Hello?"

When I reached the corner, I felt a chill that raised goose bumps on my arms. Whether they were caused by a drop in temperature or just the good old-fashioned creeps, I had no idea. Before I could lose my nerve, I stuck my head around the corner, but the hallway was empty.

Way to spook yourself out there, Styx.

I backtracked a few steps to the door of Kelly's room and raised my hand to knock.

"There must be some kind of mistake, Joe." Kelly's voice was muffled through the door. "Her room is right down the hall. Go talk to her."

What was Joe doing in Kelly's room? *Did they do this often?*

Eavesdropping shamelessly, I lowered my hand and pressed an ear to the door.

"I've got nothing to say to her," I heard Joe say. He still sounded pissed. "Here's the keys to her car." A faint jingle reached my ears. "As soon as my cab gets here, I'm gone."

Kelly was silent for a moment, then, "I'm really sorry it didn't work out for you and Nicki."

Aw, how sweet.

Not.

I knocked a little harder than I might have a few seconds earlier.

"Who is it?"

"Who do you think it is?" I snipped. "The Ghost of Christmas Past?"

There was a pause, and then Kelly opened the door. Joe was standing with his back to me, glaring out the window into the night. He didn't spare me a glance.

"Sorry to break up the party, Kelly, but I need to talk to you." Not wasting any time, I grabbed her by the hand and pulled her out into the hallway. As I did, I heard a noise behind me, like a sigh, and felt something touch my hair.

Spooked, I turned to look, but there was no one there.

No matter. "There was a little girl ghost in my room," I said to Kelly, whispering. "Her name is Sarah." I didn't care to share the news of my latest ghostly encounter with Joe. He'd probably think I was making it up just to get his attention.

It's too late to play the ghost card, Nicki, he'd said. *I'm not coming to your rescue anymore.*

"Sarah's looking for her brother, Johnny, and she won't go into the Light without him. I need you to look around for Johnny and see if he's here."

Kelly's eyes went wide. For a moment I dared hope that I'd scared her into changing her mind about this spooky old house—that she'd snatch up her suitcase and join me in getting the hell out of there.

"Oh, wow," she breathed.

And I knew we weren't going anywhere.

You girls are bound to each other, two halves of a whole. Peaches's words came back to me, and for the first time actually made some sense. If we were going to send these children into the Light, it looked like we were going to have to work together to do it.

Oy.

"Excuse me," Joe said roughly, shouldering past us. He strode down the hallway toward the stairs. "I'll wait for the cab downstairs."

"Joe." I couldn't help it. It was too hard watching him walk away a second time.

He turned, face like stone. The light from the tulip-shaped bulbs showed the darkness in his eyes all too clearly.

"I didn't kiss Spider." One more shot—I'd take one more shot at fixing things. If I hadn't been all cried out, the waterworks would've started again, so I was glad the well was dry. "Why won't you believe me?"

"Because you seem to make a career out of holding back the truth, Nicki," he said bitterly.

He had me there. Including the truth about my feelings.

"I'm never quite sure where I stand with you, or what's going to happen next," he said. "And I'm tired of trying to read your mind."

It might've been an opening for me to say something dramatic, but I was hardly going to declare my undying love under these circumstances. It would cast a cloud over something that was now crystal clear, at least to me.

"I didn't kiss Spider," I repeated stubbornly. "It wasn't me. You can believe me or not."

"That's the problem, isn't it?" Joe swung his overnight bag over his shoulder, gripping the strap tight with one hand. He shoved his other hand into his pocket. "It's always your way or no way, Nicki. Believe me or don't believe me; accept me as I am or don't accept me at all; don't tell me what to do or what not to do." He shook his head, making a disgusted noise. "There's only so much I can accept in a girlfriend, and you making out with other guys is too much."

I wasn't going to cry—I wasn't. No matter how much it hurt to learn what Joe really thought of me.

"Joe, please don't leave." Kelly's plea surprised me. I'd almost forgotten she was there. "It's late, we're all tired—let's work it out in the morning. Don't go away mad."

Just go away, I thought spitefully, but I didn't mean it, even to myself. I was just angry at him for being so damned stubborn.

Joe quit glaring at me long enough to look at Kelly. His posture softened a little, and I found myself even angrier than before.

Kelly could talk sense to him, but I couldn't?

"I'm scared, Joe." To my complete surprise, Kelly walked to him and laid a hand on his arm. "Something strange is going on in this house, but it's really important for me to stay here tonight. I know you don't understand, but I have my reasons. Please don't leave us here alone."

Well, would you look at that?

Kelly had Joe completely figured out—a nice guy

like him could never refuse a direct appeal for help. I couldn't help but wonder how many times she'd pulled that ploy on him when they were married.

The thought made me wanna throw up. Joe and Kelly had a past that up till then I was willing to ignore, mainly because I'd been so busy dealing in the present. But the past was there, nonetheless. If I dwelled on the particulars, it would drive me crazy.

Joe shot me an angry look, but spoke nicely enough to Kelly. "For you, then. I'll stay for you, but I'm leaving in the morning."

I sucked in my breath and held it. He'd said it to hurt me, and had accomplished that, but no way was I gonna play that game.

"Is there an empty bedroom where I can get some sleep?" He was back to ignoring me now. "You can wake me up if you need me."

Huh. She better hope she didn't need him.

"There's another room at the very end of the hall," Kelly said, "just past the staircase." She pointed him in the right direction, and he swung that way, still ignoring me.

The set of his shoulders as he stalked away was enough to discourage any attempt to call him back, so I let him go, fuming.

"You're scared?" I hissed at Kelly, keeping my voice low. "Since when? You've been dying to do a little ghost-busting, and now you get your wish. Joe has no idea what a sucker he is for batted eyebrows."

Kelly gave me a bland look. "I got him to stay, didn't I?"

I did my best to ignore another stab of jealousy.

"You could've done it yourself if you'd handled him right, Nicki. You need to appreciate what makes Joe tick. He's an honest, straightforward guy, and he expects the same in return."

I bit my lip. "Did he expect you to run off and join the Peace Corps?" A bitchy thing to say, I know, but I couldn't help it. I didn't need Kelly's advice on how to deal with Joe—I knew what kind of man he was.

And if I thought about it too much, I'd start crying again.

Kelly was quiet for a minute. "Let's stop this before one of us says something we'll regret. We have better things to do than fight."

"Like what?"

"Like have a séance," she breathed. "Down in the basement. We'll call up Johnny's spirit and send him and his little sister into the Light."

Oh, crap.

Here we go again.

CHAPTER 17

"No, we're not going to tell Joe. His negative energy could keep Johnny from manifesting." Kelly put three white candles down in the middle of the table; one she'd stolen from the coffee table in the living room, the other two from a shelf on the wall of the basement.

"Manifesting?" Good Lord. "I don't like this, Kelly." I looked around, taking in the brass oil lamps, the purple draperies, the wall of books on the occult. The Blue Dahlia's basement was creepy.

Yet homey in a weird kind of way.

"What are you talking about? This is the perfect spot to hold a séance! I wish Spider was here." She shot me a look. "He'd know more about séances than I do."

I knew what that look meant. "I didn't kiss Spider, dammit! I was with you, down here in the basement, remember?"

"I know." Her tone was noncommittal. She slid the Ouija board aside, making room for the candles.

"What was Joe doing in your room, anyway?" If she wanted to go that route, I could go there, too.

A shrug. "I went after him and talked him into coming inside while he waited for his cab. He said he didn't want to see you, so we went to my room."

"I hope you told him I'd been with you the whole time."

"I tried, but he didn't want to listen. He was convinced he'd seen you kissing Spider."

Kelly wasn't looking at me, and I found her attention to setting up the séance table to be a bit much. She'd already lit the incense burner she'd found on one of the shelves, and was lighting the candles one at a time.

If she was worried about negative energy, she needed to be more worried about the vibes I was putting off.

"Stupid man. Like I'd actually choose a guy like Spider over a guy like him," I muttered angrily.

Kelly straightened. "What's wrong with Spider? I think he's cute."

I rolled my eyes. "There's nothing wrong with Spider, if you like that type, but 'cute' he is not." I was referring to Spider's dubious fascination with spirits, not his looks.

"So you don't want him." Her comment sounded flat to my ears. "He's not good enough for you."

"I want Joe." There. There it was, laid out on the table.

Kelly turned, giving me her full attention for the first time since we'd entered the basement. "You better be careful with Joe's heart, Nicki. Just because I left him doesn't mean I didn't love him."

I somehow managed to keep my mouth shut long enough for her continue.

"I still love him, in fact, but he doesn't love me. He never really did." Her chin quivered, just once. "So you better be careful with him. I don't want to see him hurt."

Time seemed to contract as I stared, focusing on her face, so like my own.

And yet so different.

A clapping began, as though Kelly and I were actors in a play, or a bad soap opera. *The Young and the Restless Meets the Addams Family, perhaps.*

Bewildered, I looked around, and there—in a shadowy corner of the basement—stood Sammy.

"Go away! Leave us alone!" I reached out, without thinking, to grab Kelly's arm, but my hand found thin air. I looked, and though Kelly was there, standing right beside me, I couldn't touch her. I tried again, and my hand passed right through her arm. As I watched, she turned her attention to the bookshelves as though completely unconcerned—or unaware—of what was going on around her.

"Oh, Nicki, this sisterly bonding thing is so entertaining." Sammy stepped into the light, and my breath caught. Unlike the previous times I'd seen him, now Sammy truly looked the part of the Prince of Darkness. Black and red were the colors he'd chosen—a bloodred silk shirt, unbuttoned to provide a glimpse of rock hard abs; black silk dinner jacket and perfectly creased tuxedo trousers. His blond hair was mussed and his eyes were heavy, yet satisfied, as though he'd just come from a great party.

"Don't worry," Sammy said, "she doesn't see us. She's on a different plane." *There was that damned word again.* "She thinks she's choosing a book on table rapping or some such nonsense, while you wait patiently, like a sheep, beside her." He chuckled, giving me a wink. "Fucking with time and dimension is only one of the many perks of my job."

"What do you want?" My knees were shaking and my heart was racing, but I stood my ground. As long as I could see him as an ordinary guy—albeit a very hot, very scary guy—I could deal with him.

Or so I hoped, anyway. *Until he starts trying to poke me with his giant pitchfork.*

Sammy crossed his arms over his chest and cocked his head. What could only be called an evil grin set his bright blue eyes alight.

"Kelly wants her husband back." Sammy sounded delighted at the prospect. "She's a thorn in your side, a rival for Joe's affections, a stubborn little know-it-all." He cocked his head the other way. "I can help you get rid of her."

"I don't want to get rid of her."

"You're such an adorable liar, Nicki." Sammy ran a hand through his blond hair, still grinning. "It's one of the things I particularly like about you."

He dropped his arms, took a few steps toward the table. "Lovely room, isn't it?" He gestured around at the books, the draperies, the Ouija board on its bed of black velvet. "I do so appreciate true followers of the occult—they know just how to decorate in a way that makes me feel right at home. A pentacle or two to balance things out wouldn't hurt," Sammy shrugged, "but as long as they've got the basics."

The day I believed that the Devil cared about feng shui was the day I started wearing denim overalls and high waders to fashion shows in Milan.

"No inverted crucifix, no black robes, no altar. Peaches meant well, but she could never quite bring herself to go completely public about our relationship."

My jaw dropped.

"Oh, come now," Sammy sighed. "Surely you've figured it out by now. Kelly has. You're much more gifted than Peaches was, though. I can only hope you won't be as timid."

"I'm not going to work for you." I glanced at Kelly, but she was still engrossed in her reading. "And you're not getting my sister either." I took a deep breath, squaring my shoulders. "At the risk of sounding completely corny, 'get thee behind me, Satan.'"

"Last chance," Sammy warned, still smiling. He took a step closer, eyes burning with heat. He smelled like passion and rumpled sheets, the salty warmth of mingled juices. "I'll make it worth your while."

Why was he being so persuasive? So seductive?

In a sudden flash of clarity, I accused, "You can't make me do anything I don't want to do, can you?"

His smile turned slightly sour. "An unfortunate condition of my banishment, it seems." He heaved a melodramatic sigh. "I've learned to live with it. After all, corrupting human morals is much more fun than creating an army of robots."

"Corrupt this," I said, and made an unmistakable gesture with my middle finger.

Instead of casting me into a pit of eternal fire, Sammy just laughed. "'Behold me then, me for him, life for life . . . I offer, on me let thine anger fall.'"

"I'm sure Milton would've been gratified to know Satan was such a fan."

"Have it your way, then, Nicki Styx. But don't say I didn't warn you." Sammy shook his head. "You're much stronger than your mother, and much prettier than your sister. We could've been good together."

He bowed low, mockingly, and was gone.

"We'd like to speak to the spirit of Johnny Montgomery," Kelly said. Candlelight flickered on her face, casting shadows on the draperied walls. She hadn't believed me when I told her Sammy popped in for a visit while her head was buried in a book, claiming that since she'd seen or heard nothing, I was just overtired.

I was tired, all right. Tired of arguing. Tired of fighting. Tired of tension and jealousy and stress and spirits popping up to complicate things every time I turned around.

As if they weren't complicated enough already.

She'd insisted we hold hands, but I'd only given her one of mine. The other one I kept in my lap, rubbing my thumb over the silver and marcasite ring Joe had given me for a Halloween present.

It had only been a few days, yet it seemed so long ago. We'd been having so much fun.

"We summon the spirit of Johnny Montgomery," Kelly repeated. "Please speak to us."

Joe had looked good enough to eat that night. I'd done that, and gone back for seconds.

I wanted Joe. I needed Joe. And as soon as I could manage to pry Kelly away from her stupid candles and her stupid books and her stupid ideas about saving lost souls, I was gonna march right into that bedroom at the end of the hallway and make him listen to me, and Devil take the consequences.

I shot a guilty glance toward Kelly. *She* was the consequences, or so it appeared, but what could I do if she wouldn't listen to me? She seemed determined to throw herself into this psychic stuff, and I couldn't babysit her 24/7.

"Johnny Montgomery?" Kelly wasn't giving up. "Are you here? Please speak to us."

How was I supposed to make up with Joe and still keep Kelly safe? Did I even want to keep Kelly safe? She was pretty determined to stick her spiritual neck out.

Kelly sucked in a breath. "He's here," she whispered. "There's a little boy standing by the table. Do you see him?"

"No." I shook my head, but took her word that the little boy's spirit was there. The way her face looked in the candlelight was enough to convince anybody of anything. She looked scared, yet elated.

"Johnny says you have to tell Sarah a story," Kelly said, repeating what the boy said without understanding what he meant. "He says she won't believe you otherwise."

After breathing in sandalwood incense for a good five minutes, listening to Kelly talk to thin air, I wouldn't believe anything I had to say either.

I sighed. "Why doesn't he just tell her himself?" This séance thing was so cheesy. I believed Johnny was there, but what was the problem? He was a ghost, Sarah was a ghost—why didn't he take his little sister by the hand and drag her into the Light?

"He says she can't see or hear him. Nobody could, until now."

Wow. So ghosts couldn't necessarily see each other—how weird. I'd assumed they were all on the same plane.

Plane? Oh man.

"Johnny wants to tell us a story." Kelly's face softened. "That's so sweet," she said (not to me). "Tell me, Johnny."

Then she was quiet, listening.

"Of course we will," Kelly said. "I promise." Her eyes met mine, briefly, then went back to the empty chair. "Nicki will tell Sarah what you said. Then you can both go into the Light."

"Nicki will tell Sarah what?" Being talked about as if you were invisible was a little strange, particularly when you were being talked about by someone who *was* invisible.

"Johnny wants you to remind Sarah of the time he took her fishing," Kelly said. "Sarah got her dress all muddy, and Johnny got a hiding for it. He wasn't supposed to take her down by the river."

"A 'hiding'?"

Kelly shrugged, a little smile tugging at the corner of her mouth. "I think he means a spanking."

"Oh." Good times in the nineteenth century, I suppose.

Something brushed my ankle, and I shrieked like a banshee, grabbing at Kelly, who shrieked, too.

But it was only the cat, the one I'd petted earlier in the courtyard. Unconcerned by our shrieks, the furry little beast leapt up onto the table and lay down, tail twitching in a self-satisfied manner. If I didn't know better, I would have said the cat enjoyed a grand entrance.

"Bad cat," I scolded as soon as I had my breath back. "Get down." I shooed at it halfheartedly. "Get out."

"Her name's Tabby," came a voice. I jumped again, gasping, and there was Sarah, peeking around a chair. She glanced a little fearfully at Kelly until she realized her appearance hadn't registered with anyone but me. "She plays with me sometimes."

"Hello, Sarah," I said.

Kelly straightened, saw where my eyes were trained, and looked there, too.

I'd barely gotten my breath back, but I kept my voice gentle and made an effort to get straight to the point. "Johnny's here, Sarah," I said. "He's come for you."

Her face turned bright with joy. "Where is he?" she cried, grabbing her nightgown with both hands. She began bobbing with excitement, craning her neck to look behind me.

"He's here, Sarah. You just can't see him."

Her face fell.

My heart fluttered in sympathy. "But my sister can see him." I gestured toward Kelly, hoping to restore Sarah's smile.

But the little girl frowned at both of us, distrustful.

"How can she see Johnny if he's not here? She can't even see *me* when I'm standing right in front of her." Sarah was deeply disappointed, becoming more downcast by the second. She ignored Kelly and took one last look at the empty space behind me, as though her brother might be hiding there, then stared at the floor.

"Sarah doesn't believe you can see Johnny," I murmured to Kelly, fearful of saying anything to frighten Sarah away.

"He's about ten years old, with brown hair and lots of freckles," Kelly said. "And he says he called you Sissy."

Sarah's head lifted. Her lower lip trembled.

"Johnny wants to go into the Light, but he doesn't want to leave you here alone, Sarah," Kelly said. She was facing the empty chair, not knowing exactly where to look.

Sarah watched her, still mistrustful. "No!" The little girl snatched up one of her braids and began stroking it beneath her fingers, unconsciously soothing herself. "I don't believe you! Outside this house it's dark, and it's scary. I'll wait for Johnny. He'll come."

"We can prove Johnny's here, Sarah," I said. "You can't see him, but he's here."

"*Why* can't I see him?" Sarah burst into tears, her question turning into a wail of grief and frustration. It didn't last long, though, subsiding into sniffles. She swiped at damp cheeks with dirty hands, leaving smudges.

"Don't do it, little goth girl." A whisper raised the hair on my arms.

"Did you hear that?"

Kelly looked at me, puzzled. "Hear what?"

"These children belong to my Master," Psycho Barbie whispered, *"and he wants them."*

Ah. Finally, the light of comprehension dawned. Sammy had told Kelly he wanted something from this house, but it wasn't *something*—it was *someone*. Two little someones, apparently.

"Keith Morgan's girlfriend is here, Kelly."

"Where?" She looked around, peering into the dark corners, tightening her grip on my hand.

"Obey his wishes, or pay the consequences."

"Go to hell," I said boldly, glancing around the room.

"Nicki!" Kelly was obviously shocked that I'd say a bad word in front of children, ghostly or not.

I looked at her, thoroughly exasperated and more than a little creeped out. The darkness in the basement made it impossible to see into the corners, where Psycho Barbie and her master were probably hiding.

So did I shut up, or did I do my best to send Sarah and her brother into the Light?

I took one more look at those mussed pigtails and those smudged cheeks, and the answer was clear.

"Sarah, do you remember the time Johnny took you fishing?" I looked at Kelly, hoping she'd fill in the details. "You got your dress all muddy, and Johnny got in trouble for taking you."

Sarah dropped her head, wiping her nose with the back of her hand. She nodded, remembering. "Mama was mad. She said Johnny should know better . . . everybody knows the air's bad down by the river," she said softly, to no one in particular. The woebegone expression on her face touched my heart. "But Johnny and I had fun while we were there." Her cornflower blue eyes met mine, questioning. "How did you know that?"

I nodded toward Kelly. "Because Johnny told my sister."

"He teased you with a worm," Kelly said. "And then he pretended to swallow it."

Sarah smiled, and it was like the sun coming out. "He said it felt all squirmy inside," a girlish giggle, "but he was foolin' me. He had it in his hand the whole time. I didn't want Johnny to get in trouble—I told Mama it wasn't his fault, that I made him take me fishing." Her cheerfulness faded. "But he got a hiding anyway, and I didn't."

"Johnny says you can make it all better if you come into the Light with him," Kelly said softly. "He promised your mama he'd look after you. He doesn't want to leave you here alone."

Sarah began to cry again, silently, fat tears sliding down her cheeks. She was so young—so innocent. So sad.

"You don't have to be afraid, Sarah. The Light is a wonderful place, where everybody's happy, all the time." I spoke the words with the confidence of one who'd been there. "The brightness is caused by love, by happiness." *How to explain something so unexplainable to a frightened child?* "Your mama won't be mad at either of you. She'll be so happy to see you—you and Johnny both. You can be together again in a place where nobody's mad at anybody, I promise."

"Johnny sees it." Kelly was staring at a spot where I supposed Johnny was standing. There was a note of awe in her voice. "He sees the Light."

I looked only at Sarah, and she looked only at me.

Keeping my voice soft, I asked, "Do you see it, Sarah?"

Sarah blinked, and another fat tear slid down her cheek. "I'm afraid."

I smiled at her, wishing I could do more, like give her a hug. "No need to be afraid. Just turn your head and look."

And finally, she did.

An instant smile transformed her face. "I see Mama," she whispered, "and there's Johnny!" Sarah stood up straight, lifting her hand as if returning a wave, and then she was gone.

Just . . . gone.

The silence was profound, as though the entire house was holding its breath. My heartbeat thudded in my ears.

"He's gone," Kelly breathed. "Johnny's gone."

"So is Sarah," I said, relieved.

Chalk one up for the freaks of the world. Long may their freak flags wave.

CHAPTER 18

"We did it!" For the first time ever, Kelly gave me a spontaneous hug.

I returned it, but kept it brief. I wanted to get out of that damn basement before all hell broke loose.

"Okay, okay, we did it. Now let's blow out the candles and get out of here."

"I have to end the séance first," Kelly said.

"Um, excuse me, but in case you haven't noticed, it's over." I rose from my chair.

"Hardly," said Psycho Barbie, emerging from the shadows. "Your stupid sister has given me an opportunity. I'd be a fool not to take it."

The cat who'd been lying on the table jumped up with a hiss.

"Good kitty," I said weakly, certain my heart would never bear the strain. "Sic her."

The cowardly beast jumped down off the table and slunk away.

"What—" Kelly took one look at my face and shut up, mid-sentence. At least I thought that's what happened, until I realized that not only was Kelly not talking, she wasn't moving.

Fucking with time and dimension is only one of the many perks of my job. Sammy's comment popped into my head, and sent a chill down my spine.

"You were warned, little goth girl," Barbie said spitefully. "You think you're so cute and stylish, don't you, with that pink hair and that 'out there' style." I didn't like the way she was smirking at me. "You look like an idiot. A reject from an old eighties video." Then she laughed, a tinkly, nasty laugh that made the back of my neck prickle. "Is that a flock of sea gulls in your hair or did you just forget to brush it?"

I opened my mouth with a scathing retort, but managed only, "Get away from us."

"I think not. Your sister's little ritual has made me stronger," she said. "This is going to be fun."

And while I watched, Psycho Barbie's face became mine. Her perfectly coiffed blond hair became dark, pink-streaked, and spiky. Her chic black dress became a short denim jacket over a ruffled poet shirt, her pearls a funky necklace I'd picked up at a garage sale last year.

"What kind of thing is that to say, Nicki?" Kelly's voice startled me.

I turned to answer, but she wasn't looking at me—she was looking at Barbie. "Your hair doesn't look so hot at the moment either."

Oh, shit. *Kelly thinks Barbie is me.*

"At least I have a sense of style," Barbie said snottily, using *my* voice. "You look as drab as a potato farmer. Always do. They make other shoes besides Birkenstocks, you know."

Kelly's chin went up. "What's your problem?"

I tried to tell her, but it was no use—my mouth was moving but nothing came out. When I tried to grab Kelly's shoulder, my hand went right through her.

With a rising sense of horror, I realized that I'd become like the ghosts who came to me for help—nobody could see or hear me.

"My problem?" The plastic surgery queen was enjoying herself, I could tell. "*You're* my problem. Everything was fine until you showed up." Barbie clasped her hands theatrically in front of her and said mockingly, "Oooh, poor me, I've been in a car accident." Her fake falsetto was evidently supposed to mimic Kelly's voice. "Take care of me, Nicki; save me, Joe! My mommy's dead. Boo-hoo, I want my mommy."

Kelly's gasp tore my heart.

"You think I don't know what you're up to, Kelly?" The horrible creature who looked just like me dropped the mocking falsetto, but kept talking. "You came to Atlanta hoping Joe would take you back, didn't you?" It smiled an ugly smile. "You must've been royally pissed when you found out we'd been sleeping together. He said I was better than you, by the way."

"Bitch," Kelly said. Tears glittered in her eyes, but didn't fall.

Barbie/Nicki gave a careless shrug. "The truth hurts." She trailed a finger over the Ouija board, still on the table. "And here's another truth for you. Joe told me he was still married to my sister, but I didn't care. I slept with him anyway. Seduced him, in fact. But after what happened tonight, I'm sick of him and his goody-goody ways. You can have him back—he's all yours." Slyly, Barbie added, "Hope you don't mind sloppy seconds."

The door at the top of the stairs creaked open, and there stood Joe, silhouetted in the light that spilled in from the florist shop.

"That's what I am to you?" The raw hurt in his voice bit like a knife into my heart. I tried to speak but it was useless and he didn't see me. He saw only the creature he *thought* was me.

Then the creature laughed, and I knew it had won.

"You knew what I was like when we started, Joe. I warned you, that day in the coffee shop," it said.

That's right—I had warned him.

Are you trying to tell me you'll break my heart? he'd asked.

You can keep your heart, I'd answered flippantly. *It's not the part of your anatomy I'm interested in.*

But that was before I knew what real love meant.

Joe paused at the top of the stairs, as though he had something else to say.

Or maybe he just wanted me to take one more long, last look at something I'd never have again.

Then the door slammed shut, creating a draft that almost blew out the candles.

Kelly took off up the stairs, swearing at me over her shoulder as she brushed past. "Dammit, Nicki. What the hell is wrong with you?"

And then I was alone in the basement with Psycho Barbie, candlelight flickering on the madness in her eyes.

Or maybe it was just a reflection of the tears in mine.

"End the séance," came a whisper. *"End the séance, Nicki."*

I looked around wildly, wondering who else was in the basement.

"She's just a spirit, she has no substance. Send her away."

It was a woman's voice, raspy and low. I didn't recognize it.

"You're stronger than she is, even with the help of her master. Send her away."

The basement was dark, and I saw no one except Psycho Barbie, who morphed before my eyes back into her sleek blond self. The smirk on her perfectly made-up face made me itch to slap her.

"Focus, Nicki, focus. Speak the words and end the séance," came the raspy whisper.

The words? What words?

Hell, I'd make something up.

I cleared my throat, thrilled to find my voice working again. "Go away. The séance is over."

Psycho Barbie laughed again, mockingly.

"Your anger makes her stronger, Nicki. She's feeding on it."

I ceased to care who or where the whispers were coming from. Somebody wanted to help me, and I could use all the help I could get.

Doing my best to get a grip, I said shakily to Barbie, "I . . . I command you to leave." Truly improvising, I added, "I banish thee!" Who knows? Biblical language always seemed to work in horror movies.

Psycho Barbie's laughter faded. The flash of hatred in her eyes could've sparked a forest fire.

Emboldened, I went on. "I banish thee, O Spirit, and command you to go."

"In peace," came a whisper from the shadows.

"In peace," I added hastily. "I banish thee, O Spirit, and command you to go in peace."

Barbie's face got even uglier.

"May the peace of the Light be upon you." I was babbling now, grasping at vague memories of exorcist movies. "And the Force be with you."

The table between us started to shake, causing the candles to flicker.

"In the name of the Being Behind the Light"—I wasn't going to be hypocritical enough to claim I knew exactly who—or what—the Being was—I command you to go in peace." Besides, who knew what would happen if I chose the wrong name?

Psycho Barbie opened her mouth and hissed at me like the cobra she was.

At least I thought the noise came from her, until the stupid tabby cat leapt up onto the table again. I was ready to strangle it until I realized it was hissing at Psycho Barbie, facing her down just like I was.

Good kitty. Sic her.

Barbie didn't like the cat. Her attention shifted from me to it, eyes slitted with rage.

My heart was pounding, and I willed it to slow down, welcoming the brief opportunity to get my fear and anger under control. If Barbie was feeding on my negative emotions, I needed to close the buffet.

"Go," I said, as calmly as I could. "Go back to wherever

you came from, and stay there. You don't belong here."

"That's what they told me at the country club," Barbie said nastily.

Surprisingly, I felt a pang of pity. She must've lived a very isolated life—the rich man's mistress, kept in the shadows while her lover lived his life among society's elite. A status symbol to the men, scorned and despised by the women.

"That must've hurt your feelings."

"Like you care," she scoffed, but her voice lacked its usual edge of spitefulness.

Encouraged, I tried even harder to let go of my anger. I needed to generate good feelings, not bad ones. Knowing Psycho Barbie's biggest weakness was her vanity, I decided once again to use it. "Those people were just jealous because you're so beautiful."

Her face changed, some of the anger leaving it. "I am beautiful, aren't I?"

"You had everything those rich married women wanted," I went on. "Young, pretty, a wealthy boyfriend . . . all the perks of the good life without the responsibilities of kids and a mortgage." I'd seen enough HBO movies to improvise. "Pure jealousy, that's all."

"Those rich bitches were no better than me," Barbie said. "What made them think they were? Just because they were married didn't make them saints. They whored themselves for money, just like me." Her cynicism held a note of pain.

"Just jealous," I repeated. I had no doubt the married women of Buckhead Country Club viewed her as a threat. "But you don't have to worry about those women anymore. You don't even have to think about them."

Her image flickered, wavered like the candle flame.

The cat shifted into a sitting position, allowing its fur to settle. It stared intently at Barbie, tail twitching.

"You must be tired," I said to the wavering image. *I sure as hell was.*

"Speak the words, and send her away," came a whisper from the shadows. *"Now, while she's weak."*

As firmly as I could, I ordered, "Go in peace." For good measure, I added, "Get some beauty sleep."

Barbie looked confused, uncertain. And then lo and behold, she faded away until there was nothing left of her except the faint smell of Chanel No. 5.

I slumped in relief, grabbing the edge of the table for support. The black velvet tablecloth was soft, well-worn.

A small *mew* came from the cat. She rubbed herself against my arm, softer than any velvet, blessedly warm and alive.

"Good kitty," I said weakly. "Good kitty."

Then I looked around the basement for the source of the helpful whispers. "Hello?" The shadows were too dark. "Is anyone here?"

Silence met my questions. Scooping up my new best friend, I carried the cat up the stairs to the light switch and flipped it on.

The basement was empty. Nervously, I went down again, still carrying the cat, and blew out the candles. One last look around revealed nothing but books and purple draperies, and then I was *so* outta there.

CHAPTER 19

Once outside, I put the cat down and let her run off into the night. Then I scooted across the front porch and let myself into the Blue Dahlia, unsure of what to do next.

Find Joe? Find Kelly? And tell them what, exactly?

I dashed away tears as I ran up the main stairs, glad all the lights were on. The door to the bedroom at the end of the hall was closed, but I doubted Joe was in there. I doubted he was still in the house at all.

He hated me now, and so did Kelly.

More tears threatened as I stood in the hallway, wavering. Kelly I could handle, somehow. I was pretty sure I'd be able convince her that Psycho Barbie had said those horrible things, not me. But if I somehow managed to make Joe believe I hadn't said or done the things he thought I had, I'd piss off the Devil himself, and he'd go after Kelly.

Plus, I'd be breaking Kelly's heart.

Which I'd apparently been breaking for some time now.

But even if I didn't care about breaking Kelly's heart—she'd thrown Joe away first, after all—I'd be putting her in danger by pissing off Sammy, who wanted me to choose him.

Choose him, save her. Choose her, lose him.

Life sucked.

Then the door at the end of the hallway opened.

Without thinking, I ducked into my room, not wanting anyone to see a crybaby idiot standing in the middle of the hall.

"You don't have to take orders from Nicki," Joe was saying to Kelly. "You're a grown woman. You can do what you want."

Shamelessly, I stopped to listen, door still half open.

"Just because Nicki knows how to work it doesn't mean she knows everything."

How to "work it"?

"She's hot, she's wild, she's enough to turn any guy's head. But Nicki's high maintenance. You've got depth of character, Kelly, real substance."

High maintenance?

"Don't underestimate yourself. Nicki's the kind of girl most guys just have fun with, but you're the kind of girl they marry."

The sick feeling in the pit of my stomach made me wish I could turn back time to earlier that evening, when I naively thought Joe liked me just the way I was.

I couldn't believe he was talking about me like this.

How could I have been so stupid?

I threw open the door, letting it hit the wall with a bang. "The kind of girl you have fun with?" My anger flared, white-hot. I'd been agonizing over *them* while they chatted over my lack of marriageable qualities?

My gaze flicked scornfully past them to the open door of Joe's room. That was twice now I'd caught him and Kelly behind closed doors. An ugly suspicion made me say things even uglier. "Now I see why you were so quick to believe I'd cheated on you with Spider. Breaking up with me clears the way for you to get back with Kelly, doesn't it?"

Joe's face reddened, and Kelly had the nerve to look shocked.

"Funny you should mention Spider," Joe said. He was glaring at me, ignoring my question and its implication. "Kelly and I were just discussing him, and how she'd like to get to know him better."

"That's not what I heard," I said sarcastically. "Maybe we 'high maintenance' types are hard of hearing."

"You *are* high maintenance," Joe ground out.

"And you're a liar," I shouted. "Fuck you, Joe!"

And in the time-honored way of pissed-off women everywhere, I marched into my room and slammed the door as hard as I could, putting the seal on my relationship with Joe.

It was better this way. Wasn't it?

I heard footsteps, loud and heavy, go past my door. A few moments later another door slammed somewhere downstairs. The front door, maybe.

I was so worked up that it took a moment to realize I wasn't alone.

Sitting on my bed, ankles primly crossed, gloved

hands in her lap, was my dead grandmother, Bijou Boudreaux.

"*Now* you show up?" I swiped at my cheeks, angry at the tears, angry at the world, angry at the weirdness that was my *life*. "Now is not a good time."

Bijou gave me a regretful smile. "There will never be a better one, dear. I'm truly sorry to visit while you're upset, but it's time for you to learn the truth." The ostrich plume on her black hat bobbed as she tilted her head.

It was on the tip of my tongue to say something extremely disrespectful of my elders and totally unsuitable for little old ladies to hear. My head hurt, my heart was broken, and I knew my face was a wreck.

But I looked at Bijou's expectant expression and thought about her waiting here, alone in this house, for God knows how long until her story was told.

So I sagged back and let my shoulders hit the wall, sliding down until my butt hit the floor. "Let's hear it."

"Thank you, dear." Bijou acknowledged my exquisite manners with a gracious wave of an ostrich plume. She was wearing a black cocktail dress, just as she had at the funeral, a study in formal mourning right down to her black silk gloves. A big jet pin, black and silver, pinned her scarf to one shoulder.

I let my head fall back, staring at the ceiling while I blinked back tears, trying not to think about what had just happened. The ceiling had a faint crack, like a spiderweb, near the light fixture.

Bijou patted the bed with a black-gloved hand, inviting me to sit next to her.

I knew I was being bitchy, but I couldn't seem to help myself. "I'm fine right here, thanks."

Bijou actually smiled, the first one I'd seen yet. "You remind me so much of your mama. Nobody could tell her what to do either."

"My mother's name was Emily Styx," I said. "And she was a sweetheart, thank you very much."

The old woman's smile faded. "Were you happy, Nicki? Did Emily Styx hug you and tell you how special you were? Did she tuck you in at night and bake cookies with you and take care of you when you were sick?"

A lump rose in my throat. She'd done that, and more.

"Did she love you even when you did things you shouldn't have done, and did she forgive you when you said things you shouldn't have said?"

Memories of my teenage years came flooding back. All that angst I tried to disguise under layers of black clothing and black eyeliner, all that youthful arrogance, all that gloomy "coolness." I was so goth I used to dot my i's with frowny faces.

I don't know how either of my parents put up with it.

"Did she stick by you in bad times, and laugh with you when times were good?"

I swiped angrily at a tear that slid down my cheek. "Of course she did. What's that got to do with anything?"

Bijou shifted her ample behind on the bed, refolding her hands in her lap. "You were the lucky one, Nicki. Kelly didn't have any of that."

Bitterness rose in my throat. "So what if I had a happy childhood and Kelly didn't? Is that my fault?"

I was tired of feeling guilty for things I had nothing to do with.

"Poor Kelly," I said mockingly. "Poor little foster child. Nobody loved her, nobody hugged her . . . blah blah blah." My head was pounding, my heart torn in two, and nobody seemed to care about *that*, now did they? "I've tried to be a good sister to her, but she's got her own agenda."

Bijou said nothing, and somehow that was worse than if she had. The expression on her face was one of pity, but it wasn't for Kelly, it was for me.

I *so* did not need anyone's pity.

"How about we just cut to the chase, hm? Why don't you just tell me what Kelly and I are doing here, and why?" I crossed my legs, Indian style, and leaned forward, elbows on my knees. "What's with the cat and mouse? What the hell is going *on*?"

Bijou opened her mouth, then closed it again. I waited, impatient, certain that if she started out with "Once upon a time . . . " I'd scream.

"I had to see for myself which one of you girls was the strongest," Bijou said. "I had to see how you were with each other, and how you were with this house. I had to see how well you could resist temptation, and what was in your hearts."

I stared at her. It was amazing how the dead could seem so alive . . . so real in the physical sense. Face powder had caked in the wrinkles around Bijou's eyes. "Why?" was the obvious question.

"Because the house belongs to you now."

Huh?

"The house was to go to Peaches, and now it belongs to her daughters. I drew up my will that way. But I couldn't let you and Kelly have the house until I knew."

My brain was having a hard time making sense of Bijou's words. "Knew what?"

"Whether you were up to the task." The old woman paused, looked away. "Whether you truly had the knack."

The knack. The gift I never wanted. It was days like this that made me wish I'd never been sent back from the Light . . . I'd had enough of "doing unto others as I'd have them do unto me." Why couldn't somebody else "do" for a change?

"You put us in your will after only meeting us once?"

Bijou shook her head, smiling sadly. "I put you in the will when you were born, Nicki. It's the only way Peaches would agree to give you up, by knowing someday you'd have a reason to come back."

I stared at the old woman, numb. "You made her give us up."

Bijou didn't flinch. "Yes, I did. It was for the best."

Best for who? I pondered that question while my feelings stayed on hold. Considering what I'd seen in the room beneath the stairs, my mother had been dabbling in the black arts, and her best buddy was Satan. Maybe giving us up for adoption hadn't been such a bad idea.

"Something happened a few months ago," Bijou said. "I don't know what, but Peaches became convinced that both you and Kelly were in danger. She insisted on searching for you, and finally got access to one set of adoption records. That's how she found Kelly." The old woman's lower lip trembled, then steadied. "I think she knew something she wasn't telling me, and I think she died because of it."

"It was a car accident. It was nobody's fault she died."

Bijou dabbed delicately at her eyes with the black hankie. "Some people believe that there are no such things as accidents, that everything happens according to divine plan."

I had a mental flashback to the moment I'd had a few months ago . . . when I died. That brief flash of understanding about how all things are connected.

Bijou drew in a deep breath, squaring her shoulders. "I believe your mother died trying to protect you girls," she said calmly. "And now she's gone." Her voice changed, became the no-nonsense tone of a lecturing grandma. "You have to help Kelly. She's going to stay here, and she's going to need someone to look after her."

"How do you know she's going to stay?"

Bijou gave me a withering look.

"Oh." The family curse . . . the knack . . . whatever.

"She thinks she's strong, but she's not. She can't handle this house on her own."

My jaw dropped. "I'm not staying here."

"You don't have to." Bijou cut me off with a raised hand. The ostrich plume gave a delicate wave. "But you can still be her sister, her confidante, her—"

"Bosom companion?" I couldn't resist the snark, remembering Leonard's earlier description of Bijou and Odessa's friendship. This afternoon seemed so far away.

"Yes," Bijou replied, drawing herself up. "Her *bosom companion*. Someone she can talk with about her life, and the world of spirits, who won't think she's a total . . . " Here, Bijou teared up.

I'd made an old lady cry. Could the day get any worse?

" . . . a total freak." The black hankie was in use again. "The way the world treated your mother. If Peaches had only had someone her own age to confide in, to rely on, things might have been different." She turned her head, displaying a carefully coiffed helmet of gray hair, the beauty parlor standard of little old ladies everywhere.

I sighed, scrubbing my hands over my face. There were smears of mascara on my fingers afterward, but whatever.

"That's how the Devil will win with Kelly, you know," the black hankie was waving in the air, "he'll isolate her. He culls his victims from the herd like a wolf among the sheep." The ostrich plume was bobbing. Bijou was getting pretty worked up. "You've seen him, haven't you? I know you have."

Reluctantly, I nodded.

"But you were too strong for him, so he'll go for the weak one. You have to help Kelly grow strong enough to resist him."

I closed my eyes, utterly exhausted. Since when had I become the "strong" one? After a sleepless night of ghost-busting, betrayal, and redemption, I felt like the leftover potato salad at a church picnic.

"You and Kelly are stronger *together*," Bijou insisted. "Look what happened with Sarah and Johnny—it took the two of you, together, to put those poor children to rest. Don't you see? The war between good and evil has begun . . . don't let your mother's death be in vain. Don't let the Devil win."

"No disrespect intended, but if you know so much," I opened my eyes, "then how do I get rid of him?"

Bijou shook her head, jet earrings flashing. "The Devil can't be gotten rid of, dear." She leaned forward, straining the buttons on her black silk dress. "He can only be overcome, time and again, by what's in your heart."

"My heart's defective," I mumbled.

Why did these things always happen to me?

CHAPTER 20

Hot water sluiced over my head and splattered on the tiles beneath my feet. The Scarlett O'Hara bedroom had its own bathroom, with a walk-in shower and all the modern amenities.

I'd spent a sleepless night in the antique four-poster bed, trying hard not to give in to the urge to call Joe on his cell phone, wherever he was, and beg him to understand, to take me back.

It was better this way. It really was. If he believed I was some kind of horrible person who kissed strange guys every chance I got, the kind of person who would say the kind of things Psycho Barbie had said to Kelly, then I was better off without him.

The running water covered the sound of my crying, and washed away my tears as quickly as they fell.

Just because I left him doesn't mean I didn't love him, Kelly had said. *In fact, I still love him.*

I turned, letting the water cascade over my shoulders as I buried my face in my hands.

Nicki's the kind of girl guys have fun with, but you're the kind they marry.

I lifted my head, sobbing, toward the ceiling. Steam was already rising, carrying with it my foolish dream of thinking Joe might be the "one"—the one guy I could trust not to break my heart.

And now, to add insult to injury, I had to help the woman who'd helped him break it.

I leaned into the shower stream and squeezed my eyes shut, letting the water hit me directly in the face.

If I had to do unto others, I'd rather do what Kelly had done to me and steal Joe away from *her.* I'm sure if I turned it on strong, I could give my sister a run for her money in the boyfriend department.

Unfortunately, my second chance at life had come with specific instructions. I'd been told to "do unto others as you would *have them* do unto you," not *as* they did to me.

I could ignore those instructions . . . but I had a feeling I'd regret it if I did.

Besides, I didn't want a man I had to steal.

I turned so the spray hit my shoulder, feeling hot water stream from the top of my head to my toes, and wiped my eyes.

And she'd had him first.

That thought made me wanna cry even harder, but I bit my lip and struggled to look at the bright side.

Joe was a good man, and he'd be good for Kelly. She'd

been through a rough time—the car accident, the death of Peaches so soon after their meeting, a twin sister who couldn't be more her opposite. Like me, she'd been given the unfortunate knack of talking with the dead at a time when she needed all her strength.

Bijou was right, Kelly was vulnerable. The Devil would get her if I didn't take care of her. Joe's steady presence in her life would help keep her safe, just as he'd helped keep me safe.

Until now.

So I leaned against the shower wall, tiles hard against my wet cheek, and let my knees carry me down to the shower floor. The steam was so thick I could barely see my hand in front of my face, but it didn't matter.

I was crying too hard to see anyway.

When I came out of the shower, the bedroom was empty, thank God. No unexpected visits from bitter-eyed blondes or sad little girls or lonely old ladies. The mirror on the wall was still broken, a souvenir of Barbie's ghostly rage. My overnight bag was in the chair.

So I did what I always did when I needed a mental boost.

Look like a million bucks, feel like a million bucks.

Luckily, I'd packed my second favorite pair of jeans and a bright pink, floaty chiffon top that went perfectly with my pink highlights. I wore a black bra, liking the way it could be seen through the pink.

Joe might prefer substance to fun, but that didn't mean I was gonna quit being myself. Let him eat his heart out.

I'd brought some strappy black sandals with low heels,

perfect for jeans. I took extra time with my makeup and used a little gel to get my hair just right.

When I was finished, I stared at myself in the mirror, satisfied with the results. Any sign of earlier tears could be taken as the result of a long night. I checked my watch, tempted to call Evan, but it was still early, and it was Sunday. Evan and Butch loved to sleep in on Sundays.

Besides, Mr. Fairy Godfather might talk me out of my plan to keep a healthy distance away from Joe. At the very least, I'd end up crying and ruining my makeup.

So I squared my shoulders and went downstairs, loins girded and bra securely fastened.

"Hey." Joe was sitting on the couch, waiting for me.

My heart gave a solid *thump*, then settled into a fast gallop. *So much for my hopes of distance.*

He looked like he'd had a worse night than I had, if that were possible. His dark hair was mussed, dark circles beneath his eyes, heavy shading of whiskers on his chin. Tired and sad and vulnerable, and utterly, impossibly gorgeous. Man gorgeous.

No fair.

"I thought you were gone," I said stiffly.

"You sure are quick to think it," he answered calmly. His eyes held mine, and I knew there was a double meaning behind his words. "Is that what you want?"

I swallowed, hard. "No." *I couldn't do it.* "But that's the way it has to be." *I had to do it.*

Joe didn't move. "Is there someone else?"

I was proud of how steady my voice was. "No. I already told you, that wasn't me you saw kissing Spider."

His eyes searched mine. He still didn't move from the couch.

"Kelly seems to think we need to talk. She thinks we're being tricked by an evil spirit who wants to drive a wedge between us. Is that true?"

I was shocked to hear the truth stated so calmly. After all the drama of the night just past, I'd given up on the voice of reason. And I sure hadn't expected it to come from Kelly.

"I—"

I didn't know what to say. If I told him the truth, I'd be back to square one emotionally, and Sammy would point his priapic pitchfork at my sister.

"Because if it's true, I'm really disappointed you didn't shake some sense into me and make me listen. After what we've been through together, I should be able to believe anything."

Joe rose from the couch, took a step toward me. "If you say you didn't kiss Spider, then you didn't kiss Spider." He shook his head. "It's just, when I walked into that kitchen . . . " His gaze hardened and he looked away. "It was like getting kicked in the gut. I was so jealous, so angry." He took a deep breath, eyes returning to mine. "I'm disappointed in myself for how I reacted." Another step. "But I'm *really* disappointed you would think that I'd ever prefer Kelly to you, or that I'd start seeing her again behind your back."

Tears threatened, but I blinked them away.

"I want to be with you, Nicki. Only you. I was stupid not to believe you last night. But if it's really over, if you don't love me anymore, tell me now, and I'll leave you alone."

My throat was too tight for normal speech. "I never said I loved you," I whispered.

Joe was right in front of me now, just a few inches away. I fought the impulse to sway into his arms, or the impulse to run away, I wasn't sure which. He looked deep into my eyes and gave a slow smile.

"You didn't have to," he said. His smile deepened. "You've been a goner since the day we met, just like I have."

His hands touched my elbows, gripped them and held on.

"I can't choose you," I blurted, afraid. "If I choose you, Sammy will go after Kelly and corrupt her. He'll turn her into a servant for his army." Or something like that . . . it was hard to think with Joe so close.

His smile faded, but he didn't let me go, even when I made a token effort to pull away.

"Kelly's a big girl," he said. "She's tougher than you think." He drew me closer, ignoring the tears that spilled from my eyes. His body was big and warm and male, and the thought of holding him again was oh so tempting.

"And you don't have to choose me." He lowered his head, lips a mere inch from mine. "I choose you."

And then he kissed me, and Kelly was on her own. There was nothing except this man and this moment and this kiss; the feel of his arms around me, the graze of stubble on his chin, the smell of warm cherry chocolate melting into the sweetly scented puddle of love that was me.

When I could breathe again, face buried against Joe's neck, I made myself give him one last chance. "Are you sure?" I murmured, all teary-eyed and weak-kneed. "Are you sure you want to be with a girl who sees dead people and has a bad temper and lives a crazy life?"

Joe's laugh made both of us shake—he was holding me so tight I wasn't sure where one of us stopped and the other began.

"Do you think I'd sit on a sofa all night in a spooky old house if I didn't?"

"You did?"

"All night," he said. "I was afraid to knock on your door for fear you'd hand me my nuts on a platter, but I wanted to be close by if you needed me. I want to be with you, Nicki."

I pulled back, making him look me in the eye. "What about those things you said about me to Kelly?"

He sighed. "You mean when I said you were hot, wild, and high maintenance? Which part of that was untrue?"

"Well . . . " *When he put it that way . . .*

"Yeah, you see dead people and you live a crazy life," he admitted. "But underneath all that hot wild craziness, you're a really good person."

He was smiling, his eyes crinkling in the way I found totally irresistible.

"A good person?" I pretended to be insulted, but I was touched, both by the personal assessment and the fact that he'd been watching over me on the couch all night.

"And gorgeous. Did I mention gorgeous?" He couldn't seem to stop smiling. "Besides, I'm the one with the bad temper—I punched your friend Spider in the mouth, remember?"

"He's not my friend," I said, smiling a little despite myself. Joe actually seemed a teeny bit proud of himself for punching Spider out. "He's Kelly's friend."

"Kelly and I had a long talk last night," he said. I tensed, but he ignored it. "She's pretty smart, your sister. You should listen to her sometimes."

I opened my mouth to argue, but Joe shook his head. "She pointed out that the way we were both acting was completely out of character—I'm not usually such a jealous ass, and you're not usually such a heartless bi—" He stopped himself, smiling a little. "You're not usually so heartless when other people's feelings are concerned. Particularly people you care about."

I could hear the tick of the hallway clock, so much slower than the beat of my racing heart.

"I'll fight the Devil himself for you if I have to, Nicki. As far as I'm concerned, he can go play mind games with somebody else."

He kissed me again, possessively this time, and I didn't mind one bit.

And when it was over, I rested my forehead against his and murmured, "I guess we've just had our first fight, hm?"

"I guess so," he answered, "but I don't mind as long as there's makeup sex involved."

I mock slapped at him, but he batted me away easily.

"I love you, Nicki Styx."

The words took my breath away, but I found enough to answer him. "I love you, too."

I didn't think his smile could get any bigger, but it

did. And then he kissed me again, and nothing else mattered.

Until the kiss was over and he said, "Now go talk to your sister. She's in the kitchen."

"You're kinda bossy, you know."

"I know." Joe gave me a final squeeze, then spun me around and pointed me toward the kitchen, patting my bottom for good measure. "And don't forget about the makeup sex."

I gave him an arch look over my shoulder, incredibly relieved that things were back to normal. "You're gonna pay for your bossiness, mister."

He grinned at me, unashamed. "I hope so."

CHAPTER 21

I stopped in the kitchen doorway, nervous about what to say to Kelly. Last night she'd told me she still loved Joe—how was she going to feel about us being back together?

She looked up from her pile of books. Her brown hair was pulled into an untidy knot, and there were tired bags beneath her eyes.

"You look nice," she said warily. "I was beginning to think you weren't coming down. Feeling better?"

"Much." I gave her a smile. "Can we talk?"

"Sure." She closed the book she'd been reading.

Still nervous, I turned toward the coffeepot. "Coffee smells good."

By the time I'd poured myself a cup and tasted it, Kelly had cleared a spot on the table by stacking some books and was waiting for me to sit.

As I slid into the chair across from her, I said, "Look, I'm really sorry about the things that were said in the basement last night—you know it wasn't me who said them, don't you?"

"I didn't know it at first," she said, "but by the time I got upstairs I'd figured it out. Joe and I were on our way down to get you out of there when you . . . " She paused, then went on. " . . . when you saw us in the hallway."

I drew in a deep breath. "I'm sorry about that, too." I'd acted like a jealous ass, and I knew it.

"When I told you I still loved Joe, I think you took it the wrong way," Kelly said. She cradled an empty coffee cup between her palms. "I do love him, but not that way. I never really did—I know that now. Besides," she smiled, "in case you haven't figured it out yet, he loves you."

I couldn't help but smile back. "I know. He just told me."

She relaxed in her chair, grinning broadly. "About time."

"You really don't mind?" If Kelly and I were going to make a go of this twin sister thing, we needed to be of one mind, at least when it came to Joe.

"It's okay," she insisted. "I want you both to be happy." She was telling the truth. I could read it in her eyes—the same brown eyes that stared back at me from the mirror each morning.

"Thanks for giving me the benefit of the doubt, Kelly, and for telling Joe he was being tricked." I owed her big-time for that.

She shrugged, like giving me my life back was no big deal. "No problem," she said, smiling. "Thanks for not pointing out that my hair's a mess this morning."

We grinned at each other, back on equal footing.

One problem down, one more to go. Time to talk about Sammy.

Kelly changed the subject before I did. "I've had a revelation."

Revelation—there was that word again.

"All this paranormal mumbo-jumbo is interesting," she waved a hand toward the books, "but it really *is* dangerous, isn't it?"

I looked at her, even more relieved than I'd been a moment ago. "Yes. It is." I took a sip of coffee. "When you open a door, like we did last night with the séance," I shuddered, remembering the strength it had given Psycho Barbie, "you better be sure what's on the other side. The dead don't need encouragement to stick around. They need closure."

"What about their families?" Her voice was thoughtful. "Don't their families need some kind of closure? Some kind of comfort to help them through the grieving process?"

I shrugged, staring at the brown liquid in my cup. "As far as I'm concerned, the living have lots of choices. They can pay two hundred bucks an hour for a shrink, just like I did."

There was an awkward pause. "I never saw the Light, Nicki. When I was in the accident, when I was in the hospital, I never saw the Light like you did. Not even last night, with Johnny, although I saw his face when *he* saw it." Kelly kept her eyes on the table. "And I've only seen two spirits, Keith Morgan and Johnny. You see them all the time."

"Three spirits."

"What?" She looked up.

"You've seen three spirits. You saw Albert at the hospital the morning he died. Are we in some kind of competition?"

"No." Kelly's voice was thoughtful. Her fingers played on the rim of the empty cup. "I'm just saying that I think my gift is different from yours. I don't have your strength of conviction, and maybe that's why I don't see as many." She gave me a half smile. "Anyway, I'd like to stay here a few more days." She toyed with the handle of her cup. "Why don't you and Joe go on back to Atlanta without me?"

I frowned, remembering Bijou's comment about how Kelly was going to stay in Savannah. The old lady had been right, which somehow didn't surprise me.

"Besides, something else happened this morning that really made me want to stick around."

I met her eyes, bracing myself.

Kelly smiled shyly, a pleased smile. "Spider kissed me."

"Spider kissed *you*." I said it out loud because it was a nice reversal of the words I'd *been* hearing. "Are you sure it was him?" A lame joke, but it felt good to be able to make it.

"He came back super early this morning," her cheeks were turning pink, "to get his camera and stuff. Then he told me he couldn't sleep for thinking about me, and he didn't want me to leave Savannah just yet, and then he kissed me. I know you think he's too much into the spooky stuff, but he's sweet, sensitive—I really like him."

I was happy for her, but I couldn't resist a little more

teasing. "A cute psychic with a Mother Teresa complex, and a gloomy nerd with delusions of gothdom—you're perfect for each other."

Both of Kelly's eyebrows shot toward the ceiling, but she was still smiling. "Okay, I guess there was a compliment in there somewhere."

Spider didn't seem like a bad guy, and his knowledge of the occult might come in handy. He might be going a little too far with all the ghost-busting stuff, but he *had* cautioned us about the Ouija board . . . at least he knew there were lines that shouldn't be crossed. Maybe if I talked to him, let him know what was going on, he could help me keep Kelly out of trouble.

"Get off that couch, cat!" Odessa's voice made Kelly and I jump. A door slammed somewhere in the rear of the house. "Git! Not that way—go on, now, git!"

A few seconds later the cat came running into the kitchen. It froze when it saw Kelly and me, green eyes wary.

"Pretty kitty," Kelly cooed. "What a pretty kitty."

The cat's tail twitched.

"Kitty, kitty, kitty . . . " Kelly obviously liked cats.

"Her name's Tabby," I offered, hearing heavy footsteps coming through the pantry.

Odessa came through the doorway, her expression furious yet determined. Tabby took one look at the big black woman and bolted. Two leaps and a bound, and she was in Kelly's lap, safe beneath the table.

"What did you just say?" Odessa was now glaring at me instead of the cat.

"Good morning to you, too, Odessa," I answered sweetly.

"Don't give me none of your sass, girl. It's too early in the morning for that foolishness. What did you just say?"

"I said, 'Her name's Tabby,' but I wasn't talking to you."

Odessa was silent for so long that it made me nervous.

Kelly was stroking the cat, scratching its ears. "I'll put her outside, Odessa. Is there something we can feed her?"

"How did you know the cat's name was Tabby?" Odessa was obviously not a morning person. She ignored Kelly's question.

"Leonard told me," I lied, just to be ornery. I didn't have to explain myself—or my ability to talk to the dead—to anybody.

"Huh." Odessa crossed both arms over her ample middle. "I'll be damned."

"Don't say that!" My knee-jerk response surprised everybody, including me. "Not in *this* house."

Odessa started to laugh. It began as a chuckle, deep in her throat, and progressed to a full-blown, bone-deep, satisfied laugh.

"If that don't beat all," she said, between chuckles. "You got the knack."

Kelly was smiling, enjoying Odessa's amusement, but I didn't find the old black woman's warped sense of humor very funny.

"Yeah, well." I wished I could think of something scathing to say, but all I could come up with was, "Kelly does, too."

Odessa laughed even harder, slapping her hands together with glee. "Miz Bijou was right. Blood will tell," she said, shaking her head, "every time."

"What's so funny?" Joe came into the kitchen, looking rumpled and sweet. He'd changed into a clean white T-shirt and combed his hair. "Did I miss something?"

My heart leapt, skipping a beat, confirmation that everything was just as it should be. I stood, brushing past a still chuckling Odessa, and wound my arms around Joe's neck. His arms came around my waist, and I kissed him, right there, in front of everybody.

"You haven't missed anything." I kissed him again, squeezing him tight. "How about some coffee?"

"Coffee! That man need more than coffee, girl." Odessa moved toward the stove, shaking her head. "Go ahead and pour him a cup while I fix up some biscuits and red-eye gravy. Some of that ham would go good with grits, and I got me some fresh eggs here in the refrigerator." Odessa was talking more to herself at this point than anyone else, but it didn't matter.

Joe was smiling, Kelly was still petting the cat, and all was right with the world.

CHAPTER 22

"It ain't like Leonard to miss a Sunday breakfast." Odessa poured Joe a third cup of coffee, shooting another anxious glance toward the door. "He's here every week at eight-thirty, just like clockwork. I done told him last night I was makin' biscuits."

"Maybe he overslept." Kelly wiped the last bite of red-eye gravy from her plate with what was left of her biscuit.

"Huh." Odessa turned back to the counter. "That man ain't gonna miss a meal over an extra forty winks."

Having just eaten one of the best Southern breakfasts of my life, I was privately inclined to agree.

"You cook for Leonard every Sunday, Odessa?" My tummy was full, I had Joe by my side, and I was finally relaxed enough to make small talk. "The Blue Dahlia isn't even open on Sundays." I'd read the Hours sign in the front window during our breaking and entering session.

"Miz Bijou always had Leonard over for breakfast on Sundays," Odessa said gruffly. She shrugged, stirring a pot of buttered grits. "No reason to stop just because she's gone."

"Why don't you call him," Kelly suggested.

Odessa shook her head. "He a grown man. I ain't his mama."

But I could tell by the way she checked her watch for the umpteenth time that she was worried.

"I'll go next door to the flower shop and see if he's there." Kelly slid from her chair and picked up a stack of books. As she did, something fluttered to the floor. "I need to put some of these books back anyway."

I bent to pick up what had fallen, and the hair on the back of my neck stood on end.

Another tarot card. This one showed a woman in a blue gown, with a crown on her head, and was labeled "The High Priestess."

"Where did that come from?" Joe craned his neck to see the card. "Don't tell me, I know. Spider man left it." He was smiling, obviously teasing Kelly. "He uses them to increase his spidey-sense."

"He didn't plant that card last night, Joe." Color rose in Kelly's cheeks at the mention of Spider. "This one must've fallen out of one of the books," she added defensively. She put the books back on the table and pulled out the guide to tarot that she'd been reading last night. Ignoring Joe's eye roll, she looked up the High Priestess.

"'Secrets,'" she read aloud. "'This card represents knowledge, intuition, mysteries kept from the world to be passed only to those who seek. The curtain behind the priestess represents the unknown, while the priestess herself sits between two columns—one black and one white—symbolizing both darkness and light.'"

A pained hiss came from Odessa. She jerked away from the stove, clutching her arm.

"You've burned yourself." Joe was at her side in an instant. "Let me see."

Odessa tried to pull away, but he wouldn't let her.

"Nothing a little lard won't fix," she said, wincing. "I got me some bacon fat in the refrigerator."

To which Joe replied, "Over my dead body."

"Don't say that!" I burst out. When all three of them looked at me strangely, I added, "It creeps me out."

"At any rate"—Joe was in full doctor mode now, with no time for my creeps—"the first thing we do is get this under some cold water. If it starts to blister, we'll need some antibacterial lotion and a sterile bandage. Do you have a first aid kit?"

"What do you think this card means?" Kelly's whisper caught me by surprise.

I watched Joe as he ushered Odessa to the sink. My first thought was of Bijou. I hadn't told Kelly yet that I'd even seen the old woman, much less the things she'd told me. Secrets seemed to be her specialty.

"Bijou," I whispered back.

Kelly's eyes widened. "Did you see her? What'd she say?"

"Not here."

The entire exchange had taken only a few seconds. Joe was manhandling Odessa into holding her arm under running water while she gave him a hard time.

"I've burned myself before! I don't need no snot-nosed white boy tellin' me what to do!"

"That's Dr. White Boy to you," Joe returned calmly. "Now hold it right there while I get a piece of ice."

"Are you okay, Odessa?"

Kelly was rewarded for her concern with a rude comment from the injured party. "Do I look okay?"

Odessa kept her arm under the running water, though, as Joe rummaged through the freezer.

"Where's the ice maker?"

"Ain't got no ice maker—that's what them trays are for," Odessa snapped.

Joe cracked one of the trays with an efficient twist of the wrist, then plucked one of the cubes free. "Put this on that burn," he said to her. "It's going to hurt like hell at first, but you'll thank me later."

"Huh." Odessa's face was twisted with pain, and she took the ice cube from Joe's hand without saying anything more.

I'd burned myself with an iron once, which was why I now preferred wrinkle-free fabrics and big dry cleaning bills.

"Is there anything we can do?" I felt bad for Odessa.

"You can stop hoverin' over me," the old woman said. Pain obviously made her cranky. Of course, so did everything else.

Joe took a quick peek under the ice. "It doesn't look too bad, Odessa." He flashed her his best bedside grin. "Probably just leave you with a teeny new beauty mark."

"Huh," she said, but this time she lacked conviction.

"We'll be right back." Kelly scooped up the stack of

books. "Nicki and I are going next door to check on Leonard."

Crap.

"And don't worry about the dishes, Odessa. We'll get them. It's the least we can do after you fixed us that great breakfast."

Double crap.

I followed Kelly out of the kitchen and through the dining room to the front porch.

"Tell me about Bijou," she said as soon as we were outside.

I would've, but one glance toward the open door of the Blue Dahlia took my thoughts elsewhere.

The lights were on. Leonard was obviously there.

But why was the door open? And why was he so late for breakfast?

Kelly and I saw the same thing. We glanced at each other, and I knew we were thinking the same thoughts.

"Leonard?" Kelly went in first, calling out cheerfully. "Are you in here?"

No answer.

"Leonard?" I came all the way inside the store, heading toward the counter. The register was unlocked, the drawer open and empty, but there was nobody around.

Not a good sign.

"Don't touch anything," I blurted. The business training I'd gotten before opening Handbags and Gladrags kicked in. Robbery 101—Fingerprints: Keep the Scene Clean.

"Nicki, look." Kelly was staring at the door to the basement. "It's open."

Crap, crap, crappity-crap-crap.

Kelly put the stack of books on the counter and started toward the basement stairs.

I called Leonard's name as loudly as I could. "Leonard?" There was no need to go down those stairs if he answered, now was there? "Leonard, are you down there?"

Unfortunately, he didn't answer.

"We should call the police," I said, none too eager to be the first person on a crime scene. Leonard was an old man, alone in the shop. What if the robber had taken him down there to mug him in peace?

"He could be hurt." Kelly started down the stairs. "We have to at least check."

"Stop, Kelly." I tried to grab her, but it was too late. "You're being incredibly stupid!"

What if the robber was *still* down there?

"Leonard?" Kelly called out loudly. "Leonard? Are you here? It's Kelly."

"And Nicki," I shouted, letting the robber know there were two of us. "And the police are on their way!" A lie like that couldn't possibly hurt—even though I'd left my cell phone in my purse.

Kelly was already halfway down the steps. She stopped short, her hand on the railing. "What . . . what are you doing down here?"

Thank goodness. Leonard was down there after all.

Kelly took the last few steps down into the basement, but by now I was right behind her.

"I've been waiting for you," a man said just as I reached the bottom step.

I looked over at him, and my blood turned to ice.

The guy sitting at the velvet-covered table wasn't Leonard—it was Sammy.

"I need your help, Kelly," he said, effectively ignoring me. He leaned back in his chair, fingers idly stroking the edge of the Ouija board on the table in front of him. "And in return, I'll give you what you most desire." His smile was meant for Kelly alone, eyes intent upon his prey. "A visit with your mother, the lovely Peaches Boudreaux."

"Get the hell out of here," I said, stepping closer to Kelly. "Leave us alone."

"Nicki!" Kelly gave me a glare that would've shriveled fruit. "Stop it."

"Don't listen to him, Kelly. He's not some poor lost soul in need of help! He's the Devil."

"You don't know that!" I couldn't believe she was arguing with me over this. The lure of Peaches must've been awfully strong.

"I *do* know that." I turned my attention back to Sammy, who was watching with a smile. "I don't know what game you're playing, but you need to pack up your toys and go home. You're not welcome here anymore."

Sammy put a hand to his heart in mock horror. "You're casting me out?" He gave a theatrical sigh. "Story of my life."

"Nicki . . . " Kelly's voice held the first hint of doubt. Progress was wasted, though, when she froze—all movement stopped—as though a mannequin from Handbags and Gladrags had remembered its place.

"You're out of your league, dear heart." Sammy smiled at me coldly. "I can make Kelly believe whatever I want her to believe, for a little while. By the time she figures me out, it will be too late." Pale blue eyes gleamed at me in the dimness of the basement. "She'll be mine. My willing slave, just like her mother." He moued me a kiss.

"I'll burn this place to the ground before I let you have my sister," I said recklessly.

"You'd do that for *me*?" Sammy was toying with me, like a cat with a mouse. "How sweet. I'm sure I'll feel right at home."

He snapped his fingers.

"Nicki!" Kelly snatched me by the arm, turning me to face her. "What's the harm in listening to what Sammy has to say? What if he really can help us talk to Peaches?"

Tears of frustration threatened, but I blinked them back.

"I don't need to talk to Peaches! *You* don't need to talk to Peaches. Peaches is dead. If anything's holding her here, it's you! Your guilt! You have to let her go."

She stared at me, opening her mouth to say something. But she didn't say it. In her eyes, I read the first signs of hesitation, and pushed even harder.

"Sammy's a liar, Kelly. That's how he got to Peaches—he made her think he was her only friend, and then he took advantage of her."

"In more ways than one," Sammy said smoothly. "They don't call me the Father of Lies for nothing."

Time stood still.

Kelly showed no reaction to what Sammy had just said. It wasn't just my shock . . . Sammy was up to his tricks with time and dimension again.

The Father of Lies.

I turned my head, very slowly, and looked at him

where he sat—oh so nonchalantly—at the velvet-covered table.

"What . . . " I licked suddenly dry lips. " . . . what are you saying?"

"Oh, Nicki," Sammy said, leaning back in his chair. He was all in black today, in a lightweight silk jacket over a black cotton tee. He could've stepped from the pages of a fashion magazine, been a model for Armani. "You're so good at secrets. Surely you can figure this one out? Don't you see the family resemblance?"

It was so monstrous, so unbelievable, that my mind just wouldn't go there. "You're lying."

Sammy shrugged. "That's the problem with lies. Nobody wants to believe you when you speak the truth."

"Tell her, then," I shouted. "Speak the truth! Tell Kelly who you really are!"

"I'd rather wait until she's in my bed," the Devil said wickedly. "It gives a delicious little twist to the words 'Daddy's little girl.'"

My heart sank to the level of my shoes. I wanted to rip his blond head off, despite the way my hands were shaking; I wanted to run, to snatch Kelly and drag her away from this evil man, this evil place—but there was nothing I could do.

"It's not too late to save her, you know." Sammy plucked my thoughts from the air.

He touched the Ouija board in front of him with the tip of a finger. "You could come to work for me, help me recruit a few more souls."

I'd been doing my best to ignore the board—it had come to symbolize all that was ugly, all that was evil. I hated it.

He picked up the planchette. "You're the one I want," Sammy said, giving me his best rock-star grin. "Last chance."

Last chance.

Last chance to go back to Little Five Points, to Evan, as a person in charge of my own life. Last chance to run Handbags and Gladrags as an honest business person who knew how to succeed, on her own, without selling out. Last chance to have Joe, all to myself, for ever and ever, because he loved me for being myself.

Last chance to save my sister's soul. Even if she didn't wanna be saved.

"Haven't you given up yet, you old goat?" Bijou's voice came as a complete shock, yet there she was, stepping from a dark corner. Her black dress and feathered hat blended perfectly with the shadows, her face a pale, round moon in the dimness.

Sammy sighed, looking annoyed. "Really, Bijou, this is getting tiresome. Aren't you supposed to be dead?" He wiggled his fingers at her in a fine display of rock-star arrogance. "Run along."

"We had a deal, Samael." The way Bijou said Sammy's name gave me goose bumps. "You've tempted them and you failed. Peaches is dead, her contract is up. The girls are free now."

"But I'm not finished yet," Sammy said mildly.

"Nicki knows that the only way to win against evil is to never play the game." Bijou was talking to Sammy, but looking at me. Her eyes were dark pits of sadness, full of hard-won wisdom. "Do the right thing, Nicki—every time—and things will work out."

Easy enough for the old woman to say, but I was only

twenty-nine and had no freaking idea what the right thing *was.*

Sammy's lip curled into an ugly smile. "Nicki may be a lost cause, but she's not the only player in this game." He released a heavy sigh, as though pained. "I can see a demonstration of my power is in order."

A cold breeze ruffled my hair, bringing a foul stench with it. My stomach churned.

"Hello, little goth girl." Psycho Barbie's voice made me jump. The basement was getting awfully crowded. Barbie was standing beside the table, smirking at me.

"Don't be so full of yourself," Sammy snapped at her. "I'm very disappointed in you."

Barbie's model-straight posture wilted before my eyes. She looked fearful, uncertain. "I did what you asked me to, Master. I tricked everyone—no one knew it was me."

Sammy's gaze flicked scornfully over the blond woman at the table. "Stupid bitch." He gave a careless nod in Kelly's direction. "The sister figured it out, and so did the boyfriend. You're useless."

It was sickening to see a beautiful woman grovel. "Please, Master, I'm sorry. I'll do better next time." The fear on her face was plain to see.

"There will be no *next* time," Sammy spat.

My veins filled with ice.

"Your contract is up, and our bargain is over. I should've taken you a month ago instead of giving you an extension. You're dead, Saundra, and it's time to pay up."

Saundra. Her name was Saundra.

"That which you fear the most shall become your world, from now until the end of time. Here." He thrust something at her, from which she recoiled. "Take it. Take it and embrace your fate."

It was the mirror—Kelly's scrying mirror—glittering as it caught the light. Like a robot, Saundra took it from Sammy's hand, terror distorting her features.

"After all," Sammy murmured, a smile turning up the corners of his lips, "beauty is only skin deep, and your skin has been dead for weeks."

Saundra looked into the mirror and screamed, a high-pitched, horrible scream that made me want to cover my ears.

Then, even more horribly, I began to see why she was screaming.

The skin of her face and hands turned a mottled shade of greenish-black. Her eyes began to bulge from their sockets. Fluid began to weep from the corners and drip from her nose. A putrid smell arose in the room, making me want to gag.

I wanted so badly to run away, but I couldn't leave Kelly standing there like a statue. She had no clue what was going on around her, and I envied her for it.

"Do something!" I said to Bijou, who stood calmly by, watching. "Make it stop!"

Sammy laughed, a nasty laugh. He ignored both Bijou and me, enjoying the fright show too much to be distracted.

"There's nothing we can do, dear," Bijou said sadly. "This poor soul made a bad bargain, and the cost of it has nothing to do with us."

Saundra's screams had faded to whimpers, but still she stared into the mirror. Her face was lopsided now, one side drooping more than the other as the putrefying flesh separated itself from the bones. The hand she rose to hold it in place was swollen, the fingernails an ugly bluish-gray, the white tips of her French manicure emphasizing the decay.

"Behold your ultimate fate, Nicki Styx." Sammy raised a hand toward the sobbing, gibbering corpse. "Food for the worms, that's all you mortals be." His speech became more antiquated when he was being diabolical. "Unless you'd like to partner with me. I can offer you much, much more."

"I've seen how you treat your partners," I said boldly, though my knees were shaking. I wanted so badly to throw up, but I didn't want to add to the whole Exorcist vibe.

Besides, the creep would probably enjoy it too much.

Refusing to look at Saundra again, I closed my ears to her mad whimpers, refused to hear how they clogged in her rotting throat. The face that was once so pampered and smooth, taut from countless surgeries, was no more. The thing that sat at the table was the stuff of nightmares, and I was sure I'd see it over and over again in my dreams.

For now, I'd seen enough.

Sammy sighed, disappointed. He waved his hand as if waving at a gnat, and the thing that once was Saundra disappeared. The odor of decay lingered, but I did my best to breathe shallowly and ignore it.

"Let's see what Kelly has to say then, shall we?"

"What's going on, Nicki?" Kelly's voice made me jump.

Time was back on track.

"Never mind." She frowned at me, reading the strain in my face. "If you see something I don't see," she glanced at Sammy uneasily, "then maybe I should listen to you." She paused. "I trust your judgment." She lifted her chin in the way I already knew so well. "Sammy, I think you should leave."

Sammy slammed his hand down on the table, making the candles rattle.

Kelly and I both jumped, clutching at each other.

"How utterly boring you've all become."

He rose from the velvet-covered table, a sneer on his handsome face.

"Milton was right: ''Tis better to reign in Hell, than serve in Heaven.' You do-gooders suck the fun out of everything. I'll leave you to it, then."

And he was gone, just like that.

Kelly gasped and squeezed my arm, then gasped again as she saw Bijou, standing in the basement shadows. I wasn't sure how Bijou had suddenly managed to appear to us both, but I felt a surge of relief to know that Kelly could see her, too.

"Do you see her?" I asked, just to be safe.

"I see her," Kelly whispered.

The sharp sting of her fingernails grounded me in the moment—let me know I wasn't crazy—even though I'd be bruised tomorrow.

Bijou took a few steps forward, resting a black-gloved hand on the back of the chair. The chair where Sammy had just been. Her ostrich plume gave a graceful wave as she nodded to Kelly.

"Don't be afraid," Bijou said. "You girls did well." She smiled broadly. "I can tell you everything now. Better yet, everything will be all right."

Easy for you to say.

"What's going on?" Kelly was in shock, not yet used to seeing people appear and disappear before her eyes, I suppose. "Where did she come from? What just happened?"

"The Devil tried to trick us," I said tiredly, "and our crazy dead grandma sent him on his way with a bug in his ear."

"I can hear you, you know." Bijou Boudreaux apparently never forgot her manners. "It's impolite to talk about someone as though they weren't there," she said primly. "And it wasn't I who sent him on his way with a bug in his ear." Bijou looked at both of us, beaming. "It was the two of you, and the love you have for each other."

Kelly's tension eased. She relaxed her grip on my arm.

I wanted to rub where she'd bruised it, but didn't wanna hurt her feelings.

My shaky knees, however, were another matter, and they'd reached their limit. I stepped backward and sank to the ground, letting my butt find the bottom step all by itself.

Sammy was gone. The Devil was vanquished.

All because I'd been willing to do the right thing, and because Kelly had trusted me enough to do it.

It couldn't possibly have been that easy.

Could it?

CHAPTER 23

"Sit, girls." Bijou gestured toward the velvet-covered table. "I have a story to tell you."

"Not another story," I groaned. I wasn't up for this. I wanted out of this basement, and out of this house.

Kelly looked at me, questions written all over her face. If she didn't get the answers she needed, she'd be looking for them somewhere else, and who knew what kind of cosmic trouble she might stir up next?

"Okay, okay." I hauled myself up from the bottom step. I started toward the table, but found myself hesitant to pull out a chair. "Can we move this thing first?" I gestured toward the Ouija board. The mirror was gone, taken with Saundra into whatever hell she inhabited.

Kelly was the one who took the board away. She seemed to have no fear of it, and put both board and planchette on the floor against the wall, where I could no longer see them.

"We should break that thing into kindling," I murmured.

"No," she said.

I opened my mouth to argue.

"It needs to be left on the steps of a church for a priest to deal with." Kelly wasn't kidding. "That's the only way to destroy a Ouija board."

Bijou spoke up. "You're absolutely right, Kelly." She was still standing, black-gloved hand on the back of her chair. "Not very many people know that."

Kelly shot Bijou a shy glance, looking pleased with herself.

I hadn't known that. "Where'd you pick that up?"

"The Internet, of course."

Of course.

Kelly and I both sat down at the table. As I looked down at the velvet tablecloth, I had the oddest sensation. *This was where my mother once sat.* The worn spots on the velvet near the edge were from her hands, and the tiny burn hole in the fabric was from the time she dropped a lit match when she was lighting a candle.

I knew it . . . I could almost see it . . . and then it was gone.

"Please be patient with me," Bijou said. She looked away, vulnerable in her old age, all wrinkled skin and sagging jowls. "Let me tell you about your mother in my own way."

She'd been reading my mind. I knew it, without a doubt.

"Once upon a time," Bijou began, "a young man was born with a problem. It wasn't lack of money, for his family had plenty of that. It wasn't a dread disease or a hideous deformity." She stepped behind her chair, resting both black-gloved hands on the back. The bags beneath her eyes looked darker in the shadows, pockets of grief and worry. "The young man's problem was that everywhere he went, he felt he didn't belong, particularly with his family. In fact, he had a very strong suspicion that they'd be better off without him."

Who was this guy and why did we care?

Tempted as I was to speak my thoughts aloud, I bit my lip. Kelly seemed fascinated, and I was willing to give the old woman a little bit more time to get to the point.

"The young man decided to disappear." The ostrich plume in Bijou's hat was perfectly still. "He decided to create his own place, a place where he belonged."

And they all lived happily ever after.

"But the young man was weak." Bijou's fingers were gripping the chair back pretty hard. "There was one thing about his old life that he just couldn't leave behind. His baby daughter."

Kelly made a sympathetic noise.

"So he took his daughter and he moved far away. He changed his name and he changed his life, and his daughter's life was changed along with his." One of Bijou's hands came up to toy with the black lace at her throat. "And not always in a good way."

This was all very interesting, but I'd been through a lot that morning and I wanted to get out of the dark basement.

"Okay, Bijou, what is it you're trying to say? What's the point of this story?"

Kelly nudged me under the table to be quiet, but I'd had enough.

"Can't you just tell us straight out?"

Silence, just for a moment. Then Bijou reached up and pulled off her hat, bringing a gray wig along with it.

"You must forgive an old man," Leonard said, bald pate gleaming. "Sometimes I have trouble getting to the point."

Kelly made a strangled noise, and I'm sure the choked gasp I gave wasn't much better.

"What the *hell*?" Those three words were the only ones that came to mind.

"You're . . . " Kelly couldn't even finish her sentence.

"Please." Leonard held out a black-gloved hand. He looked ridiculous standing there—gray wig with an ostrich feather in one hand, overdone makeup, a woman's clip earrings gleaming from his ears. "Let me explain."

Kelly stood up, agitated. "What happened to Bijou?" She was in shock. "Why did you lie to us?"

Leonard's reply was put on hold as heavy footsteps sounded on the basement stairs.

"Nicki?" It was Joe. "Are you down here?"

"I'm here!" I shouted.

Joe's feet, then Odessa's, appeared as the two of them came down the stairs. Joe stopped dead at the bottom, obviously as shocked to see an old man dressed in drag as we were.

Drag was drag, whether it was a tasteful black mourning dress or a shiny sequined gown.

"Leonard!" Odessa scolded. "Get your wig back on, honey. You look like a plucked chicken."

"You knew about this?" Kelly rounded on Odessa, obviously not expecting that one.

Odessa met her gaze evenly. "You need to keep an open mind, child, and listen to what he has to say." A look passed between them—the angry young white woman with long brown hair, the ornery older black woman who outweighed her by a hundred pounds.

Kelly said nothing, but her chin rose. Odessa and Leonard were gonna have to do some fast talking.

Odessa glanced at me, and surprisingly enough, seemed satisfied by what she saw in my face.

Either that or she was just happy I was keeping my mouth shut.

"Y'all come on up outta this basement. Leonard hasn't had breakfast yet."

"I'm not going anywhere until I have some answers," Kelly said firmly. She turned her back on Odessa and took a seat again, next to me.

"Yeah," I said, in a weak show of support. "We want answers."

What I really wanted was a stiff drink.

"Why are you pretending to be Bijou Boudreaux, Leonard?" Kelly wasn't wasting any time.

Joe came up behind my chair. I lifted a hand, and he took it, resting his other hand on my shoulder.

The world became a more stable place. I felt I could cope with just about anything with a man like Joe behind me. I'd already dragged him through hell, but he still had my back.

Leonard did as Odessa ordered and slapped his hat and wig back on, but they were crooked. He knew it, too, because he was still fiddling with it while he answered.

"I wasn't pretending, dear. I *am* Bijou Boudreaux, wealthy widow and well-respected member of the community. Past president of the Savannah Historical Society, in fact." A final twitch of an ostrich plume, and Leonard was a well-dressed elderly woman again. "But I'm also Leonard Ledbetter, florist. I'm your grandfather, and proud of it."

"Are you gay?" Evan might have a fit over my stereotyping, but I was entitled to be blunt.

"Heavens, no, dear." Bijou smoothed her gray wig a final time. "Most of us aren't, you know. You'd be surprised how many men like to wear women's clothes. I adore women—wearing their clothing only increases my appreciation for the fairer sex." Bijou/Leonard beamed over Kelly's head at Odessa. "Particularly when one is surrounded by the fairest of blossoms."

Huh?

"Let me tell you my story, and then you may judge," Bijou said. "When I came to Savannah in the late fifties, it was a different time—a less forgiving time. The South has never been known for its tolerance, you know. But I fell in love with this beautiful old city. The moment I saw this house, I knew I'd never be happy anywhere else. I wanted to live my life quietly, to raise my daughter in peace."

"What happened to Peaches's mother?" I had to ask.

Bijou shuddered delicately. "Horrible woman. Never wanted to be a mother." A black-gloved finger shook in my direction. "Don't look at me that way, young lady. I left her well-provided for, never fear. She was as glad to be rid of us as I was of her."

"Huh." Odessa's opinion of Peaches's mother was made quite clear, and reminded me that she, too, was a part of this story.

"My little Lila and I were so happy here, in the beginning. Just her and me, a simple man and his daughter. I hired Odessa to cook and clean for us, to help me with the baby during the day while I worked in the shop." Bijou smiled, remembering. "In the evening, when it was just Lila and me, I could dress as I pleased, and no one the wiser except Odessa and my little Peach."

Odessa stepped closer to Leonard, as though drawn by the memories.

"But it became harder and harder to keep my secret, you see." Bijou looked away. "The more I dressed this way, the stronger my urges became. When the time came when I was inevitably caught, dressed as a woman, I bluffed my way out of it by pretending to be Bijou Boudreaux, Leonard Ledbetter's lady friend." Bijou smiled a sad smile. "And then I realized that I could get away with it—I could actually live two lives, one as a man and one as a woman—and no one would ever know."

"Except Odessa," Kelly pointed out.

"Except Odessa." Bijou shook her head. "I don't know how she's put up with me all these years."

"It wasn't easy," Odessa said bluntly. "But it was

better than being lynched. A black woman living with a white man who wore women's clothes was a stretch for most folk."

Still is, particularly when they're in their seventies. But to each his own.

"A black woman working for a white woman, living in her home, now they ain't nobody who cares about that."

"What about Peaches?" Kelly wasn't done with her questions. "Did she really make a bargain with the Devil? What about this room, this house, the spirits?"

Bijou's face fell. "It was all my fault. I failed to protect my darling girl. I was so caught up in living my own life, consumed by my new happiness, that I didn't teach her, didn't train her properly when she was young. The world of spirits overwhelmed her, because I didn't give her the tools she needed to stay strong."

"Train her?"

"Yes," Bijou said simply. "It was obvious from the time she was a little girl that Peaches had the knack, just as I did." Bijou shook her head, and the ostrich plume waved. "I thought I'd have more time."

"So you've been living a double life, all these years?" Joe sounded like he was having a hard time grasping things, and I didn't blame him. "Peaches knew, Odessa knew, and everybody was okay with it?"

Bijou gave a ladylike shrug, nodding.

"Why did you lie to us about being dead?" That really bugged me. "Couldn't you have just told us the truth from the beginning?"

Tears rose in Bijou's eyes. She dabbed at them with her ever-present black hankie. "I tried, dear. I tried to get you to come to Savannah from the beginning, remember? When you refused, I thought perhaps it was for the best. But when Kelly called I—" She waved her hankie. "—I panicked. I needed time . . . time to figure out what to do."

"You lied to me," Kelly said. She was ready to cry, too.

"I couldn't help myself," she said. "You both look so much like her, and I missed her so much. I wanted you to come to Savannah."

At that, Bijou broke down completely.

Surprisingly, Odessa reached out and enfolded him in her plumpness, pressing the old man's face against her neck.

"Go on, now," Odessa said gruffly over her shoulder to Joe, Kelly, and me. "That's enough for the time bein'. Go on upstairs to the kitchen, and we'll be up in a minute."

"One more thing," Kelly said, "and then I'll go."

I stood up, ready for a break in the drama.

"What about the children, Sarah and Johnny? If you have the knack, then why didn't you send them into the Light a long time ago?"

"Yeah." I hated being duped, and felt like a fool for not realizing that the woman who'd been sitting on my bed last night had been a real person, not a ghost. "Was that just some bullshit move to distract us, some trick to keep us here?"

Bijou lifted her head from Odessa's shoulder. Her lipstick was smeared beyond repair, the dark circles beneath her eyes made worse by melted mascara.

"If I weren't so upset, I'd be highly offended." She

sniffed delicately, dabbing at her eyes. "Those poor children have been trapped in this house for nearly a hundred years, but I didn't have enough skill to bring them together—why do you think I've immersed myself in all this?" She waved a hand toward the bookshelves that covered two of the basement walls. "It took the two of you, together, to set them free."

Oh, man. Even Ripley's Believe It or Not would never believe this.

CHAPTER 24

"Please, Nicki." Kelly's eyes were red from crying. "Please. For me."

We were sitting on the bed in Kelly's room, decompressing after the shocking events of the morning. Joe was in an overstuffed green wing chair over in the corner. I glanced at him, silently asking his opinion, but he only shrugged.

"Okay," I sighed, "but you're going to be disappointed."

Her answer was a watery smile. She blew her nose noisily into a tissue and stood up.

Joe started to rise, too, but I stayed him with a hand. "It'll be okay, baby. We'll be right down the hall."

He looked at me, clearly concerned. "You sure you're up to this, Nicki?"

What a sweetheart. I kissed him, savoring the warm

feel of his lips on mine. His steadiness was the perfect counterpoint to the craziness that was my life.

"I'm sure." Turning to Kelly, I said, "Let's go."

Together, Kelly and I walked down the hall to the room Peaches had called her own. The house was quiet except for the faint clatter of dishes in the kitchen—Leonard and Odessa were lingering over breakfast.

I put my hand on the doorknob, hesitating, then opened the bedroom door.

As I'd thought, the room was empty. The floral peach bedspread was neatly smoothed, the matching curtains open to the sunlight streaming across the hardwood floor. I stepped inside, with Kelly close behind. Deliberately, I shut the door, hearing a faint *snick* as the latch caught, and then the silence was complete.

"Peaches?" There was a faint catch in Kelly's voice, but it didn't disguise the hope in her tone. "Are you here?"

Silence. Kelly took a few steps toward the bed, scanning the room. "Peaches?" After a moment she glanced at me over her shoulder. The look she gave me was . . . well . . . desperate.

I couldn't help it. *What did I have to lose, after all?* So, with a sigh, I gave in.

"Mama," I said. "We're home. Your girls are home."

And then, before my eyes, a mist started to form near the bed. Kelly saw where I was looking, and her eyes went there, too.

"Is she here?" Her voice quivered, and without thinking I stepped up and took my sister by the hand.

"She's here," I said, ready to cry myself.

And there, standing beside the bed, was Peaches.

Her form was wispy, semitransparent. Not nearly as solid as the other times I'd seen her. But I could see the vivid pink of the dress we'd buried her in, the dark halo of her hair, a bright flash of red fingernails as she lifted a hand in our direction.

"I'm so proud of you girls," she said. "You did it. You set things right."

Swallowing past the lump in my throat, I squeezed Kelly's hand. "She says she's proud of us."

Kelly bit back a sob. "I wish I could see her."

"You can talk to her. She can hear you." My fingers were turning numb, but I didn't care.

"I'm so sorry," Kelly burst out. "I'm so sorry about the accident. I should've kept my eye on the road. I was talking too much and not paying attention and it was all my fault . . . I'm so sorry."

Why hadn't I asked Kelly how she felt, gotten her to talk about it? *Some sister I was.*

"It wasn't your fault, darlin'," Peaches said. "It was my time, that's all. Sammy warned me, but I didn't listen. The Devil always get his due."

"She says it's not your fault," I murmured. "She says it was her time, that it was Sammy's fault."

"But why?" *Good question.* "Why did she have to die?"

Peaches smiled, a sad smile. Her form was more solid now, more real. "I didn't keep my end of the bargain, girls. He promised to leave you two alone if I gave him the souls of those two poor children in return, but I just couldn't do it. I tried to put it off by keeping Johnny and Sarah here, with me, as long as I could. It was selfish of me, I know, but I didn't know what else to do."

"You kept Johnny and Sarah here to protect us?" I wasn't sure that made a lot of sense.

"If I let them go into the Light, he'd go after you," she said simply. "But I couldn't let them go into the Dark either. As long as they stayed in this house, you were safe."

"They're gone now," I said, aware of Kelly's rapidly growing bewilderment. "Aren't they?"

Peaches nodded. "They're gone, thanks to you and Kelly. You released them, and the guilt and sorrow that's hovered over this house like a shroud is gone, too."

I had to ask. "Does that mean Sammy will be after us again?"

"Oh, I'm sure he will." Peaches gave a little shrug. "But I think he may have met his match in the two of you. You're not helpless little girls anymore, now, are you?"

She was right. I looked at Kelly, realizing that her hand was still in mine. "She made a bargain with the Devil to keep him away from us, but she couldn't bring herself to keep it. So he killed her."

"You drew his attention when you came into the knack, Nicki." Peaches was still talking. "He told me he'd waited long enough for me to hold up my end of the deal. That you and your sister were too valuable to waste. He said he was going after you."

"So you went looking for us." She nodded. "You were going to warn us about him."

"Yes." Peaches took a step forward, hand outstretched, but didn't try to touch us. "I was hoping you'd let me teach you, let me show you what *not* to do, that maybe by knowing what happened to me, you'd be strong enough to resist him." She shook her head, looking rueful. "I didn't need to fret, though, did I? You girls are strong enough without me."

"What now?" Kelly looked worried. "How can we help her? What does she need to be at peace?"

Peaches took another step closer, this time focused on Kelly. "Tell her I'll be just fine, Nicki." She kissed the tip of her fingers and blew Kelly a kiss—I watched as Kelly smiled, faintly, as though she felt it. "I know where the Light is; he can't keep me from it. Now that I know you girls are going to be all right, I'm bound for glory."

"She's already at peace, Kelly," I whispered, barely able to speak past the lump in my throat. "She's going into the Light."

At least now I knew for sure who'd be waiting for me when my time finally came . . . my wonderful parents, Dan and Emily Styx, and my mama, Lila "Peaches" Boudreaux. She was already fading, while the sunlight, framed in the window behind her, grew brighter and brighter.

"One more question." I had to know. "Sammy . . . is he . . . is he our father?"

Peaches's laugh tinkled in the air like tiny bells, fading in the distance. "Oh, please, Nicki," I heard her murmur. "I may have had poor taste in men, but I never dated demons from Hell. He's the Father of Lies, not the father of twins."

"Then who—"

But Peaches was gone, the scent of her perfume the only trace that lingered.

EPILOGUE

"So your grandmother, Bijou Boudreaux, is really a man. And your mother, Lila Boudreaux, who went by the name Peaches, was a psychic who was possibly—occasionally—influenced by the Devil." Butch took a sip of his freshly shaken martini. "Is that right?"

"Bingo!" Joe was more than slightly intoxicated, and he deserved to be. "Give the man a cigar!"

"Good Lord, Nicki." Evan handed me another glass of red wine. "When will you ever even *try* to be a normal person?" He took a sip of his own martini and grimaced. "For heaven's sake, you're almost thirty."

"Listen to you," I said. "Where were you this weekend, Boy Toy A-Go-Go, maybe?"

Evan shot me a resentful look. "Butch was working the door. I had to go."

"Right." I took a sip of my wine. "Being supportive of your man and all that."

"That's right," Evan said, giving me a look.

"Of course," I said, returning it.

"How's Kelly?" Butch brought us back on point—he was smarter than his muscles gave him credit for. "Have you talked to her since you got home?" He was mixing drinks at the buffet I used for a bar—he and Evan had been waiting for us when we got home.

"Yeah. She's okay. Odessa is giving her a hard time, but she can handle it. Leonard is a bit much, but he's a sweetheart. Kelly's enjoying herself." I smiled, picturing the scene—Odessa giving them both orders, Kelly refusing to take them. "Savannah's not that far away."

"What about Spider?" Butch put a brawny arm around Evan's waist and gave him a squeeze. "Is he a good guy or a bad guy?"

I shrugged. "Time will tell, I suppose. Bijou and Odessa have promised to keep an eye on him, but Kelly wants to find out for herself."

"More power to her," Joe said, and promptly fell over. Thankfully, the couch was right there, under his cheek. His light snores began almost immediately.

"He's really tired," I said, giving Evan and Butch a rueful grin. "Poor baby." I bent over, smoothing a dark lock of hair from Joe's unconscious forehead. "He's been very busy taking care of me."

"Thank God," Evan said. He drained his martini in one gulp, plunking the glass down on the coffee table. "Somebody sure needs to."

Butch was thoughtful. "So Peaches's death was no accident."

I sighed, taking a sip of wine. "My near death experience drew the Devil's attention. Once the 'knack' kicked in, my ability to see spirits—to steer them away from the Light—became a tool he wanted to use. He wanted Peaches to corrupt us, help sway us in his direction, but she wouldn't. She tried to get to us first."

"So he killed her."

"That's what she said."

"Wow. The Devil plays dirty."

The only way to win against evil is not to play the game.

I couldn't help but wish Peaches had never played.

"Gives a whole new meaning to your nickname, devil doll." Evan looked at me strangely.

Just hearing those two familiar words sent a chill down my spine.

"Yeah. Don't call me that anymore, okay?"

"Okay. I'm sure I can think of plenty other names to call you."

"Skank."

"'Ho."

Feeling better already, I raised my glass in a salute. "To the freaks of the world—may our flags ever wave."

"Here, here," said Butch, with a sip of dry martini.

"Amen, sister," Evan finished, with a hand to his heart.

I looked around my living room, at the familiar walls, the worn velvet sofa I'd bought at a garage sale, the battered old chest I used as a coffee table. The Blue Dahlia was a cool old house, and Savannah was a charming old city, but there was no place like home.

Little Five Points, Georgia, was stuck with me.